The Annika Brisby
Series, Book Two

Dark Urban Fantasy Paranormal Romance

the SILVER THREAD

EMIGH CANNADAY

Find a Pronunciation Guide at emighcannaday.com/pronunciation-guide

For those who still believe.

Contents

Fans Only

VIP SECTION

Dying to know when the next book will be released? Love going behind the scenes?

Join Emigh's reader group!

As a VIP you'll have access to exclusive content, deleted chapters, a private Facebook group, author updates, the hottest new Fantasy and Paranormal Romance reads, and be notified of new releases before anyone else.

Sign up at emighcannaday.com/mailinglist

A Partial Map of the Estellian and Ellunian Empires

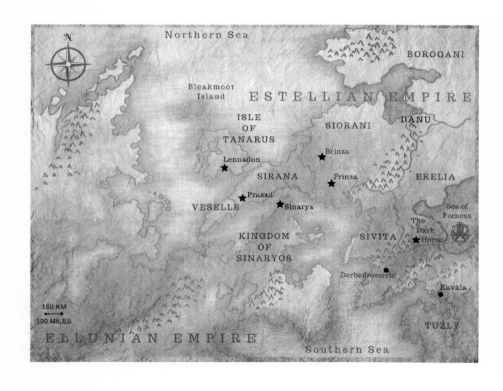

CHAPTER 1
The Largest Meadow

Talvi hoisted the saddle from his horse's back and sent the weary animal into the white pasture, where two over-fed mares stood. Out of habit, he peered through the falling snow, looking for his twin sister's grey mare, but he knew it was pointless. The mare was dead. Yuri was undead. He might never see her again.

It was a late winter snowfall, thick and heavy and wet; the kind that covers every twig and branch of every tree in a soft layer of cottony fluff. The trees of the forest surrounding his home were mostly made up of silver poplar and white birch. Their trunks and branches appeared ghostly and pale in the snow. Talvi might have appreciated the beauty around him more if his boots weren't soaked from walking so long in it. He decided Ghassan could wait just a little bit longer for his well-deserved hay and grain, and let the saddle, reins, and bridle slip from his hands beside the barn door. He was too exhausted to bother hanging them up properly. He trudged through the deep snow towards the sprawling hacienda across the quiet yard. Although he and his companions had covered hundreds of miles of terrain on foot, these last few steps seemed the longest. For almost three months he slogged through snow and sleet with his closest friends and family. They had traversed bleak plains, winded through frozen forests, and crossed icy rivers. The foothills of the mountains were treacherous in some areas, and they had barely escaped not one, but two avalanches. And even though he was a wanderer by trade, Talvi detested winter travel unless it was the short ride into town to warm his spirits at the pub. It was his opinion that during winter, any sane creature belonged in front of a fire, where they should be pacified by good food, good wine, and if they were truly blessed, good company.

He came to a robust side door, lifted the latch, leaned his weight against it, and put a false smile on his face before stepping into a wave of heat that caressed his numb cheeks and nose. As he entered the cozy kitchen, he could hear the squeals and laughter of his mother, his older sister, and her small children from down the hall. Talvi passed through the room to find them reunited with his brother-in-law, Asbjorn, who had not even had a chance to take off his coat or hat.

Asbjorn had been missing for a year on the wrong side of a broken portal, and it was feared that he might not return. It was discovered that he had been trapped on Earth, with no way to get back to his family. Now he had managed to cram both his children and his wife into one enormous bear hug, while two fairies hovered above them, visible only as soft, small orbs of orange and purplish-blue light. Talvi's mother had his older brother Finn in her arms, and his cousin Zaven smiled happily beside them, already having gotten his welcome home hugs.

"Oh, you're here; you've finally returned home!" Althea exclaimed. She let go of Finn after kissing his cheeks, and turned to her youngest son, embracing him close. "Where is everyone else?"

She glanced over Talvi's shoulder toward the kitchen to see her husband Ambrose joining them, but no one else was there.

"They're on a different schedule," Asbjorn said, looking first at his wife, then at his in-laws, and then back to his small children whom he still held tight. "There is much to tell that little ears need not hear. And my, how they have grown in all this time."

"Daddy, you need a bath," Stella pointed out, pinching her tiny nose as she made a sour face. "You're smelly!"

"Then your tale must wait," said Talvi's mother, wiping her eyes as she let go of him. She had expected all of her friends and family to return home together, and happy as she was, she still felt her heart sinking. Stella reached out for Talvi, urging him to take her from Asbjorn's arms.

"You need a bath too, Uncle Talvi," Stella informed him as he held her on his hip. "You smell like Daddy."

"I believe I shall *not* have a bath. I think you *like* how I smell," he teased, nuzzling her with his overgrown sideburns, which made her squeal and squirm. But rather than pawn his niece onto someone else and make a dash for the wine cellar, he only looked at her, studying her. He had only been gone a few months, a fraction of her lifetime, and yet she looked so different. She seemed older. But perhaps it was just he who had changed, he whose perception had shifted.

"Where is the girl with hair like the fairies?" Stella asked in her sweet little voice. Even though Talvi's body was beginning to warm up, he was abruptly chilled by Stella's innocent question. The fairies shared a sympathetic glance as they waited to hear Talvi's response.

"You mean Annika?"

His niece nodded. Talvi was surprised she even remembered Annika.

"I believe she went home," he said, trying to give a confident smile while he shifted her weight in his arms.

"But why didn't she want to stay? I thought she liked you a lot," Stella demanded.

Talvi's throat swelled in response to his little niece's precociousness, and his eyes stung. He didn't know how to respond. Stella's simple question had such a complicated answer. It wasn't as though Annika had simply said 'later' and taken off. She had been sucked through the same broken portal that Asbjorn had come flying out of. Her body had been ripped out of Talvi's protective arms . . . arms that had never let her go unwillingly until that one moment. That one moment had played over and over in his dreams, in his waking life, until it was no longer a painful memory. It was his painful, every day existence. Thankfully, his best friend, Runa, was close by to answer for him. She chose her words carefully before she spoke in her wispy wood-nymph voice.

"I think she *did* want to stay, but she is not from here, so she had to go back. She missed her family," Runa explained, trying to sound as optimistic as possible, but in reality, none of them had any idea if Annika was safe with her family or not. Runa's answer must have been less than satisfactory to Stella, because she was at that age where children begin to ask 'why' over and over. Talvi tried to answer as best as he could without saying too much, but he began to grow exasperated with her. Small children were not his area of expertise.

"Darling," Anthea said as she turned to Asbjorn, "let's bring the children upstairs, and I'll prepare a bath for us. I was just about to do the washing, so there is plenty of hot water available for when the others should like to take their baths. The washing can wait another day."

"Thank you," Zaven and Finn both said at the same time. Talvi handed his niece back to Asbjorn before returning to the kitchen with everyone else.

"Would you like a cup of tea, Dardis?" Althea offered, reaching for the kettle. There were two small orbs of light; one purple, and one orange. Without hesitation, the lights burst with a flash, resulting in two human-sized fairies now standing in the kitchen.

"That would be lovely," said the purple-eyed faerie through her chattering teeth. Her tiny pointed nose was still bright pink from the cold, making her look slightly like a circus performer. She pulled up a chair next to the hearth to enjoy her tea while she thawed out.

"Would anyone else like some tea?" Althea asked.

"I suspect Finn has gone to fetch something a bit more warming than tea," Zaven said, nodding his head toward the cellar door, which was ajar. Sure enough, Finn returned quickly with a heavy, lumpy sack in one hand and a distinctly-shaped bottle in the other. Talvi recognized it immediately, and snatched it away from his brother; his spirits lifted for a moment. Wine was for every day, but his father's precious faerie brandy was only enjoyed on special occasions.

Finn set the sack on the counter, and then took out the special brandy glasses from the top shelf of the china cabinet. Talvi uncorked the long, narrow-necked bottle, poured a glass for everyone, and then held his own glass to his nose. It made his mouth water, this divine drink that he had missed for so long. Made from peaches and apricots, there was nothing else quite like it, thicker than wine, but lighter than mead, and within a single sip, he could feel it flood into his arms and legs. By the third taste, it had reached his fingers and toes. It was definitely more effective than tea at warming him up.

He leaned against the counter next to the sink, which was serviced by a pump rather than hot and cold water faucets. His father tended to the fires while his mother tended to what would soon be cooking over them. It was her way of saying 'welcome home', and a more appreciated way of mothering her grown sons. The fairies huddled at the hearth beside her; their delicate, tiny limbs warming quickly by the heat. Talvi was content to tend to nothing more than his brandy glass. It was comforting, hearing his parents' playful bickering, the fire crackling, and the beginnings of an excellent dinner. It seemed like a distant memory, not the present moment.

"Chivanni, would you be a dear and put these into the broth?" Althea asked the orange faerie as the carrots and potatoes she was rinsing in the sink began to pile up. She glanced at Talvi's gaunt face with deep concern. "We must be certain there are plenty of extra helpings tonight. My poor boy looks nearly starved to death."

"It's not from lack of things to eat," the faerie said, and gave a little wave of his slender hand. The chopped vegetables rose and casually float over to the hearth single file, before sinking into the pot of near-boiling water without so much as splashing Althea.

"Then what is it from?" she asked, growing more concerned for her son.

"Lack of appetite," Chivanni answered discreetly, and Althea gave a subtle nod of understanding. Ambrose topped off Talvi's glass before setting the narrow bottle on the counter.

"Shall we drink to your recent marriage, then?" he asked with a wry smile as he raised his glass. Talvi glanced at his wedding band. Nothing slipped past his father.

"You ask as though I would object at drinking to anything," was Talvi's smart-alec response. He raised his glass to his lips, nearly spilling the precious brandy as his mother gasped and dropped the knife she had been using onto the cutting board.

"Talvi Anatolius, you didn't!"

"He certainly did," Finn replied, grinning at his brother.

Upon his mother's insistence, Talvi set his glass on the counter and held his left hand out for inspection. The lamplight from above made the ring shimmer with an ethereal glow, and she smiled at the tiny phrase inscribed inside the platinum band.

"*Mo reis to comp anya vlatzee*," she read softly. "How lovely that you had it written in Fae."

"We performed the ceremony on the solstice, just as it was written in the stars," Dardis informed her after taking another drink of her tea.

Althea let go of his hand, and took a step back to eye her youngest son; wild-haired, clad in black, and looking like nothing but trouble. Even though his eyes had dark circles under them, they still managed to cast a mischievous twinkle.

"The one child I never thought would settle down, and then you do so without my knowledge? For shame!"

Talvi gave a little smirk and shrugged.

"Mother, I did no such thing. You were given three hundred years notice that I was to be married this winter," he quipped, grinning so wide that his chapped bottom lip split open and began to bleed. Althea held her tongue, and turned her back to him, hiding how upset she was.

"I doubt you *will* settle down anytime soon," Ambrose commented, seeing his wife's response. "You are not certain where your bride is, are you?" Talvi's brazen smirk melted away.

"He has it narrowed down to two continents," Zaven answered for his cousin. Talvi licked his bottom lip before emptying his brandy glass in one large gulp, distracted by the bloody aftertaste. For not having a drink in months, he still felt uncomfortably sober. He knew Annika's primary home was in America, but he also knew it was a very large country. Finding his new wife might take the better part of forever.

"You have had less to work with in the past, and still been victorious," Runa pointed out, refilling Talvi's glass.

"I assume you are not staying long," his father said.

"Asbjorn and I are leaving in the morning. Finn has already promised to look after Ghassan in my absence, however long that may be," Talvi said quietly, glancing sideways at his cousin, then his brother. He was dreading what was coming next.

"You've not even taken off your boots and you're ready to leave again?" Althea asked, her voice shaking. "And how can Asbjorn part with Anthea and the children so soon? Couldn't you at least wait until Yuri returns, and then search for Annika?"

"It's not likely that Yuri will return anytime soon," said Talvi, feeling an old, deep anger beginning to awaken. A wave of bitterness washed over him, and the comfort of finally being home was lost.

"But at least she is still alive," Ambrose said, his voice breaking. Again, Finn and Talvi's eyes met. There was so much to tell.

"No, Father," Finn began to explain. "She walks, but not in the world of the living."

Talvi caught a glimpse of his mother's expression. Her mouth was a thin line across her face; her eyes were liquid pools of the darkest brown.

"Then what has become of her?" Ambrose asked quietly. "Show us what you aren't saying."

"The worst, Father. Nearly the worst," Talvi said, and he finished his third glass of brandy before looking deep into his father's eyes. Though his mind was laced with sorrow and strong brandy, he managed to relive a few memories of his journey, opening his mind so his father could see for himself. Ambrose witnessed his two sons, his youngest daughter, his nephew and many of their friends fighting for their lives against the powerful Pazachi. This sect of druids had strayed from their ancient beliefs of living in harmony with nature. Nowadays, they viewed living by example as weak. Over the past few decades, they had become exceedingly twisted and violent in their efforts to maintain a sense of control over nature, as well as those living among it.

Ambrose saw swords clash and spells cast, he saw fire blazing, arrows flying, and blood-stained snow. He felt his heart flounder as he watched his oldest son, Finn, be impaled just above the heart, followed by his daughter Yuri being struck down dead by a bolt of lightning, then falling onto the cold ground. His spirits fell further as he saw her brought back to animation as something undead; a vampire.

Talvi realized he had never seen his father come so close to crying. Ambrose took a moment to collect himself before he spoke.

"I had no idea such misery would befall anyone," he said, looking pained to say it as he stared into his brandy glass. "How has it come to this?"

Even without looking into his eyes, Talvi knew what his father was thinking. Ambrose was known to others far and wide as an elf of great wisdom and fairness. His counsel had been sought to settle countless disputes throughout the region. In his eyes, all problems had peaceful solutions, and there was always a middle ground that could be reached, if one was willing. Violence was a last resort to him; he saw it as an act of desperation.

"We knew the risk of bloodshed when we embarked on our journey. Everything is all or nothing with them," Talvi muttered. "They want the impossible, and the frightening thing is that they believe it *is* possible with enough force."

"Were you truly unable to negotiate?" Ambrose knew the answer, but he prayed he was somehow seeing things wrong. From what he could tell, it was not the Pazachi who had struck first. It had been his youngest son.

Talvi took a long time before he replied with the answer that he felt summed it all up. He spoke slowly, carefully, not to insult his father's intelligence, but to be perfectly clear.

"The Pazachi . . . *don't* . . . negotiate."

"It still doesn't make sense why Yuri wouldn't return," Althea said as she continued dinner preparations with help from the fairies. "Konstantin has always been welcome here; we have never discriminated against him for being a vampire. Why should she stay away?"

Finn cleared his throat, and began to explain.

"After we defeated the Pazachi, we discovered that they had created a mechanical portal that ended all portals, so that theirs would be the only one that led anywhere. It was created with some of the strongest black magic I've ever encountered, and it's the reason why Asbjorn and countless others were trapped in other worlds for so long."

"And then we smashed it with the diamond from Annika's ring!" Chivanni interrupted, and his orange wings fluttered with excitement. "Dardis and I broke it apart ourselves!"

"When it broke, all the missing people came flying out," Dardis added. "But then poor Annika was pulled into it, and it fell to pieces before any of us could go after her."

Talvi felt like someone had twisted a knife in his chest as he heard those words. That cursed moment never got easier, no matter how many times he saw it relived in his mind. Annika's hands slipping out of his, her face disappearing into a black void. Her expression of terror was his last vision of his new bride, and it haunted him relentlessly.

"So there we were, bloodied from battle, with the Pazachi prisoners, and the missing people, all crammed in this tiny cave," Chivanni added. "We told them that the Pazachi were responsible. They were relieved to be back, but some of them were quite distraught."

"I can only imagine. There are many worlds I'd never want to be detained unwillingly in," Ambrose said, and added a few small logs to the hearth fire. "But why hasn't Yuri come back with you?"

"We were discussing what ought to be done with the prisoners," said Finn, setting down his brandy glass. "Some of us were in favor of bringing them here, but there were too many children for them to safely make the journey we just made. Yuri and Konstantin claimed that there ought to be no prisoners taken at all, only executions. They are convinced that for every Pazachi converted back to the true Druid path, another two will rise in their place. Yuri's exact words were, 'If it were my choice, I would only show mercy to the young children, and send the rest of them to the afterworld.'"

"Has she lost her heart? That goes against everything we have taught her to value," Althea said, wiping her eyes.

"No one ever claimed it to be a simple task, to rehabilitate the prisoners," Talvi said, feeling so disgusted that he and his brother should have to upset their parents with such terrible news of their sister. "But it's the right thing to do, in order to stop this violence. Yuri would rather make them martyrs, and create even more hatred."

"Surely she was only speaking in a fit of passion," their mother tried to reason. "You know how she can say unkind things when she is upset."

"She is Konstantin's future bride now," Finn explained in a hollow voice, so foreign to him. Normally it was so warm and inviting. "Lines have been drawn, and she stands with him. Before we departed, we knew how much he hungered for Pazachi blood. I believe that he used us as pawns for his own personal gain, because he wanted that cursed mechanical portal to be his and his alone."

"He claimed that the so-called 'worthless pieces' should be taken back to his lair for study, but we drew swords over it," said Talvi, with contempt in his voice. "He was offended that we wouldn't be content to simply hand over the pieces to him. He took us to be fools."

"Then what has become of the dreadful machine?" asked Ambrose.

"We couldn't decide who should be responsible for it, so we divided it amongst ourselves. This way it could be studied, but could not be reassembled and put back into use," Finn said, trying to look hopeful.

"A wise decision," admitted Ambrose, "but that still leaves the prisoners and the travelers unaccounted for."

"We guided the travelers back as best as we could as we made our way home," Finn said. "They were the least of our concerns. The prisoners will be relocated in the spring, and are in safe hands. No vampire will be able to harm them. Although they lost their way, they are being guided back to their true path by our friends and some very trustworthy souls that we met along the way."

"You sound quite certain," Ambrose said. He seemed unsure, but said nothing more to elaborate. He looked like far too much was weighing on his mind. Talvi took this as a sign that there had been enough talk for the time being, and started to put on his wool mittens.

"Where are you going?" Althea blurted out. He stepped over to his mother and kissed her on the cheek.

"It's beginning to grow dark," he reassured her, gathering the largest carrots which Dardis had set aside. "I'm only putting the horses up for the night before I take that bath."

Outside the bright and warm kitchen, the snow was still falling in giant, fluffy flakes. The air was as moist and heavy as the snow on the ground, and Talvi could feel his toes beginning to freeze once again through his leather boots. Arriving at the stable, he gave a sharp whistle as he pulled the wide doors open. Ghassan emerged as a shadowy figure from within the trees, perking his ears as he caught the scent of the carrots. The two pudgy mares followed close behind, along with Finn's palomino stallion Galileo, and all of them hustled towards their stalls, where they whickered and grunted for their dinner. They pressed their warm noses to Talvi's coat pockets until he surrendered a carrot to each of them. Examining Ghassan, Galileo and Asbjorn's horses next to the mares, Talvi noticed how thin they appeared in comparison.

He divvied out the oats and hay, giving extra-generous portions to Galileo and Ghassan, and made sure there was plenty of fresh water in each stall. It seemed strange to him, to be doing something so normal and routine, yet nothing would ever be normal and routine again. No more straw pull with Yuri to see whose fate it would be to treat the other at the local pub, and he wore a wedding ring after swearing his entire life that he would never marry anyone, no matter what was written in the stars.

After closing the last stall door, he stood in silence, listening to the sounds of the horses eating. They had none of these concerns, no troubles at all, just contented nickers and happy neighs intermingled with the swishing of tails as they focused on their food. Talvi walked over to where he had left the saddle and bridle from earlier, and hung them up before latching the barn doors shut for the night.

His stomach growled as he entered the house through the kitchen once again. The smells were beckoning to him, gnawing at him, but nothing sounded better than getting out of his cold, wet leather boots and pants, and settling into the hot bath that awaited him. He had brought a lantern with him into the bathroom nearest the kitchen, and was happy to discover that someone had already started a fire in the wood burning stove, which had warmed the room up nicely.

Against the exposed stone wall, there was a tall walnut cabinet lined with shelves. Each shelf was well-stocked with jars of lotions, oils, salts, sponges, and other bathing luxuries. A long, dark blue robe hung from a hook on the side of the hutch, and a thick, fluffy towel was already sitting out for him. Talvi squinted in the lamplight at the labels and then set the lantern down to carry a bottle and a jar over to a bench beside the large claw foot tub. He knelt down and put the stopper in the drain, then turned on the faucet. From the jar, he poured in a handful of bath salts scented with herbs and flowers, and from the bottle, he poured a thick liquid into the base of the tub, which instantly began to fill the tub with puffy, cloud-like bubbles.

Talvi went back to retrieve the robe, towel, and lantern, and set them on the bench. He shoved another log into the stove before peeling off his clothes, and sighed in relief as he stepped into the scented suds. He eased himself in until he was completely submerged, letting the heat seep into his skin. From underwater, he heard the muffled sound of the oak door opening and closing, which was not that unexpected, given that the enormous house only contained three bathrooms.

He rose back to the surface and there stood Runa, snuggled up in thick socks and a brown bath robe that was way too big for her. It dragged along the floor behind her like the train of a bridal gown as she approached the bath tub.

"Did you start the fire for me?" Talvi asked as he wiped the water out of his eyes and let it roll down his cheeks. "That was so sweet of you to do."

Runa looked confused for a moment, and then smiled.

"No, I started it for myself. I'm about to take a bath in here," she said, and pulled a wooden comb out of her pocket. She began to run it slowly through her blonde waist-length hair as she sat on the bench beside the long tub.

"I think you missed your chance," Talvi said, and winked at her. "I'm planning on a nice long soak, so it may be a while." Runa raised a pale eyebrow at him.

"If you're going to be so selfish and unkind with me, then I won't share what I've brought."

"Come now, Runa, don't be such a spoilsport," he said, and sent a little splash of water in her direction, making her squeal as she recoiled from it. "What did you bring me?"

But she just turned up her little button nose and ignored him, focusing on combing out her long dirty hair instead. Talvi sat up and leaned over the side of the tub, dried his hands on her robe, and reached down to grab a small silver case from his pants pocket. He removed a cigarette from the case and lit it on the candle burning in the lantern, before dropping the case on top of his pants and resting his head on the back of the tub.

"I'm sorry I stole your bath," he apologized, taking a long drag and blowing a few smoke rings. "I didn't know you meant it for yourself."

"It's alright," she said, not looking too upset about it. "I forgive you." She slid her comb back into the pocket of her robe and surprised him by reaching down for his cigarette case.

"Runa, you rarely smoke," Talvi chided his dearest friend. She put a cigarette in her mouth and he brought the lantern close enough for her to light the end of it on the candle.

"Well, it's been quite a day, quite a winter, really," she said, half joking, half serious as she took a dainty puff and began to cough. "It's difficult to see your parents so upset. Remember last autumn? Remember when we went to a little book store in Sophia without a care in the world? And now look where we find ourselves."

"Indeed," Talvi agreed. He set the lantern back in place and tapped the ashes of his cigarette into the base of it. "Even with the prediction of all that has happened, I never imagined it would come to this."

"Nor I, but all will be well, in time," Runa said in her wispy, sing-song voice before taking another delicate puff, this time coughing less. Talvi watched her in silence. He wanted to master that very essence she carried. He wanted to own it and keep it in a jar, just like the bath salts on the shelf.

"How is it, my dear Runa, that you seem immune to all things melancholy, hmmm?" Talvi asked, looking up at her from the water. Steam rose up thickly from the surface, and he wondered if his frustrations were as visible as the vapors. In the firelight, his eyes were nearly black with ferocity, and the embers of rage crackled from someplace deep within. "What is your secret? I want nothing more right now, than to rip something to shreds."

Runa didn't reply right away. Instead, she lifted her slender legs over the side of the tub and let them slip into the hot water beside Talvi's feet. She took her time finishing her cigarette before she responded.

"Perhaps I can help curtail those violent urges," she suggested with a little smile. The flames from the stove gleamed in her dark brown eyes. Through the steam hovering around them, Talvi watched as she began to pull back the collar of her robe. With her other hand, she slowly reached inside of it. His eyes widened at her seductive gestures. What exactly did she have in mind to curtail his violent urges?

Runa withdrew a wine bottle, already uncorked, and grinned widely.

"Oh Badra's beard, you had me flummoxed!" he hissed, and splashed more water at her while he sat up again, reaching for the wine.

"*I* flummoxed *you?*" she asked naïvely, holding the bottle just out of his reach as she wiped bubbles from her face with the oversized sleeve of her bath robe. "Whatever did I do?" She took a generous drink from her seat on the bench before handing the bottle to her friend. He didn't answer immediately. Instead, he took his time savoring the full-bodied red wine.

"I thought for a moment that you might be laying your charms upon me," Talvi admitted peevishly, before setting the bottle on the bench. Runa gave a little shriek that dissolved into laughter, which made Talvi's face flush deep red. That in turn made Runa howl even more.

"Oh Talvi, I love you to bits, save for that *one* bit," she finally sighed, and searched under the water with her foot for that one bit of his. "I believe I am immune to *this* as well as all things melancholy," she said, and gave a strategic little poke with her toe.

Talvi scrambled to his knees and sent a massive splash her way, drenching her robe. Rather than be annoyed, Runa just gave a shrug before pushing it off of her shoulders and slipping into the nearly overflowing bathtub. A rogue wave of bubbles and water spilled over the edges of the tub, soaking Talvi's dirty clothes and the rest of his cigarettes that lay on the floor. He retaliated against the invasion by grabbing Runa's legs so her torso and head slid underwater, and then he tickled her stomach with his free hand. She tried half-heartedly to kick him, but he had her legs pinned securely over his shoulder and she didn't stand a chance. He could see her laughing from below, letting large air bubbles escape her mouth and bobble up to the surface. Just before she was about to run out of air, Talvi stopped tickling her and scooped her up with his free arm.

"Are we even now?" he crooned as he released her legs and sat back in the tub, still holding her close. "I've no more cigarettes, thanks to your wood nymph nonsense."

"You started it by stealing my bath!" choked Runa, and rested her wet head on his shoulder.

"Perhaps we can share it as we're sharing this bottle of wine. There's certainly enough room for us both. Truce?"

"Truce."

Talvi gave her a little squeeze and then closed his eyes. After going months without a drop of alcohol, the wine and the brandy from earlier were hitting him hard. The non-stop travel and eating next to nothing had left him completely spent, and he hadn't allowed himself to feel the full extent of it until now. He let himself become lost in the fog of his mind, where all he wanted, more than anything he had ever desired, was his wood nymph wife. He must have been dreaming, because he was finally warm, and his mind felt more at ease than it had in weeks. He let his long sideburns graze against Annika's forehead, hearing her breathing near his neck. He could feel her long red hair brushing against the arm that was curled around her back, dancing against his ribcage. His breath deepened as he guided her hips against his in the hot water. The wood stove was blazing now, and he felt a bead of sweat roll down the side of his face as his stomach growled again. He nuzzled into Annika's neck once more, letting his ravenous hand crawl up her legs and over her hips, before gripping her waist firmly. The fire was begging for more fuel.

With her small hands, she tried to push herself away from him, but that only made him pull her even closer against him, locking her up in his iron grip. He clutched her tight as he tried to breathe in her scent. Warm, wet skin met his lips, but it wasn't her neck that he tasted. It felt like her, but it didn't smell like her. It didn't taste like her. He felt a sharp pinch below his hip bone and his smoldering eyes blinked a few times before opening wide. He wondered what was wrong with Annika. All of the color had drained from her hair and had darkened in her eyes.

"Talvi, snap out of it! I'm not her!"

He loosened his grip, and then there was Runa, wrenching herself away from him until she was backed against the other end of the bath tub. Her long white-blonde hair, pale as it was, clung to her chest as the tumultuous water lapped against her skin. Her brown eyes still had their gleam, but she looked ready to bolt out of the bath tub if he came after her again. She was a small white rabbit, and he, a black wolf possessed by a dozen different shades of hunger.

"Runa, I'm so sorry. I don't know what just happened. I didn't mean to lose control and hurt you like that." Talvi felt light years beyond awful and awkward and embarrassed. In all their years of knowing each other, sleeping under the stars, swimming in hot springs, and having all sorts of adventures together, there had never been any kind of desire between them, other than the desire to remain the best of friends. Sure, Runa was an adorable wood nymph, but it had never once crossed Talvi's mind to seduce or ravage her. He'd never handled her that way in his life; she was like a sister to him.

He reached into his wet pants that still sat in the huge puddle under the tub, searching for a distraction. Water dripped from one corner of the small silver case as he popped it open. Luckily, there was one cigarette that was only slightly damp, and he propped it beside the lantern to dry, before laying out the others alongside it.

"You didn't lose control," Runa excused, looking relieved. She motioned for him to pass the wine back. "You didn't hurt me, either. You just drifted away for a moment."

"I'm unsure of where exactly I drifted," he replied, too embarrassed to look at her. He took a lengthy swallow from the bottle and then passed it her way.

"Finn told me that some demons exist only in the water," Runa said with a grin, before she set the wine on the bench and reached for a shampoo bar. "Perhaps one swam in with the bath water and possessed you."

"Then it's a good thing you have Zaven to keep you warm tonight instead of me," Talvi cautioned, "since I'm so prone to possession."

"It was a joke, Talvi. I think you miss Annika more than you realize," she reasoned, resting her small hand on his knee. Her brown eyes could not have pled any harder than at that very moment. "I know you're trying to be strong, but I know how you ache for her. She was here with you the last time you were at home. It may have triggered something painful that you're feeling. The subconscious has strange ways of expressing itself, and I believe you are being much too hard on yours. I'm not angry with you. You just . . . you startled me, is all."

"I thought I could handle it, this kind of emotion, but then my lust got in the way."

Still brooding and sullen, Talvi listened quietly while Runa shampooed her hair and rattled off the many ways she could have defended herself if she truly felt endangered. He found the first cigarette set against the lantern had dried sufficiently enough to be enjoyed, all the while he kept wondering if he was indeed possessed. While the moment had passed, its aftershock still reverberated in the back of his mind. Dipping into her mind with his own, he was grateful to see that Runa truly wasn't upset with him.

They traded the wine bottle back and forth with the shampoo and soap, and it seemed that the water demon was eventually washed away along with the scrubbing of arms and toes in the shared bath.

"Runa," he said quietly, "promise me that we shall always enjoy a bottle of wine together this day of the year. What day is it, anyway?"

"Well, let's see . . . " she said, scrunching her face as she counted. "I do believe it's the eighteenth of March."

"Ah, that's easy enough to remember," he said, but he was not smiling.

"What's wrong now?" she asked. "Oh, I'm sorry. I *promise* I will always enjoy a bottle of wine with you on this day of every year."

Talvi shook his head and smiled.

"Runa, you didn't even have to speak the words, and I still knew that you would make that promise to me. But you see, in a way, that is much of what adds to my unhappiness. You and I have so deep of an understanding that you don't even have to speak a promise for me to know it exists between us. You trust me so much, and I trust you. Yet, my own twin sister betrays me, betrays our family, our friends, and likely the entire elven race. I trust fewer souls today than I did a year ago, and that brings me nothing but pain."

"I understand it brings you pain," she said, looking thoughtful. "But could you not perhaps look at the matter in terms of unveiling a great truth, though it is painful to see?"

Talvi raised an eyebrow with interest as she continued,

"You are not alone in being sorely disappointed by the actions of your sister and Konstantin. You forget that she has been my friend just as long as you have, and it hurts me as well. Yes, there was the prophecy made three hundred years ago . . . but that did not mean that either of you had to follow its implications to the letter. You both had the freedom to choose your paths in life, which is why I never took it literally word for word. If Yuri desires to achieve power by turning her back on what is good and right, then sadly, that is her choice. But then, that is the reason why I am with you now, and not with her. Your demon possession problem still seems safer than being around vampires."

"Oh Runa, I adore you so much," Talvi sighed, smiling at her. All the awkwardness of earlier had dissolved. He took her pruney little hand in his. "Come with me to America."

"And what would I do, aside from being about as useful as a third wing on a raven?" she asked, rolling her eyes as she smiled. "Entertain you and Annika with my silly stories? Teach her some samodiva songs? I suppose she ought to know them, being my distant niece."

"How convenient she plays the guitar," Talvi chuckled. "I think you ought to do it. Goodness knows your sister and mother may not be back for some time."

"Yes, you are right in that," Runa said. A mischievous smile played on her wine-stained lips. "I think they are both preoccupied with affairs of their hearts."

It took Talvi's eyes an extra second to widen in surprise, as the bottle of wine was empty, and its effect was especially potent after the faerie brandy from earlier, combined with an empty stomach.

"Is *that* why Hilda chose not to come home with Finn and the rest of us? I thought she stayed to help take care of the refugees. Have they parted ways? Is there someone else?" he asked, leaning towards her. It had been widely assumed by his family for years that Finn and Hilda were officially an unofficial sure thing. Apparently not.

"It's my opinion that there is," Runa said, "although I couldn't get her to admit it to me out loud. But a sister knows these things."

"Who is it?" he demanded, but Runa rose from the water and stepped out of the tub, smiling while she proceeded to wrap herself up in Talvi's dry blue robe. Then she took his fluffy dry towel and covered her clean, wet hair in it.

"If you don't tell me, I'll refuse to come to dinner. I'll go on hunger strike, and it will be your fault when I starve to death!"

Runa started to walk slowly to the door, and then stopped.

"You'll do no such thing," she said in her coy, airy voice, and opened the door. "Your mother made potato soup, your favorite. Mmm, I can smell it in the hall."

"Runa . . . tell me!" he insisted one last time.

"Oh, and I think I smell fresh beer bread, with roast pepper spread. I know how much you love that," she said, and stepped into the hallway. She peered down toward the kitchen. "And I think I see baked squash and turnips sprinkled with that rosemary infused goat cheese Anthea makes." She stepped out into the hall, and took the towel out of her hair, using it to fan the scents into the bathroom. Talvi's nose caught multiple whiffs of all these delicious things she was describing, and now his stomach was growling . . . no, roaring at him in deprivation.

"I'm certain I'll see you at the dinner table," she laughed, and disappeared, leaving the bathroom door wide open to bring in more of the potent scents coming from the kitchen. Talvi punched the surface of the water in frustration at being bested, because Runa was right. There was no chance of a hunger strike that night. There was also no chance of leaving the bathroom in a dry robe or a dry towel, either.

CHAPTER 2
The Face of an Angel

"Annika!" cried Talvi, and readied himself to dive into the portal that she had just disappeared into. But his brother and cousin held him back from the murky abyss before them.

"It's too late," Finn said, fighting to restrain his brother. Talvi looked up, and there was a great trembling of the man-made wheel which surrounded the mysterious gateway. He shielded his face as the golden blocks imbued with rubies and sapphires began to fall from place one by one, and the foggy portal which had swallowed his wife shriveled smaller and smaller, until there was nothing left besides the rubble of jewels and gold on the cave floor.

Talvi sank to his knees, overcome with grief at his sudden loss. It hadn't mattered how tightly he held onto his bride of only one week, she had been ripped from his arms by supernatural forces which no one could control. He leaned forward, clutching his chest, where her scent still clung to his blood-spattered jacket, and he sobbed into his hands and the musty grit underneath them, oblivious to the pandemonium around him.

His eyes snapped open, but he didn't feel awake in the slightest. He felt much like he did the previous evening in the bath with Runa . . . possessed by some unseen force. This was the same grueling nightmare he had dreamt every night for two and a half months, the same one that caused him to toss and turn in his restless sleep. Even the familiarity of his massive wooden four post bed offered little comfort, warm as it was. He looked around his room at all the things he had collected in his lifetime, surveying his desk littered with various papers and paints, his music collection piled near the Victrola, the tall floor mirror that stood close to a set of armoires. If he chose to stay, he could return to his normal life at home, where all that was required of him was to chop firewood, mind the horses, help with the maple sugar collecting, and plant the massive gardens when the snow thawed. But there was a woman out there he was trying to find . . . again. He threw back the covers and hurried to dress in a pair of wool trousers and a thick sweater, letting the cold air wake him up.

He was lost in his thoughts as he began to walk around his room, gathering thing he might like to have with him for the next few months, or even years. He found himself reaching for an object, then changing his mind and leaving it. He did this more than a few times. There were few material possessions he cared for in this room. The only thing he wanted was *her*.

Talvi shoved his chosen belongings into a black canvas messenger bag and shut the door to his room behind him, walking down the long hallway. There was a faint sense that this might be the last time he walked down those steps, but then, it was just a stray thought among a gargantuan list of thoughts.

The seemingly endless hallway did in fact, end at a landing, where the steps continued downstairs, but Talvi had one more stop before breakfast. He stepped through a partially open door on the right and entered a room filled from floor to ceiling with books. It looked like a library, but there was a bed off to the side, and a chest of drawers near the end of the bed. All of the light in the room poured through one massive arched window that reached close to the ceiling. The heavy curtains had been pulled back to reveal the snowy wonderland outside, saturating the room with the brightest sunlight possible. In front of the window stood a telescope and a large desk and chair, and there on the desk sat a small stack of books. Finn sneezed as he stood on a ladder and pulled out two dusty volumes from the bookshelf farthest from the door.

"*À tes souhaits,*" Talvi said, passing by an overstuffed chair and ottoman as he made his way across the room.

"*À votre bon cœur,*" Finn replied, tucking the books under his arm and wiping his nose with a handkerchief. "I really need to dust in here."

"You'll have plenty of opportunity to work on that before it's time for spring planting," Talvi said, squinting as he looked around. It was really an insane amount of books, and he wondered if Finn would truly be able to dust every single one of them by the time the snow melted. He was rather thorough when it came to things like tidiness.

"I don't expect much opportunity for such a leisurely pastime," muttered Finn.

"You call that leisure? Badra's beard, Finn . . . you can be such a bore."

Finn gave a wry smile at his brother, then neatly folded his handkerchief and put it back in his pocket before climbing down from the ladder.

"Well, if I was just like you, our parents probably would have left us on someone's doorstep years ago. Besides, I'll be plenty busy, what with spring almost here, and I have no idea how long it will take me to unlock the secrets that are held in those blasted stones." He tipped his head toward a medium sized chest on the floor. There were three heavy locks sealing it shut. He frowned a little bit, and added the two books to a small stack on his desk, before turning back to his brother.

"When you find Annika, I want you to have her read these books. I believe she'll find them very informative and helpful."

"Right," he said, looking at his brother skeptically. "The very moment she's in my arms again, I'm going to sit her down with that pile of books and tell her to have a good read. I think you and I both know the odds of that happening."

Finn grinned, blushing ever so slightly.

"Well, catch up first, of course," he said, shifting his composure. "You know, Talvi, there has been something nagging at me about those missing travelers we encountered. It might have some relevance as to where Annika ended up."

Talvi riveted his eyes to Finn's.

"I didn't think of it at the time, but now I find it extremely odd that of all the portals between Earth and Eritähti, not one of the misplaced travelers came from the Paris embassy. It doesn't make sense, and I don't believe it could be a coincidence. I know you have your mind made up to begin your search in Sofia, but I believe you'll find more answers in Paris."

"Perhaps," Talvi replied, mulling over the idea. It seemed a long shot, but Finn was too great of a scholar for his advice to be ignored.

"I see you're not wearing the bracelet that Hilda gave you all those years ago," he observed, recalling his conversation with Runa the previous night. Finn glanced down at his left wrist, and then back at his brother.

"Not for some time now," was all he said, matter-of-factly. Unlike his myriad of books, his dark brown eyes were impossible to read. He didn't seem like he wanted to elaborate much on the matter, and he quickly changed the subject. "In any case, and I know you know this, but *please* be careful," he advised. There was a worried look in his face. "Something sinister is afoot. I can feel it."

"I feel it too," said Talvi, glancing briefly at the locked trunk on the floor. "I promise I'll be careful. I'll send word back to you as soon as I can."

"Oh, that reminds me," Finn said as he retrieved a scrap of paper from his pocket. "I don't think you have a copy of this." He handed the paper over and Talvi gave it a look, but nothing registered.

"What is this, some sort of secret code?"

"No Talvi, it's those electric mailing addresses that Asbjorn was telling us about," Finn answered, looking excited for a change. "Don't you remember him saying that he set up a mailbox for each of us? He says it's one of the fastest ways to communicate in the modern world. This way you can write to me from America and keep me informed of how things are going. I would still have to get to Sofia to access the message, but it's so much faster than writing paper letters and sending them via our standard methods. It's *instant!*"

"I assume it requires a computer?" Talvi asked, wrinkling his nose in disdain.

"Yes, Talvi," his brother joked, brushing his loose brown curls away from his eyes, which had begun to twinkle. "I have a feeling you will be forced to learn to use them . . . *frequently.*"

Talvi rolled his eyes and set his bag down next to the pile of books on Finn's desk. For as many things that he loved about Earth, computers had somehow failed to fascinate him as much as telephones, refrigeration, high speed rail, and laser light shows at rock concerts.

He stuffed the books into his messenger bag and walked down the last flight of stairs. There was only one thing Talvi wanted to do before he ate breakfast and said his goodbyes. He made his way to the reading room down the hall, and walked past the two brown velvet chaise lounges. There were dozens of potted plants in the room taking advantage of the tall windows; ferns and ficus and spider plants draped their leaves for display, while vines wandered along the walls. The sweet, clean air was a seductive perfume that begged him to lie down and get lost in a book.

He resisted the temptation and stepped to the darker side of the room, where a portrait hung of his twin sister and himself. Yuri was dressed like an Egyptian goddess, with a glittering green serpent held around her arms. Talvi stood beside her, draped in black, silver and green. It seemed he was whispering a tender secret in her ear. There was a terrible ache in Talvi's heart as he remembered the day the portrait was done. It was his gift to his sister on their two-hundredth birthday.

From the doorway behind him, Talvi heard a soft voice ask, "Do you remember what you were telling her?"

Talvi looked down into Chivanni's eyes.

"I was telling her I thought she had shit on her slipper," Talvi replied, and scratched his head. "The artist had an obscene number of cats in his studio."

"Such lies you tell me," he said and frowned, crossing his slender arms.

"He was a very skilled artist. He made me look very convincing, did he not?"

"I don't care how skillful the artist was, there is no way anyone could look so pure and innocent when they are saying something so foul."

"I beg your pardon, Chivanni, but have you forgotten whom you are speaking with?" Talvi snickered and took a digital camera from his pocket. "You of all should know that's one of my specialties."

The orange-haired faerie was quiet as Talvi snapped a few pictures and tinkered with the buttons on the camera. In his many years of knowing Talvi, Chivanni had seen him dish out plenty of hurtful comments from those same lovely lips. It wasn't that long ago that he had seen Dardis become the recipient of a cruel insult, but it had been forgiven quickly enough. Talvi was being quite honest that delivering them was a specialty of his. Chivanni looked at his friend in silence, as he took another photo of the painting. He wondered if he were making a mistake to ask to tag along with Talvi in an unfamiliar world. But then, he knew their friendship was solid; that was the circumstance that would keep him safer than anything else. Chivanni had seen the results when someone lost his respect. The last thing anyone wanted to be was an enemy of Talvi Marinossian.

Talvi slipped the camera back into his bag, took a step back, and curled a sleek, strong arm around Chivanni's narrow shoulders. Without looking away from the portrait, he confessed, "In this painting, I'm Osiris, and I was telling Yuri that I shall never love another as I love my sister Isis. And now, like the Egyptian gods and pharaohs, our time has passed, and only this image remains. Nothing will ever be as it once was."

Chivanni hugged him back, but could say nothing. He was afraid Talvi was right.

Usually, but especially in wintertime, the kitchen was the heart of the Marinossian household. This morning was no exception, but it almost felt festive. So many different smells hit Talvi's nose all at once, and if he hadn't been hungry earlier, he was ravenous now.

"Since you missed so many holidays, we're helping you make up for it," his older sister informed him as he came over to investigate. Sure enough, it looked like she was doing just that, as she pulled roasted curried squash and a baked brie out of the oven. There were pumpkin and apple pies cooling on the counters, along with a persimmon pudding, while candied almonds, dried cherries and roast chestnuts were being scooped into small dishes by Dardis and Stella. Ambrose was just coming up from the cellar with a bottle of spiced rum. Chivanni sliced a loaf of olive bread and brought it to the table along with some plates. Anthea followed with the brie while Talvi carried over the curried squash, making sure to set it close to his usual spot at the table. His mother poured him a cup of tea, set the creamer next to his cup, and urged him to sit down before resuming her delegation of breakfast duties.

Talvi slid onto his end of the long wooden bench, just a spot away from where Asbjorn was feeding Sloan a slice of pumpkin pie.

"I hate to leave him so soon, but at least I'll be home much more quickly this time," Asbjorn said, wiping his son's cheek with a loving hand. Talvi poured in a bit of cream and held his tea cup in his hands, studying his brother-in-law's face. Although they had traveled together for weeks and weeks, it wasn't until yesterday that he had seen Asbjorn's eyes light up, and felt his spirit truly be at ease. He had been kept away from his family for a year, and now he was expected to leave again. Even though life was not always fair, it had been exceptionally unkind to Asbjorn.

Talvi took a sip of his tea, conscious of its warmth as it traveled from his mouth, down his throat, and into his stomach. He imagined it was Annika sitting beside him instead of Asbjorn, and he couldn't bear the thought of having to part with her right after being reunited.

"You don't have to leave him at all," Talvi said abruptly. "Stay home with your family. I see no reason why I can't be the one to take your dossiers to London. I've read your report nine times. There's nothing more that you can share that I don't already know. Besides, I need to make a stop in Paris for an American passport. It wouldn't be any trouble." There was a brief silence, when all that could be heard was the fire crackling in the hearth.

"I appreciate the gesture, Talvi, but Merriweather was expecting me, not you. This was my assignment, after all. It would be unprofessional of me if I didn't deliver my own report."

"You're worried about offending someone who is renowned for routinely breaking embassy protocol?" he asked, helping himself to some of the warm olive bread. "Bollocks to Merriweather."

"Don't say bollocks in front of your nephew," Anthea scolded as she set silverware on the table. "It's such crass modern slang."

"*You* just said bollocks in front of him," Talvi said with one side of his mouth full of bread, and winked at his sister, "which indicates that it's perfectly acceptable for *me* to say bollocks in front of him. Say, Sloan, *bloody bugger bollocks*. Did you know your mum hates those words?" The little boy gurgled and smiled as he clapped his hands. A look of indignation crept across Anthea's face, but it melted away as she sat beside her husband. Talvi motioned for her to pass the honey, but she hesitated as Stella crawled into her lap.

"Mummy hates bloody buggy bollocks," Stella giggled.

"She does indeed," Talvi said, beaming with pride. Anthea's mouth was a thin line, but Zaven was absolutely enchanted by his cousin's antics. He, along with Finn, kept waiting for Anthea to blow her top, but she never did. Asbjorn just shook his head and grinned.

"I suppose I shall miss these colorful pleasantries when you are gone," Anthea finally said, and pushed the jar towards her brother. When he reached for it, she clasped his hand tightly. He looked over at her, and saw her lower lip tremble. He smiled softly to her, before she let go.

"I can't ask you to fulfill my obligations," Asbjorn said, trying to give him a chance to back out of his offer.

Talvi drizzled a bit of honey into his tea and stirred it in slowly before looking back at his brother-in-law.

"How convenient that you didn't ask."

"I'd like to come along and see what all the fuss is about," Chivanni blurted out. "If I were traveling to a new world, I would want an old friend with me." Talvi looked over at his ginger-haired friend, who had remained human-sized ever since dinner last night.

"But Chivanni, I have no idea how long I'll be gone. I'll be responsible if anything happens to you."

"You'll be back by next March," Runa stated as she sat down in the chair beside Finn. "I don't think one year is so terrible."

Talvi gave her an endearing smile and felt touched.

"It's not the worst idea in the world," Ambrose said, bringing a pitcher of eggnog with him as he joined the rest of the family. "Chivanni has already helped you a great deal. His abilities could be a valuable asset on Earth."

Talvi recalled the story he had told his father, of how it was the fairies who had created his and Annika's strange wedding bands, and it was the fairies who had married them, and it was the fairies that had been responsible for breaking the strange machine that had caused so much chaos with the portals between Earth and Eritähti. He wouldn't be where he was today if it hadn't been for the unwavering support of his dear friends. He supposed American culture wouldn't be any more risk than what they had already encountered, what with the forest of flesh eating trees, the avalanches, the vampires, and black magic-wielding druids gone wrong. In comparison, America would probably be a lot of fun.

"Please?" Chivanni asked, furrowing his delicate eyebrows. His large, cinnamon-brown eyes pleaded as best as they could. "Please Talvi, please let me come with you."

"Only if you promise you will do as I say," he said, passing his plate to be filled with the decadent breakfast laid out before him. "Your aunt will have my head if anything happens to you."

Chivanni nodded in agreement, swearing his promises, and fluttered his wings, hugging Talvi tightly before passing his plate around the table.

After extra helpings of everything, and extra-extra helpings of eggnog with a generous ratio of rum, Talvi couldn't help but wonder if this would be the last time he saw his family. He sensed that he was not the only one with this thought, as the meal refused to come to an end. His mother would pass around a dish or a plate from time to time, as if there was a soul who might miraculously still be hungry. His father seemed hesitant to light his pipe, even though he always enjoyed one after every meal. And remarkably, Stella had stopped accepting sweeties and instead wandered off to play.

"Brother dear, we will all miss you terribly, but I for one am glad you are off so soon to search for Annika," Anthea said, desperate to keep things cheerful. "I'm certain by now she must be feeling quite unprepared."

"Unprepared for what? She's not exactly a helpless sort of woman. She can look after herself well enough."

"But is it just herself whom she is looking after now?" his sister pressed.

"What*ever* are you suggesting?" he asked, raising a suspicious eyebrow. His older sister was really beginning to annoy him.

"Oh how can you be so daft, little brother of mine?" Anthea scolded. "You've met your destined lover, you've married the dear girl with the blood of a samodiva . . . do you not remember what comes next for you?"

"I've conveniently put it out of my mind," he sneered back, but Anthea ignored him and began to quote from memory,

"Within this body lie two unborn souls, both clever and strong in spirit. They shall be as one, until their three-hundredth year. Then they shall cast their gaze upon their destined lovers, becoming night and day, mirrors of one another. The first male twin to be born shall be married at dawn on the same day as his conception. His bride shall be from a distant land with the blood of a samodiva and the voice of a siren. Thereafter this union, through his bride's altered body, she shall cultivate and give birth to a voice that will liberate one soul at a time, thusly anchoring these lives to the world of the living."

Cultivate and give birth . . . Talvi repeated in his head. A bit of color drained from his face as his sister's mouth began to turn upwards again.

"If you believe I'm to become a father, it's not true," he insisted. "I always know when a female is expecting, and Annika was definitely *not* when we parted ways."

"I have to say, I suspect otherwise," Anthea said, looking pleased to have gotten her brother back for saying 'bollocks' in front of her children. "You of all elves should know how complicated things become when humans and elves intermingle, especially since our family has human blood in our veins. We all had our doubts that you would ever settle with anyone, yet you return home wearing a ring that you cannot remove. That means that Annika was destined for you. And if it is indeed true that Yuri has died and come back as a vampire, then surely she will become Konstantin's bride, and a mistress of the underworld."

"A mistress of the underworld?" Talvi mocked, but his sister ignored him.

"Oh hush, you! It's the best translation we've come up with— it's an ancient Druid dialect. Now if I may finish. 'The second male twin born to you shall be married at moonrise on the same day as his birth. His bride shall be from a nearby land with the blood of a demon and the face of an angel. Thereafter this union, through his bride's lifeless body, they shall bring peril to one soul at a time, thusly anchoring these lives to the world of the dead.'"

"For the past three hundred years, we were all so focused on protecting our dear Yuri from harm that we neglected to consider what might happen beyond that," Ambrose admitted before turning his eyes to his son. "On the day you were born, Talvi, we were caught off guard to say the least. We were expecting two boys all along, so naturally we thought there was room for error with the prophecy when the first baby was a female. We even picked out the simplest of names for our second male twin, in hopes that Yuri might live close to home and tend fields. But *you* were our first male twin, thus you were destined to be our Talvi."

"And then to prove it further, along came a young lady from a distant land with the blood of a samodiva in her veins," Finn added. "I remember the day you first came home and told me about meeting her. You were enchanted with her."

"She even sang for us the very first night she spent under this roof," Althea pointed out. "It was quite lovely, like what I would expect the voice of a siren to sound like. We knew Annika's arrival was anything but a coincidence. We knew she heralded great changes to come, but we also knew that we could not alter any of your destinies. No matter what we did, your fates were sealed."

"I disagree," said Talvi. "Yuri made her own decisions freely. No one forced her to become what she is today and shall become in the future. She had more choices available besides one particular story told by an old woman three hundred years ago. There are plenty of discrepancies within it, so why do you still insist upon taking it word for word?"

"Why do *I* insist on taking it word for word? It used to mean *everything* to you!" his sister snapped back. "I don't wish to part with you on bad terms Talvi, but I do hope that you would pay more respect to what the rest of us hold dear, even if you no longer do."

"We all feel hurt by Yuri's actions, but we keep looking for another message that perhaps we're simply not seeing," Finn said to his brother. "I think all of us were convinced that it was just an innocent infatuation Yuri had with Konstantin. We felt that if we tried to discourage their relationship, that it would only make Yuri more determined to keep it alive. You twins are so foolhardy sometimes . . . you would cut off your nose to spite your face. We wanted so many times to intervene, but really, it wouldn't have made any difference. None of us ever imagined that Konstantin would be the one to bring peril into our lives. We welcomed him into our home. We trusted him."

"And now we shall pay the price for it," said Talvi as he slowly pushed back his chair and rose to leave the table. "I daresay the face of an angel is the best mask a demon could ever wear."

CHAPTER 3
Merriweather

"What the bloody hell?"

Talvi clutched the strap of his bag as he came to a halt in front of what used to be the Paris embassy. Instead of a stately, centuries old building of stone, there was nothing but a fenced off narrow lot in the Latin Quarter. It was empty except for a large dumpster.

"This is the right address, isn't it?" Chivanni asked, standing fully sized to his right. Even full size, Chivanni still only came to Talvi's shoulder. Barely.

"Indeed it is," Talvi frowned. He had been visiting this building throughout most of his life. It was similar to the Louvre or the Eiffel Tower in that it wasn't a place likely to have a change of address.

"That makes two for two," the faerie said, trying to stay positive. "Are we off to London, then? Third time's the charm."

Talvi pursed his lips at such naïve optimism, and jammed his left hand into his pocket, pulling out his cigarette case and a book of matches. He could feel his blood pressure skyrocketing as his heart thumped harder and harder. He couldn't believe his luck. His first idea was to find the bookstore in downtown Sofia where he had met Annika. They found it had been closed after the owner died unexpectedly. A little harmless breaking and entering showed that all of the books had been auctioned off by the time Talvi and his friend got there. Even the shelves and the cash register were gone. The only things left behind were cobwebs and dead ends.

Talvi's second plan was to get to the Paris embassy as Finn had suggested, where they might be able to help him find his wife. It was a hub of travel, with a customs office, dormitories, a library, and even a passageway in the basement level that linked up with the Metro, as some of the tourists from Eritähti were more sensitive to daylight than others. It had been built around another portal where travelers could safely pass between the two worlds undetected by humans. Unlike the humble little samodiva cave that Talvi used most frequently, the Paris portal had been cloaked not by trees and a waterfall, but by magnificent marble, alabaster, and hand-carved wooden staircases. It wasn't hidden in the mountains outside of Sofia. Instead, it had wide steps leading right to the brass knockers on the front door. It had been built as intelligently as the London embassy had been, with the idea that sometimes the cleverest way to hide something is to not bother hiding it at all.

Talvi struck a match and took a few long, silent drags off the neatly rolled cigarette as he looked around. He began to walk along the fence toward the locked gate surrounding the empty lot, still fueled by his frustration. He found a heavy cement block and smashed the lock from the flimsy chains easily enough, and slipped through the metal fencing with Chivanni close behind. They walked carefully through the rubble, looking for clues, but the only thing he turned up was a brass paperweight of a miniature globe. Talvi clenched his jaw at the irony of the situation he found himself in. Here was this entire world resting in his palm, and yet, in this world where he stood, he had lost not only a woman, but an entire building as well.

Talvi let out an angry yell, making Chivanni jump in fright. He was about to hurl the paperweight into the dumpster when something caught his eye. He lowered his arm, and stepped closer to look at the corner of the dumpster. It was faint, but there was no doubt what was smeared along the side of it. Dried blood. He crouched on his hands and knees and leaned closer, and what he smelled made his stomach turn. It wasn't that it was foul, but it was terribly unpleasant.

"Annika was here," he said quietly. "That's her blood."

Chivanni was beside him in an instant.

"Are you completely certain? How long ago do you suppose?" Chivanni asked. Talvi narrowed his eyes as he took another sniff.

"It's been at least two months. The stain has faded quite a bit, but I'm positive it's hers."

"It doesn't look like enough blood to be too serious of an injury," Chivanni observed, trying to be hopeful, but it didn't stop Talvi from continuing to inspect the rubble for the next hour. After poking around and finding nothing, he finally agreed that the injury didn't seem life-threatening, and that Annika had probably made it to America well enough, given that she had started to exhibit elf-like healing powers before they had been separated.

Talvi led his friend back the way they had come, and stepped into a cafe around the corner for lunch. He ordered a bottle of Bordeaux as well, and inquired about the missing building. The waiter was able to answer his questions too easily. There had been a fire a couple months ago, the building was razed, and that was that. Talvi said very little and ate even less. Instead, he subdued himself with the Bordeaux while Chivanni mapped out the nearest train station.

"Try not to get discouraged," the ginger boy assured him as he poured the last of the wine into Talvi's glass. "I think we'll have more luck in London. Things always work out for you. I've seen it happen so many times. Wherever you land, you always land on your feet."

The elf turned to look at his friend, and for a brief moment, a soft smile passed across his face. He wanted to believe him, he really did. Chivanni packed up what was left of Talvi's uneaten lunch, which was most of it, and one train ride, two bottles of wine, and three hours later, their taxi pulled up to a thirteen-story building in the heart of London.

"Well, the building is still here, that's of some comfort," Talvi muttered. Snow was beginning to fall, and they hurried to the solid doors, and rang the cold metal buzzer.

Talvi wasn't expecting the door to open as quickly as it did, and he and Chivanni were ushered inside a small foyer with three carved wooden doors. One was on the left, one on the right, and one directly in the middle.

"Why, Talvi Marinossian, it's been ages," greeted the elderly doorman, clad in tweed. "What brings you to London?"

"I'm here to see Merriweather."

"You don't have an appointment," the man said, raising a suspicious eyebrow as he shut the doors and locked them. Even though he was much older, he carried a formidable presence.

"Do I ever, Gerald?"

The doorman chuckled to himself, looking a little relieved.

"Rarely, but I would give notice next time, if I were you," he said. "We're rather drowning in our workload as of late."

"Has it anything to do with the Paris embassy?"

"I'll need your password before I can answer that."

"My password?" asked Talvi. "You've never asked before."

"I've never had cause to," Gerald replied in a kind, but firm voice. "However, we must insist on this formality. Doppelgängers are getting to be more troublesome these days."

"Doppelgängers?" Talvi repeated. "Very well then; *lemon meringue*. Now what the hell happened in Paris? The embassy has utterly vanished."

"Yes it has. There was a fire, a terrible fire," said Gerald, and he pulled out a key from his pocket to unlock the door on the right side of the small room. "The chief inspector has attributed it to outdated wiring; however, we are conducting our own investigation."

"How is that going?"

"As I said earlier, we are struggling with our workload," Gerald sighed as he ushered them along. "So I'm afraid the investigation isn't receiving as much attention as it could be. If only there were someone who excelled at gathering information; someone who had just returned from his hiatus and was available for the job, perhaps?"

"Yes, if only," Talvi replied, acting disinterested.

He gave Talvi a curious look, then led him and Chivanni through a narrow hallway to an elevator. He inserted a smaller key into a little brass box, before selecting the floor. The polished brass elevator doors closed and there was the lurch upwards, until they landed on the thirteenth story.

Chivanni had never seen this section of the London embassy before, and now he was mesmerized by the sights as he and Talvi walked along a landing of an open room that rose up three more levels, illuminated by giant chandeliers powered by electricity, and skylights overhead. On the crowded main level below, there were large reading tables and desks with computers set up, most which were occupied by non-humans. The trolls were easiest to spot among the many elves, but there were also quite a few wood nymphs, fairies and other magical folk.

Chivanni grasped the wrought-iron railings on his left, passing rows and rows of books on his right, as they walked along the aisle. A spiral staircase in the far left corner of the large open room led to the main floor, but they stopped at an office in the far right corner instead. The only thing on the empty reception desk outside the office was a heavy layer of dust. The door beyond the desk was closed, with a metal name plate attached to the front of it reading: *Merriweather Narayanaswamy, Director of Modern Intelligence.*

"Perhaps your friend would like me to give him a tour of the building whilst you meet with Merriweather in private?" Gerald offered discreetly, as if he had done this more than a few times. Talvi nodded and sent Chivanni on his way, then slipped silently through the door. He was careful to not make a sound as he shut it behind him, gently turning the deadbolt.

A woman sat at a huge desk covered in very tall and very neat stacks of papers and folios, with her back to the door. She wore a long-sleeved maroon sweater dress, and high-heeled black boots. Her thick black hair was pulled to one side in an elegant chignon, and she was holding a telephone to her pointed ear, taking notes on a pad of paper.

"I'll let you know what I find out. Ta-ta for now," she said, and hung up the phone. She swiveled her chair around and let out a laugh as she recognized who was standing in front of her desk.

"What*ever* did the cat drag in?" she mused, and leaned back in her chair with a bewildered and wry smile. She appeared older than Talvi, but not by much. "You look like you've been through the ringer . . . and then shat out of a hyena's arse."

"A pleasure to see you too, Merri," he said, flashing a conceited grin at her. He sat on the edge of her desk, plopping the report from Asbjorn in front of her.

"I honestly wish I could say the same for you," she said, studying his gaunt face and the way his clothes were hanging on him. "You look absolutely dreadful. I thought your hiatus would have treated you better, but it appears your personal matters have not been resolved. Are you alright?"

"I've had worse. Though, I haven't had a good night's sleep in months."

"It's not because of what I think it is, is it?" she asked with an incredulous smile.

Talvi shook his head and tapped the thick folio with his forefinger, and Merriweather opened it up to the first page. Her smile began to fade, and a moment later she looked up at him with her dark eyes. "Why have you brought me this? What's happened to Asbjorn and Pavlo?"

"They're both fine. Asbjorn's well at home with his family. I thought I would save him the trip and deliver his report to you in person."

"How uncharacteristically thoughtful of you," she said, looking relieved. She pulled open one of her drawers and reached far into the back of it, retrieving a small rectangular object. She stood it upright on the file that Talvi had dropped on her desk. It was an antique silver flip-top lighter with the words 'cheeky bastard' engraved on the front in a flourished script.

"Where did you find this?" he asked, snatching it and inspecting it closely. "I thought I lost it."

"It was found in my last assistant's desk after she resigned," Merriweather said, letting the corner of her mouth turn upwards. "She finally realized that it's bad luck in anyone's hands but yours. I've been holding onto it for you ever since, so perhaps that's why I'm now having a run of bad luck. I've also been waiting months for this information. Do you mind entertaining yourself while I have a quick look?"

"Not at all," Talvi said, and left his perch on her desk, putting the lighter in his back pocket. He walked over to a little bar and took two glasses from inside the cabinet, but he left the bottles alone. Instead, he brought the two glasses back over to Merriweather's desk, setting them down with a soft *clink*. Then he knelt down beside her as she skimmed over the pages, and opened the bottom desk drawer, pulling out a bottle.

"Oh yes, do help yourself to my very best scotch," she said, looking annoyed. It did nothing to stop him from pouring them both a drink. Talvi lit a cigarette with his long lost lighter and took a slow walk around her office, swirling scotch in his mouth as he gazed out the huge windows at the late afternoon London skyline. He hadn't seen this view in almost two years, but he had a feeling that he would be seeing more of it in the future. Snow was beginning to fall, dusting the rooftops with a thin layer of white.

"Has anyone else read this?" Merriweather asked, closing the folio a quarter of an hour later.

"Just a couple members of my family, and Asbjorn's colleague, Pavlo. Why?"

"Did you just ask me *why*?" Merriweather demanded, and marched over to the window where Talvi still stood with his glass in hand. "After all our efforts to maintain open relations with the modern world and our own, you go and instigate a damned war with our enemies, and then have the audacity to let your entire family read Asbjorn's report! It was supposed to be confidential!"

"My entire family did not read it," Talvi scoffed. "As I said before, only a couple of us did."

"Oh Talvi, I know how you define 'a couple'—you always allow room for company."

"There was my brother and my father, which makes two. A *couple*. And I didn't start any war," Talvi insisted, his eyes gleaming, "although coming from you, I'll take that as a compliment."

"Forgive me," she said, with her dark eyes glaring at him. Her nose was only a few inches from his. "It's not yet been declared."

"I suggest you read that report in full, Merri," Talvi retorted, trying desperately to ignore how beautiful she looked when she was angry, how long her black eyelashes were, how she smelled faintly of jasmine and spiced vanilla, how she might look if she let her hair down, and how that maroon dress hugged her in all the right places. To him, it seemed an entirely inappropriate outfit for her to wear on a Wednesday. "It's not as though we blasted in and made a royal mess of things. We did the best we could, with the information we were given at the time. I know how to tidy up after an assignment."

Merriweather walked to her desk in silence, downed her drink in one shot, and sighed as she sat back in her chair. She held her glass absentmindedly, unsure whether or not to fill it again.

"From all that I know about the Pazachi, there likely was nothing else you could have done differently. But I absolutely despise that there are loose ends, that girl being one of them."

"Those are being tied as we speak, I assure you," Talvi said gently. He knew she must have been terribly upset at the situation, to have finished her expensive drink so quickly. He also knew that was about as close to an apology as he would ever get from her. He returned to sit on the corner of the desk once again. "Don't be so vexed, Merri. I prefer it when you're laughing."

"I've much to be vexed about," she said crisply, and set her empty glass beside the documents she'd been reading. "You heard about Paris, I assume?"

"I saw it with my own eyes. Or rather, I did *not* see it with my own eyes. It's unbelievable."

"If you spent a few days here, you would believe it," she said, and motioned at the huge stacks of paper on her desk. "It's been a nightmare, dealing with the amount of travelers begging for lodging and passports and directions and currency exchanges. We're a research facility, not Waterloo Station. We can't get any headway on the Paris case, because we're doing the work of two embassies. I have no time to focus on my regular work as it is, and I don't know where I'll find the time to sort out all the details that I've just been given on this ordeal with the Pazachi, not to mention the rest of Asbjorn's report. I'll be buried in presentations and meetings for the next year. It's going to drive me mad!"

"My my, you're wound a bit tight. You'll feel more relaxed after another one of these," he said, about to refill her glass, but Merriweather put her hand over it.

"Since we were speaking about loose ends," she said, noticing her door was locked, "your quill has caused me more problems than it's solved, so don't think for one second that you have carte blanche to dip your pen in the embassy's inkwell."

"Don't you worry; I only thought that for *half* a second," Talvi said, winking at her again. "Things have changed since we saw each other last. I'm married now." That statement was met with a dubious look from Merriweather's large brown eyes.

"Oh please. *You?*"

Talvi nodded and showed her his wedding band. Merriweather looked at his ring, and then back at him in disbelief.

"You're serious, aren't you?"

Talvi nodded again.

"Who is she? I didn't think there were any elven ladies left who hadn't heard of your reputation."

Snorting at her jab, Talvi replied, "She's not an elf. She's one of those modern girls."

"You mean a *human?*"

Talvi nodded again.

"You know that's forbidden!" Merriweather hissed, looking aghast. "How could you do such a thing? Where ever is she? I'd like to give her some keen advice."

"Well, that's the other reason why I'm here," said Talvi, looking first at his empty glass, and then back at Merriweather.

"I should have known you had ulterior motives for bringing me Asbjorn's report. Did she leave you already? She must be somewhat clever, then."

"She didn't leave in the way you are suggesting," he said, and the playfulness left his face. He poured a little more scotch into his glass and began to explain. "After the battle against the Pazachi, she was . . . she . . . " His voice faltered as he saw the fear in Annika's eyes all over again. "She was pulled through their manufactured portal, right before it fell apart. I know for a fact that she ended up landing in Paris, although I'm sure she's back home in America by now. She's a very clever girl. In fact, she's the reason that the portals were mended."

"But Talvi, the Paris embassy had burned down by then," Merriweather said, softening her expression and her voice. "That portal was on the third floor. Even if she had survived that kind of a fall, she would be in hospital with severe injuries."

"Not if she wasn't *entirely* human anymore," he said cautiously.

Merriweather's brow furrowed, but she only tilted her head and folded her arms, waiting for further explanation.

"Something happened to her when we were married," Talvi continued. "Something happened to both of us, actually. Try to take my ring off."

He outstretched his hand toward Merriweather, who looked at him skeptically once again.

"I think I prefer your wedding ring exactly where it is."

"As do I, but I assure you, you can't remove it, no matter how hard you try. Go on, have at it."

Merriweather slowly took his left hand into her own, letting her right thumb pass over the platinum band as she admired it. Then, she clamped her fingers around it and yanked as hard as she could. Instead of ending up with a ring in her hand, she ended up with an elf in her lap.

"Oh, damn you! A fine trick that was! I can't believe I fell for such a desperate act!" she huffed into Talvi's neck as he groaned and scrambled to get off of her. He clutched his left hand in his right and held it against his chest, gritting his teeth from where he sat on the floor against her desk.

"Hells bells and buckets of blood, Merri; I didn't think you were so strong!" he hissed through his teeth. He let go of his hand and flexed it into a fist a few times. Blood began to trickle toward his wrist.

"You mean I actually hurt you?" she asked, and took a handkerchief out of her desk drawer. "Give me your hand."

Talvi rose to his knees and offered his hand to her once again.

"Be a bit more gentle, would you please?"

She nodded and held his hand in hers, resting it in her lap as she wiped his wrist clean. She dabbed carefully around the platinum band, folding the handkerchief to a point to get in between the thin silver inscription in the center. Without thinking of it, she tried to pull the band once more, just to clean underneath it. What happened next made her gasp at the same time as Talvi; he in pain, and she in shock. She could see the silver thread from the ring had pulled the tendons and veins of Talvi's hand with it. The blood began to trickle once again.

"It's woven into your hand?" she asked, her eyes widening as she looked at him, and then at the ring once more, before wrapping her handkerchief around his finger. She clasped his hand in hers once again, and let them rest in her lap.

"Yes," he said, having recovered from the burning in his hand. It had begun to dwindle to more of a warm tingling sensation. "It's grown longer since the day Annika and I were married. Sometimes I can feel the silver thread halfway up my forearm."

"I've never seen or heard of any kind of thread like that."

"It's no ordinary thread. It's a unicorn hair."

A gasp escaped Merriweather's lips, and her golden brown skin broke out in goose bumps. "Did Annika's ring do the same thing to her? Is that why you believe she survived her fall well enough to make it to America?"

Talvi nodded again.

"Oh Talvi, who else knows what your rings are made of?" Her dark eyes were brimming with both awe and worry.

"Aside from she and I, only my brother Finn, and the two fairies who performed the ceremony, one of which is getting the grand tour from Gerald as we speak."

"What of the other faerie?"

"Safe at home with Finn."

"Thank goodness for that. I don't think any of you should discuss it with anyone else. Please tell me that your wedding was not as well-advertised as all the other soirees you throw."

Talvi laughed and shook his head.

"Not even my own mother knew about it. I think it will be quite some time before I'm forgiven."

"She'll come around," Merriweather assured him in a gentle, comforting tone. "It's impossible to stay cross with you for very long."

"You certainly seem to be having a go at it."

"I'm not cross with you. I'm concerned for your safety."

She let go of his hand to smooth her rumpled dress from his fall earlier, then glanced at Asbjorn's report. "The anti-modern sentiment is gaining strength, and your family has never been shy about their views."

"Whatever happened to 'if it harms none, do what thou wilt'?" he asked. "It seems the old creed isn't fashionable anymore."

"I don't know, Talvi," she said, fixing her gaze on him. "We live in strange times. Not everyone likes how things are developing on Earth. That's what got you into this mess with the Pazachi to begin with, and now you may have gone and made them into martyrs, which will only strengthen their cause. Being that there are survivors and witnesses, it would be arrogant not to expect some kind of retaliation for assassinating their leaders. Please promise me that when you get to America, you will lie low for a while? Try not to call any attention to yourself."

Talvi batted his lashes at her and shot her a smirk. "I try not to make promises that I can't possibly keep."

Merriweather rolled her eyes, trying not to smile. "You know very well what I mean, you cheeky bastard. Wherever are you headed, anyway? What city does your unfortunate bride live in?"

Talvi bit his chapped bottom lip, and tried his best to look as charming as possible while he shrugged his shoulders.

"I never got around to asking her."

"Talvi Marinossian, how long did you know this girl before you decided to marry her? No, don't even answer that. I'm certain it was less than half a year."

He gave an impish grin, but said nothing.

"How is it that after all these years, you can still surprise me like this? Yet I am not really so surprised after all. Well, I take that back. I am surprised. Really, how *do* you do it?" she demanded in exasperation.

"Merri, I know how much you love playing travel agent lately, but I could really use your help finding her," he confessed in his silkiest voice as he stood up and took ahold of the back of her office chair. He still held the bloodied handkerchief in his left hand. "You're *so* good at everything you do. That's why I refuse to work with anyone else here."

"That's the reason?" she said and turned to look at up him skeptically. "You certainly had me fooled. For a moment I almost thought you were complimenting me on my credentials." She motioned to the wall above her desk, decorated with numerous framed diplomas and certificates from prestigious universities and other organizations.

"Oh, I was, but we both know not all of them are hanging on a wall, protected behind glass," he said, and tilted her chair back as far as it would go, looking down at her seductively. Then he pointed at one of the frames. "I remember the night you received that award. You worked quite hard for that one, if I recall. But this one over here, this came easily enough. Three times in a row, isn't that right?"

Merriweather tossed her head and took a deep breath, shuddering slightly as she exhaled. "I didn't get this lovely corner office by being an underachiever, now did I?"

"No, you did not," he agreed, appearing satisfied with his effect on her. He gently rocked her chair, letting one corner of his mouth curl upward. "You had a fair amount of assistance acquiring this position . . . achieving your multiple awards."

"And I appreciate all that you have done for me in the past," said Merriweather, motioning for Talvi to let go of her chair. "But if you honestly want my help finding your wife, perhaps you might try acting like you are her husband?"

"Of course," he said, embarrassed that she had called him out on his bad behavior. He returned the chair to its original upright position. "Where shall we begin?"

"Let's start with some basic information about her. What's Annika's last name, or did you neglect to ask her that as well when you were getting acquainted?"

"It's Brisby," Talvi answered. "She lives with her brother Charlie and some other bloke. They're in a band together. She plays guitar . . . quite well, I might add."

"Thank goodness for that," Merriweather said, turning to her computer as she began to type. "Musicians and artists tend to willingly promote themselves." Within seconds, she had brought up a half dozen pictures of Annika. In one of them she was drenched in blue lights, clutching a microphone. In another, she was playing guitar, dressed in a poufy rainbow colored skirt and sparkly Mary Jane heels.

"That's her!" Talvi exclaimed. "How did you do that?"

"Sweetheart, I just Googled her," Merriweather explained, typing more, opening other windows in her browser.

"Do you know where she is then?" Talvi asked, peering over her shoulder, but Merriweather minimized the browser so that all he saw was her desktop background. She swiveled her chair around to face him, crossed her legs, crossed her arms, and looked Talvi square in the eye.

"I can't get a phone number for her, but I can get you to her front door in about twenty-four hours . . . *If* you agree to my terms."

"Of course I'll agree," he said without hesitation. "What are the terms?"

"As of this moment, you are no longer on hiatus."

Merriweather's right hand reached into another drawer and pulled out a smart phone. She turned it on and began to tap a few buttons on the flat screen.

"My direct line and my personal cell number are already programmed into your new phone," she explained, and nodded at her desk buried in paperwork. "Hopefully it's crystal clear to you how valuable my time is these days, so I expect you to answer when I ring you and give you your next assignment."

"What kind of assignment? Are you going to send me to Paris?" he asked. She simply smiled and shrugged, batting her long black lashes at him just as he had done to her earlier.

"I haven't decided yet. For now, I only want you to find Annika and keep her as safe as possible without arousing any suspicion on her part. Please consider what I said about keeping a low profile whilst you enjoy your honeymoon together. Let me know if her ring is reacting the same as yours, or if there are any significant changes in either of you. And eat something, for goodness sakes. When the time comes, I'll need you in top form, not looking like a ragged bag of bones."

Talvi looked into her dark eyes, trying to eke out some kind of clue as to what she had in mind, but Merriweather's mind was an iron fortress.

"Very well. I accept. But I'll need an American passport . . . and a place for my friend and I to stay tonight. Oh, and I need to exchange some currency before I leave."

Merriweather rolled her eyes and handed him the phone.

"Prince Talvi, you are a royal pain in my backside. You're taking me out for dinner after this nonsense is over with, and then you're going to buy me a new bottle of scotch," she said, and swiveled her chair back to face her computer. She clicked her mouse a few more times until she had a map to Charlie Brisby's last known address on her screen, which she routed to Talvi's phone via text.

"There's a flight out of Heathrow tomorrow at 10am," she said as his phone chimed in his hands, "with one connection in Boston before you get to Portland. Would you like a window seat?"

CHAPTER 4
A Damsel in Distress

Talvi watched as the morning light pushed through the wooden blinds of the unfamiliar room, creating a pattern of thin stripes across the body of the woman beside him in bed. Propped up on one side, he'd been watching her sleep for the past hour, watching the slow rise and fall of her chest, trying not to reach out and caress her waist, for fear of waking her up. In those intense bursts of light, her bright red mane splayed out like a fiery sunburst on her pillow. She was the most colorful thing in that dark room. And then in the next moment, the sun was overtaken by a raincloud, and the color was washed away.

It was the perfect metaphor for how he had found his lost bride. She had been radiant and full of sass when he had first met her, but that didn't accurately describe how he had found her last night. Instead, she was timid, anxious, and awkward. When they first met, their kisses had frequently given way to the most vivid imagery of memories and life experiences. Last night, all Talvi could see when they kissed was a distorted collage of random and detached mumblings, cloudy images with no clarity whatsoever. It reminded him of how the world seems when one is about to pass out from intoxication, or of how the world sounds when one is swimming underwater. Whatever the cause, that watery abyss had doused Annika's flame, and it wasn't what it used to be.

Unable to sit still any longer, he slipped away from her side, and collected his well-worn black suede pants and a few personal items on the way to the adjoining bath.

43

"Bloody . . . bugger . . . bollocks," escaped from his clenched teeth. He had just smacked his forehead against the door frame as he entered. Wincing as he rubbed the tender spot, he set his pants, shaving soap, and blade beside the sink. He wanted to blame it on the dim lighting, his recent awakening, or the tilt of the Earth on its axis for that matter, but he knew the real reason. The old house was just not built for elves that stood six and a half feet tall.

Talvi opened all the blinds in the bathroom and it lit up with the pale grey light of a late winter morning. He turned the faucet and waited for the water to heat up before putting the stopper in the drain. He splashed some of the warm water onto his face and let a few drops fall from his chin into the cup of shaving soap, then set about creating nice, thick foam with the brush. There was a particular comfort in going through this morning routine, regardless of where he found himself when he woke up.

Glancing into the adjacent bedroom, he pursed his lips. What if she didn't feel the same as he still did? If absence typically made the heart grow fonder, it had made Talvi's heart grow completely obsessed. For months now, all he had dreamed of was finding the girl, whatever the cost. Now he had her. Now what?

He set down the cup, leaving the foamy brush inside of it. Leaning close to the mirror, he searched deep into a pair of blue and green eyes for some kind of affirmation that everything was going to work out perfectly.

Oh, Talvi Marinossian, what have you gotten yourself into this time? taunted a silent voice. He thumbed the platinum ring on his left hand and wondered if he had finally taken on more than he was capable of dealing with. It was one thing to slay insane maenads, eradicate Pazachi nut jobs, and fight off vampire attacks, but to succeed at marriage?

You're really in for it, you hopeless git! the silent voice taunted once more. The striking creature in the mirror tossed his unruly mane and boldly smirked back at him.

"Surely you jest. I've experienced worse . . . *far* worse," he said out loud to himself and gave in to a satisfying, sinister laugh.

There was a little gasp from the doorway, and he turned around to see Annika in her red bath robe, looking completely mortified.

"Are you talking about last night?"

Talvi couldn't tell if she was trying not to cry, or just squinting in reaction to the brightness of the room.

"Of course not, you silly girl," he said, smiling softly. He walked over to her and pulled her close, kissing her cheeks. "Oh, you females and your damned emotions. But I suppose if you didn't have them, I wouldn't love you quite so much."

"You wouldn't love *me*, or females in general?" she asked cautiously, still reeling from the misunderstanding. It may have seemed an insecure thing to ask, but it wasn't completely unwarranted, considering his notorious appreciation for the opposite sex.

"I was referring to *you* specifically," he said, letting her go as he began to lather up his face, "but it also applies to my mother, my sisters, and my female friends back home. I adore all of you, yet as different as you are, you are still very much ruled by your hearts. It is my observation that this common bond is universal with all females, regardless if you are an elf, a wood nymph, a vampire, or a human. Your heartstrings do tend to get pulled more easily."

"So the guy that I just caught talking to himself in the mirror is calling me illogical?"

An air of amusement passed across his face as he trimmed his wild side-burns with his straight razor.

"I never said you were illogical, although a logical woman would never question my loyalty after I have traveled the lengths I have to be with her."

Annika couldn't argue with his statement. She could only imagine what his travels entailed. She knew there was a lot of snow and ice to contend with. And judging by his looks, not much to eat. There were no heated leather seats in a four-wheel drive, with a cup holder for his gingerbread latte. It was probably a lot of half frozen vegetable soup and fighting off frostbite. Other than being on the thin side, he seemed unharmed. He had certainly felt alive and warm in her arms last night.

"I've never seen anyone shave the old-fashioned way except in movies," she said. "It's fascinating."

"I find it downright mundane, but if it pleases you . . . " Talvi responded, and went back to his task. Annika stood to the side, playing with the soft rounded tip of his soap brush while he passed the blade under his hollow cheekbones with ease.

"I know this smell," she observed, sniffing the ceramic mug with a thick cake of soap inside. Her mind made the instant connection as she caught a whiff of honeysuckle, fruit trees and cinnamon. It was his characteristic scent.

"My mother makes it," he said, rinsing the blade in the sink full of warm water. "It's the exact same formula that my father used when he taught me how to shave. I've tried others, but this is the one I keep coming back to."

"That's so sweet," Annika said, and kept watching him in wonder. Here was a creature she had thought of every day for months, never sure if she would see him again, yet there he stood. She couldn't help but stare at him, afraid that if she looked away he would disappear, and it would all have been a dream. But one glance at her twisted bed sheets suggested otherwise. Her eyes moved over to the alarm clock on the nightstand, and seeing it was blank, she ran to check the time on her phone.

"Hey, did you unplug my alarm clock? I overslept."

"I may have been involved with the unplugging of a clock," he admitted, rinsing the blade in the warm water. "I thought you might enjoy your beauty sleep. There is nothing more attractive on a lady first thing in the morning than a smile."

"You would know," she said, not amused.

He shot her a look but said nothing, and instead continued shaving while she turned on the water in the shower.

"Jeez, how can you do that without cutting yourself? You make that look so easy."

"It's not difficult," he said, passing the blade up his throat and swishing it clean in the water. "I can't recall the last time I cut myself shaving." He made a funny expression as he focused on the tricky place under his perfectly straight nose.

"Why don't you just run it under the faucet instead of rinsing it in the dirty water?" she suggested. He looked sideways at her as he rinsed the blade in the sink basin again, against her advice.

"Because this is how I shave, love. Better get used to it. You're stuck with me and *all* of my habits for the rest of eternity."

A low, wicked laugh followed this declaration, and Annika watched him in silence as he took his sweet time swishing around in the dirty water. It was almost like he was mocking her.

She suddenly realized that yes, she *would* have to get used to all these habits. She was married to this mysterious creature. There was no way she could keep trying to return to her old life now, the one where Talvi didn't exist. Sneaking a glance at her wedding ring before returning her gaze to him, she felt a little intimidated; a little scared. It wasn't the fact that he loomed over her in height, or that he was older than her by over two centuries, or that he possessed much more strength than her. It was that there was so much about him that she didn't know. All she knew was her body and her brain didn't always meet up when it came to him. She had no idea how he took his coffee in the morning, what his favorite subject in school was, or if he had even gone to school at all. She knew nothing of his childhood, really. She knew his family and liked them well enough, and she liked his close friends, but there was still an aura of danger surrounding him. Why did it linger?

She took mental note of the laugh lines on the sides of his mouth, the delicate points of his ears, the faint scars on his right index finger from getting snagged repeatedly on his guitar strings. They were such minor observations, yet they spoke volumes. His rebellious hair was a perfect indication of his personality; too wild to stay still and behave for very long. It gave the appearance that it had endured countless adventures on horseback over hill and dale, with the wind rushing through it all along the way.

His eyes, too, were symbolic of his persona. Just as he had never fully committed to one trade, one hobby, or one home, his eyes refused to commit to just one color. A hypnotic shade of green outlined their blue centers, and being the hues of water, they changed just as quickly. Most of the time they were light and twinkling, but they could flash dark with intensity, whether it was for better or worse. With the dark circles under them, they only seemed to shine brighter, with more mischief.

Annika got into the shower, and was surprised when Talvi joined her a moment later. He hummed in joy as the water warmed his skin, and held her close, hesitant to let her go, now that he had the right wood nymph in his arms.

"I missed you so much, Annika. That was the most difficult journey I've ever been on, especially since I knew you were waiting for me on the other side." He reached for her left hand with his own, and their matching rings clinked gently together. "I could feel you through the distance," he confessed, squeezing her hand, and her stomach balled up into a little knot.

"You have no idea how it felt to have you ripped out of my arms and watch you disappear before my eyes. I didn't know where you would end up, or what condition you would find yourself in when you got there. My gods, I'm so glad you're safe." He leaned in close to hold her against his chest, resting his head on top of hers. He didn't let her go or speak again for quite some time. He was taken aback when she pulled away from him and reached for her shampoo bottle.

"Annika," he asked gently. "What is it, love? What's wrong?" She refused to answer, and instead began to wash her hair.

Talvi stepped back and peered down at her. His eyes gleamed like flames under the falling water, as he concentrated all of his energy on piercing her soul, but she turned her face away from him. There was little he could gather if she wouldn't look at him. He tried to scan her thoughts with all of his ability, but it was like trying to look through the thickest fog. He wondered if it was intentional or not.

"It can't possibly be that bad, can it?" he asked. "You aren't in love with anyone else, are you?"

She shook her head.

"Have you become a lady of the evening in order to pay for your flat?" This time she took a moment to realize what that meant, before shaking her head again. He had almost coaxed a smile out her, but not quite.

"I'm just glad you're here," she finally said as she looked up at him, feeling all sorts of confused with what exactly to say. "My entire family thinks I'm nuts. No one believed anything I had to say about where I'd been all that time. All I could do was try not to think about it, but now that you're here, I just feel overwhelmed all over again by everything that's happened."

"Oh, you poor little dove," he sighed, and cradled her face in his hand. His dark hair clung to his hollow cheekbones, making his pointed ears appear even more pronounced than usual. "None of them understands what you have endured, what you have seen, or what you have to bear. None of them knows you as I know you."

"Well that's just it. You only *think* you know me," she argued as she rinsed her hair. "We don't know each other very well at all. How could we? I don't even know myself anymore."

"I disagree," he said, putting his smooth cheek against hers. "Though I'm happy to help you remember. I know you better than you give me credit for. I know you more deeply than any of your past lovers ever have. I've reached a place inside of you that none of them ever touched. Let me ignite that flame once more."

Annika turned away from him, irritated.

"Why does it always have to be about sex with you?"

"I wasn't referring to sex at all," he said innocently, but then his tone shifted to a much more devious one. "If I was, you would know." He pulled her backwards against his chest and picked up the bar of soap, turning it in his hands until there was an abundance of suds sliding between their bodies. "See, right now I only want to get you cleaned up. You are very dirty," he said in her ear, inhaling deeply. "Gods, I can *smell* you."

"I'm not *that* dirty," she warned. She kept trying to free herself from his arms, but he outmaneuvered her every time. His soapy hands slid up and down her body, coming back to the same places he had just washed before sliding under her breasts and over her waist. "I think I'm clean now," she said, trying one last time to escape the arms that held her close.

"I think otherwise."

It was like playing cat and mouse in a very, very small room. The odds were not in her favor.

"We're never going to get out of the shower if you don't stop doing that," she scolded.

"You make that sound downright undesirable," he remarked, ignoring her protest. He gave her inner thigh a squeeze, moaning as he did so. "Let's get better acquainted, shall we?"

"Talvi, I can't keep up with you. I need a break," she insisted, and he finally surrendered his hold on her and set the bar of soap down. Annika began to massage conditioner into her hair at a fast pace. "I have to be to work by ten, and then my friend Patti's birthday dinner is tonight."

"Patti as in 'Patti Cake'?" he joked as he washed his own hair at a much less frenzied degree. He was so tall that he had to lean down awkwardly under the nozzle to get the suds out of his hair.

"That's the one," said Annika, nudging him aside so she could rinse her own hair. "I haven't seen her in months, so tonight is kinda a big deal. Plus, I was hoping to tidy up a bit before I go, but now I'm out of time, thanks to you."

She hurried out of the shower and wrapped herself up in a towel before tossing the second one to Talvi. He dried his hair haphazardly with it before wrapping it around his waist. Then he followed her back into the much darker bedroom, remembering to duck under the doorway this time.

"I wonder what I could do to make up for the inconvenience I've caused you?" he asked. Right on cue, Annika dodged his question, and tripped over a large messenger bag that hadn't been in her room twenty-four hours ago, stubbing her toe.

"Arrggh!" she yelped as the pain hit her, making her almost fall over. "Where the hell did that come from? Is it yours?" she accused, hopping about the hardwood floor with her throbbing foot in her hands.

"Oh, sorry about that, love. I didn't know where else to put it." Talvi motioned to the various laundry baskets full of clothes and piles of shoes strewn about the room, some items still in moving boxes and on hangers. It was a bit of a disheveled disaster. He was concerned for her foot, but was also trying not to laugh at her. She did look ridiculous, hopping around on one foot as her towel fell to the floor. He thought it was unclear if he should try to comfort her or keep his distance. She seemed pretty irritated, the way a hornet is irritated when it's swatted at.

"What the hell is in there? Bricks? Lead? Lead bricks?" she cried.

"Actually, the correct answer is *books*."

"Yeah, well, I think I just broke my toe on your stupid bag of books," she whined, and sank onto the edge of the bed. "How am I supposed to stand at work all day and then go out tonight if I can't wear any shoes?"

"You could stay home and lie on your back, and let me take care of the work," he quipped.

Annika shot a withering look at him, but it withered him not.

"Why don't you wear these shoes with the red feathers? Then you won't have to walk . . . with a little faerie dust, you can simply fly wherever you wish to go," he snickered, picking up a pair of shoes that was sitting on top of one of the boxes.

"Don't make fun of my Manolo's!"

Talvi responded by making the shoes fly around the room, complete with rooster sound effects.

"Are you intentionally trying to pick a fight with me?" she asked as she slipped on a fresh pair of panties and grabbed a bra off the ironing board. "Because that's what it seems like."

"Of course I'm trying to have a row with you," he confessed with coveting eyes while she adjusted her bra. "Especially if it's for no other reason than reconciliation."

"You would, wouldn't you?" she said, trying not to smile, but it was useless around him. The pain in her foot was quickly fading. He set the pair of shoes down back on the box and turned to her.

"Absolutely I would," he said, looking at her with longing. She retrieved a pair of green knee-high argyle socks from her dresser drawer, but he walked over to her and snatched them out of her hands.

"What are you doing?" she asked. "I have to get ready for work."

"Like hell you do," he murmured. She rolled her eyes and reached to get a different pair, but he grabbed her arm and twirled her around so her back was pressed against his bare chest. She struggled, and tried to twist out of his grasp, but he was much too strong for her to escape. "Did you honestly think I was going to let you waltz out of here and leave me alone all day with nothing but my left hand?" he purred in her ear. He began to tie her hands together behind her back with one of the socks, letting his towel drop to the floor. "Where I come from, that's considered being a rude hostess. For shame, Annika. You ought to be punished for such bad manners. Now how shall I discipline you?"

Shivers ran up her body, and a sensation of heat flooded into her bloodstream.

"Talvi, I haven't even been at this new job for two weeks," she protested. "I can't call in sick already!"

"Of course you can," he said confidently, pulling the knot tight before picking her up. "People fall ill all the time . . . and you do feel quite feverish. I'm only concerned for your well-being."

"I can't call the store if I'm tied up," she reasoned, trying to play coy. He carried her over to the bed and lay her down sideways on top of the down comforter and twisted sheets. He looked thoughtful for a moment.

"You are quite right about that," he admitted, but instead of letting her go, he proceeded to tie her ankles to her wrists behind her back with the other sock while she kept trying to escape.

"Don't struggle like that now, it will only make it worse," he crooned. Then he reached over and picked up her phone from the nightstand, and to her dismay, he scrolled through her address book until he found the right number and dialed it. He took a long look at her, looking pleased as punch at his handiwork as he held the phone to his ear.

"Hello? Yes, I'm calling on behalf of my wife, Annika. I'm letting you know that she won't be coming in today, as she is literally unable to get out of bed."

CHAPTER 5
Wingless Fairies

Annika led her husband gingerly down the stairs, smarting from the lesson she had just learned in hospitality. She saw her older brother Charlie and her roommate James standing just outside the kitchen, having a lively conversation in strained, hushed voices. The chatter came to a halt, and they both looked curiously at Talvi, then at each other, and then at Annika.

"What the *shit*, Ani?" Charlie hissed. Typically, he was the epitome of mellow, but this morning, he looked completely unnerved.

"Huh?"

"Seriously, do either of you know what the hell's going on in there?" James appeared as bewildered as Charlie. Talvi looked around the kitchen, but he didn't see anything unusual.

"I think it's a poltergeist," Charlie whispered, and turned his head toward the sink, where a huge stack of dishes were washing themselves. Annika grinned from ear to ear and looked up at her husband.

"Did you bring anyone with you that you forgot to mention?" she asked. Her question was answered by a flash of orange light, and there stood a delicately built boy, with the brightest red hair. He smiled sweetly at her, letting a pair of orange tinted, transparent wings flutter behind him from underneath his yellow cloak, causing James and Charlie to jump backwards.

"I didn't want to take advantage of your hospitality," Talvi replied, smiling back at her. "Not immediately, anyway."

"Oh, I'm so glad to see you, Chivanni," she sighed happily as she hugged Chivanni tight, making his wings flutter even harder in response. "Where were you hiding all this time?"

"In the flower arrangement above the fireplace," he said, letting go of her slowly as he smoothed his long bangs to one side. "I wanted to give you two lovebirds some time alone to catch up. I thought I would surprise everyone with breakfast, but there isn't anything to eat, so I thought I would at least wash the dishes." Turning his large cinnamon-brown eyes to James and Charlie, he said, "I didn't mean to startle you."

"It's okay, I just wasn't expecting to see that . . . ever," James said with wide eyes, studying Chivanni's wings and bright skin. It slightly shimmered, and was so pale that he could see a trace of blue veins underneath a smattering of freckles.

"I think my coffee mug is being dried," Charlie said slowly. "Is it alright if I go get it?"

Chivanni gave a quick wave and then beckoned with his hand, and the travel mug left the towel, stopped by the coffee pot, let the pot fill it three quarters full, and then floated itself over to Charlie, where it hovered patiently. Charlie hesitated for a moment, before plucking the mug out of the air.

"I don't know how you like it, so I left you room for sugar and cream, except there's no cream," Chivanni said, and then he squealed so loud that he made Charlie jump again, spilling coffee on the floor.

"You must be in Annika's band!" he cried, pointing at the dripping mug in Charlie's hands, which read: 'Drummers Pound Harder'. "Oh please, oh *please*, will you play something for me? I want to hear your music!"

"Maybe later," Charlie smiled nervously, taking a sip of his coffee. He tried not to stare at Chivanni, but it was difficult not to. His orange and yellow gauzy garments were a complete contrast from James's tailored trousers and polished loafers, and Charlie's ripped jeans and dirty work boots.

"Honey, I am *so* sorry I ever doubted one word of your story," James said in disbelief as he walked cautiously toward a clean mug to fill it with coffee. "I knew you had some weird friends, but a *real* faerie? I mean, Chivanni can friggin' *levitate* shit!"

"Yeah, I kinda mentioned that a few times," came Annika's aloof reply, and she avoided eye contact with him and her brother as she walked toward the sink and snatched a clean mug out of the air for herself.

"I guess we can make room for another faerie around here, since he washes dishes without being asked," Charlie said. Chivanni's eyes met Talvi's with an equally baffled expression.

"Where's the other faerie?" he asked, fluttering his wings with anticipation. "I thought I would have noticed another one by now." James cleared his throat and stood a little straighter.

"You're looking right at him," he said with a dry smile. Chivanni's face only registered a blank expression.

"Then . . . what happened to your wings?" he asked politely. While James and Charlie both cracked up, Talvi's brow only furrowed in confusion.

"I don't understand what is so amusing. Where *are* your wings?" Talvi asked in his soft Londoner accent.

"A faerie is what you call a guy who like guys," Charlie finally explained, still snickering a little. Talvi and his friend looked skeptical, but did not question the matter any further. They knew they were in completely foreign territory, never having been to America before.

Charlie took a loud slurp from his mug, and then pulled a red wool hat over his sandy blond hair.

"Well, as much as I wanna stay home, I have to get going or I'm going to be late," he said, and slipped into a warm jacket that had been draped across one of the chairs at the kitchen table. "I'll see you guys later tonight."

"I thought you were taking the day off," Annika reminded him.

"I was gonna, but I got asked to do a couple quick errands today. It's cool though. I'll have plenty of time to get ready for the party," Charlie said with a grin. "I have to see a guy about some chickens."

"Oh, chickens are so nasty," James said, making a face. "You're not really going to put them in your jeep, are you?"

"Heck yeah I am, if you want me to bring home fresh eggs from work in a couple weeks," Charlie replied and he headed out the door.

"At least put down some newspaper first!" James yelled after him, hurling a rolled up copy of the Oregonian at Charlie.

"I'm surprised you're not at work, James," Annika said to him as he shut the door and sat down at a round wooden table.

"Likewise." He raised his eyebrows as he adjusted his black glasses as she stirred sugar into her coffee. "But given our unexpected house guests, I didn't want to leave them here alone in case you actually were going to go in today."

Talvi took a moment to gloat at his wife as he sat down in the chair where Charlie's coat had been.

"See, I told you that you were being a rude hostess," he pointed out. Annika ignored his comment, setting her mug beside Talvi.

"Did you want some coffee?" she offered.

"I don't drink coffee. I take tea, my dear," he said. Annika slowly pulled out her own chair and sat down next to him, giving him an apologetic smile.

"We don't have any tea."

"Have you any orange juice?"

"We're out," Annika said, and shook her head.

"Cocoa?"

Annika shook her head again.

"Hot water with a bit of lemon?"

"We don't have any lemons."

"Truly?" he asked, as if she were playing a joke on him. "I thought you took such pride in your abilities in the kitchen."

"I haven't been cooking much lately," she admitted, but Talvi didn't want to accept defeat just yet. Even though Chivanni hadn't been victorious, Talvi was determined to scrounge up something edible around the house. As soon as he opened the fridge, his hopes fell. There sat a lonely and shriveled little lime, a bottle of bloody Mary mix, and a dubious glass dish covered in plastic wrap. Even faerie magic couldn't turn that into a meal worth eating. His stomach turned slightly before it growled again, not pleased one bit at the options it was being given. He wrinkled his nose in disgust and shut the door quickly.

"Perhaps we should dine out, and then visit the market on our way home? Why don't you join us, James? I don't know that I could live with myself if that thing in the glass dish attacks you while we're out."

"Yeah, about that," James said emphatically, "I'd offer to take you guys out for brunch, but I'm not going anywhere with the two of you dressed like that." James raised his neatly groomed eyebrows once more, frowning in disapproval at Talvi's outfit. Talvi glanced down at his black suede pants and untucked linen drop sleeve shirt.

"What's wrong with this?" he replied, pretending to be insulted. "I wear it all the time back home."

"I can tell. And where exactly *is* home, the eighteenth-century French countryside?"

Talvi leaned back in his chair and pulled out his cigarette case, seeing that there was an ash tray on the table.

"That's quite brilliant, James," he said, letting one corner of his mouth curl upwards as he lit his cigarette with his silver lighter, closing it with a soft metallic *clink*. "I've never heard that once in three hundred years."

Unsure if Talvi was being sarcastic or not, James lit a cigarette of his own and turned his critical eyes towards Chivanni.

"And while I'm all for being out of the closet, you look like you just came off stage from Cirque du Soliel. As the director of a high-end fine art gallery, I have a reputation *and* an image to maintain. I can't be seen at the club tonight with you looking like those hula-hoop acrobats they have." Chivanni frowned a little. He may not have known what Cirque du Soliel hula-hoop acrobats looked like, but he was quick enough to know it wasn't exactly a compliment.

"I'd like to see *you* climb up a rope sideways. I'll bet Chivanni could do it," Annika said in his defense. "Anyway, I'm not getting dolled up just to go out for breakfast. Who do you think we're going to run into at the pancake place on a Friday morning, anyway?"

"Well that's just it," James replied, glancing at her before resting his eyes on Talvi. "You never know who you're going to run into, so you might as well look good just in case. I can handle the black suede pants and the industrial boots, but that Liberace-inspired top has *got* to go."

"If it's that important to you, I'll let you dress me however you see fit," Talvi said to James, trying to win him over. If he and Chivanni were going to be living under the same roof as him, he figured it best to start off on the right foot. "I just want to be quick about it so we can get something to eat. The last decent meal I ate was on Wednesday evening. How about if Chivanni shrinks into his normal faerie size for now, and then after breakfast perhaps we could have you pick out some more appropriate clothes for us to wear tonight. Does that sound agreeable to you?"

"Yeah, I can work with that," said James. He put out his half-smoked cigarette, got up from the table, and disappeared into the living room, heading straight for Charlie's closet.

"I think you just made a BFF," Annika snickered.

"A *what?*" Talvi asked.

"A 'best friend forever,'" she explained, sipping her coffee. "James probably would have been a stylist if he wasn't in the art scene. He has a passion for fashion."

"Why doesn't he do that then, if he enjoys it so much?" Chivanni asked.

"Paintings don't talk back or complain, I guess," Annika shrugged. "Or lead you on and break your heart."

Before the elf or the winged faerie could inquire further, James came back into the kitchen with some clothes in his arms.

"I think these should work alright for now," he said, handing Talvi a dark grey long sleeved t-shirt and a black hoodie. "They're really baggy on Charlie, so they should fit you fine. Your shoulders are broader than his, and you're a lot taller."

Talvi slipped out of his linen shirt and pulled the new one over his head and down his torso. It was a little snug in the shoulders, but it fit his slim, toned body well.

"Yeah, that is definitely a major improvement," James said as he and Annika shared a glance. There was no way either of them were going to let Charlie have that shirt back now. It looked way too good on someone else. He handed over the black zip-up hoodie and called it good.

With Talvi now looking less eighteenth-century French countryside and much more Portland native, the four of them left for Annika and James's favorite diner. Just sitting down at the table was a small adventure in itself, with a three-inch version of Chivanni flitting back and forth from Talvi's shoulder to Annika's shoulder to the table top. She lost track of how many times she had to remind him that he couldn't use his faerie magic so brazenly in public, as she and James nabbed packets of jam and salt shakers out of the air.

Talvi sat through a scrumptious brunch of vegetable quiche, seasoned breakfast potatoes, buttermilk pancakes, orange juice, tea, and toast covered with butter and jam, all the while observing James and Annika chit chat over their waffles about band practice and new song developments, shoes, workplace gossip, and what they were going to wear to the upcoming birthday party. It was becoming clear that Annika was less enthusiastic than James about all of these things. In particular, she didn't seem to be as excited about the party, even though she claimed it was for a friend of hers.

Talvi nodded and smiled at all the right times so that he would not have to partake much in the conversation, which allowed him to concentrate on what was not being spoken out loud. It was still just as challenging to see Annika's thoughts clearly, but he was able to dive right in James's mind. He relished the ability to sift through James's thoughts the way some people flip through a photo album, even though a considerable amount of what he saw was unpleasant. At least he was getting some clear information about this unfamiliar territory he found himself in.

Thanks to James's very open mind, Talvi browsed through the daily interactions of their household. While his sipped his tea, he caught glimpses of James and Charlie trying to coax Annika into joining them for band practice. He saw her through their eyes, but while her body was visible, her fiery spark was not. There were countless scenes of Annika lying on the couch, watching the television, with a drink nearby. Sometimes she was locked away in her room, playing guitar quietly, sometimes singing and working out a melody. But she rarely seemed to leave the house, and for a girl with so many pretty clothes and shoes lying all around her room, it didn't add up.

She mentioned Talvi and her experiences in his world less and less frequently, to the point that she didn't mention any of it at all. From what he could tell, no one in her family seemed to want to hear about it, or know how to accept her story. They just wanted her to go back to being her old self, but they didn't understand that it was impossible for her. Talvi thought it was rather like asking a butterfly to crawl back into its chrysalis, or telling a bird to shrink back into its shell. Oh, his poor little dove, indeed.

The waitress brought the check and Talvi made a swift interception just as James was about to take it. He reached into his back pocket and pulled out a passport and his wallet. While he counted out a few bills, Annika grabbed his passport and took a peek inside.

She couldn't help but smile as she looked down at the photo of a black-haired elf smirking back at her. His ears came to a pronounced point, though they were not too large to warrant much attention. His wild black hair had about as much attitude as the expression on his face, and even the passport photo captured the perpetual twinkle in his eye. She reviewed the information to the side of his picture, which identified him as an American citizen.

"Ha, I know this is a fake," she announced. "You were born in Derbedrossivic."

Talvi let out an amused snort. "No, I was born in Chi*cago*," he teased, trading his Londoner accent for a Midwestern American one just to tease her better.

"So my idea worked? My uncle helped you find me after all?" Annika asked, handing the passport over to James for inspection as well. James nodded his agreement at a forgery job well done before giving it back to Talvi.

"I never met up with your uncle," he replied, looking a bit confused. "I went to our bookstore, but it was closed for business. What was this grand idea of yours?"

Now Annika was confused.

"I asked Uncle Vince to give my contact information to the bookstore owner in Sofia. I wrote a letter with your description so that if you stopped by looking for me, he could help us get in touch. I figured the bookstore would be the first place you would check."

"I did look there, but it was a dead end. Literally. The owner died. Lucky for us both that I have my ways," he said sweetly to her, but Annika still seemed upset.

"Uncle Vince told me he would take care of it. Maybe he was lying."

"Isn't he in New Zealand right now anyway? Besides, if he thought Talvi was involved with you disappearing for so long, the last thing he would have done is give him a map to our door," James blurted out.

"But *he* wasn't the reason I disappeared!" Annika snapped back defensively.

"There now, let's not let this spoil such a fine breakfast," Talvi said, and kissed Annika's cheek. He glanced up and reached out to grab a little pitcher of blueberry syrup that had been slowly approaching Annika's plate, but it was too late.

"Oh, Chivanni!" she moaned. "Seriously, enough with the levitation act!"

"I'm sorry, I just thought it could use a dash more syrup," Chivanni excused when a syrupy blob fell down the inside of Annika's white blouse, staining the front along its way. The boys seemed quite entertained when Annika stood up, trying her damnedest not to reach into her bra in the middle of the restaurant and scoop out lumpy blueberry syrup.

"I'll meet you guys up front," she said, frowning sideways at the faerie now perched on Talvi's shoulder.

The bathroom was located near the restaurant entrance, and when she came out, James and Talvi weren't waiting for her. Instead, a tall, athletic, blond man in a pressed shirt, sharp suit, and perfectly tied double Windsor was speaking to the hostess. He turned around and adjusted his glasses, giving Annika a soft smile.

"Of all the breakfast nooks in all the towns in all the world . . . " the familiar voice said. "Long time no see, Ani."

"Uh, hey there, Danny. How's it going?" she managed to spit out as she looked her ex-boyfriend up and down, from his polished shoes to his neatly clipped hair. She suddenly felt at a major disadvantage, thinking he looked like a million dollars and she looked like hell. Hell with blueberry syrup drizzled on her wet shirt. She wanted to kick herself as she remembered her last words to

James before they left the house. *Who do you think we're going to run into on a Friday morning at the pancake place, anyway?*

"I didn't think I'd run into you here," he said as he walked up to her, eyeing her chest with an amused grin. "But then, I didn't think I'd ever run into you anywhere again. I thought you were avoiding me."

"I wasn't avoiding *you* in particular," she said, trying to act casual, like wearing syrup as an accessory was the latest fashion trend. "I was avoiding everybody. Didn't Charlie tell you? I had mono. What are you doing here dressed like that?"

"Trying to drum up some extra funding for my department," he said, eyeing her strangely. The awkward silence was broken by words as plain as day saying,

I can't believe she thinks Charlie would have told me such a crap story. I know something crazy happened to her in Europe. Why won't she just go talk to someone? That girl needs therapy . . . and some Thorazine.

Annika pushed Danny's thoughts out of her head and sat down on a nearby bench. She didn't have a clue what else to say to the man whom she had spent two years with before turning down his proposal only a few months ago. But instead of telling her 'goodbye' or 'nice to see you' and following the hostess to his table, Danny surprised her by sitting down beside her.

"I heard you were missing for a while over in Europe. I'm so glad to see you're safe and sound," he said with genuine concern in his eyes. "I was really worried about you."

"Oh, it wasn't a big deal. I just got lost in the woods," she said quickly, grasping for an excuse. *No one just gets lost in the woods for two months, you idiot! Only a moron would believe that!* she thought, feeling her neck grow warm. "What about you? What have you been up to?" she asked quickly.

Danny shrugged a little.

"I got another promotion at work and paid off my car early with my holiday bonus. Other than that, not much, besides soccer."

"Huh. Well, congratulations on the raise," she said, glancing around at the restaurant. She had officially run out of small talk, and she didn't know why he was still sitting beside her.

"You left some things at my house, like your rainbow skirt," he said, and suddenly he had her full attention.

"My rainbow skirt? I wondered where that was."

"It was in the closet. You also left your fancy shampoo and some other things. We'll have to do some catching up when you come over." He gave a little smile and Annika returned it.

"Yeah, I don't think you want that girlie shampoo in your bathroom the next time you bring home a date," she teased, but it seemed to be Danny's turn to feel awkward.

"I haven't brought home anyone since . . . since we broke up. I've thought a lot about you, about us," he went on. "I think about our argument a lot. We didn't part on very good terms, and it's been bothering me this whole time." She smiled weakly at him, wishing this conversation wasn't happening. "I tried emailing you when you went to Europe, and then you went missing for almost three months. When you got back and Charlie said you were pretty upset by whatever happened, I figured you would call me when you were ready. I told Charlie to let you know that I wasn't mad at you."

"It's fine, Danny. I'm okay, really. It's been so long since that argument; I don't even remember what we said to each other, but I've let it go," she told him, trying to make light of it. He sighed and turned towards her.

"Well I remember exactly what I said. I remember it like it was yesterday, even though it's been close to five months. I guess I didn't know what I had until it was gone. Your little studio is still empty, and it's not like I need a guest room or a second office. I feel like such an asshole for springing those tickets to Hawaii on you like that in front of all those people. I think I was just afraid if I didn't make a move, you might get away from me. I should have given you more time. That's all you needed, was more time."

He took a lock of her long red hair and twirled it in his fingers, and Annika felt goose bumps as she remembered all the other times he had twirled her hair just like he was doing now. "I miss how you were always singing in the shower and trying to get me to come out dancing with you, and James, and Patti," he said with a reminiscent smile.

"How can you say that?" she exclaimed. "You hate dancing, that's why I could never get you to go out with us."

He grinned a little to himself and let go of her hair only to take her hand in his. "But you were always trying to get me to loosen up. And you always came home to me. We complimented each other so well; you being the creative one, and me being the more . . . *practical* one. I always thought when we had kids, that you and I would be the perfect . . . " he trailed off, noticing the ring on her left hand. "What's this?" His eyes darted back up to hers, and she just stared at him as her face grew warm. "It's not an engagement ring, is it?" he asked, and she couldn't respond. Her mouth may as well have been stuffed with cotton. Danny's surprised eyes grew a little wider.

"So I thought we should at least hit Nordstrom, and then try some men's boutiques if we have time, because you'll never find anything at the mall that's gonna fit *your* body," James was saying to Talvi as they approached the bench. The wingless faerie clammed up as soon as he realized who was sitting so close to Annika, which intrigued Talvi. James had been talking his pointed ears off for the past ten minutes.

"Hey there, James. I haven't seen you in a while. Who's your, um, *friend?*" Danny asked, turning towards them both and casually letting go of Annika's hand.

"This is Talvi," James said, looking at Annika with the perfect *you are so busted* expression.

"That's an unusual name. Is that Norwegian or something?"

"It's Finnish, actually," Talvi replied, tilting his head to one side as he tried to size Danny up.

"Well, if you guys don't mind, I'd like to 'Finnish' talking to Ani," said Danny. "We were kind of in the middle of something important."

Annika thought she was going to die right then and there as Talvi's blue-green eyes burned like flames. She was sure his jealous side was about to make its American debut, but instead he forced a gracious smile.

"Well then, since it appears there is no smoking allowed in this establishment, I'll just wait for you outside, love," he said, batting his black lashes at Annika. Then he locked eyes with Danny and leaned just a little closer, looking down his nose to emphasize his height even more.

"Be sure not to take up too much of her time. My wife and I have a busy day scheduled, and even more plans this evening." He ran his fingers through his hair, making sure that Danny noticed his matching wedding band. Then he turned on his heel and sauntered out the door with his preternatural feline grace.

"Wow . . . " Danny whispered softly as reality struck him full blast. He turned to his ex-girlfriend, who was incapable of speech at this point. "I see you didn't waste any time getting back in the game. That's one hell of a rebound, but then, that's March Madness for ya."

He chuckled to himself and paused as if he was going to impart some witty advice, but instead he just shook his head and let the hostess lead him to a table with four other well-dressed people.

Annika was still standing there, hoping that this was all just a warped dream that she was about to wake up from. But such was not her luck. There she remained, marinating in that awkward, terrible moment. Wide-eyed and desperately holding his tongue, James grabbed Annika's hand, jerking her out of her stupor as he dragged her out the door.

"Who was that bastard?" Talvi asked them as they met up with him in the parking lot and walked towards James's car. "That was *him*, wasn't it?"

"That was Danny, Annika's ex," James said quickly, and fished a cigarette out of his black bag. "Holy shit, did you see that Brooks Brothers knock-off he was wearing?"

"It's not a knock-off," Annika said quietly as she jumped into the backseat with the now human-sized Chivanni following in tow, letting her husband have the legroom up front.

"And how would you know?" James asked as he jammed the key into the ignition and lowered the windows. He put a cigarette between his lips and Talvi leaned over to light it for him.

"Because I helped him pick it out," she said, remembering that day. A flood of memories came back, memories that, like the boxes in her room, had been shoved in a corner to be dealt with another day. She didn't want to think about it now, but seeing him in that suit triggered a series of images stored in the back of her mind; lazy Sundays on the couch, soccer games with him and Charlie, going out for beers after a win, going out for beers after a loss, fancy dinners with his co-workers from the hospital, and all her band's shows that he was too tired or too busy to attend.

"Fine, then, I take it back about the suit, but he looks like he's gained ten pounds. Did he quit playing soccer with Charlie?"

"Nope," Annika replied.

"I honestly thought for a second that those two were going to just skip the chit chat and whip 'em out and measure."

"Whip what out?" asked Chivanni. "Their fists?"

"Not quite," James answered, giving a snort. He took another drag off his cigarette and tried to catch a glimpse of Talvi's expression, but he was staring out the window, stewing in silence.

CHAPTER 6
Pretty Paper Dolls

When they reached Nordstrom, Talvi seemed to have recovered from the incident at breakfast. Either that, or he was doing his best to fake it. Annika took James by the arm and gave him a stern look.

"I know how you can get with your makeover extravaganzas," she warned in all seriousness. "But if you go overboard playing dress up with the guys, I'll sell your new Hermes man purse on eBay to pay for it."

"You wouldn't dare!" he gasped in horror, clutching his precious black crocodile bag. Annika knew then that she had him right where she wanted him. "Do you have any clue what I had to go through to get this?"

"I do," she said, smiling cruelly as she recalled the story about how James and his beloved black bag were united by a miffed Mafia mistress. "And I'd start the bidding at fifty cents just to spite you."

"You are such a bitch," he said, only half-joking. "You'd really do it, wouldn't you?" Annika's evil grin only widened. "Well it's not a purse. It's a *bag*," he snapped as he conceded to her terms. "Besides, what exactly do you mean by going overboard? It's not like I'm picking out an entire new wardrobe for both of them."

"It's not that," she said. "I don't care what you do with Chivanni, but don't dress Talvi too metro."

"Oh, who do think I am, David Copperfield?" James huffed. "Even if I decked him out like a fireman . . . " he trailed off for a moment, caught up in the vision of Talvi in uniform, holding a big, heavy axe, looking out from under the sweaty brim of a hard hat, waiting to extinguish a burning fire somewhere. "Mmm, *that* might look interesting. But, no matter how macho I try to make him look, it's going to be a challenge."

He looked up at Talvi and adjusted his trendy glasses, inspecting him as carefully as an heirloom tomato at a farmer's market.

"Just look at these pores, would you? They're nonexistent! Look at that perfect skin tone. He's a pretty boy, and I'm *not* a miracle worker!"

Rather than look embarrassed by the excessive flattery, Talvi opted for the smug smile he wore so well before James grabbed him by the arm and headed to the men's department. Compliments weren't anything new to him, not after hearing them constantly throughout his entire long life. Rather than tag along with James, Annika decided it was the perfect opportunity to find a new top since she was still wearing the blueberry-stained one. With Chivanni by her side, they wandered to the women's department as he told her about his home in Srebra Gora.

He had grown up in a small glen near a tree lined creek that flooded every spring, leaving a mass of exposed roots that made perfect places to hide or nap. He spent his days playing with his friends, exploring hollow tree trunks, and learning things from his aunt like where to find the best wild honey, how to communicate telepathically with animals, and what situations it was acceptable or not to use faerie magic. He had always envied Talvi's family for traveling through the portals between Eritähti and Earth with ease, and he eagerly looked forward to every visit his aunt paid them.

While it wasn't forbidden, it was considered extremely dangerous amongst the fairies to cross through the portals that lead to the modern world. It had changed too much to be as safe as it used to be, and trips to Earth were rare. But because of their appearance, it was much easier for the elves to walk among humans unnoticed, and Chivanni would listen to any of the heavily embellished stories that Talvi could recall from his adventures. He would sometimes beg for a story to be retold over and over again, at which point the details usually became even more fantastic and exaggerated, but he didn't mind. He adored the Marinossians, Talvi especially; they were as close as cousins, since Chivanni's aunt was faerie godmother to Talvi and his twin sister.

"I'm counting on you for some serious advice about living with him," Annika told him as they tried on scarves in front of a large mirror. "You've known Talvi so much longer than I have."

Chivanni snickered to himself.

"I doubt I could tell you much that you don't already know."

"Like what?" she urged. "Humor me."

Chivanni smoothed his long red bangs off to one side and looked thoughtful for a moment. His big brown eyes and freckles reminded her of a young Twiggy, he was that dainty.

"He takes tea every morning, with a bit of cream and honey," Chivanni said. "And if there's lemon available, he really likes that. He adores anything with lemons in it. Perhaps that's why he can be so sour sometimes," he added with a little laugh.

"Um, that's not quite what I had in mind, although I guess it's good to know," Annika replied. "I meant more about dealing with him being in your day to day life."

"Oh, well the tea is fairly important to that," Chivanni said, looking absolutely serious. "If he doesn't have his morning tea, he can be quite intolerable."

"Okay, that's easy enough," she laughed. "What else?"

Chivanni looked thoughtful again, racking his brain for helpful tips.

"It might help if you think of him more like a cat than a dog. Even though his sun and moon signs are in Scorpio, his rising sign is Leo, the lion. That's why he naps as often as he can manage, and is so proud of his mane. Do you have cats and dogs as pets here on Earth as we do back home?"

Annika nodded, curious to see where Chivanni was going with the comparison.

"Then you know that while dogs are eager to please, cats merely grace you with their presence. Talvi has never sought to serve a master of any kind, so don't expect to put a lead and collar on him. It's best not to nag at him or boss him around. If there is something you want of him, let him conclude it was his idea, and he will gladly serve it to you on a silver platter. Don't tell him no or deny him something he desires, unless you are prepared to deal with his sullen resentment. You may as well save yourself the inevitable melodramatics and agree with him from the start, because ultimately he will have his way. Hmmm, what else? Oh yes—don't ask for his opinion unless you truly want it, because he will be brutally honest. And don't ever lie to him. It drives him mad. When he does become upset, he'll need extra coddling. He tends to brood over things."

Annika grinned even wider. Chivanni was right. He wasn't telling her anything she didn't already know.

"You make him sound like such a spoiled little brat," she remarked.

"He *is* a spoiled brat, at times," Chivanni said with a pensive smile. "Though once you've learned to see beyond those traits, you will be showered with steadfast love and protection from him. He's very generous and big-hearted, and fiercely loyal. There's no one else I would rather have for a friend."

Annika looked carefully at the boy before her. It was so easy to assume that the red-haired boy was human. Aside from his wings and that shock of bright hair, he could fit in well enough among a crowd if he dressed differently. But if a person were to study him more closely, they would notice that his skin held an unusual sheen to it that was best described as iridescent. His large, wide eyes, light brown as they were, reflected so much light that they seemed to glow. His porcelain smooth skin had no lines in it whatsoever, unless he was smiling. And although he was the thinnest boy Annika had ever met, he wasn't feeble or weak at all. In fact, his little body seemed incapable of ever running out of energy.

"All right, it's your turn, you winged faerie," James said, having found Annika and Chivanni at the jewelry counter. "I put a ton of clothes on hold for you to try on."

"I can't wait to see what you do with him," Annika gushed as she laid eyes on her husband. Talvi was now wearing a maroon fitted button down shirt with black jeans, and stood holding two large bags of new purchases. "I love what you've done here! Such a masterpiece . . . encore, encore!"

"Thank you, thank you," James said with a curtsy. "These two are just a pair of vintage driving moccasins in need of a little polish. Can you believe how this one turned out? He's drop dead *gorgeous*." James gave Talvi another once-over, took Chivanni by the hand, and disappeared with the other shoe in need of polish.

"What the hell is a driving moccasin?" Talvi demanded once James and Chivanni were out of earshot. "Is that some type of wingless faerie slang?"

"No it's not slang, babe. It's a shoe," Annika grinned.

"You have no idea how much you owe me for this," he said, giving the bags a bit of a jiggle.

"I know Nordstrom is expensive, but—"

"I wasn't referring to the money," Talvi clarified. "I just want you to know that the reason I'm here isn't to play dress up with your friend."

"I know that," Annika replied. It looked like there was more that Talvi wanted to say, but he was unsure of how to go about it.

"The bloke in the suit at the restaurant, Danny—he's the one who gave you that incredible ring, isn't he?" he asked, looking at his wedding band strangely. "I never thought in all my life that I would actually *meet* him. I rather liked him as a fictitious character in my head, not a living, breathing person that I might ever meet, let alone the fact that he's got some wits about him *and* is chummy with your brother. How often do they get together, anyway?"

"Well, they're co-captains of their soccer team," Annika said, picking up her pace a little. "They have practice every Saturday morning."

"*Every Saturday*? Bloody hell!" Talvi groaned, looking even more annoyed. "He doesn't come over to visit, does he?"

"He hasn't in a long time."

"Did our generous donor discover what Chivanni and I did to your old engagement ring?" he asked, still frowning a bit as he looked at his wedding band again. Annika stopped walking, and turned to him.

"Of course not," she told him gently, realizing better why he was cranky. If there was one deep and personal thing she knew about her husband, it was that he didn't like owing anything to anyone. "That ring brought us together, you know that. You're the one that said everything happens for a reason. If he never gave it to me, I would probably still be living with him. Then I never would have met you. And besides, what we're wearing isn't the ring that he gave me anymore. It's just a chunk of platinum that you had the fairies change into something a million times more beautiful and meaningful than what it started as."

Annika recalled how she had given Talvi her engagement ring from Danny, and it had been melted down and forged into what was now permanently attached to their hands. It didn't matter how hard they pulled; the rings would only come off if their fingers did too.

"I don't know why I didn't think of it like that," he said and took a deep breath, letting it out slowly. "Lucky me for marrying such a clever, clever girl." Annika took his hand and together they walked slowly past the racks of clothes, keeping their eyes out for James and Chivanni.

Talvi chuckled to himself and leaned down close to her.

"Speaking of which, I think we need to get away for a while. Why don't we find a dressing room nearby so you can see what else I've collected this after-noon? I'll give you a little clue . . . it's not in these bags."

Shivers ran down Annika's legs as he nipped at her earlobe.

"This isn't the place," she whispered, astonished that it had only been three hours since their last interlude and he was already hounding her again. "If I get banned from Nordstrom, James will never let me hear the end of it. Let's hurry up and find those two so we can get out of here. We still have to stop by the grocery store before we can go home."

"You'd better make it snappy, then," said Talvi, giving her a nuzzle. "I'm about ready to throw you over my shoulder and find the nearest stairwell. I've had hardly any time alone with you, and it's driving me mad. Newlyweds are supposed to go away on long honeymoons for a very particular reason."

Annika grew weak in the knees as the nuzzling turned into a warm kiss that made the hair rise along her neck. She knew being taken to the stairwell wasn't an empty threat, coming from him. A hand curled around her waist, pulling her so close that it was obvious what else he'd collected that afternoon. She could imagine being pressed up between her husband and the wall, her clothes being roughed up by his determined hands. To her dismay, her daydream was abruptly shattered by the sound of James's shrill voice addressing a saleswoman nearby.

"It's not too late to pretend we got lost," Talvi suggested. The hunger in his eyes was unmistakable. "Where shall we run off to? A dressing room? A hotel? Rome?"

"We can't do that to Chivanni," Annika hissed, but the truth was that she would love to be alone with Talvi in Rome. "The poor thing is probably wondering where the heck we are. I know James can be a tad pushy."

"A *tad* pushy?" Talvi asked, letting her go. "He doesn't dress you very often, does he?"

"Um, well, sometimes he does . . . " She racked her brain, trying to think of a defense, but James really had none for his overbearing personality. "Okay, so he's about as pushy as a bulldozer. He grew up in New York. He's an Italian queen. What could you possibly expect?"

"I honestly don't know what to expect from an Italian queen," replied her husband coolly. "I've only known a Spanish princess, and she was much more obliging than your friend."

"I'm sure she was," Annika said, having a pretty good idea of how well he was obliged. She knew that Talvi had sown enough wild oats to supply a flour mill, but that reputation was supposed to have been left behind in a parallel universe.

They watched as James marched up to the clerk behind the sales counter and spoke to her, making a lot of wild gestures with his hands. She handed him a pair of scissors, looking a little scared. He disappeared into the dressing room and there was more bickering. Finally the door swung open and Annika was baffled at who stumbled out. A very cute boy in slim-fitting dark blue jeans and a lightweight green sweater was peering at himself in a full length mirror in wonder. His transparent, shiny wings had been pulled through two slits in the back of his sweater and were folded down behind him. His flaming red hair was no longer competing with his clothing. On the contrary, his sweater complimented his hair perfectly. James looked very pleased with himself and walked back to the clerk, handing her the pair of scissors. Chivanni turned in anxious circles, looking for someplace to hide. He kept trying to cover his orange wings, but they were in plain sight as he crept over to where the other two were waiting for him. He looked scared as he tip-toed over to them, clutching at Talvi's arm for protection.

"Chivanni, I've never seen you . . . in the fifty-eight years I've known you, I don't think you've ever worn any modern clothes before," Talvi said, mystified at the transformation as he absentmindedly handed a few large bills to the sales girl. The faerie kept trying to cover his wings, looking very uncomfortable.

"What's the matter?" Annika asked. "You look great!" Chivanni's cinnamon brown eyes grew wide and watery as he craned his neck upwards to look at his friend.

"I want my cloak back!" he wailed, and grabbed Talvi's shirt, burying his face in his chest. "I've never felt so exposed!" The elf wrapped his arms around the winged faerie and rubbed his back, trying to fend off the impending tears.

"It's called coming out, and I'll bet you've needed to do that for a long time, you winged faerie," James said with authority. He took the change and receipt from the clerk and joined them. Chivanni stared at him, watery-eyed and confused. James seemed to grow impatient at his level of naïveté.

"You know, coming out of the closet—revealing to the world who you are, and if they don't like it, tough shit. They can just go to hell," James explained.

"We can't have him revealing what he really is to the world," Talvi pointed out. "It would be best for him to stay inside of the closet. At least we could give him his cloak back to cover his wings."

"Oh, yeah, because that bright yellow cloak was so subtle," James said sarcastically. "As long as you don't float shit around, no one will care too much about your wings. We'll go to the Alberta Street fair next month and you'll see what I mean."

"But . . . but . . . " the winged faerie protested to the human faerie, as Talvi curled his arm around Chivanni and coaxed him towards the door.

"But nothing. Stop trying to hide who you really are and just be yourself!" James insisted from behind, walking next to Annika. "I for one am glad you got rid of that damned cloak. You've got a cute little . . . set of wings."

When they arrived at the grocery store, it was Talvi's turn to take James aside and tell him a few things.

"First thing's first," he said, giving James a stern look. "Neither Chivanni nor I eat animals, and since we are guests in your home, I would hope that there is no cooking of them whilst we are staying with you."

"You're seriously asking me to give up meat?" James replied in disbelief.

"He doesn't mean tube steak," Annika joked, nudging James in the ribs with her elbow. He rolled his eyes at her and then turned them back to Talvi.

"I'm only asking you to not bring dead animals in the house," Talvi said, curling his protective arm around his winged friend's shoulders. "I can tolerate the smell when I must, however, you may have noticed that Chivanni is quite sensitive. He would likely cry for days if anyone cooked or ate an animal under the same roof where he sleeps. It's so easy to forget that other living creatures have feelings when you call them pseudonyms such as veal. And until you've tasted his cooking, I don't think I would complain very much about having a gourmet chef in the house."

James glanced at Annika, unsure of what to make of the request.

"He *is* a really good cook," Annika assured him. The compliment made Chivanni's wings flutter slightly as he smiled, and James gave a reluctant shrug.

"What the hell, I'll give it a shot," he muttered, and started to head for a shopping cart.

"I wasn't finished speaking, James," Talvi said in a polite, yet firm tone. "Chivanni has certain dietary needs and he can only have clean food. He can't eat anything with chemicals or he'll become very sick. And he doesn't know how to read English, so you'll have to help me look at the labels and make certain nothing contains any preservatives or hormones and the like. Organic would be best for him. And we'll need quite a few liters of spring water. He can't drink anything from your tap, and I'd rather not, either. I'm told it contains chemicals as well as residuals from all the medications that humans take."

"Oh for fuck's sake," James whined, tossing his tousled hair as he rolled his eyes a second time. "That's Charlie's area of expertise, not mine. I don't pay attention to that shit."

"It's not so complicated," Talvi insisted. "This is part of who Chivanni is. Did you not in fact tell us all earlier that if someone doesn't like you for being different, tough shit? They can just go to hell, right? I'm quite fond of that philosophy myself." The light in his eyes danced merrily as James realized he had been bested by the best. "Perhaps it would be easier if you and Chivanni focus on the produce, and leave the rest to Annika and I. You can't really go wrong if you're gathering things such as lettuce and bananas."

"If I'm gathering *what?*" James asked, grinning wide.

"Lettuce and bananas," Talvi repeated, making James smile even wider.

"I'm really sorry, Talvi, I still didn't understand that last thing you wanted me to get."

"James, are you bloody deaf? I said *bananas!*" he cried in exasperation. James just laughed and shrugged, loving the way he said bananas in his English accent.

"Okay, I heard you that time," he sighed happily. "Can I start getting those ba-*nah*-nas already, or is there something else I need to know about Chivanni?"

"Oh, yes," Talvi said with a mischievous smirk. "He bites on occasion, so you better get on his good side while you still can. I'll let you figure out the rest on your own." With that they split off into pairs, each with their own cart.

Compared to riding horseback together over hill and dale, dueling gypsy songs on their guitars, dancing in elaborate ballrooms, and being rescued from flesh-eating trees and bloodthirsty vampires, doing something as domestic as grocery shopping with her husband seemed incredibly lame to Annika. But then again, it was interesting to see what kind of things he was putting into their overstuffed cart, when they finally were put there. Talvi wasn't joking at all about Chivanni's dietary needs, and he spent most of the time reading every label on every item that Annika handed him. She began to lose track of how many of her favorite foods were disqualified and handed back to her. Her favorite cereal, her favorite ice cream, and her favorite potato chips were all replaced with brands and flavors she had never tried before.

"When you said Chivanni would get sick if he ate the wrong thing, how sick are we talking here?" she whined when Talvi handed her a few approved jars of peanut butter instead of the brand that she'd been buying for years.

"It depends," he replied, spying some almond butter and snatching it off the shelf as well. "It could be as mild as a runny nose and a rash, but if he were exposed to a large dose at once or small doses over a long period of time, he could very well die. His entire family was killed when they were sprayed with pesticide, which is why he was raised by his aunt. Being that I am responsible for his welfare, I can't afford the risk."

Annika shivered and vowed not to complain about the groceries any more, and instead asked Talvi to show her how to read a label properly.

"So, I have to ask, now that we're at least somewhat alone," Talvi asked casually as tried to choose between orange marmalade or blackberry jam, "is there anything else you wanted to talk to me about? Any particular concerns you've had since I last saw you? You do seem a bit preoccupied since we were last together."

Annika grabbed both jars out of his hands and set them on top of three large containers of organic orange juice and six boxes of all-natural black licorice candy.

"Nope," she lied, turning around. The very public jam aisle was the last place she seemed to want to have this very private conversation, but Talvi was determined one way or another. He knew she was trying to avoid answering him, and she knew that he wouldn't simply let it slide, either. He would dig to the deepest depths to find out what she didn't want to say. Talvi wondered how long Annika could hold out on him, and he wondered how much longer it would be until James and Chivanni joined up with them again.

"Annika, you're certainly not the first individual who's experienced this type of anxiety before. My sister had a very difficult time dealing with it as well, but you would never know it to look at her now," he said delicately, putting his hand on her shoulder. Talvi smiled as he continued, "There was one time when she and I were much younger; we encountered a tribe of maenads, and I thought she would never be the same after that disaster. It took her quite some time to reconcile, but eventually she did. And now Yuri's just as good with a sword as I am."

Annika turned around to face him, utterly confused. "Yuri?" she asked. "I thought you were talking about Anthea."

Talvi snorted in amusement. "How could you think *that*, when you know how different my sisters are? Anthea's a homebody; she would certainly never venture anywhere near maenad territory! Besides, she's got those two maggots to look after, and now that Asbjorn's home, she wants more. Just what I need; another stinking, squirming larva crawling underfoot when we come home. Aren't two enough? My sister was actually upset when Father told her that the twins in our family run in the males on *his* side, because that means she won't have a chance at them. It will either be my brother or myself. Why would anyone actually *want* double the mess, double the fuss, double the noise, and double the amount of lost sleep, when one screaming larva is bad enough?" And just as if to prove his point, at that very moment, a baby in the next aisle screeched so loud that it threatened to shatter every glass jar in the entire store. The painful pitch made Annika and Talvi both grimace.

"My poor mother . . . can you imagine *twins* making that horrendous sound at the same time?" he said, still recovering from the severe audial intrusion. "There's not enough faerie brandy in the world to drown out *that* racket!"

"No, there's not," Annika squeaked. Talvi felt certain that the shaking in his wife's hands wasn't from the coffee she'd had at breakfast. What was going on with her?

"For some reason, it's difficult for me to read your thoughts as clearly as I used to, so you'll need to be a little more open with me about things. I want you to know that you can talk to me about anything, and I'll understand." When he glanced up at Annika, he was not expecting her to look white as a sheet, gripping the handle of the cart to keep herself steady.

"What's wrong?" he asked, worried. "You look absolutely terrified."

"It's just . . . I don't think I can deal with . . . with . . . "

"With maenads? Good gods, love, *you'll* never need to worry about them," he chuckled, and began searching for the maple syrup.

CHAPTER 7
The Little Dove Feathers Her Nest

After the groceries had been put away, the foursome reassembled upstairs in Annika's room to help Talvi and Chivanni unpack. James folded his arms across his chest, frowning a little as he summed up the situation. Since her return, he had only dared peek his head in her room, never fully capturing the splendor that one unemployed and depressed person can create.

"Annika," he said, rubbing the bridge of his nose under his glasses, "I don't even know where to start." He looked around the bedroom, making lists in his head of what needed to be taken care of first. There were dirty dishes cluttering up her computer desk that needed to be brought to the kitchen; empty vodka bottles and juice boxes that needed to go in the recycling bin; trash that needed to be taken out; a thick layer of dust to contend with; papers to be filed; and mountains of shoes and clothes to be put away, along with other boxes of belongings.

James tossed his head a little and finally walked over to the three laundry baskets filled with clean clothes, and he began to hang them in the closet.

Annika pulled open some of her dresser drawers and added those clothes to the pile that James was working on, giving Talvi some room for his things. The past three months had been spent getting used to the idea that she may never see him again. It had not been easy, getting back on her feet after being swept off of them.

"What are all these papers?" Chivanni asked, as he approached her desk.

77

"Are they important, or shall I dispose of them?" He picked through envelopes, sticky-notes, the backsides of bills, and receipts that all had a few lines of scribbling on them.

"They're just ideas for songs," she said, coming over to join him. "You don't need to worry about that."

"It's really no trouble," he said, while Talvi lifted one of the envelopes.

"*It comes as no surprise, and I find love only gets in the way,*" he read out loud just before she snatched the paper out of his hand. "Hardly the musings of a new bride," he teased.

"It's not ready yet," she said peevishly, adding the envelope in her hand to the pile of papers on the desk. She shuffled them all into one pile and put them in the top drawer of her desk, shutting it harder than necessary. "I've had horrible writer's block. The music's no problem at all, but the lyrics just aren't coming to me."

"They'll come out of the woodwork when they're good and ready," Talvi assured her, "Give them time. It will be worth the wait."

And then he said no more. Annika thought for sure that he would have teased her further, and said her song lyrics sounded cheesy, but instead he had only smiled and let it go.

Meanwhile, he had taken a small metal box covered in strange writing out of his messenger bag. He opened it cautiously before reaching into it. First his fingers slipped in, searching around for something. Apparently unable to find it, he reached in further. Then further still, until his entire right arm was shoved into this box. James stopped hanging clothes and watched skeptically, as there was no place for Talvi's arm to go, except through the bed . . . but it was definitely inside the box.

Talvi rolled his eyes in annoyance and began taking out things right and left, scattering them upon or around the bed as they swelled up to their normal size.

"What the fuck? That box is like Mary Poppins' magic carpet bag," James remarked, watching in wonder.

"Where do you think the concept came from?" asked the elf. "This is known as a 'Faerie Poppins Box.' It was invented by a faerie named Poppins over five hundred years ago. They're becoming quite popular, because they're so cold."

"Cold?" James repeated. "'Cause it's made of metal?"

"No, I think he means it's *cool*," Annika informed him, smiling a little at Talvi's misuse of slang. She and James looked on with interest as Talvi unpacked a guitar case, a wooden longbow, a quiver filled with arrows, a black-handled knife, a few sets of clothes, Annika's mp3 player and digital camera, and a small mountain of books in various thicknesses and strange languages that she couldn't read. The few she was able to decipher sounded incredibly interesting, with French titles such as *Transformations: A Guide for New Vampires and Their Loved Ones*, *Various Demons and the Objects they Possess*, *The Art of Mind Cloaking*, and one that caught her eye, simply titled *Samodivi* in Macedonian.

"Funny you should notice that one above all others," he said, seeing her glance at the book. "That's the same one Finn insisted I bring *specifically* for you, from his personal collection."

"He did, did he?" Annika pondered why Finn would pick that one particular book out of the tens of thousands he owned, just for her. To say Finn had a lot of books was like saying the Pacific Ocean had a lot of water, and she would never forget the day she stumbled upon him reading in his bedroom, surrounded by bookshelves that stretched higher than the arched windows, all the way to the ceiling. He had invited her in, set her down directly in front of him, and asked her what it was like to be a modern girl. It was the most memorable interview Annika had ever experienced.

She snatched her camera, having not seen it in months, and walked over to her desk, inserting the memory card into the computer after she sat down. A slide show of evidence began to play, and Annika motioned for James to come over and watch it unfold while she gave him a little narrative of her adventure. It had been so hard for her, to not have any proof other than her ring. She needed her friends and family to understand her . . . to believe her.

Her photo montage started with a few shots of the Balkan Mountains, then one of Uncle Vince and his friends huddled around a table loaded with dishes of food and glasses of vodka, smiling brightly. Then there were some scenes of downtown Sofia. Then more mountains. And then everything changed.

There was Runa, braiding her long blonde hair next to a wood burning stove. And Talvi's older sister Anthea smiling sleepily at a table while two small children with pointed ears were eating out of a bowl on the kitchen floor. There was a shot of Talvi walking through the barn with two large pails, silhouetted in black, and then many pictures of adorable, cuddly barn kittens. There were a few shots of Runa, Hilda, Sariel, and Yuri lying in the hay, snuggling with the kittens. Then there were Anthea's music rooms, filled with dozens of different instruments from all over the world. When the next photo appeared, James reached over and hit the pause button on the computer screen.

"Who is *that?*" he asked, and Talvi and Chivanni wandered over to join the viewing.

"Oh, that's just my brother Finn," Talvi answered.

There he stood beside his brother, mirrored almost perfectly, each of them with a bow in their hands. Talvi's was in his right, and Finn's was in his left. They both had their opposite elbows drawn back, and were grinning over their shoulders at the photographer. They were unmistakably brothers, but Finn was taller, with relaxed brown curls instead of wild black hair. The smile on his face was warm and kind, rather than devilish and wicked.

"*Just* your brother Finn," James mocked, adjusting his glasses as he admired the photo. "Annika, will you email this to me? I need a new screen saver for my laptop. And my phone."

After taking a moment to send the photo to James, Annika resumed the slideshow, displaying a ballroom filled with elves and wood nymphs, with fairies mingling within the crowd, and also floating above it. Then there was Talvi, sitting at his desk, making love to the camera with his bedroom eyes. A sheepish laugh escaped when she saw the next few pictures of her in his room. She was wearing nothing but an annoyed look on her face, which grew less annoyed with each new photo. Then she was sitting on Talvi's lap, both of them smiling at the camera.

"I think we can skip past a few of these," Talvi suggested discreetly, trying to hide his blushing face. "The troll photos are at the very end of the roll."

"It's a digital camera, sweetie. There's no roll of film," she explained, as she turned the screen away from James and Chivanni, searching for the last few photos she wanted her roommate to see. When she returned the monitor to its previous position, James took off his glasses and rubbed his eyes, leaning in close. There stood a giant green-skinned troll, over eleven feet tall, covered in wool clothing, with huge fanged teeth jutting up from his smiling lower jaw. His huge barrel chest was puffed out with pride, and in front of him stood Runa and Annika, with carefree smiles on their faces even though they were less than half his height.

"That is *insane!*" James said in a squeak of a voice.

"No, that is *Ohan,*" Talvi corrected him. "He's a troll."

"Gee, ya think?" James asked sarcastically, squinting at the image again before putting on his glasses. "I need a glass of wine. I think my brain's going to explode."

He went back to gather Talvi's new clothes in one of the baskets that he'd emptied, and with Chivanni's levitation skills, the two fairies followed the dishes and wastebasket down the steps and into the kitchen.

Once they were alone, Talvi reached into the metal box a final time and withdrew a hemp sack that jingled when he set it on the rug. He gave Annika a wink before he opened it up, revealing key chain after key chain full of gold and silver rings of all different sizes. Some would barely fit on an infant's finger; others were larger, thicker, and wider.

"Where did all of this come from? You told me that you don't have a job." She kneeled down next to the sack and sank her fingers into the metal rings, lifting up a large handful. There was a chorus of different pitches as Annika let the rings fall from her hands back into the bag with a *plinkity-plinkity, plink*.

"I have had many jobs, my love," her husband snickered, watching her with amusement as she picked up another handful of gold and silver rings. "You only asked me if I had a regular job, and I told you I did not. For one thing, I was on hiatus when you asked me that question. For another, my jobs are very irregular, but I'm very good at the things I do. Therefore, I find myself appropriately reimbursed."

"Then how come all of your family and friends mentioned at one point or another how lazy you are?" she pointed out, still playing with the treasure. "I can't even remember how many of them told me that."

"As I said, I am *very* good at the things I do," he explained, raising one eyebrow at her. "And coming home to relax afterwards is one of them. It is only logical to expect that I would like an extended rest when I'm home. Wouldn't you agree that when one travels constantly for the greater portion of the year, one would also enjoy sleeping in front of the fire as often as possible? Besides, you speak as though I brought my life's savings with me. I only brought a small portion," he said with a slight shrug. "I'm certain we'll get by just fine while I'm here."

"This is '*getting by*'?" Annika squeaked, looking into the bag one last time before he tied it shut. They had never really spoken about what he did to earn his keep, and that might be something a wife should like to know. "What did you do to earn this much money?"

"This and that," he chirped mysteriously, and shoved the burlap sack into the little metal box just as James and Chivanni came back.

"Hey, I found this down in the basement behind the washing machine. Is it yours?" James asked, cutting through Annika's state of wonder. He was untangling the chain of a silver necklace. He held it up, letting the light catch on two jeweled fish swimming in opposite directions to form a circle. One of the fish was deep blue; the other a dark shade of blood red. "It looks antique."

Talvi's mind darted to another reality as he and Annika looked at the amulet swaying from side to side on its silver chain. The image of a young man in a horned helmet flashed into Talvi's vision. He saw Nikola's ice blue eyes as clearly as if he were standing directly in front of him . . . and he could see his matching amulet. He swallowed back his jealous thoughts as he remembered Nikola explaining the powers that their twin amulets possessed.

It's a very complex combination in a single amulet. The sapphire is a stone with many supernatural powers. It will protect you against both violent physical and psychic attacks. It will ward off the sorcery of your enemies, and even accidental death. The garnet balances yin and yang energies. It will increase your psychic abilities, courage, and confidence, and will fend off evil spirits while you sleep. It will help protect your aura, and if that's not enough for one little stone to do, it will also keep you safe while traveling . . .

"That's the amulet Nikola's grandmother gave you," Chivanni said, with his eyes growing wide. "But why ever did you take it off?"

"I think I took it off to clean it, and then I misplaced it . . . I'm not sure."

"Perhaps you should put it back on," he suggested. "It has been imbued with many valuable attributes. Nikola never takes his off."

"Who's Nikola?" asked James with piqued interest. His eyes had widened in curiosity, especially at seeing the subtle changes in everyone's demeanor at the mere mention of this person's name. Who was this absent person who was able to make Chivanni's wings flutter, Annika's cheeks blush, and Talvi's eyes flash?

"Oh, Nikola is the sweetest boy . . . " the faerie began, clasping his hands together and getting a starry look in his eyes. "He is so kind and thoughtful. He rides an elk and can shape shift into a wolf, and he can make it rain on command. He even saved Annika's life."

"Reeeeeaaaaally?" A wide grin had spread across James's face. "Annika has never mentioned any of this to me. How could you hold out on me like that?"

"Because you didn't believe my story to begin with, so why would you believe that I was attacked by a vampire and then rescued by a druid?" There was more than a little sharpness in the tone of her voice.

"It wasn't that I thought you were lying, Annika," said James quietly. "I just found your story pretty difficult to believe. It's kind of *out there*, you know?"

"Well, I was attacked by the vampire *twice*, but Nikola got rid of him for good."

"Nikola was simply in the right place at the right time," Talvi sneered, clenching his teeth in anger. "I would have loved nothing more than to rip that vampire's throat out with my bare hands when I had the chance. However, it is in poor taste to do that sort of thing in front of one's birthday guests."

James started to say something, then stopped, then started again, but stopped. For being a person with an opinion about everything, he suddenly didn't know how he felt about that last statement. Talvi looked like he meant business.

"I must say, I am glad that you didn't lose such a precious gift," Chivanni said, and carefully lifted the amulet out of James's hand. He slipped the thin silver chain over Annika's head, and let the amulet settle itself against her chest for the first time in three months.

"Nikola said you weren't supposed to take it off. No wonder you were feeling so dreadful all this time." He gave her a little kiss on the cheek and smiled sweetly at her.

"What? You can read minds like Talvi does?" Annika asked.

"Not exactly. It's more of seeing auras and sensing the energy around someone," he said, placing his dainty hand on his hip. His large eyes grew very sympathetic and concerned as they scanned the space around her. "James mentioned to me at the grocery store that you haven't been yourself since you returned."

"And you really think that my necklace has something to do with how I've been feeling?"

"Of *course* it has something to do with it, love," Talvi said, gazing at the sparkling garnet and sapphire embedded in silver. He hated to admit, but it was a beautiful necklace, and it probably wouldn't be the last time that someone other than him would give his wife such lovely gifts. "You'll feel better soon, I'm certain. Did you stop wearing it when you left us?"

"Well, yeah." Annika seemed stunned, and it occurred to Talvi that perhaps she had never considered there was such a strong connection between her and her amulet.

"I recall Nikola saying that there would be an adjustment period while the amulet got to know you a little better," said Talvi. "Perhaps there was a withdrawal effect when you took it off. Powerful forces will sometimes do that to you. Why, they can even drain you a bit."

"He did say it was meant for me," Annika admitted, touching the amulet. It felt slightly warm on her chest, as if it were radiating its own heat. "And he said it would be stupid to take it off, but I just thought he meant in your world, not mine. I mean, it's not like there's anything around here that I need to worry about."

"Oh, my little dove, you have so much to learn," Talvi snickered, and put his arm around her, kissing the top of her head. "This amulet of yours will maintain the same qualities, regardless of which realm you find yourself in. The parallel worlds of Earth and Eritähti mirror one another very closely, and all of us are connected to everything, whether we care to admit it or not."

"So, you mean there isn't anything really separating our worlds, besides, oh, say, *time* and *distance?*" Annika joked.

"Just like the silver threads in the rings we wear, our two worlds are much more interwoven than they appear," Talvi affirmed. "It will do you well to remember that more often."

CHAPTER 8
The Evening News

The light of a television flickered in the dark hotel room, making everything appear more garish than it really was. The curtains had been drawn back from the windows, and outside only the last bit of indigo remained in the sky over Prague's oldest quarter. Soon the moon would rise above the city, and it would be time to go out yet again to soothe this discomfort that could only be described as an unquenchable thirst. Yuri could feel the gnashing in her veins, the crawling of her skin; it was a sensation that mystified any worthy description, other than the worst hangover of her life. Her body hurt, her aching head was sluggish, and her mouth was dry. She craved only one thing, and lying in bed all night was only going to make it worse. She sat up in the king-sized bed and focused her eyes on the television while she pulled on her boots one at a time.

"What's that on the animals?" she asked the figure standing beside the window, seeing a close up shot of birds suffocating in a thick, tar-like substance.

"There was another oil spill," came the reply in a Slavic accent as thick as the oil on the birds on the television. Konstantin had remained as still as a statue, watching the twilight shift into night over the city below. Now he turned his green eyes toward the flashing screen, watching with disdain as the footage switched to beached dolphins and sea turtles, dead or dying on the stained sand. "Another casualty of the modern world. It never . . . *ends*," he said, shaking his head slowly. His long blond hair barely moved as he stepped closer to where Yuri sat on the side of the bed. She changed the channel and was met with a view of soldiers hiding behind rubble, throwing a grenade. She changed the channel again to see an enormous man stuffing chicken wings into his mouth with his fat, greasy fingers. One more channel flip, and they were watching a middle-aged couple embracing as an announcer read off the list of unpleasant side effects that could be caused by taking this male enhancement prescription.

Konstantin reached over to take the remote from her, and turned the television off, leaving the two of them to sit in silent darkness. Only the sounds of the city streets crept in the windows from below.

"One day, humans shall be wiped from the surface of the Earth as steam is wiped from glass," he mused. "But until that day comes, we feast. Shall we?" he asked, reaching out his hands for Yuri's. She took them, noticing that he didn't seem cold to her anymore.

"Could we stay a bit closer this evening? I'm so tired," she pouted as he pulled her to her feet. Her head was throbbing, and there was no way she wanted a repeat of the previous evenings. She'd had her fill of stoned and drunk young backpackers, picked up from hostels around the city. It was remarkable, how many of them smelled so strongly of patchouli that she could taste it through their unwashed clothes. It made Yuri want to wring their necks, which was what ended up happening more often than not after she had swallowed their tainted blood. While Konstantin had disposed of their bodies, she had been his lookout, but the smell of hippie still clung to her like barnacles on a boat.

"You're only tired because you're so young," Konstantin assured her, and helped her into her long red wool coat. "Over time, you will require less rest, and begin to rise earlier. And vampire or not, it's rarely wise to dine in the same place as where you rest. You'll get crumbs in the bed."

"I don't think I can tolerate another young tourist," Yuri said, wrinkling her nose while Konstantin fastened up her buttons. The thirst was starting to scream inside of her.

"Leave it to my future bride to have such refined taste," he said, kissing her so passionately that she forgot all about her headache. "I have a better idea for breakfast tonight, if you think you can control yourself this time, my Scorpio sphinx. We are running out of good places to hide bodies."

"I promise, I won't kill anyone else," Yuri said with a little smirk. "As long as they're not hippies. I don't know if you noticed, but I *hate* hippies."

"What if you could taste the blood of a young man who ate only strawberries for a month, hmmm?" Konstantin said, letting his green eyes shine in anticipation as he brushed a bit of lint from the front of her coat. "What if you could drink from a woman who tasted like Brazilian rum? Would you enjoy that, Yuri? Could you mind your manners well enough to not kill them this time?"

"Yes," she whispered, consumed by the thought of quenching her thirst in such a divine way.

"Then prepare to fall in love with me all over again," he said, and offered her his arm.

Now they were walking through the door of an upscale restaurant, but instead of the pungent and nauseating scent of cooking food, Yuri only smelled different types of alcohol, and above everything else, fresh blood. Her pulse quickened and her breath deepened as Konstantin helped her out of her coat. She lifted her nose to the air, catching hints of fruit, spices, and flowers. It felt like she had been starving for weeks, and now there was a smorgasbord of delights awaiting her just around the corner. When he handed Yuri's coat to the host at the door, the discerning male vampire did not immediately hang it up as expected. Instead, he watched Yuri's reaction to the tantalizing scents, and then focused his eyes upward onto Konstantin.

"You can't dine here. No children under ten years allowed. You know the regulations on that."

Konstantin smiled kindly at the man, trying not to look too condescending.

"I *do* know the regulations on that," he said patiently. "But surely you know that you can make an exception for us."

"I don't care who you are, or who you are escorting. No children under *ten*," the host snapped back in frustration. "There is a saying where I'm from; 'The guest who seeks special attention muddies the host's tea.'"

Konstantin's green eyes flickered brightly in disapproval, but he gave a soft smile.

"I appreciate that you are following orders, however, we are not ordinary guests. Please allow me to introduce myself," he said to the man with an air of amusement. "I am Konstantin, underboss to Vladislav, of *la familia Vladislava*. This is my future bride, Yuri Marinossian. Now, tell me your name, so I know what vampire enforces the regulations of *la familia Vladislava* so obediently."

Their host bowed his benevolent head and replied in the most submissive voice, "My name is Phillip, your excellency. Please, accept my deepest apologies for my unparalleled ignorance."

"I am not the one you must seek forgiveness from," Konstantin answered, still looking amused as he glanced at Yuri. "My bride to be is the daughter of Vladislav's right hand. I am merely the left hand."

Yuri gazed into Konstantin's glittering green eyes, at his high cheekbones, and his straight, blond hair that fell to his elbows. He could have already sucked their host dry and left his head on a platter, but he possessed an unusual measure of self-control. Indeed, she was falling in love with him all over again, exactly as he had promised.

"Of course," Phillip said, still bowing his head. "Miss Marinossian, however can I repeal this injustice I've done to you?"

"You can start by hanging up my coat," she replied, and watched with satisfaction as Phillip beckoned for Konstantin's coat as well. He dashed away with them, and when he returned, he grabbed two menus and led them to a table nestled in a private corner, away from the commotion of the kitchen or the clatter of the bar.

"It would be my pleasure if you would allow me to pay for your meal this evening," Phillip said to Yuri. She smiled to herself, and then turned her dark brown eyes up to him.

"I may be Konstantin's future bride, but I am eternally my father's daughter," she informed him. "He is known for being exceptionally honorable and just in his rulings. I know my beloved would enjoy nothing more than to treat me to a fine meal, but I see no reason why you couldn't bring us a complimentary dessert afterward."

"Of course, as you wish," Phillip said with a gracious nod of his head.

"Oh, and Phillip . . . " Yuri said, just as he was about to turn away and leave them in privacy. "There's a saying where I'm from as well," she said, staring into his eyes, into the core of his being.

"Never mess with a Marinossian."

CHAPTER 9
Patti Cake

"Patti knows that our reservation is for eight sharp, right?" Charlie asked anxiously from the passenger seat of James's car. "Maybe I should call and check in with her."

"Oh my god, Charlie, she knows what time to meet us! I've already confirmed with her twice!" exclaimed James from behind the wheel as he concentrated on the road in front of him. The cold rain was coming down harder than the usual Portland drizzle, and he had his windshield wiper blades running at full speed. "Hey, screw *you*, buddy!" He waved his middle finger to the driver who had just cut him off. "I friggin' hate Friday night traffic downtown!"

"I was wondering who exactly this Patti is," Talvi asked from the back seat where he sat beside Annika. "Though now I believe she's Charlie's girlfriend. Have I got it sussed or what?"

"I don't know what 'sussing' is." Charlie said, ignoring his insinuation.

"It means having something figured out," Talvi explained.

"What's up with the English accent anyway?" Charlie asked, trying to change the subject. "You're not from there."

"No, but my father used to work in London quite often, so that's where I learned the language. While I was in Cornwall, I picked up Fae from the fairies as well," Talvi boasted. "Chivanni says my accent is hysterical, since his tribe

89

speaks a completely different dialect." At that, the winged faerie in the back seat snickered loudly in agreement.

"It's true . . . " Chivanni said, nearly shouting to make his small voice heard. "He sounds like he's got marbles in his mouth when he speaks Fae back home."

"So what else did you do in England, besides have tea parties with Cornish fairies?" Charlie snorted in amusement.

"Oh, my mother typically would plan something very educational for us children whilst our father was in meetings," Talvi started to explain, allowing himself to take in the view of the city as they crossed the Burnside bridge. The high rise buildings shot up from the west bank of the Willamette, glittering and wet underneath the low, dark clouds, while the rain drops reflected the traffic lights.

"We usually visited museums and galleries of all sorts, and monuments or sacred spots like Stonehenge, but I always loved it when Father took us to football games at Old Trafford."

"Old Trafford?" Charlie asked, sounding bewildered. "You like soccer?"

"No. I like *football*," Talvi grinned. "I might be Manchester United's oldest fan, with the exception of my brother and father. We were cheering them on back when they were still called Newton Heath."

"But that was like, a really long time ago," Charlie said slowly. "Like when people still rode around in carriages. Or I suppose that since you're an elf, you're really old and have super powers just like Chivanni's?"

"How very astute of you Charlie. You're catching onto things rather quickly," Talvi remarked, wiggling his fingers at him. "So when are you going to tell me about your girlfriend Patti, or shall I simply use my super powers to read your thoughts about her?"

"What? You can't do that," Charlie argued, turning around in his seat to look at Talvi.

"Well I see what draws you to her . . . she's a lovely girl," the elf said, looking smug. "Her hair is rather short for my taste, however. Is she really as clumsy as a three-legged giraffe?"

James let out an unabashed guffaw, and even Annika couldn't help laughing. She loved her friend Patti dearly, but it was true that she was one of those tall, gangly tomboys that never seemed to grow gracefully into her body.

"How do you know that when you've never met her? Who told you?"

"No one told me, Charlie; it's my super powers," Talvi said with a sly grin. "Why don't you just tell her that you fancy her and get on with it?"

"She's not into me like that. We're just friends," Charlie said, before facing forward in his seat.

"Perhaps you simply haven't discovered what it takes to win her affections."

"If you're thinking of wine and roses and candlelit dinners, forget it. She's not that kind of girl."

"I've never known a lady who didn't appreciate the red carpet treatment," Talvi said with authority. "See, the trick is to figure out which direction to unroll that carpet, and then you offer your arm and escort her along the way."

"You make it sound like a cake walk," Charlie argued. "It's not that easy to figure out what a chick wants."

"Nor is it as difficult as you make it to be," Talvi explained patiently. "You simply have to decide if she's a vixen you'd like to pursue. And if she is, then you might have to get off your foxy bum and actually woo the lady, Charlie. If she's interested, wooing becomes rather enjoyable." Talvi paused, and a wicked grin spread across his face. "And if she's *not* interested, wooing can become great sport."

"*Wooing* her? That sounds so cheesy," Charlie said sarcastically.

"Ah, but it works," Talvi said with a wink. "I had to woo your sister here nonstop for a full two weeks before she finally—before she was wooed."

"You don't really think what you did is considered 'wooing a lady,' do you?" Annika howled.

"Come off it, love. You relished every second," Talvi snickered. It was true; he had said and done some outrageous things to her when they first met. There were too many for Annika to remember them all, and the methods he'd used certainly weren't going to be found in any books on chivalry. She recalled how he had introduced himself to her. He had knelt down on one knee, taken her right hand in his, and then given it more foreplay than she'd had in a year.

"Okay, okay," Annika finally admitted as James turned into a parking garage. "I agreed to marry you, so obviously something you did worked."

"If you want a woman's attention, Charlie, do something unique and memorable for her," said Talvi, squeezing his wife's hand. "If I only ever give you one bit of advice about the fairer sex, it's this: Venus favors the bold."

James parked the car, but he didn't get out with the others.

"For shit's sake, I can't find my phone!" he said, feeling along the floor of the car. "I know I had it with me when we left."

"We'll help you look," Talvi offered. "Why don't you two go on ahead?"

As they made their way down the stairwell to the sidewalk outside, Charlie asked his sister, "Do you, um, do you really think I should take any advice from Talvi?" Annika pulled the hood of her coat over her head, but Charlie wasn't as concerned about keeping his hair dry. "I don't want to screw things up with Patti just because your husband gave me a bad tip, you know what I mean?"

"Well, he does know what he's talking about," she said, hopping over a puddle on the sidewalk. "I know he dated a lot of girls before he met me. He's kind of well-known for that back where he's from."

"Yeah, and you also hinted that he acted like a jerk," he reminded her. "I don't want to treat Patti like that."

"Oh, I was just being mean," Annika excused, although she knew there were plenty of people who probably agreed with her brother. "He just, well, he said things to me that no one has ever said to me before. But you know me. I wouldn't go and marry the first guy that said what I wanted to hear."

"I didn't think you would just go and marry any guy at all, no matter what he said, without any of us getting to know him first," Charlie said, looking at her curiously. "And it's so soon after breaking up with Danny. It takes time to get to know people, Ani. It's like you're a different person now."

"What do you mean?" she asked, looking over her shoulder for her husband. He and James were almost a block behind them. Annika picked up her pace a little to keep up with Charlie's longer legs. He wasn't nearly as tall as Talvi, but anyone over five feet seemed tall to Annika.

"You're completely in your own little world," Charlie said, facing forward, "and you've gotten a lot better, but you don't know how hard it was to listen to your story when you got back. What did you expect, when you told us a story about being trapped on the other side of a broken portal with elves and fairies? We thought you were *nuts*! I had to constantly lie to Mom and Dad, and tell them you were doing okay when you were anything but okay. I've never seen you so depressed before, and I know you haven't been totally honest with anyone about what exactly happened while you were gone. I didn't tell Mom and Dad about the drinking, but they know you weren't working or paying your bills. I told them you had mono. When I asked Danny what to do, he said you really needed to see a psychiatrist and get on some kind of anti-psychotic meds, but he didn't think you'd do it."

"You talked to Danny about whether or not to put me on anti-psychotics?" she cried, aghast. "You had no right!"

"Of course I did! He's my friend, and you freaked us all out!" Charlie snapped, walking faster. It was the first time in ages that Annika had seen her brother so genuinely upset. "And given that I see him every Saturday at practice, it's kind of impossible not to talk to him."

"Well you could have made something up," she muttered.

"Well I guess I was just sick of lying so much," he grumbled, and slowed his pace considerably. "You don't know how hard it was to have Saturday brunch at Mom and Dad's and look at their faces. It was bad enough watching Mom cry every day while you were missing. The search parties never found a single clue after you went on that hike and didn't come back, and, well, all we could do was hope for the best."

Charlie stopped walking, and turned to look at his little sister. There were tears in his eyes that he was trying to blink away. Seeing him like this made Annika's heart break a little, and she felt guilty to have been the cause of so much pain for so many people. She could catch a glimpse of what life must have been like while she was missing; Saturday brunches with her chair sitting empty, and probably not much fun because her dad and brother were too sad to crack jokes throughout the whole meal like they always did. She didn't know how to tell anyone about the battle that had occurred, or about being married to an elf, because they wouldn't understand. She kept waiting for the right moment, but it never arrived.

"I'm not mad at you, Ani. No one is," her brother went on. "We're so happy that you're home safe, but no one was ready for the crazy tale you told when you came back. I mean, James and I can't argue for a second about that wacko Faerie Poppins box that Talvi keeps all his shit in, and you can't really ignore Chivanni's wings or him levitating dishes around the house, but I guess I'm still not used to the fact that you married someone so soon after breaking up with Danny. We don't even *know* Talvi. For all we know, he kidnapped you and you've got Stockholm Syndrome. I don't really think that, and James seems to like him alright. It's just . . . it's just a big adjustment."

Annika looked at her brother and took a deep breath. She wanted to say something wise to alleviate his fears, something profound about how when you know you're supposed to be with someone, that you just *know*, but she couldn't force the words out. It was all a big adjustment for her, too. It was one thing to wear a ring and tell James and Charlie stories about her elven husband from a parallel world, and it was another to have this elven husband appear unannounced after being separated for three months. That left a lot of wide open space between them . . . and a lot of room for doubts to creep in. But for the moment the doubts were far, far away.

Charlie ducked under the awning of the classy bistro they had their reservation at, and opened the door for his sister, ushering her out of the cold rain.

Annika was unprepared for the sensations that met her inside the restaurant. She hadn't left her house much since her return, other than her recent return to work. It was one thing, to spend her time at a music store, where she was the new girl. That meant she got stuck with the day shifts, which didn't make her much as far as commissions went, but it also didn't make as much noise either.

In comparison, the restaurant was insane and chaotic. A wine rack ran up to the ceiling and there were lockers built into the walls bearing the names of diners who obviously visited so often that they needed their own lockers. The dim lighting and exposed brick complimented the sleek lines of the tables and booths, but it wasn't the chic atmosphere that caught her off guard. It was how strong and intoxicating the sounds and smells were, as though everything was amplified a by a dozen. It was stronger than she remembered from her days as a waitress. She was inundated by what smelled like a hundred ingredients bombarding her nose, and what sounded like a hundred conversations all happening in her head. Her eyes darted around, trying to find a face to match each random voice.

I'm going to be so pissed if that busser doesn't have their table set, their hostess was thinking as Charlie inquired about their table reservation. *Oh, good, some of their party is already seated.*

Maybe I should get a paternity test before I tell her? came from a man sitting across from a beautiful woman. It sounded like he was saying this right there in the lobby, but the couple was sitting at a table in the middle of the dining room.

"I need you to start that filet right now, and butterfly it!" came from the expediter back in the kitchen, even farther away.

Annika tried hard to ignore the excess noise, having practiced at home around her brother and James. Their thoughts weren't complete open books, not all the time, anyway; she was only getting glimpses of what they had on their minds. But it was still staggering how much she was able to pick up on, both silent thoughts and spoken conversations.

Her nose gathered whiffs of the different wines and cocktails people were drinking, the scents of garlic butter cream sauce over sautéed sea scallops, and even the pungent aroma of blue cheese stuffed olives coming from the bar. They followed the hostess to their table in the back corner where three people were already seated. It was very private, and thus could not have been more perfect. Annika thought her head would have exploded if they had been seated anywhere else.

"Look who finally crawled out of the Bat Cave!" said a woman with teal dreadlocks and horn-rimmed glasses. A tan girl with a blunt black bob who had been talking to her turned around and her eyes opened wide. She leapt up and hugged Annika tight.

"Annika, you made it! I haven't seen you in *forever*!" she scolded. "I guess you finally got over that case of mono."

"Yeah, I'm feeling a lot better," Annika assured her, and settled into the chair beside her after greeting the other two members of their party. "Thanks for asking, Patti."

"Hey Jack, hey Jill, and happy Birthday, Patti Cake," Charlie wished the girl with the black bob while he took a seat next to Jack. He noticed that Patti's right hand was bandaged up in white gauze. "What happened this time?"

"Oh, Charlie . . . " she began with a sheepish grin and glanced down at her bandages. "You know what a klutz I am. One of the line cooks was showing me how to make my favorite entrée during my break today and I burned the crap out of myself. And of course it had to be my right hand, and the jerk manager on duty would only let me take two tables at a time. He said I couldn't handle more, so I didn't make any money today."

"Aww, I'm sorry to hear that," Charlie sympathized. "I hope it's not too serious."

"You're such a sweetheart, Charlie," she said, and gave him a wide grin. "It could have been a lot worse, but it still hurts like hell, so Jack ordered us a bottle of 'special medicine' tonight." With her left hand, she picked up a glass of red wine and toasted the young man sitting between Jill and Charlie before taking a generous sip.

"So what do you think of Jack's prescription?" Annika asked, looking at the bottle. "Was 2004 a good year for special medicine?"

"Abso-friggin'-lutely," Patti sighed happily, sinking comfortably into her seat. "It's commonly known on the wine list as a Malbec, and I highly recommend it. I don't know why I drove my car, though, because at this rate I'll probably need a ride home tonight."

"I can like, drop you off on my way home, no prob," Jill drawled. "But all my boarding gear's in the back and I'm warning you right now that the passenger seat is majorly covered with dog hair."

"Oh Jill, that would be awesome. You know I could care less about the dog hair," she grinned. "In a few hours, I don't think I'll care about too much at all."

"Damn, who are the hotties with James?" Jill asked Annika when he walked through the door with Talvi on one arm and Chivanni on the other. He must have been in heaven, because he looked like he was floating on a cloud. "Is he dating two at a time now?"

"Ha! He wishes he was," Annika hooted as the trio approached their table. James reluctantly let go of his arm candy as he made the introductions.

"Okay, so everyone, this is Talvi and Chivanni. Boys, this is Patti, Jack, and Jill. Patti and Annika used to work together at the restaurant, and Jack and Jill work at the art gallery with me."

"*Enchanté*, Patti Cake," Talvi said, taking her left hand in his right before placing a kiss on it. He let it go and did the same to Jill, then shook Jack's hand before fixing his attention back to Patti as he took the seat between Annika and Chivanni.

"Tell me, birthday girl, however did you manage to receive such a delightful name?"

"My last name is Kaeke, which is a type of Hawaiian drum," she explained, rummaging through her purse as she tried to hide her blushing face from Talvi's hypnotic gaze.

"It's actually two drums that are made from coconut trees," Charlie chimed in. "And when you play it, it's supposed to be a kind of language, so that you can say whatever you want without using your voice."

"How fascinating," Talvi remarked, still eyeing Patti inquisitively as she reapplied her lip gloss. "I've always taken an interest in unusual names and their meanings, but I believe Miss Patti Cake is the bee's knees, hands down."

"Hell yeah, she's the bee's knees," said Jill, giving Patti a side hug. "Are you like, her surprise birthday blind date since she can never find a guy taller than her to go out with, or are you here with Chivanni?"

Charlie tried not to scowl as James snickered under his breath. Annika just watched with intrigue to see how the conversation played out.

"I'm here with Chivanni," he said, touching his faerie friend affectionately on the shoulder. "We're staying at James's house with Annika and Charlie."

"Okay, well that settles that," Jill said, shaking her teal dreads with a disappointed grin.

"I love your sweater, Chivanni," Patti said. "That shade of green looks so nice with your hair."

Chivanni beamed with happiness. One thing about fairies, though, is that when they're exceptionally happy, their wings tend to flutter and beat merrily, and Chivanni almost knocked a tray out of a waitresses' hand with his orange wings.

"Holy shit!" exclaimed Jack. "Are those wings? They look so real!"

"Of course they're real wings!" he said defensively. "I'm a faerie, and all fairies have—" Talvi clamped his hand over Chivanni's mouth and bent down to whisper in his ear as Jack, Jill, and Patti looked on curiously.

"Chivanni just came out of the closet today," James explained, watching what appeared to be a lovers' quarrel between the faerie and the elf. "He's been a little touchy."

"Aww, that's understandable," Patti said, giving a supportive smile as Talvi ended their private chat. "Congratulations on coming out, Chivanni. It gets better."

"His wings are actually a movie prop," Annika added, hoping desperately that her friends were buying the story. "They look neat though, don't they?"

"Oh, okay. I get it now," Jack said with a snort, and took a sip of his wine. "He's a faerie, so of course he needs to have real wings."

"I don't understand why they're so amusing to you," Chivanni said with a little frown as he looked away from Talvi. "Every faerie I know has them, besides James." There were a few more guffaws and sniggles from Jack and Charlie.

"Chivanni, I love that you're being so literal about being a faerie. I think your wings are totally rad," Jill said, adjusting her horn-rimmed glasses. "Can you make them flutter again?"

"He better not," Talvi said sternly, looking at his annoyed friend, "or we'll have to leave early and miss out on all the dancing to come after dinner. If there is anything Chivanni enjoys more than cooking, it's dancing."

"Oh, then you better behave yourself," James said, trying not to laugh at the pouting faerie on his left. "We're going to a club later that's impossible to get into."

"If it's impossible to get into, how are we going to get in?" Chivanni asked, crossing his slender arms as he slunk down in his chair.

"I'm going to use my faerie magic, since you can't use yours," James announced. Chivanni scowled even more, but the warning look from Talvi told him he was walking on thin ice.

"What kind of faerie magic can you even do?" he asked James, wrinkling his freckled little nose in displeasure.

"I may not have wings, but I know one of the bartenders at the club, and I got him to put us on the VIP list for tonight. Cheer up, you sourpuss. Don't be so sensitive."

"Weren't you the one telling him to be himself earlier?" Talvi reminded James. "He's very sensitive and delicate. That is who he is. Just give him some time, and he'll cheer up when he's ready." He reached over to tap the faerie lightly on his nose. "Although it is a shame how darling you look when you pout, Chivanni. I almost wish you were cross more often."

The red-haired boy tried his best to sneer, but he failed miserably, rolling his eyes as a renegade grin danced over his lips.

"So, hey Talvi," Jill began, leaning in on the table a little closer to him. "Are your ears, like, real?"

"Well they're not imaginary," he said with a wink.

"Can I touch them?" she blurted out. Talvi looked a little surprised, but Jill was already reaching over his empty bread plate for his left ear.

"If you flick them, you'll regret it," he warned playfully, leaning a little closer. She traced his ear with her finger, examining it carefully before rubbing it between her fingers. Talvi felt a shiver run up his spine as he closed his eyes in pleasure.

"There's no way these are fake," she realized, moving to caress his other ear. "And it can't be plastic surgery 'cause I don't see any scars. That is so rockin', man!"

"I think you just found out what makes him tick," James said, seeing the response in Talvi's body language. He watched Talvi gently take Jill's hands away from his head, and turn to her with flushed cheeks and bedroom eyes. He looked slightly inebriated.

"You'll make my wife insanely jealous if you keep that up," he told her, running his hand seductively through his hair.

"Oh, I'm sorry," Jill said with a sheepish grin. Then the grin was replaced with a puzzled expression. "Wait a minute . . . so you're not . . . does that mean . . . ?"

"He's my husband!" cried Annika with a laugh, before turning to Talvi. They smiled at each other and held up their left hands simultaneously, revealing their matching bands.

"No way! You're *married?*" Jill exclaimed, giving Annika a dirty look as she sat back down, like she'd been tricked.

"Surprise!" Annika laughed. Luckily, she was able to steer questions about the wedding away from being answered at any length, and kept Jill and Patti preoccupied with the story of how Talvi and his brother created their rings with Chivanni's help.

"We won't be able to make any birthday toasts if the rest of you guys don't decide what the hell you're drinking," said Jack as their server came over for their drink order. Annika excused herself to the bar, claiming that the drink she had in mind would be too complex to explain to anyone but the bartender.

When she returned, she tried her best to join in the discussion as it drifted from Jack's day at the art gallery, to Jill's latest adventure snowboarding, and Charlie's upcoming soccer game. Annika faded in and out of the conversation as she sipped on her drink, getting tangled in her private thoughts. She found herself back in the jam aisle of the grocery store with Talvi, hearing him tell her how twins ran in his family. She then went back in time to almost twenty-four hours ago, right before her husband had arrived at her door, where James had reminded her that her portion of the electric bill was about three months late. That in turn had reminded her that it wasn't the only monthly event in Annika's life that was about three months late. Motherhood hadn't been a concept she was interested in, but now she found herself considering it a possible reality. There weren't any other conditions she could think of that covered every symptom she had; nausea, cravings, and the heightened sense of smell. When she saw the care Talvi took to help Chivanni read the menu, since the faerie couldn't read it for himself, she had to wonder; would he really be such a horrible father?

Drinks arrived, toasts were made, and when the entrees came to the table, the delectable smells made Annika's mouth water. She was about halfway through her seared pheasant with blueberry sauce when she excused herself for a second time that evening. And Talvi knew that ladies tended to spend a bit more time freshening up than fellows did, but Annika had been gone long enough that her dinner was starting to get cold.

"Jill," he asked after a while, "would you be so kind as to check on my lovely wife? I fear she may have gotten lost." Jill wasted no time heading to the bathroom, and was gone for almost as long as Annika had been absent. When she finally returned, carrying a take-out box, she looked sympathetic as she sat in Annika's empty chair beside Talvi.

"I hate to be the bearer of bad news, but she's not feeling too good," Jill explained as she emptied Annika's remaining dinner into the box. "You'll need to take her home."

"Is she sick?" asked Charlie, sharing a glance with James, like this wasn't anything new to him.

"Yeah, she's praying to the porcelain god in the ladies room," Jill explained, and closed the take-out container. "There's no way she's going out dancing with us later."

"I swear, she must have an ulcer," James said, looking from Charlie to Talvi. "She needs to go to the damn doctor already."

"How long has this been going on?" asked Talvi as he folded up his napkin and set it beside his plate.

"Ever since she got back," said Charlie, rolling his eyes. "Do you want me to call you a cab? Because James has a thing about his leather seats. He'll have a cow if she pukes in his car. "

"Oh, I love cows," said Chivanni, clapping his little hands. "Especially tiny calves! They're *so* adorable. Can we have a little spotted cow at your house?"

"I don't think he meant that literally," said Jack, and Chivanni seemed very let down by this actualization. He really did adore little spotted cows.

"Maybe you can come to the dairy farm where I work when the calves are born," Charlie said, seeing how upset the winged faerie was. "We have some spotted cows that are almost due." This got Chivanni's wings fluttering again, though Talvi seemed not to care as much this time.

"Here, take my car," Patti said, and handed Talvi a set of keys. "I'm getting a ride with Jill tonight, and my car already looks like someone threw up on it. It's the hooptie parked in a meter stall about halfway down the block."

"A hooptie?" Talvi repeated. "What type of automobile is that?"

"An ugly one," Patti answered. "It's camouflage, but you can't miss it. It's got a bright orange door."

"I see . . . " Talvi said slowly, looking at the keys in his hand. "So Annika's waiting for me to drive her home?"

"Dude, there's no way she's gonna drive herself," Jill said. "She's blowing chunks."

"Are you coming along for the ride, or can you behave yourself?" Talvi asked Chivanni.

"Hmmm, dancing or vomiting . . . dancing or vomiting. I think I would rather go dancing," he replied. "And I promise; no faerie magic."

Talvi left enough cash to cover dinner and a generous tip, and excused himself from the rest of the party as he gathered his wife's leftovers, and then gathered his wife.

This ought to be interesting, he thought to himself as he escorted Annika down the sidewalk, wondering what exactly a 'hooptie' vehicle was. He found it soon enough. It was quite a piece of craftsmanship, painted in brown, black, and olive green camouflage, except for the passenger side door, which shone a blinding shade of blaze orange. Patti wasn't joking when she said it looked like someone had gotten sick on it.

Yes, this ought to be very interesting, as I have no bloody idea how to drive.

"No no, that's for the turn signal," groaned Annika from the passenger seat. She had the window rolled down, hoping some fresh air would help, but it also let in the cold rain. She didn't really care though. She felt awful.

"You said it was to turn on the headlights, love," Talvi said through tightened lips.

"You pull the end to turn on the lights," she insisted again, clutching her stomach. "And you push all the way up for the right turn signal, and then all the way down for the left turn signal. You seriously haven't ever driven before?"

"There's a first time for everything, love," he said, trying his best to sound confident. He followed her instructions to the letter, though it was some time before he was able to master how much to press on the brake and the accelerator, and they were traveling along just fine when Annika abruptly said,

"Pull over!"

"But there isn't any place—"

"There's a driveway right there! Just pull over!"

Talvi turned sharply to the right and there was a loud crash. They had rammed the car smack into a huge tree . . . beside a driveway. Annika unbuckled her seat belt and opened the passenger door, and immediately heaved while Talvi leapt out to tend to her. Being that there wasn't much he could do, he gathered Annika's hair in his hands so it wouldn't get messy, but there was nothing left in her stomach to make a mess. Every time he thought she was going to say she was ready to go, she would lean forward and dry heave some more. Within a few minutes, Talvi could hear a siren, and a squad car with two police officers pulled up in front of them. He turned around and saw an old woman scowling at him from her front window. No, it probably did not look too innocent from her point of view, with Talvi holding Annika's hair back as she rested on her knees, bobbing forward. He smiled and waved to the woman with his free hand, and she yanked the curtains shut.

"License and registration?" one of the officers inquired.

"Registration for what?" Talvi asked, still standing beside Annika. He gave her his handkerchief to wipe her mouth.

"The vehicle registration, sir," replied the second officer, helping Annika back into the passenger seat. "And we'll need to see your driver's license."

"It's not my bloody vehicle," he said irritably. "I have no idea where the driver's license and registration for it would be."

Annika sighed and turned to open the glove compartment. The entire drawer fell out of the hinges, dumping dozens of papers, baggies, a scale, and candy wrappers onto the floor of the car. Her hand flew to her forehead as she let out a groan, but this time it wasn't the nausea.

"Sir, I'm going to have you step over to the side of your vehicle," said the second officer, and tried to lead Talvi away from his wife, but he refused.

"It's not *my* vehicle, I tell you," he insisted. "Can't you see my wife is ill? I just want to get her home!"

"I'm going to need a tow truck and a canine unit dispatch," the officer said into his radio, and took out his handcuffs. "Sir, please turn around and place your hands behind your back."

CHAPTER 10
How I Met Your Mother

"Ring . . . ring . . . ring . . . "

"Come on James, you always pick up your phone," Annika muttered to herself. "Where the hell are you when I need you?" He was likely still out with everyone else, making a night of it.

Annika hung up the phone, and hesitated. If all her friends were out at a noisy bar, none of them would hear their phones. Who did she know that would be home on a Friday night? Danny would be, but there was no way in hell was she going to call him. She pondered the thought of sleeping on a cold, hard bench for a few minutes before she dialed the only other number that would be guaranteed to answer.

"Hello? Who is this?" a deep, muffled voice answered.

"Dad, it's me. I'm um . . . I'm at the police station."

"What the hell for?"

"Well, it's complicated."

"What the hell did you and Charlie do now?"

"Please Dad, just come get us."

"Fine . . . I'll be there as soon as I can," her father grumbled.

Annika sat down in the chair by the phone for what seemed an eternity, until an officer led her through the door to the lobby, where her dad and Talvi were both waiting. The two men couldn't have looked more different; Talvi incredibly tall and thin, with thick, black hair and smartly dressed, while her dad was of average height, hiding his larger than average beer belly under a Green Bay Packers sweatshirt, with a Trail Blazers knit hat pulled over his thinning sandy hair. Yet both of them shared the most painfully awkward expressions she'd ever seen. She quickly signed herself out and the three of them walked out the doors of the police station in complete silence.

"Dad, I'm so sorry," she said, not looking at Talvi as they climbed into her dad's jeep. Her father made no immediate reply as he drove away in the opposite direction from their house.

"Where are we going?" she asked.

"Home. I'm too tired to drive all over town and drop you kids off. You two can sleep at our house, and deal with your friend's car in the morning."

"Mr. Brisby, I, I sincerely apologize for inconveniencing you this way," Talvi said. "I'm so sorry to have disrupted your evening. I never should have borrowed Patti's car. I wasn't thinking."

Annika saw her father shake his head a little, and then was surprised to hear him chuckle and say, "You were thinking alright, pal. Just not with the right head."

Annika's eyes opened wide and she stared at Talvi, who seemed just as shocked. "Your mother's going to shit a brick when she finds out about this. The way those hens at the salon cluck, it won't be long at all before the whole roost hears about Faline's daughter and son-in-law getting arrested for 'lewd and lascivious behavior.'"

The rest of the car ride was free of conversation, and even with the decreased traffic, it seemed to take forever to reach Annika's parents' home.

They walked into the small, dark house and she started to head up the stairs to her old bedroom. Her dad followed behind her, pointing to the living room when Talvi stood in the entryway looking confused.

"You get the couch, buddy," her dad said. "And just to let you know, I'm a light sleeper and have a brown belt in Jiu Jitsu. Catch my drift?"

Talvi nodded, and Annika scurried up to bed. There would be no unintentional *or* intentional daughter-defiling going on under that roof tonight; that was for sure.

Annika awoke to the familiar smell of bacon frying and coffee brewing. Ah, it was Saturday morning at her parents' house. She washed her face and trotted down to the kitchen, where she found Talvi sitting at the table with a breakfast plate, a cup of tea, and a glass of orange juice, chattering away with her mother as if he were the boy from next door. They both looked up at her as she came into the room. It was surreal, to see them sitting side by side at the kitchen table.

"Well, well, well," her mother said with a wry smile, putting her hands on her hips over her purple pajamas and pink robe. "That's a fine way to meet your *husband*, young lady! Although after your un-ladylike behavior last night, I don't think I can call you that anymore," Annika felt her face grow warm, but she soon recovered.

"I think everyone in this room is aware that we were wrongfully accused," she smirked, and smoothed her wrinkled dress.

Her mother walked up to her, apparently not as upset as she had expected her to be. Then she surprised Annika by giving her a huge hug.

"Sweetie, I'm so sorry for what you must have gone through while you were missing in Europe," she said, hugging her tighter. Annika shot a confused look to her husband from over her mother's shoulder. "Talvi told me everything."

"What do you mean, *everything?*" Annika asked as she was released from the embrace, and glanced from her mother to her husband with suspicious curiosity.

"I explained how you must have fallen and struck your head whilst hiking, and that I found you wandering about the woods near my family's home, babbling *en français*," he informed her with a radiant smile. The light was absolutely dancing in his eyes. "You couldn't recall where you lived, and since my eldest sister is a doctor, I brought you home with me, so that we could at least look after you until your amnesia wore off. Your excellent French led us entirely in the wrong direction in our efforts to get you home. We wasted months scouring the missing persons reports from France instead of Bulgaria or anywhere else. I finally brought you to Paris to see if anything would trigger your memory, and shortly after we arrived, you disappeared on me and had your parents come collect you. And here you went and told them you were with fairies and wood nymphs the entire time, and had gotten married to an elf." He gave an amused little laugh at her shocked expression and turned to her mother. "I get that all the time because of my ears, but I was born this way. I suppose

Annika's creative side likes to color things up a bit, even if it's at others' expense. Was she this much trouble when she was younger, Faline?"

"Heavens, no," her mother said, shaking her head. "Come on; let me have another look at this ring he had specially made for you." Still recovering from her husband's tale, Annika held out her left hand for inspection, while her mother tucked her light brown hair behind her ear as she squinted at the twinkling band.

"That ring is gorgeous. What kind of writing did you say this was inside of it, Talvi?"

"Oh, nothing you would recognize," he said cheerfully. "It's an ancient language that most people have never heard of, although my bookish brother and I speak it at home with a few friends of ours. He's an absolute fiend when it comes to studying rare languages. The phrase on the ring is an old saying which doesn't translate very well, but it means that true love is capable of crossing any distance. Even if she couldn't remember where she lived, your daughter was still charming enough to win my heart for eternity." Faline cooed at the romantic explanation and walked back to the stove as Annika poured herself a cup of coffee and sat down across from Talvi.

"And has your bookish brother ever needed your dad to come get *him* out of jail?"

"Well, actually . . . um . . . never," Talvi said and fussed with a few strands of hair. "Finn is very responsible. He would never find himself in that situation. I believe Annika is a bad influence on me. I've never been in trouble with the law before."

"That's right, blame the victim," Annika said as she rolled her eyes, then stirred some sugar into her coffee. "I don't think last night was that big of a deal, in the grand scheme of things."

Faline's eyes opened wider.

"You don't think getting arrested is a big deal?" she asked, opening a cupboard to take out a few more plates. "You'll have to repay your dad and I for the fines, by the way. You know we can't afford that right now, Annika. We're still paying off the last minute plane tickets to Paris we bought to bring you back home." She set the plates on the counter with a *clunk* beside the stove, and started to fill one of them with food.

"Don't trouble yourself over the fines and the tickets, Faline; I'll take care of my wife's debts as soon as I'm able to exchange more of my currency," Talvi said as he winked at Annika.

"Do you mean to tell me that you're a well-to-do trouble maker?" she asked, putting a plate of hash browns, scrambled eggs, wheat toast and applewood bacon in front of her daughter, which Annika started nibbling right away.

"Only if it will improve your opinion of me," came his snappy retort.

"You know, money doesn't solve everything, but it definitely helps," Faline said, snickering to herself, before returning to the kitchen to fix her own plate. "There's bacon on the stove, if you want any, Talvi."

"Thank you, but I don't eat animals," he replied as he slathered jam on his toast. "I do appreciate the gesture, however."

"Oh, are you a vegan?"

"Aren't those the vegetarians that don't take things like cream or honey?" he asked, eyeing his heavily buttered and jammed toast, and then his wife, who nodded. "I am most decidedly *not* that. I can't imagine a world where I willingly deprive myself of cream and honey. I enjoy it far too much." He turned towards Annika when her mother wasn't looking and sank his teeth into his toast with far more sensuality than was necessary.

"Is it a religious thing, then?"

Talvi chewed slowly while he thought of a response, all the while inching his foot up the back of Annika's calf from underneath the table.

"One could call it that, for lack of a better explanation," he said politely before taking another bite of his toast. He was now coaxing his foot up her knees, towards her thighs. She would have enjoyed it more if she wasn't starting to feel sick again. She set down her last piece of half-eaten bacon, and heard her stomach make a familiar sound.

"Fair enough. Help yourself to seconds, although you could probably have thirds, you skinny thing. There's plenty of food," she said, fixing a plate for herself.

"Why, thank you, Faline," he said in between taking licks of buttery jam from his fingers with deliberate strokes of his tongue. "I usually do help myself to seconds and thirds. My appetite tends to be quite insatiable."

"You sure don't look like you eat that much. You must have a hollow leg."

Talvi snickered to himself and ceased licking his fingers, pulling his foot out of Annika's lap just in time as Faline set a pitcher of orange juice in front of him. He poured the women each a glass before refilling his own.

Annika gnawed at her toast as she waited for the unpleasant feeling in her stomach to pass, but she knew it wasn't going to go away. She'd felt it dozens of times over the past few months, and last night had begun exactly like this.

Maybe this time would be different. Yeah, right. She knew what was coming next.

"Are you feeling alright sweetie?" her mother asked, smiling at her daughter. "Did you drink a little too much last night?"

"No, I didn't have—" Annika clapped her greasy hand over her mouth and bolted from the table to the bathroom upstairs. She heaved again and again, until she thought her stomach was empty. She ran the faucet and gargled before rinsing her mouth out, but when she returned to her chair, she didn't feel any better.

"Are you alright?" Talvi asked from his spot across the small table. "You don't look very well at all." He narrowed his eyes in concern, trying to determine what might be the cause, before he took another sip of his juice.

"Well I think I've figured out why you two got married so fast," her mother said with a suspicious look in her eyes. "You're pregnant, aren't you?" There was a crash of glass as a puddle of orange juice spread all over the floor underneath Talvi's chair. He stooped down to blot up the mess with his napkin while Faline helped collect the pieces of broken glass.

Annika moaned while another wave of nausea came rolling up in her stomach. It was one thing to be paranoid of being pregnant, but it was something completely different to have her own mother say it out loud. It made it more real than ever before. She clamped her mouth shut and found herself kneeling in front of the toilet once more, vomiting until she swore her mutinous stomach was attempting escape from her very body. Slow moving footsteps approached and someone passed through the open door, before shutting it for some privacy. She opened her eyes to see Talvi kneeling beside her with a glass of water.

"So, are you certain there's nothing else you wanted to tell me?" he asked. He handed her the glass and smoothed her hair back, away from her face.

"I'm sorry Talvi," she said reluctantly, as she was both literally and figuratively backed into a corner in the little bathroom, "I don't know for sure, but I do know that I'm late. I'm really, really late."

"How late?"

"A little over three months."

"I—I don't know what to say. I'm a bit surprised that this didn't come to my attention sooner," he said, stunned. "I thought surely I would have noticed if you . . . if you were . . . it's just that, this is *not* the sort of thing elves miss. We always know when a female is expecting."

"You do? But how can you tell?"

"It's difficult to explain," Talvi said, tilting his head to one side. "It's something one doesn't see with their eyes. We simply *know* it; we can *feel* it. But with you, perhaps circumstances are different. Strange things happened during our handfasting. Perhaps this is some sort of delayed anomaly caused by it. Are you experiencing any other symptoms?"

"Yeah," she said, still afraid to look at him. "Ever since I got back, I throw up all the time, and I've been obsessed with blueberries. I put them on everything lately. But Thursday night, right before you showed up, I realized what the reason was. That's why I know I'm not hung over . . . that's why I asked the waitress to put some pineapple juice in a martini glass; so no one would ask why I wasn't drinking. I didn't want to deal with it."

Talvi took a deep breath, exhaled, and then took another deliberate breath. He didn't want to deal with it either, but at least now he knew what she had been trying to hide from him since his arrival. He thought back to his last meal with his family, and his older sister's teasing less than two weeks ago, that he was destined to get married and have lots of babies with his wood nymph wife. He wondered if this was the very moment he'd tried his entire life to avoid. If it was, he couldn't let Annika see how apprehensive he felt. He put on his most valiant smile.

"When Anthea was pregnant, she couldn't eat cinnamon-date bread the entire time without getting sick, and it's her favorite breakfast." He reached up for the hand towel and wiped her face with it. "And you wouldn't believe the bizarre food cravings she had . . . certainly nothing as lovely as blueberries. She ate the most revolting things. The smells kept Finn and I out of the kitchen for months."

Annika knew how Talvi felt about kids long before their conversation in the jam aisle. Back at his house, a world away, she'd seen him avoid his young nephew like the bubonic plague. He made it pretty clear that children were nothing more than squirming, smelly little larvae that served no purpose but to keep him from his precious naps and beloved bar-hopping.

"How can you be so calm, after the way you were talking about getting twins like it was some horrible curse?" she wanted to know, finally able to look at him through the tears forming in her eyes. "You know neither one of us is ready for . . . *kids!*"

"I doubt many parents are ever truly ready," he assured her. "Even Anthea has her bad days. Now please don't cry, my little dove . . . you'll only agitate yourself further."

He held her close, rubbing her back, and she briefly imagined what their life might be like in the not so distant future.

Annika saw their home as a wreck, with obnoxious, noisy, bright plastic toys scattered everywhere and two black-haired tykes chasing each other around the fireplace with rusty scissors. Her guitar and bass were dusty from lack of playing, the walls were decorated with finger paints and sticky residuals of food, while the floor was enhanced with trash and papers and stains. It was a similar version of her bedroom a few days earlier, except with more diapers and less vodka bottles. But on second thought, maybe the vodka would stay. She was by no means ready to lose countless nights' worth of sleep because crying babies kept her awake all night. And the thought of a post-twin body was upsetting as well. She had places to go, things to see and do, dreams to create, and a needy infant or two were not part of those plans. She was sure her husband was thinking the same thing, just keeping it to himself. But with every protest she voiced, he only assured her they would get through it together.

When Annika finally felt better enough for Talvi to coax her out of the bathroom, they found Charlie and her father sitting at the table, wiping the last bit of scrambled eggs and hash browns from their plates with slices of toast. Her brother had already taken the liberty of finishing hers off for her. Given that he was wearing his dirty soccer practice clothes, it wasn't much of a surprise.

"Hey jailbird, I came by to give you a ride home since your husband totaled Patti's car," Charlie said with his mouth full of Annika's abandoned toast.

"It's *totaled?*" She felt even more lightheaded and unfocused as she slid back into her chair. "I thought it just had some damage to the front bumper."

"Are you kidding? Talvi parked it into a tree. It's totally wrecked," Charlie replied as though it almost gave him pleasure to do so. "She already talked to the insurance adjuster. The front axle is bent and the engine is pretty messed up, but since she only has liability insurance, the damage isn't covered. I've offered to give her rides to work when I can, but she's still freaking out about not having a car."

"I'll get her another one," Talvi muttered, and his hand instinctively reached for the silver case in his pocket. It was astounding to him, how quickly things could spiral out of his control.

How long have I been here? he wondered. *Oh, only about thirty-six hours. Bravo, you git. Bravo.*

"Talvi, what line of work are you in, exactly?" Faline asked as she began to clear plates. Talvi took out a cigarette and tapped one end against the silver case a few times before putting the case back in his pocket.

"Mergers and acquisitions," he replied without missing a beat, and kissed Annika on the head before putting the cigarette in his mouth. "Good thing it pays well, because being married to your daughter is getting expensive. Now if you'll excuse me, I know you don't allow smoking in the house." He sauntered out the front door in his cat-like way of moving, leaving the Brisby family to exchange plenty of glances among themselves.

"He's not seriously going to buy Patti a new car, is he?" Charlie asked, with his mouth hanging open. "That's insane!"

"I don't think he meant a Mercedes, Charlie," Annika replied, wrinkling her nose. "And shut your mouth when there's food in it. You're gonna make me puke again."

"I never would have taken him to be an investment banker," Faline said, picking up a piece of broken glass that she had missed from earlier.

"He doesn't seem to have a problem taking risks," Annika's father said, grinning ever so slightly, "so I guess I can't be too surprised."

"What the hell did you do after you left last night? Rob a liquor store?" Charlie asked, but, no one volunteered an explanation.

"That's fine," he shrugged. "It'll be in the paper anyway. They always print the police reports." He waved his finger triumphantly at her before wiping his hands and face off with his sleeve. "I'll know whatever you did soon enough, along with everyone else in P-Town *and* the 'Couve."

"What? Oh no!" Annika and her mother wailed simultaneously, and her father grumbled something indecipherable before shoving his nose further into his copy of The Oregonian.

"Man, I can't wait! It's got to be good if *you* guys won't even tell me," Charlie said, wiping his greasy mouth on his sleeve. "Well, are you ready to get out of here and face your doom?"

You don't even begin to know what kind of doom I'm facing. Annika thought bitterly amidst her nausea.

Here she had broken up with Danny because he wanted her to settle down and get married and do the whole kid and family thing relatively soon, and now she found herself entangled in all of those commitments. She began to wonder if maybe it had been her destiny all along, regardless of who she ended up with, to not pursue her passions. Maybe she was just being selfish. Maybe she was supposed to be like so many other women, putting everyone else's needs before her own. She'd fly to PTA meetings in her faerie dusted red-feathered Manolo Blahniks and sit next to women with the same matching haircuts and yoga pants, who talked about her behind her more fashionably dressed back. They would ask her to volunteer at the school book fair, and then recruit the twins into Scouts. They would think she was a raging alcoholic for suggesting that school functions might have better attendance if cocktails were served at them. They would be appalled that she didn't agree that every child should receive a blue ribbon at the annual art show, because let's face it . . . they weren't *all* little Picassos. She would find herself regretting that she never became the song-writer that she had always dreamed of becoming. She would probably find herself regretting a lot of things.

Maybe it was her destiny after all, because she just wasn't dedicated enough to be a real artist. The past few months had been proof of that. Why had she wasted so much time wallowing on the couch in self-pity, when she could have been recording her own songs and booking gigs? Pop stars half her age and not nearly half as talented were more successful than she was.

What if Danny had been right all along, and she was destined to be just another starry-eyed shoe gazer? She did live in Portland, where it was impossible to throw a rock without hitting an artist or musician of some kind. Maybe it was finally time for her to walk away from that silly pipe dream and become a bonafide grown up, like Danny was always telling her to do.

"Go for the sure thing; never bet on a wild card," he'd always told her.

Charlie had his keys in hand, signaling that he was ready to roll, and Annika felt a long, lithe arm curl tight around her shoulder. It was Talvi, back from his smoke break, coaxing her along as he began to head towards her parents' front door.

"Mr. Brisby, you have my word that I'll reimburse you in full within a fort-night," Talvi said to her father as they headed out with Charlie. "I'll tend to the matter as soon as possible."

"Well, it doesn't have to be all at once, but if you paid back your share of the fines first, I might not make you sleep on the couch next time you're here. I know you kids have a lot on your platter as it is," her father said with a repressed grin. "And Talvi . . . "

"Yes sir?"

"You can call me Jonathan."

Charlie waited until the front door had shut completely before he burst out laughing.

"What the hell was that all about, Talvi? I didn't know that *you* got arrested too! What were you *both* doing that you *both* got arrested?" he hooted, but neither of the two made a peep. His laughs died down quickly as he came to his own conclusions without the aid of a printed police report. "Never mind. Hey Ani? What the hell is wrong with you? I know you're not hung over."

"She's not feeling well," Talvi said, helping Annika climb into the back seat of Charlie's messy jeep. There were crumpled newspapers and feathers all over the floor, although some of the feathers were settled on his duffel bag full of sweaty towels that needed desperately to be washed. Talvi coaxed Annika to lie down with her head in his lap, smoothing her hair carefully, trying to make her as comfortable as possible. Talvi was so preoccupied with her, that he didn't notice the tense expression on Charlie's face.

"Listen, I want you guys to see Danny at St. Vinnie's first thing on Monday. This has been going on long enough."

"What has been going on long enough?" Talvi asked.

"This chronic 'food allergy,' or whatever she's had since she got back," Charlie said, waving to his mom with a forced smile as he backed out of the driveway. "I thought for a while that maybe it was all in her head, but let's get some blood tests done and see if we can find something. Maybe Mom's right and you're just pregnant."

Annika moaned, partially at what Charlie was suggesting, and partially because her stomach was still cramping up painfully. Even breathing felt like a chore. Talvi looked down at her without his typical impish smile.

"Are you referring to the same Danny from your football team?" Talvi asked, but he already knew the answer.

"Yeah. Ani's going to go see him first thing on Monday morning. That's all there is to it. And if she doesn't, I'm telling Mom and Dad." Annika groaned again in compliance.

"What does she need to see *him* for?" he asked Charlie before looking down at Annika.

"Danny's a pathologist," Charlie answered. "He'll do some blood tests and find out what the hell is going on with Ani."

"Ah," Talvi answered, and felt his own blood starting to boil. The last thing he wanted, besides to be a father, was to have a former fiancé and modern mad scientist poking and prodding his not-completely-human wife, testing her like a guinea pig. He jotted this down in his mind right next to the car accident, getting arrested, owing Annika's parents thousands of dollars, owing Patti a car, and simply said, "How splendid."

CHAPTER 11
A Ray of Light

When they got home, Chivanni was timidly clearing the kitchen table where James was sitting with his cell phone glued to his ear in one hand, and the other clutching a fistful of his perfectly tousled dark hair in frustration. The way that Chivanni was tiptoeing around made Charlie wonder if it had been announced that Mount Hood was about to blow up at any second. But the possible eruption wasn't geological in nature. It was Italian.

"Listen, Jack, you call that incompetent fuckwad right back and tell him to get that shit here as soon as possible!" James screamed. "Ground shipping could take all week! Doesn't he realize there was just a blizzard in Denver, or am I the only person on the planet who watches the Weather Channel?"

Here he paused, letting Jack get in his two cents.

"Yeah, the music *does* blow more than the northwesterlies," James agreed after a moment. "But the roads will be a friggin' ice skating rink! Call him right now, give him the gallery's account number, and tell him to send it air instead! I needed that shipment *yesterday*! I swear, if I wanted to take it up the ass like this, I'd just go out with Jerry again!" He snapped his phone shut, chucked it into his crocodile man-purse, and took off his glasses. Rubbing his forehead, he said, "Well *you* look like shit," as he looked at Annika through his repositioned glasses. She covered her mouth with her hand and ran into the bathroom down the hall, but Talvi didn't run after her this time. Instead, he helped Chivanni

115

with the dishes, grateful to have anything to distract him from what his wife had been trying to hide since his arrival.

"Trouble at work?" Charlie asked his roommate calmly as he hung up his coat in the mudroom near the kitchen door. He had long ago grown immune to James's frequent outbursts and rampant name calling, but their houseguests weren't quite as accustomed.

"I'm just stressing out a little," James said, frowning as he took a cigarette out of his bag. "You know that huge show I have at the gallery in less than a week?"

"Yeah?"

"Well, the artist *just* shipped his pieces. Like, they're totally going to get delayed in this blizzard! I'm so pissed off, I could spit nai—" He stopped as they all heard her heaving into the toilet again from down the hall. "What the hell's wrong with her?"

"She's not feeling well," Talvi said, glancing in the direction she had run.

"There's no way she's hung over, not with her tolerance. Maybe it's food poisoning again," James said, frowning as he grabbed a lighter and headed to the porch to smoke.

"Yeah, food poisoning," Charlie said with a slight grin, making quotation marks in the air with his fingers.

"Hey guys," Annika said weakly from the doorway, looking more pitiful than ever. "Can one of you call work for me and tell them I'm still sick? I'm going to go lie down for a while." She headed for the staircase, but she was hoisted up into a pair of strong arms before she could take another step. Talvi carried her upstairs and walked into the bedroom, and for a good long while, he wasn't sure if he was in the right place.

The furniture had been rearranged, the bed was made, all the laundry was put away, and the rug had been cleaned. Talvi's books had been neatly lined up on an elegant set of antique oriental bookshelves, and his beautiful longbow was mounted on the wall above the shelves, with his quiver on the top shelf. He pulled back the bed covers, getting a whiff of freshly washed linens, before setting Annika down and tucking the blankets around her.

A few minutes later, Chivanni and James drifted into the room; Chivanni with a glass of water, and James with a bottle of aspirin, which he set on the clutter-free nightstand closest to Annika.

"I called the music shop for you and they seemed okay with you not coming in again. And I'm sorry for snapping at you down there," James said as he took off his glasses and rubbed them clean on his shirt sleeve. "I didn't mean to tell you that you looked like shit. I mean, you *do* look like shit, I just didn't mean to say it out loud."

"It's okay. If I look the way I feel, I'm sure it's like shit," she said, smiling at his honesty. It was usually blunt, but always reliable. "What happened to my room? Did you do this?"

"Yeah, what do you think of it?" James grinned, putting his glasses back on. "Do you like the matching lamps we found to go on the nightstands? We picked those up at an estate sale this morning. How about those bookshelves? Aren't they fantastic?"

"*We* who?" Annika asked, eyeing him a little suspiciously. James was not the type of guy to use the pronoun 'we' in back-to-back sentences.

"Chivanni and I, who else? I had no idea faerie magic was so practical! I think I'm in love."

Chivanni blushed a little and busied himself with straightening a painting on the wall that wasn't crooked to begin with.

While Annika checked out her new lamps, Talvi peeked in the bathroom to find it magically transformed as well. The fluffy oversized towels were folded up on a cushy chair beside the large built-in bath tub, and a long wrought-iron table was perched beside it, holding soap, shampoo, and pillar candles. It looked like a room at a luxury spa resort.

Talvi returned to the bed and sat down next to his wife, smoothing her hair away from her face while James handed her the glass of water.

"We'll let you have some rest now," James said courteously. "I mostly wanted to see your reaction to your room. I'm taking Chivanni to the gallery with me, and Charlie just left for work. So if you need me to bring anything else home for you, now's your chance."

"Well, there is one thing I'd really, really, really love for you to pick up for me," Annika said, after taking a long drink of water. "Can you get me a . . . um . . . a pregnancy test?"

Both Chivanni's and James' eyes widened as they looked her, and then at Talvi, and then back at Annika.

"Shut the fuck up! So *that's* why you've been blowing chunks for the past few months? Holy shit!" James blurted out. Chivanni couldn't even speak. He just looked at Talvi, wide-eyed.

"Charlie wants me to get some blood tests done at the hospital on Monday, but I don't think I can wait a whole day and a half," said Annika, taking another drink before she set her glass on the nightstand.

"No . . . " James said, still completely baffled. "I don't suppose you would want to wait to find that kind of thing out. Alright, well, text me if you need anything else." He turned to leave, grabbing Chivanni's arm as they left the room in a hurry. For a while, neither Annika nor Talvi spoke.

"I'm so selfish," Talvi sighed after a long moment of silence. "I really wanted you all to myself for as long as possible. I don't want to share you with anyone." He crawled alongside her and reached under the covers, resting his right hand below her navel. It felt strange and comfortable to her at the same time. "I don't understand why I'm not able to sense precisely what is happening to you. I feel *something* changing inside; it just doesn't feel like you're expecting," he said, repositioning his hand and pressing in a bit more.

"Can you tell if it's deformed conjoined twins with fetal alcohol syndrome? Because that's what I think it is."

Talvi rolled his eyes at her and shook his head.

"That tickles," she said, squirming a little. "You can't really tell just by touching, can you?"

"Typically, I don't even need to do that much," he said. "I can usually sense it without touching, though using one's hands will tell for certain. My mother first taught me how to do this on the animals back home, and even Anthea had me check with Stella and Sloan. I've never been wrong before." He now put both hands on her, frowning a little in concentration.

"So what is it supposed to feel like?" she asked.

He paused for a moment.

"All that comes to mind is a ray of light."

She immediately pushed his hand away and rolled to her side, facing the wall instead of him. It bothered her to no end that he sounded so relaxed about the same topic that had her stomach in knots. And that screeching baby at the grocery store was definitely not a ray of light. It was a pain in the ass.

"Why did you push my hand aside?"

"I don't want to think about this anymore."

"Oh, because pretending nothing is wrong resolves things so bloody well?" he asked. "You won't be able to drink yourself to incapacitation this time."

"What's that supposed to mean?" she hissed.

"You know perfectly well what I'm referring to," he prodded coolly. "I may not be able to read your thoughts as well as I would prefer, but I am still capable of listening to those of your friends and family. Surely you didn't think that they would go unnoticed by me. I think you need to face some demons that have been following you around ever since our battle with the Pazachi. Having to defend yourself in a matter of life and death is nothing to be ashamed of. It appears to have been eating you alive from the inside for months. I'm so sorry for what you must be going through, but the pain doesn't disappear when you cast it in shadow or drown it with alcohol. The best thing to do is to bring it out into the light and let it go. I know your friends and family won't understand, but you can talk to me, Annika."

There. He had finally said it; he said the thing that she had never dared mention aloud. Steely-eyed and resolute, she didn't reply right away.

"We killed that girl's parents . . . " Annika whispered, half expecting the room to cave in on her as she spoke. "I saw Justinian cut off her mom's head, I watched you shoot her dad through the heart, and I watched her find their bodies. I guess that messed me up a little, not to mention that I killed people myself. They could have been her aunt and uncles . . . who knows?" She started to sob, and Talvi curled his arm around her a little tighter, trying to think of something comforting to tell her.

"Would you rather that we were the ones who were dead?" he said quietly, rubbing her back. "Would you prefer it if she stood with her father over *your* body? I don't think you do. Nothing will change what happened that day, Annika. It doesn't matter to them if you live your life in sorrow or in joy, but surely it matters to you, and those who love you. The Pazachi didn't give us a choice. They didn't want to negotiate; they made that very clear from the beginning of the whole ordeal. You have to understand that they would never have surrendered to us. They didn't want peace . . . they wanted power. They were under the influence of incredibly dark magic; they were blinded by their greed to have power over every race, over every realm, even over nature herself. Nothing would have been enough to satisfy them."

No, Annika didn't want to trade places with the people who had been killed, but something still bothered her even more than the lives that were taken. It was the life that had been left behind to suffer through the aftermath of that nightmare.

"What about the girl? We made her an *orphan*! I've never seen anything so messed up! We ruined her whole damn life! How can we ever make up for doing something like that?" Annika was now crying harder.

"I'm not certain that it will ever be possible to make amends to Denalia," he said softly. "I feel terrible for what she must endure, yet I accept that I am not completely to blame, either. Her parents had just as much a part in ruining her life, if you want to call it that, as Justinian or I did. I accept the price one pays for taking a life and harming another one so severely . . . but she would be beyond help even if her parents were still alive. She has been brought up to follow a very destructive path. A child should be free to play and discover how the world works in their own ways, not be forced to learn the darkest magic that exists. It's chilling, the shell of a girl she is, as though she's not even human."

"What happened to her after I went through the portal?" she asked as her tears died down. She was racked with even more guilt now that the orphaned girl had a name. Talvi shifted uncomfortably on the bed and pursed his lips. With great caution, he gently began,

"Well, if she had been younger like the other children, we would have left her to be cared for under Takashi and Natari's guidance. After we disarmed the survivors, they were relocated to a different area of the forest. Tak and Natari were quite confident that they could rehabilitate the young ones," he said, finally able to look her in the eye, "But Denalia is a girl of fifteen, not five, and unfortunately she's been taught to fight from an early age. Her level of skill, her immaturity, and the situation she's in make her an extremely dangerous weapon."

"She's a *kid*, not a weapon!" she said bitterly as tears started to run down her cheeks.

"She is not a mere child, Annika," explained Talvi. "She's the daughter of two of the most powerful Druid extremists that have ever existed. You'll recall that they were rumored to be a myth; their manipulative ways were so unlike the other Druids. They have desecrated what it means to be a human son or daughter of Mother Nature, and Nikola was not alone in cursing them. They wanted to completely sever the connection that our worlds hold with each other. They care nothing for the human race, which is rather ironic and twisted, being that *they* are human! Denalia was trained to be a killer like them, and leaving her in that environment would only breed a deadlier desire to follow in her parents' footsteps. We thought it would be best to send her with Pavlo, Justinian, and Sariel."

"Oh, so after you guys killed her parents, you had a vampire and your thug friends kidnap her?" she sneered. "You really think that you're doing her a favor?"

"Those 'thugs' are *our* friends and family, Annika. It *is* for her own good, believe it or not," he said sternly. "We acted in her best interest—you just don't see it because you're letting your emotions get in the way. It's a terrible tragedy that's happened to her, and as such, the road to her recovery isn't going to be easy or pleasant. I truly wish the circumstances were different, but they are what they are."

Annika couldn't make sense of what he was saying, other than her being too emotional, and him thinking it was right to kidnap orphans. It seemed beyond cruel and unfair. It seemed sick and wrong. The whole misfortune of Denalia's ruined life made her see her husband in an entirely different light . . . kind of a shadowy, dingy, and gritty light. She turned away from him, settling on her side.

"I think it would be a good idea if you left me alone for a while," she said. She knew she should get in a nap before band practice. But there were too many thoughts racing through her mind for her to relax.

"But we still haven't resolved . . . you know . . . that *other* matter," he reminded her.

"What's to resolve?" she asked, turning to look at him just long enough to glare at him. "I know you hate kids, and I'm sure as hell not ready for them right now. It's not like I have to keep it. Besides, after what you did to Denalia's family, do you really think I would want to have a baby with you?"

Her comment struck Talvi harder than he was prepared for. His eyes stung, and his stomach felt like someone had punched him just enough to knock the wind out of him. It took him a few moments to regain his composure.

"I would do it all over again, if I were faced with the same decisions," he said quietly as he stood up to leave. "I thought you knew me well enough to know that I would never want anyone, especially my own children, to live in a world overrun with evil."

CHAPTER 12
Snow

"Sariel, keep up with us! We must get to the forest before the storm hits!" bellowed a huge man through the wind. Snow was blowing all around her, whipping loose strands of her long dark hair into her frozen face.

"I am well aware, Justinian!" she growled back to the knight, struggling with the weight of her own frosty sword and ice-laden cloak. Sariel had the spirit and tenacity of a lioness, but those qualities seemed to have left her when she needed them the most. Her boots felt like they were made of lead, not fur-lined leather, and her lithe body felt like a cumbersome weight she was barely in control of. She found herself exhausted as soon as she had risen that morning, just as she had been for the past few weeks. It had been decades since she had ever traveled in such harsh and physically demanding conditions. As far as she was concerned, the storm had already been hitting them for the past hour, and the only reason she didn't let herself sink into the snow was because the tree line was perhaps only another half hour away. As soon as they were safe within the forest, out of the wind, she could finally sleep. Oh, there was nothing in the world she wanted more now than to curl up in her blankets and close her eyes. And when they woke up, they would pass through the forest, and cross to the other side of the mountain range, where the spring weather would greet them. It wouldn't be more than another two weeks travel.

Right now, they were up to their knees in frozen white foothills, with a range of mountains rising up behind them in the near distance. Thank goodness the heavy cargo they had been carrying was finally disposed of, piece by piece along the way. They had left the objects at various locations; one tumbled down a cliff and into a streambed, one was thrown over a waterfall, and one was dropped into the center of a frozen lake. It was too cold to bury them in the solid ground, and even though they were made of pure gold and encrusted with precious stones, there wasn't a metal smith in the world that Sariel would dare take them to. It had been sworn upon that something so foolish and dangerous would never happen. Death first.

She rolled her pale blue eyes as she felt another growl in her stomach. They had only eaten a few hours ago, but then, it was hard work to walk through the snowdrifts when her legs were so much shorter than her companions. Her hunger had never been so insatiable as it was lately. She allowed herself permission to dig through her satchel and find a half-frozen chunk of cake-bread. It would do, but it wouldn't alleviate the unusual twinge below her stomach. No matter how much she ate, it never went away. One day it wasn't there, and then one day it was, and it never went away. It wasn't unpleasant; sometimes it felt as if she was about to start her cycle. But after nine-hundred years, she knew her body, and this was different.

She gnawed on her cold snack, watching herself fall farther behind Justinian, but she didn't care. She turned to her side and looked up at an unarmed and blindfolded young woman, who had the luxury of riding the only horse in the group. Even though she sat like a princess, bundled up in her white furs, both of her hands were bound with thick hemp rope. It seemed an absurd measure for a fifteen-year-old girl, but this was no ordinary girl. She hadn't said more than a handful of words in the past week, no matter how hard Sariel tried to crack her shell and get through to her. She seemed to be praying every time Sariel looked at her; bound hands clasped and her lips constantly chanting the same foreign words over and over under her breath. It bothered Sariel, wondering what the girl was thinking in that twisted mind of hers. It bothered her that a child should be brainwashed from birth to go against her very human nature to feel love and compassion for others. It bothered her that she could see no positive outcome for this girl, even though she wanted desperately to maintain some sliver of hope that Denalia could reclaim a normal life. She daydreamed of reforming the girl, of teaching her respect for nature and all living things, rather than manipulating the world they lived in. She imagined all the power that the girl possessed, being used for good instead of evil, but it didn't look very promising.

The three of them were followed closely by another figure, and even in the blinding white snow he still managed to appear shadowy. His entire body was completely covered in dark wool clothing, even his face and his fingertips were shrouded from the sun. Sariel wondered if vampires felt the cold the same way she did . . . if they could get hypothermia and frostbite just like she could.

"Sariel, you are a samodiva, are you not?" Denalia asked from her horse. It was possibly the first question she had asked in a week.

"I am," she replied.

"Is it true that when a samodiva marries a man, you become human like him so you can be his wife and bear his children?"

"Yes," Sariel answered, looking up at the blindfolded girl. "Why do you ask?"

"I think you are human now," Denalia said. It wasn't really a question or an opinion as much as she seemed to be stating a fact. Sariel smiled a little, glad that the girl was finally opening up to her.

"But I am not any man's wife," she explained, trying to hasten her way to the trees.

"You are Justinian's wife, even if you are not formally hand fasted to one another," Denalia said simply, with little emotion in her voice. Rather than be annoyed at her, Sariel instead felt a warmth inside that chased away some of the cold in her fingers and toes. Then the warmth burned enough that it became another growl in her stomach. She assured herself that dinner was not far away now.

"What makes you think that?" Sariel asked, walking a little closer to Denalia.

"Even though I can't see, I can hear what goes on between you two when you believe I'm asleep. You're not as strong as you used to be, either. It's because you're a human now, carrying his human child," said Denalia.

Sariel stopped in her tracks, taken aback by her words, but before she could say anything there was a sharp pain in her chest, and she knelt down to catch her breath. The darker figure rushed over to her side, but Justinian was too far ahead to notice, and it was too windy for him to hear anything.

"I'm alright, Pavlo," she said, wincing a little from heartburn. "It's normal."

"It doesn't look normal." The vampire said as he peered through the dark veil that protected his face and knelt down beside her. She scooped up a little snow and brought it to her mouth, hoping it would soothe the burning sensation.

"You don't spend a lot of time in the company of pregnant women, do you?"

she replied, and swallowed another mouthful of snow. She looked up at Pavlo. All she could see of him were his perpetually sleepy, sympathetic, hazel eyes. He shook his covered head and blinked slowly, and she imagined that he was likely smiling just as serenely under his veil.

"Denalia, how long have you known this?" Sariel asked from the ground. There was no reply. She and Pavlo looked up to see a horse with no rider.

"Justinian! She's gone!"

Panicked now, Sariel and Pavlo searched through the snow frantically, hoping to make out Denalia's tracks in the drifts, but there weren't any. She couldn't have gone far, and to do so in these white-out conditions alone, with her hands tied up would be suicidal. They called out her name, to no avail, and there they were, left behind, fumbling in the deep powder for an escapee who left no tracks, only a single, tawny feather.

CHAPTER 13
Male Bonding

Talvi came down to the kitchen to fix himself a cup of tea. He set the kettle on the stove and cranked the heat to high. Other than the sound of the gas flame igniting, the rest of the creaky old house was silent. James and Chivanni had gone to the gallery, and Charlie was shut away in his room. The only thing making noise was the occasional car driving past the house through the wet street. Talvi wandered from the kitchen into the living room, taking a look around at the patches of crumbling plaster, the water stains on the ceiling indicating the need for a new roof, and the stone fireplace that looked like no one had used it in about a decade, except as a place to burn bad memories.

If only Annika's heart could be mended as easily as this plaster wall . . . he thought, picking at one of the damaged spots. White dust crumbled onto the wooden floor below. He wanted to make things better, but he also knew he couldn't force Annika to confront her problems. It didn't matter when or how he brought them up, if she wasn't ready to deal with them. He had perhaps pushed too far, too soon, and adding parenthood to the mix of emotions had certainly not helped. It bothered him that he honestly couldn't tell what was going on with Annika. He had always been able to read her mind fairly well, but ever since their wedding ceremony, he felt like he was receiving a series of jumbled thoughts. Perhaps it was also the amulet she now wore, which served to help cloak her mind. Regardless of what it was, it was working . . . too well for his liking.

The whistle on the kettle sounded, and Talvi poured himself a cup of tea and added just a hint of honey and lemon, before returning to the living room. He sipped in silence, wandering from room to room, inspecting the place. It was far easier to distract himself with the shortcomings of this house than it was to think about the ones in his relationship. And it was far more complicated to imagine where he was supposed to live with his new wife, and perhaps a new family. Annika didn't belong on Eritähti, as much as she had grown to care for her friends there, and he didn't belong in the modern world, as much as he loved his extended visits. No matter where they lived, they would be out of place.

Talvi sat down on the sofa, staring at the television, which was turned off. He had only just arrived in America, and already it was turning upside down on him. Part of him wanted to be back home, back to his ancient mountains and steadfast rivers. Back to his favorite pub, where the bartenders kept pouring beer in his mug as long as he kept pouring out entertaining stories. He could go back to being almost as free as a summer breeze. But that was not his style, to run from problems. He liked to meet them head-on, but his way usually involved his bow, his blade, his fists, or his charm. Being diplomatic was more of his father's or Finn's area of expertise.

The door to Charlie's room swung open and out he strolled, slowing down as he realized Talvi was staring at a blank television screen.

"Um, do you want me to show you how to work the television?" he asked.

"I wasn't really interested in watching a program at the moment."

"Do you mind if I play a game then?" Charlie asked, and plopped down on the couch next to Talvi.

"Have at it." Talvi watched as Charlie aimed one remote at the television, and then picked up a game controller.

"You might like this one," Charlie said, as the word FIFA flashed onto the television screen. "I'll even be the Blackburn Rovers so you can have your precious Manchester." He passed a second controller over to Talvi and proceeded to school his new brother-in-law at video soccer.

As Talvi learned the ropes on scoring virtual goals, he also learned that Charlie had decided to go into sustainable agriculture about halfway through earning a degree in history. They talked about small farming practices and what would be planted next at the organic farm where Charlie worked, and what would likely be planted in the gardens back at Talvi's house. Though it was still difficult for him to wrap his head around Talvi's age, the history buff in Charlie listened with awe as he described in great detail what it was like to be born right as the Industrial Revolution was beginning to grip Western Europe. Talvi explained how, during his family's visits, he watched firsthand as it carved up the English landscape that he loved so much. It wasn't only humans who had been affected by the changes. He spoke about entire faerie glens that were wiped out by pesticide applications, countless pixie dwellings that were destroyed by the changes in agriculture, great owls whose trees were cut down after living in them since time began, along with displacing the other creatures of the forests and meadows and moors. Endless numbers of his family's friends had dispersed and scattered, many never to be seen again.

He shared with Charlie what he thought of the great cities he had visited; Paris, London, Rome, Cairo, Tokyo . . . there was so much art and culture to be enjoyed, but the land was chewed up and stained black by the rampant use of fossil fuels, and trees were no longer the sacred beings that they used to be. They were mowed down to make room for concrete and glass structures. Animals were penned up in their own waste, fattened on grain and then slaughtered, at a much higher tax on mother nature than it cost to grow vegetables to feed a hundred times as many people. And what for? For feeding the endless ocean of hungry mouths, for clothing and housing the people that did not get thrown in the dumpster. Talvi had seen an article about that in a newspaper at the airport, and never was so grateful that Chivanni couldn't read English.

"That's what prevented your sister from coming home for so long," Talvi explained. "There's a movement rising back in my world, one that would like to sever all connection between Earth and Eritähti, because of all these reasons you humans keep giving them."

"You should come to work with me sometime; maybe even on Monday," Charlie said during a pause in the game, and turned to Talvi. "We're not all like that, you now. There's a lot of us mere mortals working pretty hard to change the way things are."

"I appreciate the invitation, but what about your orders to take Annika to be examined by her former flame? I think I should be present for that."

Charlie smirked to himself.

"You don't need to worry about Danny. He's not a douchebag. The whole thing will take five minutes. She can swing by on her way to work. This leaves you free to spend a day on the farm with me."

CHAPTER 14
One More Night of Freedom

Annika woke up with a jolt and found herself in the dark, moist with feverish sweat, like she'd been fighting some kind of infection and the fever had only just broken. She couldn't believe she had really slept away the entire afternoon, but the sky proved her wrong.

She walked into the dark and deserted downstairs and warmed up a plate of the quiche that Chivanni had made earlier, and found Talvi on the living room couch with a book, reading by candlelight. An empty box of his licorice candy lay on the coffee table. He didn't look up at her when she sat down beside him.

"Are James and Chivanni still at the gallery?"

"Mmm hmm," he hummed slowly and turned a page.

"What about Charlie? He must have given Patti a ride to work."

"Mmm hmm."

"I'm sorry I was such a grouch," she said after she'd eaten a bite, noticing her audience wasn't paying attention. "Are you still mad at me?"

"Mmm hmm."

She sighed, watching his eyes pass over the rows of unfamiliar text. He flipped another page, devouring it visually. "How about now?" she asked as she slowly ran her hand up and down his thigh, but he ignored her, not missing a beat in his reading.

"Mmm hmm," was all he responded with.

She wrinkled her nose a little. Surely this should have gotten his attention.

"You must be pretty mad if you won't even respond to me," she kept waiting for him to scratch his head so she could see that he was lying, but he never did. The more she thought about what he had said to him earlier, the worse she felt as she gazed at him in the dim light.

Maybe I think because he's a guy, that his feelings aren't as easily hurt as mine. He's been nothing but calm and understanding, and I've been a total bitch. I should be ecstatic that we're together, not looking for things to tear us apart again.

Talvi flipped through a few more pages in the long, awkward silence that filled the space between them.

"I guess what I said was really mean," she admitted out loud finally, after finishing her dinner.

"It was downright vicious," he said, looking right at her. "I didn't think you had it in you to be so cruel." He set his book down on the coffee table, but his eyes did not leave hers. They had no anger in them, but they weren't twinkling either.

"I'm sorry for lashing out like that."

"It's human nature to do that when you are injured or frightened, Annika," he said simply. "But I suspect that you are less human than you care to admit. Perhaps you've been trying to fit back into your old skin, but you find it can no longer accommodate you as you are now. You can't keep living in an abyss of melancholy. I wish you had inherited Runa's immunity to it. Nothing seems to weigh her spirits down."

He kept looking at her, waiting for her to talk more about the things that she was scared of saying out loud. His expectant gaze was so intense, she had to look away.

"Maybe you're right," she said, and swallowed hard. Before she had met him, her life felt so certain. She was Annika Brisby, with a pretty defined role among her friends, her family, and in her band. She was determined to make something of herself and her talents, and to hell with anyone who suggested otherwise. After she had met Talvi, those things had begun to seem less concrete. Her friendships felt shallow, her music seemed insignificant, the world around her was overwhelming, and she felt somewhat detached from her former life.

"Maybe I'm trying to be something I'm not," she mused, and fiddled with her wedding band. "I thought I could just go back to my old life like nothing happened, but something *did* happen. I'm trying to be Annika Brisby, and I'm not that girl anymore. I'm Annika Marinossian now. I just don't know what that means. I don't know who I am. I don't know *what* I am."

"I don't know what to tell you," Talvi admitted. "All I know is that things become complicated when humans and elves intertwine their lives. That's why they don't do it. Look at us now . . . look how complicated things have become in so little time. I say, we've really outdone ourselves, don't you think?"

Annika sighed. If there was one thing she knew about her husband, it was that he never did anything half-assed. He was Mr. All or Nothing. She supposed that made her Mrs. All or Nothing.

"So what are we going to do about it?"

"We'll see how things play out, and we'll get through it together," he finally said. "You know, my parents didn't give me much advice about being married, but my mother told me that we should never go to bed upset with one another." He reached an arm out to invite her to curl up against his chest, and she jumped at the opportunity.

"Aww, that's a sweet thing to say," she said as she cozied up in the crook of his arm. "What did your dad tell you?"

"He told me to be certain that the sofa was comfortable, just in case. So I thought I would look into that possibility," Talvi said, and raised an eyebrow at her. "Just between us, I don't think it matters where I sleep, as long as you're in my arms."

A warm tingling sensation blossomed at both ends of Annika's body, causing her to forget about their argument. She wondered how he could know the perfect words to say, like it was something he learned in sensitive husband school. He must have studied hard, because all she knew was that she felt much better than earlier.

Talvi had gone back to reading his book, and at first Annika thought she might follow along with him, but when she examined the yellowed pages, the text printed upon them was in a language she had never seen.

"What language is this?" she asked. "It kind of looks like a blend of Arabic and Swedish."

"I suppose it does, now that I think about it," he said, turning a page from left to right instead of right to left. "It's Karsikko."

"I didn't know you were a linguist like your brother," she said, wondering what native Karsikko speakers looked like, and where they were from.

"I do not have the interest nor the discipline in languages that Finn has," Talvi admitted. "I only know fifty-six, nineteen of which I'm fluent in." Annika felt her ego take slight injury when she heard this new fact. She'd always been proud of her knowledge of French, Spanish, and Macedonian thanks to her mother, but his fifty-six blew her measly four completely out of the water.

"So what's Karsikko? I've never heard of it. Who speaks it?"

"I do," he said, still trying to focus on the book's contents. "It's my native tongue."

"Then why did everyone at your house speak perfect English while I was there?" she said, somewhat puzzled.

"When you are a guest in someone's home, aren't you more comfortable if they speak your language? Personally, I think it's extremely rude not to, unless you don't know it."

"But how come you never told me you spoke so many languages?" she pestered. "How come you never told me that your native language is Karsikko?"

"You never asked," he said with the faintest smile, and went back to his book. There was so much about him that Annika didn't know . . . so many mysteries and quirks and preferences and personality traits that she had no idea about, not to mention all the ones that he didn't know about her. So what if he had no idea how she liked her coffee? There was plenty of time to learn those kinds of things. But what was he like before she'd met him? At the core of his being, who was he, really?

Annika closed her eyes and imagined him surrounded by a dense forest of the tallest white birch trees she had ever seen. Here, in his native home, he was truly a free and wild creature, free from any obligations to anyone or anything. She saw him riding Ghassan, clad in his black suede traveling outfit, carrying his longbow, moving with ease through the woods, communicating with the animals around him. He had the power to heal with his touch, he could ask a tree how it was doing and it just might tell him, and he was equally as capable of sleeping on a bed of leaves as he was on satin sheets. He could shoot a moving target from a galloping horse, he could recite texts from memory that had put her to sleep in literature class, and he somehow managed to be on a first name basis with her parents mere hours after being arrested for molesting her in public. He had captivated her at first glance, something which no man had ever accomplished. It was too easy to forget that he wasn't human.

She opened her eyes to see this exotic creature from another world sitting next to her, holding the worn book in his careful hands.

"What's that book about, anyway, since it's got your attention so well?" she asked of his reading material.

"It's a history of the relationship between the Kallo and Näkki elves. We were originally the same race, but the Näkki chose to interbreed with demons in order to acquire their powers. That's why they're so physically different from us, what with their yellow eyes and sharp teeth. They offer sacrifices to their demon gods for their dark gifts. They're very similar to vampires."

"Do they get along with each other?" she asked, deeply intrigued.

"Well now, that's an interesting question," he said, and closed the book. "They were at war against each other for centuries, until quite recently."

"Aww, they must finally be getting along. That's nice."

"No, it's not," he said, looking serious. "It means they're likely to direct their aggression elsewhere."

"Like where?"

Talvi gazed at her for a long time before he gave a response.

"I don't wish to speculate, and I wouldn't concern myself about it if I were you. All I can say is, I can't think of a safer place to be right now than here. That spur-of-the-moment, secret wedding of ours turned out to be much more convenient than we ever could have planned."

Questions about vampires and evil elves bounced around in Annika's mind, but then the side door of the kitchen opened and in bounced James and Chivanni, with a cardboard box hovering behind him.

"You guys were gone for a long time," she said, sitting upright. "I was starting to think you forgot about band practice."

"We stopped at the wine shop," James said, nodding his head at the cardboard box, which was now headed for the countertop. They watched as Chivanni made a little hand motion and twelve wine bottles rose out of the box, and arranged themselves in a row on the counter. "I wanted to be ready to celebrate whatever your results are. Or help you forget them. Either way, we're prepared." He picked up a plastic bag and waved it in the air, and Annika trotted into the kitchen, leaving Talvi on the sofa with his book.

"Okay, so I already read the directions, and they say you should wait until first thing in the morning to take them for the most accurate results," James said, handing over the instructions. "But I think you should take one now, because oh my *god* I'm dying to know!"

"*Them?*" she asked, looking up at him from the unfolded paper she held. "How many did you get?"

"Three boxes with two tests each," he said, setting his crocodile bag and car keys on the kitchen table. "All you have to do is pee on a stick, and then we'll know in three minutes!"

Annika's brain felt on overload, having another huge dose of reality knock her upside her head. Deformed twin elf babies began to haunt her mind again.

"James, what am I going to do if it comes out positive?" Annika asked. "How are we ever going to be successful if . . . " she trailed off, realizing it wouldn't be that long before her free time might be a thing of the past. She felt regretful that the most productive thing she'd done for the past three months was support the nearest liquor store and watch every zombie movie ever made. Sure, she'd written a few songs, but they weren't perfect yet. She could have done so much more with her time, besides feeling sorry for herself and debating her sanity, dwelling especially on a messed up teenage druid girl named Denalia.

She closed her eyes and saw herself in a filthy fur cloak, caked in dirt, spattered with blood, with both hands holding a sword. She could see lightning flashing, and trees crashing down around her. There were bodies strewn about all over the ground, lying in the mud, being rained on. She saw Denalia kneeling down beside two of them, grieving for her parents. She saw herself in the reflection of a bathroom mirror in a Paris coffee shop, washing mud off her face and rinsing blood off her shoulder.

A cold shiver jolted her out of her trance, and James's voice brought her back to the present moment as he rattled off the names of people from some of their favorite bands.

"All those people have kids," he said, as he inserted a corkscrew into a bottle of Montepulciano. "It can't be that hard."

"Yeah, but they're all rich enough to have nannies when they go on tour," Annika said, still very unconvinced. "Or they just fly home to check in with the fam."

"Well how rich do you need to be?" James asked as he set the bottle on the counter to breathe and took four wine glasses out of the cupboard. "You see how loaded my family is, and we hardly speak to one another. I think I only inherited this money pit out of my aunt's spite for her ex-husband. I mean, it's not like she refused to give back his record collection; it's a friggin' *house*!"

"Yeah, I don't want the kind of headaches—*ahem*—I mean, *money* that your family has," she agreed. "And I don't need a private jet, or a membership at the yacht club, or an island shaped like a palm tree. I don't care about drinking thousand dollar bottles of wine. I just want to go out for dinner or coffee once in a while, record this new album, try to play more gigs and see some awesome shows of other bands; maybe travel a little more . . . " Annika trailed off. There were a lot of things that she wanted to do.

"Judging by what your new hubby calls 'spending money,' he's got to be loaded," James whispered, pouring a taste of the wine into his glass. "I can't believe how much he spent on clothes and shoes for him and Chivanni. And now I hear that he's going to buy Patti a new car? You could hire a nanny whenever you want, and still do all the things you wanna do. I'll bet you don't even need to work. Why don't you just quit your job and let him spoil you rotten? He seems to want to do that, and it's not like we need your employee discount that bad. I don't really *need* another keyboard . . . although I sure wouldn't mind upgrading to one with seventy-three keys," he said wistfully, and swirled the wine in his glass while taking a deep whiff of it. Annika didn't find the matter as simple as James did.

For one thing, Annika didn't like the idea of being a kept woman. It was one thing to let a man hold open a door or offer his coat on a cold night, and it was another to have to ask permission to make a large purchase, or to be given an allowance. She was accustomed to having her own money from an early age. She had paid for her own guitar lessons with babysitting money she'd saved up, because her parents wouldn't give in. Her mother especially didn't want her falling into a lifestyle of playing music in bars, being leered at by men twice her age. But Annika wasn't the type to stay home cleaning house, folding her rich husband's socks during daytime television commercials. She also wasn't the type to have a maid do it for her either while she spent her allowance from him. Her rich hubby could fold his own damn socks, thank you very much.

But the other concern Annika saw was that most of the bands James had mentioned were made up of men, not women. And all but two of the musicians that she knew in town who had kids were men, and they had wives or girl-friends or baby-mommas that stayed home instead of coming to the shows like they used to. After having their first baby, every single one of the new mothers Annika knew sort of just . . . disappeared. From what she could tell, men had it too easy when it came to being parents. They didn't have to worry about singing their heart out while being kicked in the ribs for hours at a time. They didn't have to cancel shows because of Braxton-Hicks contractions. They didn't have to bother taking extra breaks during band practice to accommodate morning sickness, a shrinking bladder, or to nurse a hungry, screaming baby. Loud music and sleeping babies belonged in opposite corners of the world, and Annika wasn't ready to walk away from her corner yet.

"I'm sure everything will work out fine. I'd be such an awesome uncle. I'll teach your kid naughty words like Versace, Prada, and credit card debt."

"You and Charlie would definitely be the coolest uncles in the galaxy," she said, smiling as she imagined any baby's first words being Versace.

"I'll even quit smoking if the tests turn out positive," he said, and tasted the wine in his glass, swishing it from one side of his mouth to the other. "But honey, I can't give it up until after Friday when this damn show is over and done with. Just look at my face! I'm already starting to break out from the stress. I thought this shit was supposed to stop after high school."

"Thanks James," Annika said, touched by the gesture. She knew there was no way in hell he would ever quit smoking, but he rarely suggested the idea, and that meant something, coming from him. "Things generally do work out for the best, don't they?"

"God, I hope so," he said dubiously. He poured the Montepulciano into the four glasses, which prompted Talvi to abandon reading on the sofa and join them.

"Jack and Jill keep telling me the same thing about this show, but it's kinda hard to have faith. I can't plan anything when there isn't any art to make plans around."

Annika was quiet for a while. It wasn't as though James was telling her to move out because crying babies and dirty diapers clashed with his single and fabulous bachelor lifestyle. And he certainly didn't look ready to throw in the towel on their music because somebody had the audacity to reproduce.

"It's just a lot to think about," she said, glancing sideways at her husband. James just shrugged a little.

"I know it's a huge change, but no one's saying that you have to start driving a minivan and wearing sweatpants in public." Here he cringed, and in all seriousness he said, "Although I'm pretty sure they allow strollers in Armani. But if you turn into one of those self-righteous, holier-than-thou mommies who thinks they're suddenly an expert on everything just because they shot out a crotch fruit, I'll kick you, Talvi, and your spawn to the curb. I *cannot* stand women who think they're better than everyone else just because someone didn't wear a condom!"

Annika's eyes opened wide.

"James, if I ever, *ever* start acting like that, I give you permission right now to bitch-slap some sense into me," she replied, and James looked relieved.

Talvi, on the other hand did not seem nearly as relieved. He gave Annika an anxious, expectant look and asked, "Well what are you waiting for, love?"

"The tests say to do it in the morning for best results," she replied, after looking over the instruction pamphlet.

"Yeah, but you're more than a month late, so you can take it anytime," James argued. "Don't you want to know? I think we're all dying here!"

She could hear Charlie starting to warm up his drums in the practice space above the garage, and her fingers were itching to play. She saw two versions of herself in her mind. One was wearing a pair of Jimmy Choo heels, pushing twins in a stroller down the jam aisle. The other one was standing on a smoky stage, playing guitar to a huge crowd and singing her heart out, with different colored lights shining over her silhouette. She knew she could pull off either outcome just fine, but she silently begged the universe for one more chance to make something of her musical abilities.

"I don't want to worry about it until tomorrow morning," she finally said, letting them all down while she raised her glass of wine. "Give me one more night of freedom."

CHAPTER 15
Spring Leaks

Annika woke up wrapped in Talvi's arms and lay there for a moment with her eyes shut. Something didn't feel right. Whatever it was, she hadn't felt it since she was a very small child. The sheets around and underneath her were drenched. She sat up with a feeling of dread, and slowly peeled back her down comforter, but the damp sheets had no color.

"Why is it so cold?" Talvi groaned. "Put the blanket back, would you?" Instead, Annika crawled down and sniffed the strange spot. She could smell the clean cotton, but nothing else.

"Badra's beard, what are you doing?" he complained, and sighed as he propped himself on his elbow to investigate for himself. He frowned in confusion as he ran his hand over the wet sheets. "What is this? Did you spring a leak?"

"No, but I know what did," she said as a cold drop of water hit her on the head. She looked up and sure enough, the ceiling was leaking from the rain pouring outside. Given the condition of the old house, she was a bit surprised it hadn't started leaking earlier in the rainy season.

"Mmm, well, even if you have spare shingles, I'm not climbing up onto the roof right now. I'll fix it later," he said and yawned. "Now come warm me back up. Just scoot over this way to where it's still dry."

"I can't. It's morning," she said quietly, still sitting in her just-woken-up daze.

"So what's the rush? You don't have anywhere to go first thing this morning," he said with sleepy eyes and motioned for her to lie next to him a bit longer.

"Oh yes I *do* have somewhere to go. The directions said I should take those tests first thing in the morning, so I have to *go* to the bathroom."

"Ah, yes . . . " he said unenthusiastically, and sighed as he rubbed his eyes. "So much for sleeping in."

Annika slipped on her robe and went into the bathroom with her pregnancy tests and the instruction pamphlet. When she came back out, Talvi was standing barefoot on the bed dressed in his new jeans and an old t-shirt, inspecting the leaky ceiling overhead.

"Well?" he asked, looking down at her anxiously. "What's the decree of the gods, Mrs. Marinossian?"

"I have to wait three minutes," she said, putting her hands into the pockets of her robe. She was so nervous, she dug her fingernails into the palms of her hands until it hurt. "So what do you think about it?" she asked, taking a deep breath and looking up at him. Her heart was racing, and she sat down on the edge of the bed, trying to stay calm.

"I think it's going to take me a while, but I can manage it well enough," he said before sitting down on the bed beside her.

"Yeah, it'll take me a while to deal with, too," she said.

"I wasn't aware you knew anything about mending a roof," he said and lifted his eyebrow to look at her curiously.

"Huh? I thought you meant . . . never mind," Annika said as she realized they had been referring to two very different topics. "You can fix the roof?"

"Of course I can," he boasted. "You know very well the way my father punished us for misbehaving was to make us do home improvements. I was very, very, wicked growing up." He paused to snicker to himself. "I was always getting caught lying. I wish I knew what gave it away." Annika smiled to herself, because she knew exactly what gave it away . . . his twin sister had been the one to tell her this juicy secret, and she wasn't about to reveal it.

"I wonder what it could be?" she asked playfully.

"I don't know. I only hope our son or sons aren't as ill-behaved as I was. I was fairly awful."

"What if it's a girl? Or twin girls?" she asked, turning to look at him. A bit of color drained from his face.

"Then may the gods help us, because we're in even worse trouble than I thought," he said gravely. Annika studied his expression carefully as she waited for it to fade from an anxious gaze to an impish grin, but it didn't.

"I know that you don't want kids . . . " she said, taking a deep breath. "We don't have to go through with this, you know." Her husband was quiet for a moment, lost in thought, until a twitch at the corner of his mouth gave him away.

"Do you know why my eldest sister has two entire rooms for all of her instruments?" he asked. Annika shrugged.

"Because she's the oldest, so she was probably spoiled more than the rest of you."

"Yes, but why do you think that was?"

"I don't know, but I'm guessing you're about to tell me."

"What was that thing you said when you and I were having dinner with my family?" he asked, frowning a little as he tried to remember. "You know, it was that thing about showing up at parties uninvited and breaking things?"

"Oh, you mean '*crashing* a party'?" she answered, starting to smile. His attempt at slang was so endearing.

"Yes, that's it," he said, trying in earnest to look chipper. "Well, I suppose you would say that my oldest sister crashed my parents' party when she showed up. But when they finally met her, everything changed. I think they both felt extremely guilty for not loving her the second that my mother found out she was expecting Anthea. That's the reason why she was indulged with two exquisite rooms filled with every instrument under the sun," he explained, and then added as an afterthought, "Or, at least, every instrument that doesn't require electricity."

"So then, what are you telling me? That you're okay with this? I've seen you around children, and I know that you hate them, especially babies."

"I don't hate them, Annika."

"Well you sure don't like them very much."

"I'll admit that I don't like *other* people's children very much," he said, taking her hand in his, "but I'm certain I would adore ours."

Annika's eyes stung as he said this, and before she knew it, she was crying. The flood of emotion came out of nowhere. He pulled her close, which only made her cry harder.

"Aww now, don't do that, love," he said, wiping off her cheeks. "I didn't mean to make you cry."

"I can't help it," she shuddered. "Say something funny, maybe that will snap me out of it."

"Something funny?" he asked innocently.

"Yeah, like a joke."

"I know what you meant. You told me to say something funny, and I did. Why, come to think of it, I've said something funny three times now."

"I didn't hear you say anything," she said wiping her nose as she settled into her bed. He snickered very softly.

"Well I heard the wind rushing through your head, you silly girl. You're a bigger ding-a-ling than Runa. Are you certain your head's not made of wood?" He gave the side of her head a gentle rap with his knuckles as she realized he had indeed said 'something funny' three times without her catching it. And being compared to his best friend back home had never been more appropriate than it was at that moment. For all her sweet innocence, Runa was the biggest ding-a-ling she knew.

Annika sighed, and ran her fingers through Talvi's straight black hair, twirling it around like two devilish horns and gazed into his beautiful blue-green eyes. Here she had been so scared to tell him her suspicions, only to find out they were worse when unspoken. She couldn't believe how lucky she was to have someone like him in her life.

"It's been three minutes," he whispered, and helped her up. Together they walked into the bathroom where she had set all the tests on the counter, and she was shocked at what she saw.

They were all negative.

"I can't believe it!" she said, holding up one of the tests as she stared at it in disbelief. "I was so convinced after yesterday morning." Talvi looked just as relieved and perplexed as she.

"Hmmm." He partially sat on the counter and bit his lip.

"What's going on in that head of yours?" she asked. "Don't tell me you were hoping it was positive." His head jerked upwards and he shook his head vigorously.

"No, that's definitely not it," he said, still narrowing his eyes in thought. "It's something James said yesterday when you were ill. He said it sounded like food poisoning, and what with these negative test results, it made me wonder something just now. You had pheasant for dinner the night of Patti's birthday, and you were eating swine at breakfast right before you became ill, weren't you?"

"Swine?" she repeated.

"A pig. You ate part of a pig for breakfast," he clarified. "Your mother asked why I don't eat animals, and I let her believe it was for religious reasons, but really, it's because none of the Kallo elves eat animals. It makes us as ill as you were yesterday."

"So you think my body rejects it just like yours does?" she asked. "Do you think it has to do with being able to heal as fast as you do?"

"That's what my intuition is telling me. Our handfasting united us in more ways than marital bliss. There was very powerful magic involved between us that day," he said, looking at her curiously. "Just because you look like a human on the outside doesn't mean you aren't becoming something else on the inside."

Annika nodded in agreement, feeling like everything he said was making perfect sense.

"When I went through the portal from your world to my own, I cut my shoulder on a dumpster and was bleeding pretty bad. But then it healed right in front of me."

"I know. I found the exact place that you fell," he said, nodding his head. "Humans lack such healing abilities, but all elves have them. Perhaps you're still experiencing a transition of sorts . . . because you have to understand, you aren't completely human anymore. But then, you were never completely human to begin with, my little wood nymph wife."

Coming from anyone else, this would probably have sounded quite strange to Annika. But she knew she had a lineage that traced back to the ancient wood nymphs called samodivi, and she knew her strength and senses were more pronounced than ever before. Her vision seemed sharper, her ears picked up things she never seemed to notice in the past. She'd blamed the subtle changes on being away from home for so long, but then she thought back to their wedding day. That day everything had changed.

She recalled visiting James at the gallery one time when an art restorer had come in to see if an Italian painting could be salvaged or not. Annika remembered watching this woman take a cotton ball and squirt a little solution on it, then dab at the painting. In an instant, decades of yellow-brown grime had been wiped away, leaving only the bright blue of a Venetian skyline. Annika hadn't even realized that the painting was dirty until that revealing moment. Yes, that was the best way to describe how she felt immediately after her wedding. Blinders had been removed after being worn since birth, and nothing was going to put them back on.

"I'm really *not* completely human, am I?" she repeated, and she felt the silver threads from her wedding ring tingle with warmth under her skin. It seemed such a ridiculous thing to say out loud, but she couldn't argue with the evidence.

"I don't know what else it could be," he said, looking equally as fascinated as her. "But it would explain why your menstrual cycle is throwing us for a loop. Elven women only experience that once a year. The wood nymphs are the same."

"Only once a year?" she exclaimed. "That's awesome!" Annika felt another huge weight slip off of her shoulders. No more monthly cramps, backaches, headaches or any of the other PMS inconveniences she'd had for twenty five years. She wanted to scream out the window how lucky she was, but instead she just grinned like a Cheshire cat, and did a happy dance, leaping around the room, letting the relief wash over her.

"Yes, well, if elves' cycles were every month as it is with humans, I would probably have a thousand little black-haired maggots crawling around," he said and grimaced. "Talk about crashing a party."

"It's no wonder you had so many girlfriends then, if you didn't have anything to worry about," she said, and walked back into the bedroom to dress. She put on a pair of jeans and a peach colored shirt with short, puffy sleeves. Talvi looked on with a faint smile as she hopped around the room, pulling on her socks while trying to stay standing instead of sitting down. It was one of the ridiculous, illogical things she did that for some reason, just made her more irresistible to him.

"Believe me; I did have one thing I worried about quite a bit. It was only a matter of time before it happened," he said quietly.

"Before *what* happened to you?" she asked. "Elf herpes? Elf syphilis?"

He made a sour face at her.

"Annika! I cannot believe you just said that!"

"Well, if you're positive that you don't have any love children out there, what else could you mean?" she asked, walking close to him, but he only folded his arms across his chest and turned up his nose at her.

"I don't even want to tell you now; you've perverted the moment beyond redemption," he said, still playing hard to get. But it occurred to her that maybe he wasn't just being melodramatic. Maybe she had actually hurt his feelings.

"Talvi, I'm really sorry I said that. I was only messing with you. Just tell me what you were worried about, please? I'll make you some French toast for

breakfast," she bribed. He was quiet for a while before he finally reached out
for her.

"It was just a matter of time before one of those girls came along and nicked
my heart away," he said, and nuzzled into her neck. "I'm so glad it was you."

James was sitting at the kitchen table with a cup of coffee, thumbing through
the phone book when they came downstairs to make a celebratory breakfast.
Annika was used to seeing trash cans and pitchers and cups collecting drips on
exceptionally rainy days. She was not used to seeing the trash cans and pitchers
and cups float through the air and empty themselves into the kitchen sink
before returning to their places. But considering the winged faerie that now
resided underneath that leaky roof, it was not so far-fetched.

"So? Do I need to hire a child proofing service along with a roofer?" James
asked, anxious for the answer.

"You don't have to hire either one," Annika said proudly as she found a large
bowl that wasn't being used to catch leaks, and set it on the countertop. James
leaped out of his chair and hugged her tight, then let go and gave her and Talvi
a high five.

"Way to go on no baby!" he cried out in glee. "But what do you mean that I
don't have to hire a roofer?" asked James. "Look at this place. I've got to call
someone soon, before we start collecting animals by twosies! You'll have to tell
your mother I'll need to reschedule my appointment for tomorrow," he made a
grand motion at the room, showing it off like a prize on a game show. It was
true, the regular leaks had grown heavier, and new ones seemed to be springing
up all around them.

"Well . . . " Annika began, trying not to laugh as she noticed a new leak
beginning to drip directly into James's coffee cup. "It turns out that I married
an excellent handyman," she said, and took a few things out of the fridge.
"Sorry I forgot to mention that until now."

"A handyman? No shit?" James asked with a grin, not seeing the rainwater
dripping into his mug. "Hmmm . . . Talvi, what are you doing today, since you're
not going crib shopping?"

"I believe Annika and I were going to her mother's salon," he said, eyeing

James suspiciously. He had a good idea of what sort of ulterior motive was in store for him.

"Sweetie, you can't come," she said, measuring a bit of milk and sugar into the mixing bowl. "It's sort of a hens-only kind of place. No cocks allowed, besides James, and he's going later in the week."

"That's not very fair," he argued.

"No, it's not, but it's a tradition. Besides, you'd be really bored if you tagged along. It's just a bunch of old ladies getting their hair done and talking about knitting."

"That's bollocks and you know it," Talvi insisted.

"Well, there are things we hens like to cluck about that can't be said in front of boyfriends and husbands. Just deal with it. I think James needs your expertise around here, anyway," she dismissed, and went back to mixing the eggs, milk and sugar with a fork.

Knowing it was pointless to pursue the matter with her, Talvi turned to James, who looked ready for another makeover.

"So, Mr. Handyman, have you ever been to Home Depot?"

"No, I can't say that I have," Talvi replied with a wry grin, "but I'm guessing that's about to change."

"I hope you're as good as she says you are. I have a shit-ton of work I need done around this place, in case you haven't noticed."

"I'm really terrible at that sort of thing," Talvi said, running his fingers casually through his wild hair. "You don't even want me to pick up a hammer around here."

"What a load!" Annika exclaimed, waving a loaf of bread in one hand. "You were just bragging about how awesome you are, and I think you better prove it."

"Fine then. You just work on that French toast and I'll show you," he said arrogantly, and vanished into the living room to inspect the leaks in the ceiling.

"Is there anything he doesn't do?" James asked, closing the phone book.

"He doesn't lie very well, that's for sure," Annika said as she dunked a slice of bread into the mix in the bowl. "Hey, where the heck is Charlie? You'd think he would have woken up from all the racket by now."

"He went to get the Sunday paper," James said, grinning as he took a sip of his rain-spiked coffee. "He said there was an article he couldn't wait to read."

CHAPTER 16
Annika and the Inquisition

"Hi ladies!" Annika called out, shutting the door to the cozy little corner shop salon. She noticed more than a few eyebrows raise curiously from her mother's clientele, all familiar faces that she had gotten to know over the few years that they had lived in the city.

"Hello Annika," the small group of older women greeted her, two of which were seated under heated hood hair dryers, which made the small salon even warmer. "We haven't seen you around in a while."

"Don't tell me that you've been doing your own hair," a middle aged woman scolded, looking up from her newspaper long enough to take a sip of the mimosa sitting on the table beside her. She wasn't the only one nursing a strawberry-garnished champagne flute.

"No way—look at these roots Beatrice," Annika said as she hung up her coat and purse. "I'll never trust a box to do what my mom does best. Where is she, anyway?"

"Oh, Faline's in the back, getting your color ready," Beatrice said with a motherly smile. She was Faline's closest friend and co-owner of the salon, and like an aunt to Annika. "You know what a perfectionist she is with her craft. Where do you think you get it from? Heavens, child, take a seat! We need to talk."

"What's wrong? Is my mom okay?" she asked, walking behind the counter to where a mini-fridge sat. There was a bottle of champagne and a bottle of orange juice inside, and she quickly mixed the right amounts of the two in her glass before garnishing it with a couple strawberries. She sat down in the swivel chair next to Beatrice. Beatrice glanced at Annika's drink and draped a black cape around her, fastening it behind her neck.

"Your mother is fine dear, considering . . . " another woman said. The ladies leaned forward in their chairs and exchanged glances.

"Uh, what's going on?" Annika was starting to get worried.

"*You* should be the one telling *us*!" A third woman said with a smile, and they all clucked like little hens. Annika looked around at them with a puzzled expression.

"Somebody spill the beans already!" Annika demanded. Beatrice laughed and handed her the Sunday paper, strategically turned to one page. Annika caught two very distinct names right away.

2:21am: Officers responded to a complaint of lewd and lascivious conduct and a collision near the intersection of 39th and Belmont. When the officers approached the vehicle, they observed a male and female engaged in suspicious acts on the vehicle, which had collided with a Douglas fir. Annika Brisby, 25, and Talvi Marinossian, 28, were arrested and released after posting bail. Citations were also given to Marinossian for driving without a license, driving without insurance, and property damage in excess of $1000.

Annika's face grew incredibly warm just as her mother returned from the rear of the salon with some bottles in her hands. It was definitely not from the excess heat that the hairdryers were generating.

"I'm just glad it managed to get in the Sunday Oregonian," her mother said with a wry smile. "Nobody reads *that* edition."

"You know, they never really tell you exactly what they mean by 'lewd and lascivious'. There's so much they leave open to interpretation," one woman said from under a hairdryer. "I wonder what it was?"

"Did you read the words carefully? It said *on* the vehicle, not even *in* the vehicle!" Beatrice giggled.

"Ah, to be young and in love," another woman sighed.

"Harold never took me on dates like that!" a crabby woman croaked. The women all erupted in rounds of girlish laughter.

"So?" Beatrice said, turning to Annika with bright eyes.

"Well, if you want the complete story, it's not half as interesting," came Annika's reply as she settled into an empty chair. "We didn't do anything remotely lewd and lascivious. That's the only charge that was complete crap. I was sick, and he was holding my hair back. It just looked bad to the lady whose tree we crashed into. We're innocent, but there's no proof."

"Sure there's proof!" Beatrice said, grinning happily. "We all heard about that impressive morning sickness yesterday. You shouldn't be drinking that mimosa, either, missy." More clucking ensued as this statement was made, and Faline came into the main area.

"You *told* them?" Annika cried.

"Of *course* I told them. I'm the only one here who doesn't have any grand-children . . . yet."

"Well, you'll have to keep waiting," she said, and ate the strawberry garnish from her glass. "I'm not pregnant."

"Really?" Faline paused for a moment before resuming her task of setting the bottles of color on the counter near her work area.

"Really," Annika declared, all too happy to be sharing the good news. "I took six tests this morning, and they were all negative."

"I must say I'm a bit surprised, especially after that episode yesterday. Maybe you should have Danny do some blood work tomorrow, just to make sure you're alright. I know one woman who had negative home tests with all three of her kids. She needed a blood test with each one."

That was not the response Annika was hoping to hear, and she tried not to look as shocked as she felt. Her mom must have really been let down by her news, to offer such a story.

"I promise I'll call him before I leave today and make an appointment," she assured her mother. "I have to stop by his place and pick up some things anyway."

"Poor fellow," one of the ladies sighed. "He stopped by here once, you know, just to ask us how you were doing. He's a sweet man, that Danny . . . such a catch."

"Whoever his replacement is must be quite the charmer," Beatrice winked. "Aren't you going to tell us about this mysterious new husband of yours, or are you going to leave it up to the newspaper and your mother to fill us in?"

Even though she meant no harm, Beatrice's comment about Talvi being a replacement made Annika feel a bit awkward. She and Danny hadn't even been split up for three months when she'd met Talvi. At the time, she didn't even think of him as some kind of rebound; she was just living in the moment. That was really the only thing she could do when she was in the Srebra Gora forest, trapped on the other side of the broken portal. She had no idea when she was going to be able to come back home, or if she would ever be able to come back at all. Instead of making herself miserable every day thinking about a future that might not happen, she had taken Talvi's advice and found things that she enjoyed about his world; and he had definitely been one of those things.

But now that she was back home, facing the opinions and ideas of all the close people in her life, it made her question herself to no end. It didn't feel good to have these self-doubts. She struggled to think of what to say as her mother parted her hair and sectioned it off with little clips.

"Um, what do you want to know about him?"

"Well, for starters, what kind of name is Marinossian?" Beatrice inquired.

"I don't know," Annika shrugged. She didn't think it would go over too well to tell them it was some variant of an elvish name.

"It sounds Armenian, if anything, but I just assumed based on his accent that he was from England," her mother said.

"That's just where he studied English," Annika informed her mother, leaving out the bit about learning Fae from the Cornish faeries. "He travels a lot, so he speaks a few different languages."

"Oh, how fascinating," one of the women said. "How many does he speak?"

"He said he's *only* fluent in nineteen," she replied, smiling.

"*Nineteen?*" Faline repeated. This got some clucks amongst the hens. "His family must be very cultured, to send him to schools that teach so many languages."

"I have a friend who's a diplomat, and all of his children speak around six languages," Beatrice said. "But nineteen is just astounding. He must be a genius!"

"I never really thought of him as a genius, just a smart-ass," Annika said, feeling more at ease, and it wasn't from the champagne in the mimosas, although it didn't hurt. It was here in the privacy of Faline's salon that they were supposed to let loose, spilling secrets and talking about things men only wished they could hear, and might not believe unless they heard it for themselves. Perhaps she was worrying too much about what everyone else thought.

"What about his first name? I've never seen that before either," Beatrice said, taking her newspaper back and reading the police report again with a smile.

"Oh, it means 'winter' in Finnish," she said.

"It's a good thing he didn't 'Finnish' what he started, or the paper would have been very boring today!" one of the ladies chimed, and the others erupted in middle-aged giggles again. Annika blushed once more.

"Now tell us what he looks like. Is he tall, dark and handsome?"

"Yes, yes, and *yes!*" Annika yelped slightly as her mother's comb tugged at a stubborn snarl, jerking her head a little.

"I'll bet that's what you were saying right before the police showed up Friday night!" a white-haired lady piped up.

"Agnes!" Faline said from above her daughter's head, pretending to be shocked.

"It's not exactly the worst publicity for an up-and-coming rock star to get," Beatrice said, still smiling brightly. "Your mother told us he's quite well-to-do. Is it true that he's going to get your friend Patti a new car to make up for the one that he crashed?"

"That's what he said," she said with a goofy grin as her mother started applying color and foiling her hair. "Although I'm not sure if he realizes how much cars cost. He has some spending cash, but most of his money is in silver and gold."

"He sounds like he's got a good head on his shoulders, even though he's not much of a driver," Beatrice said. "Not too many people are smart enough to keep their finances liquid like that, especially in this economy."

"Yeah . . . " said Annika, sipping her mimosa again. She was pretty sure that Beatrice was thinking of something a bit different than a burlap sack full of silver and gold rings.

"What is Talvi up to today?" her mother asked. "I thought you might bring him by to meet the ladies."

"That's funny you ask. He wanted to come, but I sent him to the store with James to get building materials. The roof is leaking and he knows how to fix it." That just made the hens cluck even more about her good fortune, and they spent the next hour comparing the size of their husbands' honey-do lists.

After her long hair had been touched up in her signature flame red hue, and freed of all split ends, Annika dialed a number on her phone that she hadn't called in months.

"Hello?" a deep voice on the other line answered.

"Hey, it's me. Whatcha up to?"

"The same thing I do every Sunday," Danny replied. "I haven't changed as much as *you* have in the past few months."

Annika rolled her eyes a little and ignored his humorless tone. "Am I interrupting anything?"

"Nope. Did you just get your hair done?"

"Yep, how did you know?"

"Because it's a Sunday. You're still red, aren't you, or has that changed too?" he jabbed.

"Of course I'm still red," she laughed. "I'll never switch to another color; it suits me too well."

"You're right. It does suit you too well. So what's up?"

"Do you mind if I stop by for a few minutes and get that stuff out of your way?"

"It's not in the way," he said. It sounded by the tone of his voice that he didn't really want to give her shampoo and poufy rainbow skirt back after all.

"Well, you can always bring them to work tomorrow," she suggested. "I'm stopping by to see you there, anyway."

"Oh did we make plans that I'm not remembering?"

"No, I'll tell you about it when I get there."

"See you soon, then," he said, and hung up quickly. Annika grabbed her purse and waved goodbye to her mother, Beatrice, Agnes, and the other ladies, then made the drive down the familiar streets that she had traveled so often in the time that she had dated Danny.

It felt surreal to pull her car into the driveway next to his. She'd parked there nearly every night for two years. She hesitated at the front door. She didn't have a key anymore, but she knew he only locked the door at night. Uncertain whether to walk right in or knock politely, she finally decided on a quick warning knock before she pushed the door open. The familiar scents hit her like an old, stale memory.

"I'm in here," his voice called from the living room. Annika walked down the hall and into the room, where Danny was sprawled on the couch in a t-shirt and warm-up pants, flipping between three different cable sports channels, like he always did on Sunday afternoons.

"Well look at you," he smiled as she came into the living room. "I'm glad you didn't cut off too much. I think you'll look just as sexy even when you're your mother's age."

"You're just saying that," she teased.

"No, it's true. Your mom would be pretty hot if she grew her hair as long as yours."

154

"Danny!" she admonished.

"What? You look just like her," he said. The lively chatter at the salon had taken its toll and Annika felt her stomach growl. It was loud enough for him to hear, and he walked over to the fridge and found a box of fried rice and an egg roll.

"I just got this last night, so it's still decent," he remarked as he put the leftovers in the microwave. "You can have the rest, if you want."

"Do you want the egg roll? It's got pork in it," she said, having noticed the distinct smell of cooked meat. After the episode with the bacon yesterday morning, there was no way she could forget that scent or the trouble it caused.

"So what? You always get the egg roll," said Danny, giving her a weird look.

"Well, I think I'm a vegetarian now," Annika explained.

"Yeah right. The girl who likes her filet mignon still mooing?"

"I'm serious."

"Is *he* a vegetarian?"

"Well, yeah, but it's just a coincidence," Annika said, trying to soften the blow. Danny shook his head in disbelief and was quiet for a few moments until the microwave beeped.

"What did I do wrong?" he asked as she scarfed down the fried rice. "I just don't understand why things weren't good enough for you. I thought you were happy. Look at us. It's like we never missed a beat, sitting here like an old married couple. On Sundays, you either get your hair done or you do foo-foo girlie things with James, while I watch college ball. And at breakfast, I know exactly how you take your coffee, and you know exactly how I like my eggs done. Is that really such a bad way to spend your life with someone?"

"There's a lot more to a relationship than having a Sunday routine or knowing how I like my coffee," she said, and took a big bite of rice.

"Oh really? I'll bet Finnish doesn't know how you take yours," he said, looking like a know-it-all. He was pretty good at it.

"His name is Talvi," Annika said, trying to be polite. She really wanted that rainbow skirt back. Patti had sewn it and dyed it by hand, and it was a birthday present from a few years back.

"Well, whatever you call your new euro-trash boy-toy, I'll bet he doesn't have a clue, does he?" Danny pointed out, but she refused to answer. "I think knowing all the little things about a person counts for a lot. I thought I did a good job of remembering holidays and birthdays, and all the other things a boyfriend is supposed to do. I just don't get it. I don't understand how you could tell me that you needed more time after two years together, and then you disappear for a few months and you're already married to someone else that you barely know, that none of your friends or family knows. Charlie said it's not even legal, which is probably for the best. I get a really sketchy vibe from Finnish."

Annika knew she didn't have the answers that Danny was looking for, because nothing she said would be good enough for him. Of course it sounded like an immature, poorly-planned thing to do, but he didn't understand. She barely understood her relationship herself, when she started analyzing all the little details. Sure, it was intense at times, but all the little details were just that; little details. They would fall into place as time went on, and if she really was becoming an elf and samodiva hybrid with all their heightened capabilities, she had all the time in the world for Talvi to learn how she liked her coffee.

"Maybe you don't need to understand everything," Annika eventually said. Danny frowned a bit, and she knew what he was thinking with that analytical, scientific mind of his. Danny wanted to understand everything about the world around him. He needed to.

"Can you at least tell me what I did wrong, so I don't make the same mistake again when I meet someone else?"

"You did everything perfect. You're a great guy. But we're like orange juice and toothpaste . . . they're really nice by themselves, but it just doesn't work when you mix them together," she said, trying to keep her explanation simple. Danny gazed at her in a way that told her he thought a bit differently.

"If I had done everything perfect, you'd still be living here," he pointed out. Annika wondered where all of this stubbornness was coming from. She felt her amulet warm up against her chest, and she slowly found the exact words she wanted him to hear.

"And if *I* had done everything perfect, we never would have gotten together in the first place. We would have stayed friends, and left it at that."

He looked a bit surprised at her confession. After all, she had been the one to hit on him, and she had been the one who rationalized getting together with someone so different from herself. She thought she was doing herself a favor, bringing balance to her life by dating someone completely different than her. It seemed like a logical decision for someone as impulsive as her . . . but so much for logic.

"You're a really sweet guy, Danny," she said, meaning it with all her heart. "I really mean that. It's just, you and I are so wrong for each other. You have that thing you always say, about never betting on the wild card. Well, I just can't do that. I'd rather take my chances than play it safe."

"It's one thing to take calculated risks, and it's another to throw caution to the wind and do whatever feels good, Annika," he insisted.

"Yeah, and there's a big difference between being a devil-may-care hedonist and trusting your instincts," she said, putting her foot down. If Danny was going to trap her in this awkward conversation, then she had no choice but to level with him. "Talvi and I have a lot in common. We both love the same music, we both play guitar, and we even own some of the same books."

"Those aren't the only things you two have in common," he told her with a wry smile. "When Jeff texted me this morning at the crack of dawn, I thought it was some kind of joke. But when Adam called me a half hour later, I went out in my robe and boxers in the rain to get the paper. I didn't believe it until I read it myself."

Annika wondered how long it would take for that scandalous and incorrect police report to become old news as Danny disappeared into the living room. She hoped he wasn't fetching the article, and to her relief, he came back with a box instead. Sitting on top was a poufy tulle, silk and organza skirt, streaked with the colors of the rainbow and random strings of sequins.

He seemed hesitant for a moment, gazing at her with a funny expression before surrendering the very last of her belongings, the ultimate act of closure to their romantic past.

"I just have one question about that police report, but you don't have to answer if you don't want to."

"And what's that?" she asked suspiciously.

He paused only for a moment and then blurted out, "If I would have done something crazy like that, would we still be together?" Annika looked right at him, at the man she had tried to convince herself to stay with for so long. He was smart, good looking, had a great job, a nice car, and a nice house. She even had to admit that she still cared about him a lot, but not in the wildly passionate sense. He didn't like to go out dancing, he didn't like hiking or picnics, he thought her sense of fashion was outlandish, but most importantly, he didn't care for her music. She made him a CD of all her songs, yet he never remembered any of the titles. She knew that he'd never forget how she took her coffee, and that he would have been thrilled to have her stay at home and pamper him when he came home from work, but she wanted more out of life than a meal ticket. She thought long and hard for an answer.

"Danny, you never would have done anything crazy like that. That's not who you are. You and I are so totally different. If either of us had changed who we were to suit the other, I would have resented it for the rest of my life. *That's* why we're not still together."

She set the empty plate beside the sink, and when she looked up, a devilish spark that she had never seen had entered Danny's eyes.

"How was I supposed to know?" he leaned forward, balancing the box on his hip with one hand. "You never told me that's all it would have taken . . . " Annika's stomach did a flip as his hand reached toward her, but he only rumpled her hair and stood up a little straighter, handing over the box.

"Did you say you were coming to see me at work?" he asked her. "What's wrong? You're not still drinking every day, are you?"

"No . . . " she admitted, looking at her feet.

"Well good. I was worried about you," he said. "What else are you feeling?"

"I've been really tired on and off for the past few months, and I've also been getting something like food poisoning, but I think it's because I can't eat meat anymore. I also took a . . . um . . . a pregnancy test this morning and it's negative, but Mom said she has a friend that they never worked on, so I should probably get one of those done too."

"A pregnancy test?" Danny repeated, looking at her in a whole different way. "Is that the reason why you—"

"No, that's not the reason why I got married!" she blurted out before he could finish his sentence. "That wasn't even on the radar till a few days ago. I took six home tests, and they were all negative. I just think it wouldn't hurt to get a blood test for it, since you're going to be doing a workup anyway."

"Oh, Ani . . . " he sighed, and rumpled her hair again. "What am I going to do with you?"

"Give me a nice discount for the lab work?" she winked, and Danny shook his head hopelessly.

"What time do you want to come in tomorrow? I'd plan for an hour, to deal with parking."

"I work at noon, so how about ten-thirty?" she suggested.

"Sounds good. Maybe, if you're lucky, I'll buy you lunch."

"Oh, if *I'm* lucky, huh?" she joked as he opened the front door for her.

"Yeah. But seriously Ani, if your luck ever runs out and Finnish does something stupid like mess around behind your back, you let me know. I'll make sure he regrets it."

CHAPTER 17
TMI, Talvi

"Where the hell have you been? It doesn't take that long to get your hair done," James demanded when Annika walked into the kitchen back home. "Oh my god, we had so much fun shopping today! The girl at the checkout counter didn't know what hit her when Talvi accused her of being too rough with his caulk!"

With a glass of wine in one hand, he grabbed one of Annika's hands in his other as she balanced the box from Danny on her hip. Her eyes opened wide when they stepped into the living room, where music was blasting on the sound system.

Two shopping carts were parked off to the side. Inside of them were numerous bags of mulch and potting soil, along with some gardening tools. There were entire flats of flowers lying around the floor; petunias, impatiens, pansies and small daisies. There was plywood, sheetrock, two by fours, buckets of mudding and paint, bags of plaster, piles of cedar shingles and all other sorts of building materials strewn all over the floor.

There were all types of different power tools too. An electric table saw, a cordless drill, hammers, boxes of nails, a nail gun, tubes of caulk and a caulking gun, a tape measure, work gloves, protective goggles, and a tool belt all scattered about the room. Talvi and Chivanni were sitting in the middle of it all, laughing hysterically over the music. Annika set the box down slowly, and stepped over and around the mess until she was standing in front of them, where Talvi was flipping through the Japanese section of the user manual for the table saw while Chivanni sipped his wine and looked over his shoulder.

"I cannot believe how daft these instructions are. They make absolutely no sense, whether in English *or* Japanese," he said, still grinning as Chivanni hovered beside him, full size. "Why, the bastards even wrote it in haiku!"

"They did *not!*" James argued, but Talvi cleared his throat a little, and read this directly from the manual:

"Troubleshooting tips-
Make sure that 'power' is on,
And saw is plugged in!"

Chivanni did a back-flip in the air, as Talvi read out loud the exact same instructions again, this time in perfect Japanese, making Chivanni and James howl even louder.

"I don't know what is more disturbing, that there are bastards who can't be bothered to plug in an electric saw for it to work properly, or that there are manufacturers who are so inclined to provide instructions for these bastards!" Talvi said, reading more of the troubleshooting tips. His expression lit up once again. "Oh, Chivanni, you won't believe this one!" He hooted, hamming up his accent to sound more cockney. "I do believe I've got another 'aiku for you up me sleeve . . . wait for it!" He thought for a moment while a few sniggles continued to escape his lips, before he spoke again.

"This god-awful saw
Does not work under water
Well fuck me—I'm hosed!"

Chivanni laughed so hard that he ceased hovering in the air, and instead fell with a soft 'plop' onto the bags of potting soil below.

"It seems like you guys have done some serious male bonding today," Annika said, shifting her glance from her roommates' rosy cheeks to the numerous empty wine bottles on the kitchen counter. James and Chivanni were still laughing, though Talvi managed to look up before he responded with:

"A lovely vixen
Hath come into my vision
Oh, my heart be still!"

He stood up and took her arm, slowly spinning her around in a circle before planting a kiss on her cheek with his wine stained lips.

"I'm so glad you didn't cut off too much," he said in relief. "I think you'll look like a wood nymph even when you're your mother's age." Her stomach lurched a little as she realized he had said nearly the same exact thing as Danny had earlier.

"What's wrong, love?" he asked. "You're probably just hungry, aren't you? I noticed that you didn't have much to eat at breakfast. Well, Chivanni has been cooking a lovely meal for all of us. Charlie and Patti are due back from the art museum any time now, and then we're all going to have an early dinner before she goes to work," he said cheerfully. "Aren't you excited to see her again? I can hardly wait."

"Huh? Oh, yeah, I'm just hungry," she said offhandedly, still recovering from the uncanny remark. She took a confused look around the room. "Um, guys, I have an idea of how you got this stuff here, but how the hell did you *pay* for all of this?"

"Oh, I know we got a little carried away," Talvi said, waving a tipsy hand in dismissal. "James said he would put it on plastic, whatever *that* entails, and I'll pay him back my share after we straighten my finances."

"Talvi, you can't blow all of your money like this!" she cried. She didn't know much about power tools, but she knew that they were not cheap. "You still have to pay back my dad for the bail money and the plane tickets, and there's all those fines that will be coming in the mail, not to mention the fact that you said you'd buy Patti a friggin' *car*, and now you've gone and bought all this stuff? How much did it cost?"

"It couldn't have been *that* much," Chivanni said innocently. "James only used two little pieces of plastic to pay for it."

"Yes, they were quite small, weren't they?" Talvi agreed with a laugh.

"James!" she shouted towards the kitchen, where he was gathering the dishes Chivanni had prepared. "Please don't tell me that you maxed out your credit cards to pay for this!"

"Of course not! How irresponsible do you think I am?" James said in all seriousness as he returned with silverware and set the table. He seemed very annoyed that she of all people could have thought so little of his financial management. "I still have sixty eight dollars on one of them."

"*Sixty eight dollars?*" she screeched before turning back to her husband. "Talvi, I thought you were just going to buy some *shingles*! You're not going to have any money left in a week at this rate! What's all this other shit for, anyway? Since when do you need pansies to patch the roof? That's not going to stop the leaks in this room. Or are you just going to plant flowers under them to soak up all the water?"

161

"Oh I like that idea," Chivanni said, and with the flick of a wrist, he levitated one of the flats from the shopping cart to a soggy spot on the rug.

Annika was beyond exasperated. She didn't understand how her husband could throw his money around like it was nothing. Sure, she had a few expensive toys of her own, but at least they were paid for. She was supposed to be getting out of debt, not getting further into it. And even though she and Talvi wore matching wedding bands, Danny was right when he pointed out that they were never legally married in America. Maybe she wasn't under any financial obligation to his outrageous spending habits.

"Annika, why are you so upset?" Talvi asked her with a confused frown. "James has a lot of things that need repair around the house. I thought it would make you happy, to have me help restore this lovely place."

The first few notes of "Let's Dance" by David Bowie played overhead, and since Annika was at a loss for words, Talvi seized the opportunity to drape her arms around his neck and lead her into a loopy waltz around the room.

"Put on your red-feathered shoes and dance the blues," he crooned to her, looking smug as he customized the lyrics.

"Talvi, you can't waltz to this," she protested as he guided her haphazardly one way and then the other, narrowly missing the petunia flats and buckets of mudding that lay precariously on the floor. "It's in 4/4 time, and a waltz is in 3/4."

"You're absolutely right about that, my little dove." He immediately switched to a tango as his left leg pushed between hers, guiding her backwards. She was afraid of him stepping on her feet or tripping over a bag of plaster in his inebriated state, but he miraculously managed not to. One hand pressed into the small of her back, coaxing her hips against his while the other hand caressed the length of her arm, sliding along her ribcage. With both hands, he dipped her low to the ground, letting her hair brush against the rug as he rocked her gently from one side to another.

"Let's sway . . . " he sang softly while he pulled her back up and turned her until her spine was against his chest, and rested his cheek against hers. " . . . sway through the crowd to an empty space . . . *like your room,*" he sighed wantonly into her ear in his velvety smooth voice before nipping at her ear lobe. He continued to swing her around the room wildly, careful not to let her go flying too far.

"And if you should fall, into my arms . . . " Right on cue he let go of her. Just when she thought she would hit the floor, he caught her, grinning with from ear to softly pointed ear. Her heart was pounding so hard that she was trembling. That sexy tango might have been more enjoyable if she wasn't worried about breaking her neck. She was so distracted she didn't notice Patti trot into the room as the song ended.

"Hey guys, how's it—" Her toe caught on the corner of a piece of lumber and she was about to face plant into a cultivator, lying on the floor with the pointed ends up.

"*No! Patti!*" yelled Chivanni, and instead of getting three new holes in her head, Patti remained safe in the air, hovering above the menacing garden tool.

"What the heck . . . " she stammered in disbelief from where she was floating, as the faerie and the elf rushed over to her. Chivanni made a motion with his hand, pulling the cultivator away, while Talvi lifted Patti out of the air.

"What the heck was that?" she asked him, before turning to look at Annika and Chivanni.

"That was your introduction to faerie magic, Patti Cake," Talvi said, setting her gently on the ground. "I didn't think it would be so dramatic, but then, seeing it for the first time is rather dramatic for most humans. That's why fairies are forbidden from practicing it in front of them."

"You mean, *you* made me float in the air?" Patti asked Chivanni. "I thought your wings were fake, but they look so real." Chivanni glanced at Talvi, and then turned to Patti, taking a step closer to her.

"They're real because I'm a real faerie," he explained, letting his wings flutter until his narrow feet had left the ground. "I can't hide what I really am." Patti yelped at the sight of him rising closer to the ceiling.

"Oh my god! You're *really* a *faerie!*"

"I *know*! That's what I've been trying to tell you!" he said a little impatiently, and fluttered down to the ground as gracefully as a feather. "Talvi said I'm not to do any of my magic outside of the house, or in front of anyone besides him and Annika, but I couldn't bear to watch you get hurt. Neither could he. He's really an elf, you know. You ought to let him mend the burn on your hand. He can heal you with his touch."

"Does James know? Does Charlie know?" Patti asked, still wide-eyed at what she'd seen. She glanced at Talvi, who only seemed irritated with his friend for blurting out the truth about them.

"Pish posh, of course they know," Chivanni said, waving his hand toward the pile of materials on the floor, until they parted to make a wide, unobstructed path to the kitchen. Patti looked on, dumbfounded, as he took her by the hand

and led her out of the room, followed by Talvi and Annika. "It's better that you understand these things sooner than later. I have a feeling that we'll be seeing more of you around here."

The four of them joined James and Charlie at the kitchen table, where the last of the silverware was being laid out beside the plates, complete with cloth napkins and wine. Talvi made it a point to sit beside Patti, and he watched her try to cut her food left-handed for all of one minute before turning in his chair to face her.

"Let's get this parlor trick out of the way, shall we?" he asked, and offered his left hand to her. "I, too, have the feeling that we'll be seeing more of you around here, so I may as well follow Chivanni's lead and come out of the closet myself."

"Huh?" Patti asked, scrunching her face in confusion.

"Just give him your hand," Annika instructed. Patti was hesitant until she glanced around the table and saw the hopeful expressions on everyone's faces. She held out her right hand, and Talvi painstakingly began to unwind the white gauze. A bright red blistering patch was revealed on her lower palm, and Annika winced at the sight.

"Patti, did you go to the doctor for that?" asked Charlie with concern. "That looks a lot worse than I thought it would be."

"No," she replied, letting Talvi cradle her hand between both of his. "I couldn't afford the bill." She looked on with the others as Talvi closed his eyes in concentration for a few long moments. Finally he opened them, and beckoned her to look. She glanced down at her palm, frowned, and held it closer to her eyes, tilting it this way and that.

"I can't believe this," she said, looking mystified as she showed her hand to her friends. "You really made my burn disappear!"

"What can I say, Patti Cake? I'm good with my hands," Talvi replied and sat back as he swirled his wine in his glass. "But you must keep this secret to yourself. The same goes for Chivanni. I would hate to have to erase your memory of this if you become too chatty. It's not as tidy as one might think." He looked pleased with himself, to say the least, when Patti nodded vigorously. Annika was dying to ask him what he knew about altering people's memories, but she felt that Patti had been exposed to enough non-human events for one evening.

"How was your visit to the museum?" she asked Patti instead, helping herself to the dish of sweet potato enchiladas.

"Oh, it was fun," Patti replied, eyeing Chivanni and Talvi strangely as she spooned some sour cream onto her plate with her healed right hand. "There was an exhibit about virginity that was pretty interesting. I had no idea that there are women who have themselves surgically altered up in there so they can become 're-virginized' later on."

"Sounds like a blast," said James, sticking out his tongue in disgust as he cut his dinner into pieces. "Don't most people try to make it a point to get 'de-virginized'? I know I did."

"There was a handmade book that catalogued that, too," Charlie said with his mouth full. "Most of the stories were pretty boring. Some were really sad. Some were totally weird."

"What's weird to you?" James asked.

"I guess it depends who you're asking," Charlie shrugged, still chewing. "Some people might think my story is weird, but some might not."

"Why don't you tell me, and I'll be the judge," James said, and reached for his glass of Shiraz.

"It was with a neighbor of ours, back when we still lived in Germany," he said after he swallowed the mouthful of enchiladas, avoiding his sister's eyes. "She always asked me to come over and help her with odd jobs around the house. I was totally clueless."

"Who was it?" Annika asked. "I knew all our neighbors in Germany."

"Frau Schmidt, down the street."

"But you mowed her lawn!" his sister cried in shock.

"Tell me about it," Charlie said, and shoved another huge forkful of enchiladas in his mouth so he wouldn't have to elaborate.

"I guess her husband wasn't cutting it, was he?" James asked, lifting his fork to his lips.

"I guess not," said Annika, still surprised at her brother's confession. "My first time was with my high school boyfriend," she said and took a drink of wine. "I would stop by the practice rooms after his symphony rehearsals."

"You said you were taking lessons!" Charlie accused, covering his mouth so the food in it wouldn't go flying out. "Mom and dad were even going to buy you a violin!"

"You seem to have a recurring fascination for men with bows," Talvi teased.

"I guess I do, huh?" she said and smiled at him before turning to James. "What about you? I can't believe I don't know your story by now."

"My first was the cutest barista at a coffee shop in Brooklyn. I found out his schedule and used to walk fifteen minutes out of my way, just so he could make me a friggin' cup of coffee. I think it was a month before I finally asked for his number."

"Did he steam your latte?" Patti asked with a snort.

"Oh, he did a lot more than that," James chuckled. "I wish I'd met him sooner."

"Oh really?" Patti asked. "I ended up waiting until my third year of college. For one of my art history classes, we spent an afternoon at the art museum and we got to see all the cool stuff they keep in the basement when it's not being displayed. Our docent was a total hunk, and we kept checking each other out. When it was time to leave, I told him that I thought I left my notebook in the basement, and . . . well, you know that ancient Roman sarcophagus we saw today?"

"You did it on that?" hooted Charlie. "No wonder you like the museum so much." Patti stuck out her tongue at him.

"Trust me, it sounds way more awesome than it really was," she assured everyone. "Marble is really cold, and not comfortable at all. What about you, Chivanni? Any faerie tales worth cataloguing for art's sake?"

"I don't kiss and tell," he said, brushing his long bangs to the side of his face. An impish look had entered his cinnamon-brown eyes. "But Talvi's story is definitely worth cataloguing."

"Chivanni, you know this isn't in my repertoire of the tales I tell," he replied, casting an annoyed look toward his friend. "I'll opt out of this, if I may."

"If it was a bad experience, you don't have to share it," said Patti.

"It wasn't bad at all," he said, shifting awkwardly in his chair. "But it isn't very . . . it's not exceptionally . . . it's just not prudent." He took a bite of his food so he wouldn't have to explain himself.

"*You're* worried about being prudent?" Chivanni squeaked.

"There's nothing about this conversation that *is* prudent," James pointed out.

"Are you afraid that I'll get upset?" Annika asked, eager to learn more about her new husband. "Because I won't. I really don't mind hearing your story, if you don't mind sharing it."

"Honestly, it was so long ago, I barely remember anything about my first experience," Talvi said, playing with his hair slightly.

"Spare us your lies," Chivanni said with a naughty grin. If Talvi hadn't wanted the attention, he certainly had it now. He couldn't ignore the expectant

166

faces all looking at him. He set down his fork, swirled the wine in his glass, and looked carefully at his fingernails, smiling sheepishly to himself.

"It was the Samodivi of the East," he finally admitted with a sigh.

"Sam *who?*" James gasped. "Is that why you didn't want Annika to hear this?" Talvi snickered a little and shook his head, still looking at his nails.

"Not Sam. *Samodivi*. Wood nymphs," Chivanni explained for everyone's benefit.

"Nymphs? Like, *plural?*" Charlie asked, still looking quite surprised. Talvi nodded and lifted his head.

"Seven of them, to be precise."

"Shut up!" Charlie exclaimed in disbelief.

"You're so full of crap," Patti accused, rolling her eyes.

"Seven? But how?" Annika wondered aloud, her curiosity peaked. Talvi took a drink of his wine and continued to swirl the glass ever so slowly in his hand.

"I'd been riding east for a week, running an errand for my brother. I was supposed to be returning some books for him, or so he claimed. Anyhow, I stopped to take a nap under a sycamore tree and when I woke up, my arms and legs were bound tight."

"They tied you up?" James asked. There was a twinge of envy in his voice.

"Yes, and then they spirited me away to their little cottage in the woods." He stopped abruptly and covered his face with his hand. "Oh, this is so ridiculous. In all my years, I've only told this story to a small handful of trusted souls." He removed his hand to reveal a brightly blushing countenance, and took another long drink from the glass in his other hand, finishing it.

"Keep going. This is some good stuff. You know, for art's sake," Patti urged him, and her brown eyes watched him with fascination. Talvi took a deep breath as James filled his wine glass again.

"Well, they kept me tied up in their cellar, and they said the only way they would set me free is if I could learn to please every single one of them. And there being seven of the lasses, and myself being an inexperienced lad, that's a daunting task, believe me."

"Are you kidding?" Charlie said in awe. "That's like every man's dream!"

"Not every man's," James corrected him, but he was clearly as mesmerized as everyone else as he leaned a little closer to the storyteller.

"It wasn't a dream, it was damn near impossible," Talvi said, and a more relaxed grin spread across his face as he settled back comfortably in his chair. "The cellar was so bloody dark that I could scarcely see what I was doing. And their little game was quite misleading. They kept me tied up, so I had nothing to please them with but my mouth. When I succeeded at that, I was rewarded with a little food and brandy, but they refused to let me go. They had tricked me into staying. They only freed my right hand; my weaker hand, and forced me to learn that way as well. Again, I only received nourishment after I had completed that second task, and yet they refused to give me my freedom. After that, I was allowed the use of both of my hands, but my legs were still bound. It wasn't until the last samodiva gave her approval that they agreed to completely untie me. They gathered in the cellar and told me to choose which one of them I had enjoyed the most." Annika's eyes were nearly falling out of her head in anticipation, along with everyone else's.

"So out of seven wild wood nymphs, which one did you choose?" James hissed. "The prettiest, I suppose? Or the feistiest? Jeez, how did you decide?"

"Well, they were all quite lovely in their own ways. It was impossible for me to favor one over another, so after being surrounded by those charms for over a week whilst tied up in that dark cellar, what do you think I did?" he asked his audience with a shrug of sincere nonchalance. "I chose all seven."

There was such a thick haze of silence around the table; it could only have been cut with the newly purchased electric saw. It clung like an erotic fog, entrapping all the listeners in the incredible, fantastic tale. Annika played the vivid story over in her mind, imagining him being devoured by seven wild wood nymphs, seeing him taste and touch and experience all of them at once, and was surprised that her heart was pumping just a little harder than before. She glanced over at Patti, who had covered her mouth with her hands. Even James had taken off his glasses and lit a cigarette.

There was a loud chime and everyone was jolted back to reality as Patti dug into her back pocket to retrieve her cell phone.

"Oh crap," she groaned, reading a text message before she snapped the phone shut and rushed to the door. "I'm late for work! Dinner was delicious, Chivanni. Thanks again!" She threw on her heavy cardigan and within a matter of seconds, she and Charlie were racing out the door.

Chivanni turned his mischievous little smile over to Annika.

"If it was so delicious, why did you only eat three bites?"

"Oh, I ate something before I came home," she said. "I'm sorry Chivanni; I'll just save it for later. It's really good though."

"I could have sworn you told me you were rather hungry when you came home today," Talvi said, eyeing her curiously.

"I guess I wasn't thinking straight. It was a little chaotic when I came home today. I had some Chinese earlier and I'm still pretty full," Annika said.

"I thought you were out clucking with hens, not going for Chinese without me," he pouted. "I've been craving ma po tofu for the longest time."

Annika glanced into the living room at the box with the rainbow skirt sitting on top.

"Since I was in the neighborhood, I stopped by Danny's to pick up the rest of my things," she said, and smiled at Talvi as she pushed back her chair and stood up. He looked at the box and then back at her skeptically.

"So you mean to tell me that it took you all day to collect that parcel from him? Because James told me that it typically only takes you an hour and a half to get your hair done."

"Leave me the hell out of this," James sang, and stubbed out his after-dinner cigarette.

"He doesn't live far from Mom's place, and since I was in the neighborhood, I decided to stop by and pick up a few things and we figured out when I could get that blood work done," she said casually, and began to gather the dinner plates from around the table and help Chivanni put away the leftovers. She wasn't exactly thrilled to learn that her husband had coerced James to go so far into debt, and she was expecting his story at dinner to be cute or awkward like the rest of them. She wasn't expecting to hear a mind-blowing account of a week-long orgy with seven beautiful, feisty wood nymphs. Annika wasn't feeling too guilty about her visit with Danny.

"I fail to understand how 'stopping by' your former lover's home becomes an all-day rendezvous," Talvi said coolly, folding his arms across his chest.

"I have no doubt you do."

His eyes narrowed, but the spat with his wife was put on pause as Charlie came in and plopped down into the chair next to him.

"Patti thinks she's going to get fired," he announced. "This is the third time in a month that she's been over a half hour late."

"They can't fire Patti; she's awesome!" Annika said as she filled the sink with warm water. "Why do you think the managers call her 'Party Patti'? She's the only server I know who can run a twenty-top and not make one mistake, and she turns and burns them like a wildfire. I always hated large parties."

"Yeah, but the day she burned her hand, they were really counting on her," Charlie said, turning around in his chair to face her. "They had three large reservations they were expecting on her to take care of single handedly, but they didn't mean it literally."

"That was an accident," Annika said, adding dish soap to the water. "Those kinds of things happen."

"Yeah, but she got written up for being behind the line. You know the servers aren't allowed back there with the cooks."

"She got written up for that?" Annika said angrily as she made her way back to the table. "She got hurt on the job and then got written up for it?"

"Yep. She's been written up twice now. It's some new manager. I think he's worried about workman's comp or something."

"What was the other write-up for?"

"Her second warning for being half an hour late."

"Jeez. If she gets written up tonight, that's probably it," Annika sighed irritably.

"I guess we'll see," Charlie said, trying to be optimistic, but his typical grin was missing.

CHAPTER 18
Sariel's Baggage

The firelight flickered on Sariel's face as she stared into the flames in disbelief. She knew it was futile to try and search for a teenage girl dressed in white during a blizzard when there were no tracks to follow her by. Being a druid, Denalia must have shape-shifted into an eagle or an owl and taken flight, but Sariel was astounded that the girl had outsmarted her and her traveling companions. Or perhaps she wasn't very smart at all, to be flying around during a blizzard, when she had been blindfolded and had no sense of where she was. Her odds were slim to none, and it had been decided that there was no way she would be alive within a few short hours.

The samodiva, the paladin and the vampire had kept on their original course towards the dense forest, and just as they had hoped, it offered a wonderful shelter from the storm. They had gathered enough firewood on their way into the woods to get an impressive fire burning, but for heat that would last through the night, they needed some fair-sized logs. Pavlo had gone in search of just that, along with some warm-blooded dinner of his own. His strength had come back slowly, one woodland creature at a time, but it was nothing like it had once been.

She had bundled up in furs and wools while Justinian set about making dinner. Even though it was just another serving of vegetable stew with a piece of bread and some dried fruit, Sariel's mouth watered as if it were a grand Yule feast.

"Justinian . . . " she began, not sure how to say what she needed to say. She had only had this conversation four other times in her life, and it had been centuries since then.

"Sariel . . . " he mimicked as he knelt down to add a little more snow to the stew, gave the vegetables a stir with his huge muscled arm, and then covered them to simmer. When she didn't respond, he looked up at her. "What is it, Sariel?"

"You do know the legend of the samodivi, don't you?" Sariel asked, and immediately started criticizing herself. That's not what she meant to say.

"Of course I do," he said, wondering why she looked so serious. "One would have to live in a cave not to have heard that legend."

"It is said that a man must steal a samodiva's clothes in order for her to marry him, however, that is not completely accurate. It is a more polite way of saying—"

"I know what it means," Justinian interrupted, grinning a little as he picked ice out of his long black braid. "I may be human, and not nearly the age that you are, but I am well aware of how the world works."

"Then you know what happens sometimes when clothes go missing," she stated.

"Sariel," Justinian said, kneeling beside her, "I have been traveling with you for four months now, and you have never been this indirect. What is it that you're trying to say?"

"I thought perhaps I was only fatigued by traveling so far in such deep snow, but after today I'm sure of it." She paused and took a deep breath. "I'm carrying your child."

Justinian was silent for a moment, but his eyes were still smiling. Sariel kept waiting for him to frown, but he didn't. She kept waiting for him to object, but he wouldn't.

"That does make things easier, in a way . . . " was what he said.

"What?" Sariel asked, looking confused. "I've already raised three daughters on my own. How does this make anything easier?"

"I have been trying to 'steal your clothes', so to speak, since we began this mission. Being that it's winter, I have been required by practicality to let you keep them," he admitted, gazing fondly at her. "I planned to ask you when the weather was warmer, but if I've already given you a child, it makes it easier for me to ask you to be my wife."

"Your wife?" repeated Sariel. Justinian snickered a little.

"I'm already on my knees," he said, smiling again as he reached into her blankets and took her hand. "If you are willing to remain human to have a family with me, I am willing to risk that you might one day change your mind and cross over to become a samodiva again."

"I won't change my mind," Sariel said in all seriousness.

"I'm not questioning your honor, my dear." Justinian said patiently. "I know you left your human life behind when your first husband left this world. You brought your daughters home to the safest place you knew of, and you raised them well. I am simply saying that I am aware of your ancient history, and I would like to spend the rest of my life adding to it."

Sariel was quiet for a few moments. In all her years, there were only ever two men that had ever intrigued her enough to win her respect and her heart. One was returned to the gods nearly a millennia ago. One sat before her now. Was it finally time to lay down her sword of vengeance and hold something even more precious in her arms? The men who had murdered her husband had been the reason she had lost her fourth child, an unborn son. They had died a merciless death under her vengeful actions, but their lives hadn't quelled Sariel's anger. She used to daydream what kind of man her son would have grown up to become, had he survived. She even had a name for him, an ancient name as old as the gods, a name that had never been spoken aloud. She used to imagine that one day his spirit would try being born again, but there was never a man virtuous enough in Sariel's eyes to help her try.

Until now.

"If you want more time to consider, I understand," Justinian said, bringing Sariel back to the present moment.

"No, time is one thing that I have had perhaps too much of," she said. "I think I deserve to enjoy and savor the rest of my life, and I think I would like to do that with you and our son."

"What makes you so certain it's a son that's on the way?" Justinian grinned, barely able to contain himself at Sariel's response.

"I can't explain why; I can only feel it," she said, smiling back. "But if we want to know for certain, there are some old friends of mine that I could ask. How convenient that they happen to live on the way to my home."

"I cannot think of any other place I would rather travel to." Justinian said, and dished up dinner for himself and his soon to be wife.

CHAPTER 19
Sugar and Soot

On Monday, Annika stopped by the hospital before work, and had Danny draw her blood for testing. Rather than spend a cold and wet day at the farm with Charlie, Talvi opted to stay home with Chivanni and get started with his massive honey-do list. The first thing on his list was fixing the roof, but until the rain stopped, he busied himself with patching cracks and holes in the plaster walls. Tuesday was a repeat, except with an even bigger mess left, if that was possible. All the old, loose plaster had to be dug out of the weak spots, which ended up leaving piles of fine dust on the floor of every room in the house.

Annika thought it best to wait until her day off on Wednesday to tackle the matter of converting Talvi's money into American dollars and getting him legally licensed to drive. When Wednesday morning came around, he wouldn't even let Annika take a shower. He had literally pulled her out of bed, helped her dress, and dragged her downstairs just long enough for him to brew some tea before they left. Now they found themselves in her black coupe, battling morning rush hour traffic.

"Badra's beard, does it ever stop raining in this city?" he asked, looking out the window with a sneer. "It makes London seem dry as a bone."

"The Pacific northwest is a temperate rainforest," she pointed out. "It rains a lot. That's why it's so pretty and green here."

"Is it like this all year?"

"No. Summer is absolutely perfect, but you have to pay for it. The rain starts around autumn, and usually goes till June. Sometimes it rains for a month straight. Sometimes longer."

"Bollocks to that. I prefer a Mediterranean climate, myself. Say, why don't we go to southern Italy, at least until summer begins here?" She turned to look at him, and he raised a hopeful brow. "Just say the word, and I'll make it happen."

"Um, I have a new job, and I'm in the middle of recording an album, sweetie," Annika reminded him. When she glanced out the windshield she slammed on the breaks so she didn't hit the car in front of her. Those thoughts of southern Italy were pretty distracting. She'd never been there, but she always wanted to go.

"Why don't you let me drive, since your attention seems to be elsewhere?" he suggested.

"No. You can drive later," said Annika. Talvi waited all of one minute before asking her,

"How about now?"

"No."

"But it's later," he pointed out with a wink, and took a sip of tea from the travel mug he'd brought along.

"Talvi . . . " She was beginning to get annoyed with his persistence. "You're going to drive me insane before we get to the bank. I promise I'll teach you afterwards, *if* you stop nagging me about it."

"I'm sorry," he said, trying not to laugh at the pouty face she was making. "It's just that I've always wanted to drive a car like yours, and now that I have the perfect opportunity, you're making me wait. I hate waiting."

"We all do. Join the club."

"What club?" he asked, which made Annika shake her head and smile.

"You know, for as bad as you want to drive, I'm really surprised that you never learned how. It's not like you didn't have the time."

"True, however there are an abundance of trains and taxis and busses that take you wherever you might like to go. I personally prefer a motorcycle to get around, but whenever we did get a car, Finn always insisted on driving it. After a wild bash about town, it's much easier to let someone sober find your hotel than it is to try and navigate cobblestone streets on a Ducati whilst inebriated. I'm afraid I've ruined a few too many bikes that way. A private car with a driver is considerably less expensive."

"You make a very good point," she smiled, grateful that her husband's days of drunk driving were behind him. "Let's get this over with so that I can make you wait a little less longer to get your license, okay?" she said, and pulled into the parking lot of the main branch of her bank. She slung her purse over her shoulder and carried the burlap sack of gold coins to the front door, which he opened for her.

"Are those real?" he asked, looking around at the fake plastic trees in the lobby decor.

"Why don't you go find out for yourself while I deal with this?" she said, and he walked off to one side.

"Hi there, we need to exchange this and make a deposit." Annika said to the next available teller, setting the sack down with a soft clinking sound on the counter. An uppity looking brunette wearing a tight bun gave her a skeptical glance.

"Are those coins? Take them to the supermarket across the street. They have machines specifically for that." She pointed towards the door.

"They're not coins. It's gold. And they're rings, not coins."

"You know, if you're looking to pawn things off, you're welcome to use our phonebook over there by the courtesy phone. I don't go to those places myself, otherwise I would tell you *exactly* where to go," she said flippantly. Annika was flabbergasted.

"You know, I have an account here and no one's ever been so rude to me when I've brought you money before," she replied, putting her hand on her hip. The woman narrowed her eyes a little and crossed her arms.

"Well I don't mean to be rude, but it would take forever to sort those coins, and the machine across the street will do it in less time. You can bring the cash here and save everyone a lot of trouble."

"Yeah, I get that, but like I said, these aren't coins. It's gold, see?" Annika said, and opened the bag. The brunette stood up and peered into the bag at the myriad of key rings filled with gold rings of all different sizes.

"What is this, some kind of April Fool's Day joke?" she said as she picked up one of the key rings.

"It won't be April for another week," a male voice said in an English accent. Talvi had finished his inspection of their fake plastic trees and wandered back to Annika's side. The brunette's face melted from a snooty expression to a much more pliant one as she looked into his eyes.

"Wow, are you wearing contacts?" The woman asked. "I've never seen ones like those before." Talvi frowned in confusion, glancing at his clothes and then back at the woman.

"Contacts? What are those?"

"They're like glasses," the woman explained. "But you wear them in your eyes."

"I've never heard of such a preposterous thing," he replied, and leaned seductively over the counter, gazing into the woman's eyes until a flush spread across her face.

"Sandy, isn't that your name?" he asked, and she nodded her head in sublimation. She reached her hand upwards to touch her shirt, brushing her breast as she searched for a nametag that wasn't there. "Sandy, you're such an intelligent and lovely creature. Why are you in a place like this when you could be at home in bed? I know you have a man waiting for you. Why don't you leave early and surprise him?" he asked in that velvety smooth voice of his.

"I . . . I . . . don't . . . I don't know . . . " Sandy said, and shuddered.

"Take my advice. I wonder what your hair looks like when it's come undone and falling down your bare shoulders?" he said, completely turning up the charm. Sandy seemed to be desperately searching for a pen, or a pencil, or a paperclip. Who knew what she was looking for, but she definitely couldn't look away from Talvi's hypnotic blue and green contact-free eyes.

"Hey Sandy, are you coming to take your lunch break?" two women called, walking towards the door. When Talvi turned around to look at them, they smiled very wide grins as they walked along.

"Oh, you look busy. We'll just grab you a salad," one of them said, and the other woman kept walking right into the closed glass door, impacting it with a loud thud. Thoroughly embarrassed, they bustled outside as fast as possible while Annika watched in amusement.

"I'm going to go find the president of the bank to come help you. Don't go anywhere," Sandy said, smoothing her skirt and sweater, and walked as quickly as possible to the rear of the lobby.

"I think that extra shake is for you, babe," Annika said with an amused grin of her own. "I don't know what the heck you did to her, but way to go."

"I just showed her a few things to try with her husband when she goes home tonight," he said with an air of satisfaction. "I've given her plenty to think about, so the next time you talk to her, she should be much more relaxed." Annika was never so grateful to have such a brazen flirt for a husband.

After a little while, Sandy returned with an older woman who took a peek into the burlap sack and asked them to join her in her office. It was some time later that Annika and Talvi signed their names on various papers adding him onto her checking and savings accounts. She felt her throat close up as each account was filled to the maximum limit they could insure it for. They put the rest of the gold in a safety deposit box and let the bank president escort them to the doors with their new keys. When they passed Sandy's desk, she even smiled at them.

"Thanks for stopping by today," she said, and twirled her long hair which she had pulled loose from the tight bun.

"Guess who got his driver's license today?" Annika called out to Chivanni as they walked in the kitchen and hung up their jackets. The smell of vanilla and cinnamon made her mouth water, but what really caught her by surprise was to see Patti standing with Chivanni at the stove in an old soccer jersey and sweat pants of Charlie's.

"Oh, hi!" she said, looking up from the stove to grin at her friends. The small bottle of vanilla floated through the air and put itself back in the cupboard to her left. "I'm guessing you guys went to the DMV?"

"Yeah, and the line wasn't bad at all," Annika replied. "Talvi passed the exam with a perfect score."

"I'm surprised he passed at all, since he's such an elderly driver," Patti said, winking at Chivanni before grinning at Talvi. "I heard how old you are."

Annika snorted while Talvi tried to scowl at Patti, but it rebelled into a smile as he traded his empty travel mug for a glass of orange juice.

"So I have to ask, when did you get here? I don't remember you coming in," Annika inquired, still eyeing Patti's clothes. She was dying to know what was going on between her friend and her brother.

"Well, I finally got fired for being late Sunday night," Patti said, trying to be a good sport. She transferred two pancakes from the pan onto a plate hovering in the air nearby, and poured batter for two more. "But of course, my managers let me get dressed up and come in last night anyway, those assholes. After that I went straight to the bar across the street and ordered two shots of Jaeger. The next thing I knew Charlie was driving me here. So here I am."

"What about school? Don't you have painting class today?"

Patti trembled, wiping a few tears from her face with her spatula-wielding forearm.

"What's the point of going? I still owe half my rent for March, and April is almost here. I lost a lot of money when I burned my hand. I'm counting on being evicted now that I can't pay for April, either. On top of that, I'm taking so many classes this semester, that I really can't work any sort of full time job and still have time to get my final projects done. I'll have to drop my classes just to pay my bills, and it's so late into the semester that I can't get a refund. I've wasted all that time in school for nothing!"

Patti started to cry and Annika rushed over to hug her, while Chivanni carefully took the spatula out of her hand and flipped the pancake.

"I'll just move in with my brother for a while, at least until I find another job. He's so tweaked out all the time, I'll bet he won't even notice," she said, wiping away her tears with the back of her hand. Annika was revolted by the very thought of Patti living with her brother.

"Won't notice?" she said irritably, letting go of her. "Of course he'll notice! The guy's a friggin' crack head! He'll pawn off everything you own in your sleep!"

"What's a friggin' crack head?" Chivanni asked naïvely. "Is his head really split open?"

"Pretty much," Annika replied, feeling an uneasy knot rising up in her stomach. There weren't too many people she downright loathed, but Patti's scumbag older brother was one of them. "The guy sells crack and meth out of his house. If Patti moved in with him, she could go to jail for a really long time if he was ever busted, which I'm kinda surprised he hasn't been yet. He's such a moron."

"How can they incarcerate *her*?" Talvi demanded. "She's not involved with his business!"

"They can say she was an accessory to a crime, which would still get her a few months or maybe even years in jail, depending on the prosecutor," Annika explained passionately. "And even if she managed to avoid much jail time, there would still be an insane amount of fines to pay. It would make ours look like pocket change."

"It's my fault that this even happened," Talvi said, looking irritated, but a plan was forming in his mind. "You wouldn't have lost your job if I hadn't wrecked your car. Why can't you simply stay here? The room between ours and James's is empty, and you certainly wouldn't have to worry about theft while you were here. You could focus better on your studies, and perhaps even set up a little painting area in the living room. That way you won't have to throw your classes."

This made Patti smile a little, which relieved her friends.

"You mean *drop* my classes," she corrected him. Talvi turned to Annika with the most irresistible expression, clasping her hands in his.

"Oh please love, please can we keep her?" he begged, as though Patti were a lost, helpless puppy. "I promise we'll take care of her! Chivanni can feed her, and Charlie can take her on walks to the park, and I can teach her all sorts of clever tricks. Why, look how well she makes pancakes? She seems quite eager to please."

Annika wasn't prepared for his idea at all. She knew Chivanni would of course feed her and Charlie would love to take her on walks to the park, but somewhere deep inside it bothered her to see how brightly Talvi's eyes had lit up at the idea that he could teach her tricks of any kind. Ignoring that nagging voice, she nodded in agreement of what a great idea it was.

"Do you want me to telephone James and ask if it's alright? I know he'll say yes!" Chivanni asked and fluttered his wings so much that his feet lifted off the floor momentarily. He seemed just as excited as Talvi was. "I'll clean up after her, too!" he said as he floated the milk and eggs back into the fridge, and gave her a soft kiss on the cheek.

"Where is James, anyway?" Annika asked. "He usually comes home for lunch."

"I think he stayed at work today, *thank god,*" said Patti, doing her best impression of him. "He was stressing out so much before he left this morning that I think he's better off at the gallery. It's not exactly tranquil here." She pointed to the living room, which was now a combination of a shopping cart corral, a small lumberyard, and a wood shop with a garden store on the side. Little piles of dirt and sawdust were strewn all over the floor. And where there were not little piles, there were bigger piles. "It's really sweet that you guys want me to stay, but I don't want to add to his stress level. James seemed pretty pissed off when he left this morning. Now's not the best time to ask."

"But that's what friends do, they look out for each other," Chivanni assured her. "I know you would do the same for us if Annika had one of those cracked-heads like your brother does."

Patti looked at him in bewilderment, though a smile tugged at the corner of her mouth.

"Don't look so gloomy, Patti Cake; it will be fun," Talvi said. "And now that

I've acquired a driving license, I can take you to school when Charlie isn't available, until we find another car for you."

"This is too much to ask," Patti excused.

"You won't be bored around here, that's for certain," said Talvi as he motioned towards the living room full of potential home improvements. "We'll see to it that you earn your keep. Those flats of flowers are just begging to be planted today. Perhaps you ladies could do that after some lunch? I see the sun has finally come out. I must say, that's quite a good omen."

"Well, if you guys honestly think James will say it's okay . . . " Patti said slowly. "I really don't want to live with my brother."

Annika went over to the stove and took over pancake duty.

"I'm sure James will agree," she said, trying her best to sound as excited as her husband and Chivanni.

"Then I'm gonna burn my apron in the fireplace! Woo hoo!" Patti started to run to the living room, to find it, but her foot caught on the corner of a bag of mulch, sending her to the floor with a thud. "I'm alright!" she called, and disappeared around the corner.

"Patti darling, why don't you have a bit of lunch before you begin setting things on fire?" Talvi called out to her while Chivanni happily sent four plates and four sets of silverware floating from the kitchen counter onto the table. They magically set themselves perfectly at each place, complete with napkins.

"So, what went on last night that she's dressed in my brother's clothes?" Annika asked Chivanni with a raised eyebrow. The faerie let out a gleeful laugh as he manually turned off the stove and joined her at the table.

"Nothing lewd and lascivious, that's for sure," he retorted, and pointed to a large, gaudy, gilded picture frame on the wall. "Patti read the news article to me."

Annika glanced to the spot designated for photos and other embarrassing memorabilia, known as the Wall of Shame. Among the many incriminating pictures and odd objects taped inside the frame was a photo of Charlie sleeping under a coffee table with his pants around his ankles and an empty bottle of gin beside him, and another one of James closely surrounded by topless female strippers. There were a few more photos of themselves and their friends in compromising situations, but there in the very center was the police report cut neatly out of the Sunday paper, embellished with puffy cupid stickers and little hearts drawn in red glitter glue. Seeing it for the first time, Talvi leaned down to read the article, smiling in self-satisfaction at his fine work.

Patti returned from the living room, setting her work apron beside her before sitting down to help devour the pancakes. The four of them passed the syrup around the table while Talvi came up with a strategy for the day.

"Now that the rain has stopped, my first assignment shall be mending the roof, and after that I need to replace the entire staircase to the basement. The wood is so rotted that I can't believe no one has fallen through it yet."

"Well, we never go down into the dungeon, except to do laundry," said Annika with her mouth full. "It's creepy down there."

"Indeed, it is," he replied, and waited until he was finished chewing to reply further. "Your mission is to put those flowers into the ground before they wilt," he said with the utmost seriousness. "Make certain you water them well when you're done, so they stay as lovely as they are now."

"I don't know the first thing about gardening," Annika fussed, but after breakfast she found herself shooed outside with Patti and Chivanni with an array of different gardening tools. In the meantime, Talvi had buckled on his tool belt and was set on the task of repairing the roof now that it was dry enough to safely walk on. Even with heightened healing powers, a broken neck wasn't likely to be mended by magic. The weather was unseasonably warm that day, and it threatened to get even warmer since there wasn't a cloud in the sky.

"So Patti, are you gonna spill the beans already?" Annika asked, as they searched for the perfect spot in the front yard for the flowers. "What's up with you and Charlie?"

"Oh, I guess it looks pretty suspicious with me wearing his clothes, doesn't it?" she said, blushing a little. "For your information, I slept on the couch. You both left for the bank so early this morning that you mustn't have seen me. And I didn't want to dig through your clothes without asking."

"I wouldn't have minded."

"Sometimes you mind," Patti said, speaking from experience. They found what must have been a flower bed at one time near the sidewalk, and each took a different gardening tool.

"Well, either way, Charlie really likes you."

"Yeah, I know he does," she replied casually as she pulled weeds, surprising her friends.

"You *know*?" Annika asked. "You've known all along?"

"Do you like him as well?" asked Chivanni. Patti smiled faintly.

"I like him as a friend, but not like a boyfriend."

"Why not?" Chivanni wanted to know. "He's so amicable."

"Just because."

"Come on, Patti Cake, tell me why," Annika pleaded.

"How cliché is it to like your best friend's brother?" Patti said, wrinkling her nose. "Who the heck would I talk to about my love life? I tell you everything, and if I was dating him, well, then I couldn't tell you anything at all."

"Yeah, I guess that would be kinda gross," Annika agreed, and started to dig a small hole with her spade.

"See what I mean?" Patti said smartly. "Then I'd have to go and find another best friend, and I'd rather not. You're the nicest person I know, Annika."

"I'll tell you who isn't nice," said Chivanni, casting a little spell over the small hand trowels to turn over the soil for him. "It's that faerie queen friend of yours. Is he always so overwrought and foul-tongued?"

"What? James isn't that bad!" Annika said, and then eyed him inquisitively. "Patti said she slept on the couch, but I never thought to ask where *you've* been sleeping since you didn't take the spare room." Chivanni pretended he didn't hear this question and busied himself with ordering the shovels around.

"Chivanni, don't tell me you and James . . . " Annika said with huge eyes. The red-haired faerie glared at her as though he were beyond insulted.

"I'll have you know that I sleep in the flower arrangement on the fireplace mantle! I don't go to bed with every pretty face the way Talvi—" Chivanni gasped and cupped a hand over his mouth in shock at what the words it had just spoken. "Oh, I'm so sorry! I didn't mean it like that, Annika! That was a terrible thing to say!" He looked like he was about to burst into tears.

"It's okay, Chivanni, I know you didn't mean it," she said after the initial impact of his statement wore off. She knew it was going to take a while to shake that old reputation. Was he really as bad as she was led to believe? Annika peered up at the roof of the house, where Talvi was preoccupied with prying the rotted shingles away. She knew that she had married the king of Casanovas, but he had assured her that he had retired from that lifestyle long before meeting her. She also didn't know anyone else who was capable of unearthing so much of the juicy backstory about his past, until Chivanni had moved in. Now curiosity was getting the best of her.

"How many girls have there been, anyway?" she found herself asking.

"I certainly never kept track of them in all the years I've known him," said Chivanni, relieved to see that his friend wasn't upset at his deficit of tact. Annika pursed her lips a little. Maybe she could guilt-trip Chivanni into telling her.

"But you must have some vague idea," she pursued. "You can't say something like what you just said, and then leave me hanging like that. Can't you even take a guess?"

"Oh, if I honestly had to wager . . . " he squinted a little in thought, counting in his head and on his fingers simultaneously. "It hast to be at least five, no, probably closer to six—"

"But that doesn't make sense; there were seven wood nymphs," Annika interrupted.

"Hundred," Chivanni announced. "Yes, probably around six hundred, give or take a few dozen." Patti stifled a gasp, but said nothing.

"Give or take a few *dozen?*" Annika repeated, unable to make the number register in her head. "Jeez, they're not donuts!"

"You forget that sometimes there were two or more at a time, which does tend to add up rather quickly," Chivanni reminded her, as if it may be of some remote comfort to know. "Also, I've only known him for about sixty years, so I can't attest to what went on before we met."

While Annika was uncomfortably silent, Chivanni just continued with the tactless truth.

"He loves beautiful things, just as you do. Think of it like this: when James and I helped you organize your room, I could not believe how many pairs of shoes you had! I thought it was ridiculous, but James explained why. They're all so pretty and yet so different, and you have a pair for every occasion, for whatever mood you're in. I've seen you wear three different pairs in one day. That's how Talvi used to feel about girls."

"But shoes go on *feet!*" she insisted, unable to grasp such a vast number. "*Shoes* go on *feet!* There's no emotional attachment there!"

"I do beg your pardon, but I heard you were quite upset that Talvi made fun of those red-feathered shoes of yours. So who is to say what is worthy of emotional attachment?" he asked innocently. "He's three hundred years old, Annika. How many pairs of shoes might you have slipped your feet into after three hundred years?"

"I'm not choosing sides, but even *I* might have a couple hundred pairs if I were that old, and I'm not into shoes the way you are, Ani," Patti piped up softly, trying to ease the blow. Annika still said nothing. She was still trying to wrap her head around Chivanni's original estimate. She supposed that considering how many days there were in a year, a hundred year long case of satyriasis could indeed add up fast. But the number was still staggering.

"Talvi had quite an introduction to the sensual arts, being kidnapped by the Samodivi of the East, but he didn't intend for it to happen that way," Chivanni explained, thinking it was helpful. "His brother told him all about them, how they look for handsome fellows to kidnap, but Talvi didn't believe him one bit. So Finn thought he would be clever, and prove he was right. He asked Talvi to run an important errand for him, returning a few borrowed books to some friends of his. In exchange he'd give him a very rare bottle of faerie brandy. What he didn't tell Talvi was that these books weren't borrowed at all, but some rather old ones that he didn't want anymore! He gave him a map to the sycamore tree and told him to wait there for a day. You know what happened next."

"Oh my god!" Annika gasped. "That's a horrible story! I can't believe Finn would do that! Talvi must have been pissed off at him for years when he realized his brother had lied to him."

"He came home three weeks later and had only one thing to say to Finn."

"What did he say?"

"According to Finn, all Talvi said was, 'You owe me a very particular bottle of brandy.'"

"*That's* it? *That's* the story?"

"Well, I think the moral of the story is to listen to your older, wiser brother," Chivanni clarified.

"Wow, you actually think there's a *moral* to that story?" Patti snorted, and reached over to get another clump of flowers so Annika wouldn't see the tears of silent laughter in her eyes. She wouldn't have seen them anyway; her head was spinning too much.

"So it's his brother's fault that he was ever like that?" she gasped. "I thought Finn was such a gentleman!"

"He is, most of the time, but you can't blame him for his brother's behavior," Chivanni reminded her. "We are all free to make our own choices in life. Finn didn't instruct his brother to be led by his loins around the surrounding countryside, seducing ladies in every village along the way. Finn didn't bring female guests home so frequently that his father encouraged him to pursue his sense of adventure elsewhere . . . That's the main reason why Talvi's family never minded that he was always off traveling for most of the year. He returns every winter, and typically stays until the crops are planted in spring. At one point, his mother and older sister wanted him to leave home for good, but it was because of Finn that he was allowed to stay, as long as he moved his bed chambers to the wing farthest from the rest of his family for the sake of discretion. They did not care for the example that he was setting for his young niece and nephew. Stella picks up all sorts of bad habits from him."

"I thought his bedroom was so far away from everyone else's because he was a light sleeper," said Annika, feeling stupid on top of everything else she was feeling. Her spirits started to sink even further as she remembered the hefty hike from the front entry of his house to his bedroom door. Chivanni only shook his head, indicating Annika had been misled all along.

"Trust me, he has no trouble sleeping. But Annika, this was all ages ago. He truly has changed quite a bit in the time I've known him. You forget that he was born with that prophecy about himself and his twin sister."

"A prophecy?" asked Patti. "That sounds mysterious."

"Oh, it was very mysterious, until they turned three hundred last autumn," said Chivanni. "It was foretold that his sister would die when they met their destined lovers, so he committed his heart to Yuri and made it a point never to love any of his lovers."

"That would be enough to keep *me* from getting attached to anyone," Patti said, looking at her friends. "Did his sister die when you two got married, Annika?"

"Well . . . yeah, I mean, sort of . . . " Annika stuttered, realizing the truth. "I guess technically, she *was* dead for a few minutes."

"What an awful thing to go through. It sounds like he had good intentions, even though they were a little misguided," Patti suggested.

Annika took a few moments to review this overwhelming amount of information. She wasn't a psychologist, but she could see a connection between her husband's sexual history, and the potential of real feelings for someone leading to his twin sister's death. Prophecies like that weren't exactly something to be ignored, not among the elves of Eritähti.

"It's all in the past. As long as he sleeps in my bed at night from now on, that's all I really care about," she finally said before glancing up towards the roof where she heard him hammering the new cedar shingles into place. She was ready to shift the conversation to something lighter. "And he obviously loves me, or he wouldn't be here."

"He loves you so much, Annika," Chivanni assured her with a sympathetic gaze. "It was terrible to see how upset he was when he lost you. He couldn't sleep . . . he couldn't eat. That's why he looks so ghastly. We didn't see him smile once until we reached his family's house . . . and even then, he was still fairly miserable. His energy has completely changed since we arrived."

"I still can't believe he spent so much money just so he would have something to keep himself busy."

Here Chivanni shook his head, snickering.

"Oh, he's not looking for a hobby, Annika. If there's one thing I know about Talvi, it's that he can keep busy taking a nap. Besides, he has a lot of reading and other tasks that he's supposed to do instead of working on James's house."

"Maybe you're right," Annika said, rolling her eyes. "He did bring a lot of books with him. So if he's supposed to be reading, why did he agree to do all this extra work?"

"Because he made a deal with James that he would fix the house to make up for the money that you owed him, along with some future payments." Chivanni informed her. Right away, Annika felt irritated that people were making financial arrangements involving her without asking her.

"But James knows that I'm good for it," she insisted. "That's why I'm working at the music store." She knew the amount she brought home wasn't going to start any trust funds, but the employee discount would come in handy, and at least she was able to put her knowledge of guitars, amps and what Charlie had taught her about drums to good use.

"James told me that you didn't have any savings left," Chivanni said matter-of-factly, not realizing what a raw nerve he was hitting. "I think the way he put it was that you 'blew through it like a tornado hitting a tailor park'. What kind of park is that? Does one bring their clothes with them for alterations while you have a picnic? It sounds absolutely divine."

Patti blurted out a loud laugh, but Annika was less amused.

"No, he meant a *trailer* park. They're just places that seem to attract disasters," she muttered. She wasn't sure she appreciated his type of honesty anymore. She was getting so much more than she had bargained for.

"I don't know why it seems to bother you that he wants to be helpful around the house," Chivanni said. "I find it adorable that he's so eager to take care of you and show off his talents. You know that back home, his father made him build entire rooms as a form of punishment, right?"

Annika smiled faintly and nodded. She did recall hearing about that fact, on more than one occasion.

"It seemed that every time I stopped by, he was always working on one thing or another . . . when he was home long enough, that is," Chivanni said, sighing wistfully. "It's a good thing he misbehaved so often. His family's home is beautiful." The faerie's eyes looked up into the tall pine trees above, caught up in a daydream about his life in another society.

"So have you been there a lot? What's his house like?" Patti asked. Along with Annika, she was all too happy to lead the conversation away from their piss-poor financial planning or Talvi's recovery from sex addiction.

"He did so much of the work, I'm sure he would take more pleasure telling you all about it. You should ask him when you have at least an hour to spare for each ear," Chivanni snickered, and then spoke in an aloof tone, mimicking Talvi's accent perfectly; "*This* is the courtyard that I laid all of the tile for . . . and *here's* the greenhouse that my brother and I built for our dear mother, and here's where I painted *all* of the Roman gods on the library ceiling for my father, and *here's* the mural that my sister and I created for the foyer . . ." Chivanni trailed off as he realized this list could go on and on. "He does tend to boast, but then, I suppose I would too if I had a house as grand as his."

"With that accent of his, I could listen to him brag about his house all day," Patti said, deeply interested. "I didn't know he was an artist. He actually painted a mural on a ceiling? I'll have to ask him how he did that without breaking his neck." She stood up, setting her flower on the ground next to Annika before walking up the front steps.

"You're going to go ask him right now?" Annika called to her friend.

"No, dufus! I'm thirsty. It's starting to get hot out," Patti called back with a laugh as she walked into the house.

Annika was quiet as she and Chivanni continued to plant flowers in the warm sunshine. She was still mulling over all the information she'd learned in a very short amount of time. It truly shocked her that it was Finn who had sent Talvi in search of the Samodivi of the East. That wasn't the sort of thing he would do . . . was it?

Oh, Finn . . .

Where was the flaw in him? He was so intelligent, polite, and kind, and pretty easy on the eyes as well, with his loose brown curls perpetually falling into his dark brown eyes. He was so different from his reckless and impulsive younger brother. Finn was much more mature, a committed bookworm, but he wasn't an old fuddy-duddy either. He thought things through carefully and always seemed to consider everyone else's feelings before he considered his own. He liked to stay close to home, and while he enjoyed a few drinks at the local tavern, he was not the one known for having too many too often. The worst thing Annika had ever seen him do was lace a couple cigarettes with pixie dust and help himself to his father's best brandy, but no harm had been done to anyone.

He was also very tender, affectionate, protective and caring. So much so, that at one point Annika thought perhaps Finn wanted her to be more than just a friend.

Oh Finn . . .

"Annika? Are you coming or not?"

"Huh?" She blushed as she squinted up at Chivanni, who was hovering in front of her, interrupting her daydream.

"Patti was right; it *is* getting quite warm out here," he replied. "You should get out of the sun. You look a bit flushed." The faerie wiped his forehead with a dainty hand, leaving behind a thin crescent-shaped smear of dirt on his luminous skin.

When they came inside, they saw Patti at the kitchen counter, cutting lemons. The large glass pitcher filled with water and the bag of sugar beside it were the only clues Annika needed to see what was going on. Talvi was leaning against the counter beside her, shirtless and chatting away. He wasn't helping at all, unless it was solely in the form of moral support.

"I refuse to believe that a girl like you would be so willing to give up with only two months left in the semester," Talvi told Patti. "That seems a bit daft, when you've already invested so much time and effort into your classes."

"Well, right now I need to focus on keeping a roof over my head and my bills paid. Even if James is okay with me moving in, I can't live here for free. Maybe I can finish the semester, but I'm a year away from finishing my degree. I know that I want to be a professor, but I keep changing my mind about what I want to teach for the rest of my life. I like everything . . . painting, pottery, drawing, sculpture . . . if I went to school to become a doctor, I'd have finished by now." Patti was trying not to frown.

"How can anyone be expected to only do one thing for their entire life?" Talvi asked her. "I'm three hundred and still have yet to do one thing for the rest of my life. You know, there is a school where I live that you would love. My sister Yuri studied ceramics there and created all the dishes we use in our home. My mother used to teach weaving classes quite often. I remember brushing countless angora rabbits with Yuri when we were little. To this day, every time I see a rabbit, my first thought is, 'what kind of yarn might he make?'"

"Rabbits?" Patti repeated. "You mean she spun the yarn and dyed it and everything?" Talvi nodded.

"I believe you would absolutely adore this place. My brother Finn teaches there as well . . . physics, astronomy, biology and such. I know they've never had much luck finding painting instructors. If you were to instruct there, you may take a class for every one you teach, and if you are popular with your students, you make some income as well. Not everyone pays in eggs and cheese, you know."

"I don't care, I *love* cheese!" she cried, looking considerably uplifted. Talvi glanced up to see his wife coming towards them. He smiled sweetly and blew her a kiss. Annika caught it midair and pressed it to her cheek.

"Shit! Oww!" There was a clatter as the knife Patti was using fell to the floor.

"What happened?" Talvi asked as he turned around to join Patti at the sink, forgetting all about the kiss he'd just blown to Annika.

"I cut my stupid finger and got lemon juice in it," she groaned, trying not to cry as she rinsed her finger under the faucet. "What a week I'm having."

"Now that wasn't a very clever thing to do," he said softly, shaking his head in reprimand as he enclosed her wet hand into his. "I think you're just using me, *Patagonia*." She glared at him a little, but he just brandished a smug smile back at her.

"Who told you my real name?" she asked, eyeing Annika suspiciously, but Annika shook her head.

"So you honestly do prefer Patti *Cake*, Miss Kaeke?" he said, raising an eyebrow. She was trying her best to look annoyed, but Talvi had a way of disarming and charming that was far stronger. "Well, Patti Cake, perhaps you should skip the lemonade and bake me a cake as fast as you can. But then, I really shouldn't let you near the oven . . . you'd probably burn yourself again."

"I probably would," Patti's smile was beginning to reveal itself. "My clumsy ass will keep you busy, that's for sure. It's a good thing you don't charge for your doctoring services or I'd be in debt up to my ears in less than a week. It's not like I have health insurance."

"Oh, don't mistake me for a charitable organization," he snickered. He opened his hand and inspected her finger carefully, seeing that it had healed up. "I'm certain you have something that I would accept as payment, and it won't be trivial, either. You owe your doctor a very, very big favor, Professor Patti

191

Cake," he teased. She snatched her hand out of his and flicked his pointed ear with her mended finger.

"And *you* owe me a car, smart ass. I'll let you finish making the damn lemonade," she said, grabbing her apron off the kitchen table as she headed for the fireplace in the living room. Talvi watched her pass through the door and laughed to himself, before gazing at the cut lemons with a faint smile. When he looked at Annika, she was watching him with a faint frown. Maybe it had been all that backstory that she'd just learned, but whatever it was, she hadn't appreciated the lighthearted tone of his voice, or the length of time that he'd spent healing Patti's hand, or the believable image of him playing doctor with her, of him telling her to open up and say "ahh".

"I know you're thinking about her a lot lately," she said to him, when she was sure Patti wouldn't hear. "I can hear some of the things in your head, like how much you want her to stay."

Talvi tilted his head and looked at her strangely.

"Of course I want her to stay. She's hilarious," he turned to the pile of cut lemons and started squeezing them into the pitcher, seeds and all. "Modern girls . . . I tell you."

"What do you mean by 'modern girls'?" she asked, not liking the way he said it.

"You don't know how to make lemonade unless it comes in a packet of dry powder with a ten page instruction manual. Whatever happened to using your instincts?" he said. His tone had Annika guessing if he was just being dry and sarcastic, or if he was actually insulting her. She watched him combine the lemons with water and sugar and stir it with a wooden spoon, then pour himself a glass.

"And *that's* how it's done," he said with a satisfied smile after he took a long drink.

"It's not exactly rocket science," she said, pouring herself a glass. But when she tasted it, it was way too tart for her liking. She set her glass down and with both hands she lifted the huge bag of sugar to the pitcher, but he took it away from her.

"Don't do that," he said, sounding more than a little bossy.

"Why not?"

"I prefer it the way it is."

"But it's too sour," she insisted.

"You can always add more sugar to your glass, but you can't undo it once you've put it in the pitcher."

"You sure *act* like you want to put it in the pitcher," she snarled.

"I'll be damned if we're still speaking about lemonade," he growled as he set his glass on the counter, but he was still holding the very large bag of sugar in his other hand.

"Oh don't act so self-righteous!" hissed Annika so only he heard her. "You're so predictable, Mister Six Hundred, give or take a dozen. I know what 'big favor' you have in mind for Patti."

"Such as playing doctor with her?" he taunted in a low voice. She didn't deny the accusation. Talvi's eyes flashed in outrage for a moment, and combined with the tone of his voice, Annika felt a bit scared of what monster she might have provoked. His grip on the bag of sugar tightened with a crushing force, and Annika took a step back as he took a step closer. His lips twisted into a cruel grin.

"You're unbelievable, that's what you are," he said through clenched teeth. "Why, you're so sour, I do believe it's *you* that needs a little sweetening up." With that, he turned the entire ten pound bag upside down over her head, spilling sugar into her damp sweaty hair, into her bra, down her shirt onto her sweaty back, and into the rear of her pants and all over the kitchen floor before dropping it at her feet and sauntering back to the other room with his glass of lemonade as though nothing had happened.

At first, Annika thought the smoke she saw was coming out of her ears, but it was coming from the living room, where she could hear Patti and Chivanni coughing.

"How long has it been since you guys have used the fireplace?" she heard Patti gasp.

"Patti, do you even know what you're doing? No—wait!" she heard Talvi call out. There was a sudden *whoosh* and a black cloud of soot came billowing through the door. Chivanni looked like a giant moth as he buzzed out from beyond the dark cloud and headed straight for the kitchen sink. If Annika thought she was angry before, now was speechless. She couldn't even move; she was so appalled at the situation she found herself in. She was just about to throw a two-year-old style temper tantrum, but someone else came home early from work and stole her thunder.

The kitchen door opened and in walked James, crunching sugar crystals under his patent leather Italian loafers as he entered the room. Annika felt her heart stop for a distinct moment as she looked into his eyes. Apparently his day at work had not been fruitful, because he looked royally pissed, and his mood was zooming downhill fast. His white knuckles curled around the strap of his crocodile man purse as he looked in horror at the empty bag by Annika's feet, and then at the bottom of his shoe.

"Don't tell me you spilled sugar all over the hardwood *fucking* floor," he said in a scary voice to the alleged culprit standing in front of him, surrounded by and covered in evidence. "Do you know what an uptight *bitch* it is to clean?" If the throbbing vein in his temple was a fuse, James looked like a powder keg ready to explode. His eyes darted from Annika standing in the pile of sugar to Chivanni the soot-covered moth, and seeing the black cloud still billowing from the living room, he began to walk that direction.

"Um, James, I wouldn't go in there if I were you," Annika said as she bent down and tried in vain to shove sugar back into the paper bag. But it was too late. She braced herself, waiting for the shit to hit the fan. There was a pause, and then James came back into the kitchen, tracking soot and sawdust and sugar along with him on his shoes. There was another long, long pause. He glared at Chivanni. Then he glared at Annika. And then the shit hit the fan.

"WHAT THE FUCK HAPPENED TO MY MOTHER-FUCKING HOUSE?" James screamed at her. "I go away for three FUCKING hours and come home to *this*? Where are my fucking cigarettes?" There was another pause. "Oh my god, you have *got* to be shitting me! I just bought a pack last night!" Another pause. "ARRGGHH!" Suddenly standing in a small hill of grainy sugar on a hot sticky spring day didn't seem so bad. Out of the corner of her eye, Annika watched Talvi creep with all the stealth of a ninja through the other entrance to the kitchen from around the hall, and then leap silently up the steps, disappearing into their bedroom.

James's hands shook as he removed his glasses and sat quite stiffly in the chair at the table, setting his bag in the seat next to him. Talvi came bounding down the stairs and handed him a lit cigarette, and James snatched it away with no comment. Annika knew her friend had a temper, but she'd never seen him this angry before. He always had something to say; now he couldn't even speak. He looked almost catatonic as he took several long and deep drags, and eventually his shaking hand grew steadier. Patti stepped meekly into the doorway, and Chivanni hid behind Annika, peeking over her shoulder.

"I'm so glad I went into work today," James said in a calm, eerie voice. "Jack has an emergency dentist appointment on Thursday, the day I'll need him the most. He fell at soccer practice Saturday morning and broke his crown, and that's the only time he could get in. If that wasn't shitty enough, it turns out that Jill is really sick. She fainted yesterday with a temperature of a hundred and three degrees. I'm not even sure if she'll be better by this Friday, let alone sooner to help me hang the art and set up for the show. I sent out the invitations three weeks ago, I have the catering paid for, the advertising paid for, and the artwork that I've spent all this time, effort, and money promoting isn't even here." James took a couple more long drags, trembling a little less. "After all that good news, I thought I could at least come home and have a glass of wine, or a bottle for that matter, and a relaxing bubble bath. I wasn't expecting to find it transformed into *this*. Between the sugar, soot, and sawdust, I don't know which is going to be harder to clean, but I have to start on it right away, before we get soot everywhere . . . or ants . . . or roaches . . . or condemned. I don't exactly have a building permit." He had a strange, possessed look in his eye, and finished the cigarette, dropping the filter-less stub in the ashtray. He buried his head in his arms on the table and began to shake. Annika walked over to him, rubbing his back sympathetically.

"James, I promise everything will get cleaned up. And I'm sure everything will fall into place for your show on Friday. We'll help you any way we can. Why don't you go take that bubble bath and we'll worry about the mess? I'll bring you a glass of wine," she said softly, but he only shook harder. Patti crept a little closer with her hand still curled around the fireplace poker, and a remorseful look on her face, but her guilty façade quickly transformed when she heard a loud snort come from James. He lifted his head and his mouth was gasping for air, while tears of laughter squeezed out of his eyes.

"Holy shit. Do you realize I work with *Jack* and *Jill?*" he burst out. Annika and Patti looked at each other, bewildered at the abrupt turn James's mood had taken.

"Um, we already made all those jokes a long time ago. Why's it so funny now?" Annika asked. James was trying to answer, but he was laughing so hard it took him a few minutes.

"Yeah, but Jack . . . Jack and Jill . . . " he gasped, "Jack fell down and broke his crown, and Jill came tumbling after!" He screamed, and leaned so far out of his chair that he fell onto the sugary floor, clutching his stomach in hysterical shrieks. "Jack really fell down! He broke his mother fucking crown! He broke his crown and Jill came tumbling . . . " James kept repeating hysterically, and the others looked at each other in confusion as he began to roll in the sugar, still laughing.

"What the hell just happened?" Annika asked, looking completely baffled. "Do you think he's finally having a nervous breakdown?"

"I don't know, I've never seen one happen before," Patti said, just as unsure as her friend. "It's like he was ghost-dosed with something. If I didn't know any better, I'd say he was high, but he's been in front of us the whole time."

Annika whipped her head around to look at Talvi. "*Is* he high?" she demanded. "Did you bring along something else you forgot to unpack the other day?"

Talvi's smile gave him away as he watched James start to lick at the sugar crystals on the floor.

"I might have brought along a bit of pixie dust," he confessed.

"What's pixie dust?" Patti asked. "What the heck does it do?"

"You're looking at it," Annika said, pointing to James. He was still squirming on the floor and giggling like a mad school boy. She had tried pixie dust before, but she didn't get nearly the same results as she was seeing right now.

"I'm so sweet! I'm such a sweet boy," he said, rubbing the sugar in his hair and pouring it down the inside of his shirt.

"I didn't mean to use so much," Talvi said, trying to look serious, "But I was in such a hurry. Anyhow, I much prefer him like this than his previous state."

"How long is he going to be like this?" Annika asked.

"I don't know," Talvi said, stepping out of the way as James lunged at him with a fistful of sugar he had scraped off the floor. "Probably just a few hours."

"A few *hours?*" Patti repeated in shock. "What are we going to do with him? There's all those power tools lying around! He might hurt himself!"

"Oww!" Chivanni cried. James was gnawing on his sooty leg.

"You're a sweet boy too!" he said maniacally. "You're a little gingerbread man, aren't you?" Chivanni jumped backwards, attempting escape, but James's grip was so tight that he only succeeded in falling on the floor. James gathered another small handful of sugar and crawled over him, rubbing it in Chivanni's hair and over his neck as the small framed redhead thrashed underneath him. "You tried to run as fast as you can, but I ended up catching you, gingerbread man!" He threw his head back in a diabolical laugh before burying his face in Chivanni's neck. The real faerie gave a noise that began in a yelp and ended in giggles at being relentlessly nibbled.

"I don't think he's a danger to himself as much as he is to Chivanni," Talvi snickered. He started to head into the living room, but there came a protest.

"Talvi, don't leave! Get him off of me!" Chivanni giggled from underneath James. He was slowly being devoured by the obsessed man, covered in more ticklish nibbles that sent his wings fluttering, which sent soot and sugar swirling around the floor in a gritty grey mess. "I can't make myself small!"

Talvi sighed as he reached down and tried half-heartedly to pull James off of Chivanni, but James put up quite a fight. Suddenly he gave a loud yelp, recoiling just long enough for Chivanni to scramble out from underneath him.

"He bit me!" James cried out, clutching his hand to his shoulder. "Oh my god, he fucking *bit* me!"

"I warned you about that," Talvi reminded him, grasping him by the arms. "Everyone knows that fairies bite."

"I'm electing you his keeper until this wears off," Annika instructed her husband. "I've never seen him so bonkers."

"*Me?* I really think this wingless faerie would rather have Chivanni keep an eye on him," Talvi said with a laugh, but the faerie brushed past him and headed for the downstairs bathroom.

"I never would have given him so much dust, Talvi!" Chivanni scolded, still looking like a giant dark moth. "At least not for his first time. Besides, you're the only one strong enough to control him while I take a bath." He started to walk away.

"Oh, a fine time for that!" Talvi argued exasperatedly as James lurched forward unsuccessfully trying to escape. "Why the hell do you need to take one at this very moment?"

"Because I can't do any proper magic if I'm all sticky with sugar," he said, being a bit of a priss. "What good will the pixie dust have been, if, when he comes to his senses and sees this mess, he just goes mad again?" With that he passed through the door. James lunged after him again in one last attempt, but Talvi's strong arms held him back.

"I want that gingerbread man!" James argued. "Bring him back! I wasn't done with him yet. Let me go!"

"Stop being so belligerent or I'll tie you up with all that rope we bought!" Talvi said, trying to reason with the madman in his hands. James turned around and looked up at him.

"I don't see any rope in that tool belt of yours!" His brown eyes had never been so crazed. "What else do you have in there, pretty boy?"

"Annika, go get some rope from the other room," Talvi ordered, trying to avoid James's groping hands. But she just stood there, relishing the sight. "Be quick about it, would you?" She gave him a long, hard look. While she was relieved that her friend wasn't going to give himself an aneurysm, she was still mad at Talvi for fawning all over Patti earlier.

"I didn't make any of this mess, so I don't think I should have to clean it up," was her flippant reply before she headed upstairs to take a shower.

CHAPTER 20
Oh, Finn...

Back in the parallel world of Eritähti, in the woods of Srebra Gora, in the village of Derbedrossivic, Finn Marinossian had his work cut out for him. He, his father, and Asbjorn had spent the past two weeks collecting sap from the maple trees in the forest, bringing it to his mother and sister to cook down and make maple syrup, maple sugar, and little taffy candies with Stella and Sloan. And after the last of the snow had melted and given way to the first flowers of spring, it was time to clean out the beehives for another sweet summer of fresh honey. His mother and older sister had begun their annual spring cleaning, which they always did right before planting the gardens of vegetables and herbs. This meant nearly non-stop washing of everything in the house, and everyone's help was enlisted. If it were a small cottage, it would have been done in a few days. But it was his family's house, and like many things Marinossian, there was nothing small about it.

That meant weeks of work to wipe the dust from every inch of the sprawling hacienda that was his father's pride and joy, right after his children and grandchildren. It also was taking longer because in the past, Yuri and Talvi were home to help, along with the three samodivi and a bit of magical help from the fairies. This year they weren't there to pitch in, and Finn's aching back and shoulders were lamenting this fact every evening. There was so much extra work that he was too tired at night to bother researching that trunk of stones in his room, so there they sat, locked up and unstudied. There was just too much to do before the planting must begin in the gardens surrounding the house.

Curtains must be shampooed, floors must be scrubbed, windows must be washed, and all of this required a steady intake of wood to fuel the fires to heat the water. The leaves must be raked out of the courtyard, the fountain with the koi must be dredged of dead plants from the winter and filled back up with fresh water, and flowerbeds must be mulched. Rugs must be beaten, furniture must be wiped clean and have paste wax applied, silverware and doorknobs needed to be polished, and door hinges and water pumps must be oiled for another year of use. And just when it seemed every chore had been completed, something else was remembered. The chimneys needed cleaning. The chandeliers still had cobwebs. The mattresses needed to be turned. It just never seemed to end.

On top of all of these extra seasonal chores, there were the daily responsibilities of bringing in wood for heat, wood for cooking, and collecting more wood when the supply began to grow low. It wasn't just strolling around the forest to gather twigs. Oh no.

First, Finn and Asbjorn would scout the woods for dead and dying trees. Then, it was a full day's work to harness one of the horses, then find the chosen tree, chop it down, cut off all the limbs, secure the log to the harness, haul it back home, remove it from the harness, and repeat.

There was also caring for the horses every day, which meant lunging them for a bit of exercise, hauling water, filling up feeding troughs and mucking stalls. The mares and Asbjorn's gelding were not much trouble to contend with, and his own palomino stallion Galileo was as easygoing and laid back as ever. But just like his owner, Talvi's stallion Ghassan had a knack for causing more trouble and needing more attention than all the other horses combined. If he had just been groomed, he would run straight to the muddiest spot in his field and have a thorough roll in it. If there was an unattended bucket of water on the ground, he would playfully prance about until it had 'accidentally' been kicked over. If there was a weak spot anywhere in the fence, he leaned harder on it until it broke. He and Galileo had already been caught a few times in the mares' pasture, which would have been fine if they weren't coming into season. It astounded Finn, how much trouble one horse could cause. If Ghassan wasn't tied up just right, he unfastened the knot with his teeth and would wander off on an adventure. Twice already, Finn had found him in the village, with his head in a window of the Tortoise and Hare, most likely looking for Talvi. Or free barley and hops. The brewers always saved the darkest hops for their best customer's horses, which automatically put Ghassan at the top of the VIP list.

Ghassan was probably just having fun, but Finn wasn't laughing. Instead, he found himself cursing his brother's absence while he groomed coats, picked cockleburs out of manes and tails, and trimmed and picked hooves in the stable. If Talvi was around, he wouldn't be stuck with such a large list of chores that left his back aching every night. If Talvi was around, Finn probably would have figured out the precise way that the Pazachi had created those stones by now. If Talvi was around, things would just be easier, plain and simple.

He had urged his brother to go find Annika as soon as possible, which any good brother would have done. So why was he so irritated by his decision? Partially, because he had wanted to go with Talvi to help find her. Talvi wasn't the only one who found himself missing Annika's endearing humor and inquisitive nature. She had formed lasting relationships with her new friends and family, in particular with Runa and Finn. Based on everything Annika had told him about America, it sounded like a fascinating place to visit, from an anthropological point of view. He was envious of his brother, who might have mastered the use of a computer by now. He was deeply jealous of the art, science, music, and culture that Talvi was no doubt swimming in with his new wife.

Tethered by his responsibilities at home, Finn had stayed behind. If he thought things were tough now, he could only imagine how difficult it would be for his family if he wasn't there. Sure, Asbjorn was home, and others from Derbedrossivic would lend a hand if it was needed, but they had their own crops to plant, their own spring cleaning to complete.

He made up his mind that as soon as the gardens were in the ground, he was going to visit Sofia and make long-awaited use of that electric mailbox.

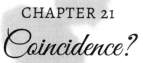

CHAPTER 21

Coincidence?

Upstairs in her own bathroom, Annika let the water pour down her shoulders for a long time as she washed her hair twice, making sure to rinse all the sugar out. The little spat between her and Talvi had left her feeling confused.

He hasn't even been here a week and we're already fighting? My brain is ready to explode! How can Talvi look at Patti the way he does, and then blow me a kiss? Could he have flirted just a little more with her, right in front of me? He didn't deny that he wants her to stay, but why is he so interested in her? Oh right, because she's got boobs.

She only felt more frustrated that her thoughts didn't sort themselves out in her head as she proceeded to put on a mud mask, give herself a pedicure, and then a manicure in the privacy of her locked bathroom. Surely he wasn't so brazen as to start making advances at other women right in front of his wife. She wanted to believe that she was just over-reacting, but at the same time, there was a fear that perhaps he had not changed his ways like he claimed.

Annika also knew that there was always going to be an aspect of their relationship that other people would never be able to understand, being that they both came from two different worlds, and really belonged to neither. That perpetual sense of displacement had brought them together, yet it had also placed somewhat of a wedge between them.

Like Charlie said, it took time to get to know someone. Annika had only known Talvi for a handful of weeks, on *his* turf, among *his* friends. Now the tables were turned.

Annika heard her phone make a little beep, which indicated she had a new voicemail. Apparently it was urgent, because she had missed three calls from him as well. With nails that were not quite dry, she carefully tapped the buttons on her phone to play her voicemail aloud on speakerphone. It was Danny, saying that he needed to talk to her as soon as she had some time. Annika wasn't quite ready to leave the safe zone of her bathroom, back into the chaotic world of downstairs, so now seemed as good of a time as any. Besides, Danny's voice had sounded anxious, which instantly made Annika wonder if those home pregnancy tests had been wrong all along. She thought about raising mentally handicapped elf twins as a single mother and found herself wasting no time getting ahold of him.

"I'm glad you finally called back," he said, still sounding urgent. "I've got those blood test results; do you have a minute?"

"Yeah," she replied, trying not to move her mouth too much because of the dry mud masque, "but you sound strange. Is something wrong?"

"Not exactly wrong . . . but not normal, either," he said, sounding uncertain. "I think something tainted your sample, because the tests I ran don't make any sense."

"What do you mean, they don't make sense?"

"Your hemoglobin levels are really high, and your T-cells are different, too. They're bigger. And your cells have so many polymorphonuclear leukocytes with enhanced phagocytic activity that it's off the chart."

"Danny, I need layman's terms," Annika said, so exasperated that some of the dried mud masque flaked off her cheeks. "I don't have a clue what phagocytic activity is."

"Okay, so it's like this. Think of your immune system as being a bouncer at a club. You need someone who can take care of the riff-raff, like viruses and bacteria. Otherwise you get really sick."

"I'm with you so far. So is my bouncer working the door, or is he flirting with the cocktail waitress?"

"Oh, he's working the door alright, but this isn't just any bouncer. He's more like Wolverine."

"Did you just say *Wolverine*?" Annika wondered how many comic references Doctor Danny used in a week. Probably a lot.

"Yeah, isn't it crazy?" he went on, almost giddy as he spoke. "I've been testing your samples ever since you came in, but I can't figure out what's causing every single one of your cells to be enhanced like this. From what I can tell, you're completely free of any diseases, and your hemoglobin is even carrying extra oxygen to all of your tissues. I've never seen anything like it. There's no logical explanation for any of this, and *I* sure as hell can't figure it out. If I told my colleagues what I really think of these results, they would laugh me out of a job."

"What do you really think?" she asked. She had never heard him sound so excited about anything work-related before.

"Oh, I don't know," he said, sidestepping her question. "I think I'd feel better if we did another blood draw on you and sent the samples out to a few different labs. But from what I can gather from your cells, you should be feeling like a million bucks, not throwing up and sick all the time. Wolverine's got your back, baby."

Annika thought about the wound in her shoulder she had watched heal in front of her eyes, and recalled how she always caught the flu by now, but she hadn't noticed even a runny nose all winter.

"So I'm not knocked up then? What about the weird cravings? I've been eating blueberries nonstop." Danny laughed a little.

"You're definitely *not* pregnant," he said. "That's the only test that came back with normal results. As far as the cravings go, blueberries are really high in antioxidants, so that might be your body's way of getting them into your system. It's just telling you what you need, to keep your blood and tissues as pure as they are."

"That makes sense, but what about me getting sick all the time?"

"The only thing I can come up with is that you keep introducing some kind of pollutant into your bloodstream. It could be anything . . . junk food, too much sugar or saturated fat, smoking, hell, even chemicals in skin care and cleaning products. Your skin's your largest organ, you know. You're probably getting sick because your body's trying to keep those toxins out, and you keep putting them back in. Your immune system doesn't want to mess with that crap when it has a potentially immortal body to take care of."

His last words rang in Annika's ear even louder than her phone had earlier.

"I'm sorry, did you say 'potentially immortal'?" she repeated. She hadn't mentioned this particular wedding present from Talvi to anyone back home, but now Danny was saying it loud and clear, with lab results to prove it.

"Yeah, I did," he said, sounding even more excited. "That's why I don't want to involve any of my coworkers. I'd love it if you could come back in for a few more tests, though, so I can get more conclusive results. I don't like assuming things without reliable evidence."

"I'll think about it," she said, and hung up the phone after promising to let Danny know of any changes in her symptoms.

When Annika ventured outside the security of her bathroom wrapped in her robe, she found her bedroom quiet and still except for the sound of a page in a book being turned. There, lying on the clean bed was her dirty, sooty, saw-dusted and sweaty husband, engrossed in another one of his books. He said nothing to her as she sat down on the edge. He didn't even glance in her direction; it seemed the book in his hands held more interest to him.

"Are you still pissed off about earlier?" she asked. "Because I'm the one who should be mad. You're the one who dumped ten pounds of sugar on me and let James think it was my fault." He didn't acknowledge that she had spoken, let alone existed as she spoke again.

"You're real mature, ignoring me like this." But he still said nothing, only frustrating her further.

"Come on Talvi, you're not giving me anything to work with here." A snarky little smile played on his lips, and he reached down for his tool belt, which had been sitting on the floor. He tossed it at Annika's feet, saying,

"The staircase for the basement needs to be assembled, so get to work."

She rolled her eyes at him.

"What is your problem?"

"I'm not the one with the problem," he said, and turned his piercing eyes away from his book just long enough to say, "*You* are."

"*Me?*" she said. That was the wrong answer, according to her rules.

"Yes *you*." He turned back to his book. "You don't trust me as far as you could throw me, you little thing."

"How can you say that when last night you were asking me where I was for two hours? That means you don't trust me either."

"It's *him* that I don't trust, not in *his* home, not when I know *he's* trying to lure you back."

"He is not," she said feebly, feeling her argument dissolve as quickly as sugar in a pitcher of tart lemonade.

"Alright Annika, he definitely wants nothing to do with you," Talvi said calmly and placed a bookmark between the pages before closing the cover. "He hasn't thought once about what he could do to win you back. He hasn't suggested that he should have been the one to be ticketed with you for lewd and lascivious behavior. That's why you were simply 'talking' with him for two hours Sunday afternoon."

"If you're not jealous, and you trust me so much, then why are you giving me a hard time?" she asked, refusing to confirm his suspicions. "You're the one who slept with over six hundred women, and now you're making goo-goo eyes at my best friend!"

He looked like there was something extremely nasty he wanted to say, but he thought better of it. He counted to ten . . . then twenty . . . then thirty, before he spoke.

"That's in the past, and nothing will ever change that," he said, selecting his words with the utmost care. "I wish it didn't upset you so much, but I'm certainly not going to feel remorse for every pleasure I had before I ever knew your name. How dare you insinuate that I would stoop so low as to pursue your dear friend, let alone anyone besides you? You have no idea what blasphemy that is to hear. How can you think that of sweet Patti Cake? How can you think that about me, after all I've done for you? Do you think finding you was a leisurely stroll through the trees? Do you think I came here because I had nothing else to do?" He waited for Annika to answer him, but she didn't. She was slightly afraid to.

"I'll have you know that I spent the past three months dodging avalanches, blizzards, frostbite and blood sucking trees to be with you! And these rings," he said, lifting his left hand towards her face, "We'll wear them to the grave unless someone cuts off our hands first. I just don't understand how you can doubt my loyalty after all we have been through. I let you and James have your fun with dressing me up like a paper doll, even though I hated it, and I thought you would be relieved to have me take care of your financial burdens, not offended. At first I wondered what else I could do to prove my devotion, but now I realize it is not my duty to prove anything to you. I have done plenty to demonstrate how I feel for you. Hence, *you* are the one with the problem, not me." Annika's stomach plummeted as she looked away from him. He made an indestructible argument, and the only one she could be upset at was herself.

"I guess I don't understand why you're with me," she said softly. "You could've had anyone."

"I didn't want 'anyone'. I wanted *you*. Now enough of that feminine nonsense. I could make the same case that you're attempting to make."

"Give me a break," she mumbled. She would admit that she was a cute girl, especially if she took the time to get dolled up properly, but Talvi had a movie star charisma that made most girls and even some boys flock to him like white on rice.

"It's true," he said, glancing at her. "Do you not recall being the apple of a particular vampire's eye back home? Or what about poor Nikola? He's still sore that he failed to win your affections. Even here, I see men looking at you wherever we go. Who wouldn't want to wrap their hands around that little waist of yours and pull you close?"

"Why don't you do it, then?" she taunted, ready to make up.

"Oh, I'm still cross with you," he said, his eyes twinkling mischievously.

"Because I wanted to know how many lady skeletons there are in your closet?" she asked.

"One hardly speaks of such things," he said. "It's in poor taste."

"Oh, but you can tell me in front of my friends that you lost your virginity in a week-long orgy?"

"You said you wouldn't get upset about that. You said you wanted to know, so I told you, even though I didn't want to. I was not exactly begging to share that story, if you recall."

"Yeah, but you're supposed to tell me everything. I'm your wife."

"I'm well aware of our marital status," he said somewhat sarcastically as he flashed his ring at her, "but that does not entitle you to have complete domain over my entire life. It's my opinion that some things are best left unsaid . . . no questions asked, and if you truly trust me, then you won't feel the need to know every little detail of my life."

"Like knowing what your magic number is?" she insisted.

He looked at her just long enough to narrow his eyes a little, then snapped, "I honestly don't know what that number is! You may as well ask me how many pints I've ever drank. I really couldn't tell you."

"How can you just *not know*?" she asked. Surely he could round up to the nearest tenth. Or hundredth. Or maybe he had a point, that knowing wouldn't do her any good whatsoever. She bit her lip in frustration. She didn't like admitting when she was wrong.

"I don't know because it was never important to me, Annika," he said, throwing his hands up in exasperation. "*You* are what's important to me! As far as I'm concerned, my number is *one*, because you are the only one that I want to be with."

Annika mulled over his response as she crawled onto the bed and sat beside him.

"Do you really mean that, Talvi?" she asked. "How can you be so sure about me?"

"Because I've never questioned what I knew in my heart. Your problem is that you ask too many questions. You waste time wringing your hands over matters which you cannot control, rather than giving in and losing yourself in the present moment. But to be fair, it does help to have a prophecy made about you being the one intended for me," he said with a soft smile.

"Will you tell me more about that?" she asked. "How old were you when you found out about it?"

"I don't think I was any specific age," he said, "It was something I was always aware of. I grew up knowing I would meet my destined love right around the time I turned three hundred. And Yuri knew the same thing about herself as well. I knew all along that it was going to cause some sort of harm to my sister, but I didn't know it would mean her death until I was around one hundred and forty or so. That's about twelve years old, if you convert it to human years. And being such a tender, impressionable age, it scared me enough to not want to care much about anyone outside my family."

A sympathetic moan came from Annika.

"That seems such a horrible thing to grow up knowing," she said sadly.

"I suppose it had its moments," Talvi said, looking faraway for a moment. "It's not the sort of thing that can be kept secret, since all of my family knew about it, and we have the ability to read each other's thoughts if they're thought too loud, too often. We didn't avoid discussing it, but we didn't address it too much either. I'm certain it's why my mother and father let me get away with so much, because I was acting out against that knowledge.

Then you came along and turned my world upside down, with that cheek of yours," he accused, but he didn't look too upset by it. In fact, he was trying not to smile. "I tried so hard to resist you, but I couldn't ignore what you did to me, even that first day we met in the bookstore. The moment I saw you, I knew who you were, and what you would mean to me. I knew the shape of your face before you were ever born. We didn't disturb the old journal very often, but my entire family knew your face. You know which portrait I'm speaking of, in the library back at my house."

"I know," Annika said. "I look so much like Magda, that even her sisters thought I could have been her."

"Yes, you gave Runa and Hilda quite a startle that day," he agreed. "I went back to the bookstore to try and find you, even though I had no idea what I was expecting to find. You were alluring and terrifying all at once, because for the very first time, I stopped worrying about my sister's life and wanted to fulfill my own. You're different from anyone I've ever known, Annika. You're a very strong woman, and I think there's a reason why we find ourselves lying here, in this bed together, speaking about this. Perhaps my role in your life is to help you unfold your wings, since you are my little dove."

Annika squeezed him tighter than ever, until he pretended to be gasping for air, which made her laugh. When she eased up on her grip, he reached out to stroke her hair, and ran his hand along her bare arm.

"I don't yet understand all that we are, or what we could become or accomplish, but so far, following my instincts has lead me in the right direction. It's what lead me to your door, after all, so why should we waste time questioning what we have now that we're together?"

"We shouldn't waste time doing that," Annika said, eyeing the caked soot and dried sweat on his bare chest and arms. "You should probably take a shower though. You're getting get the bed filthy, and the comforter just got washed."

"Why don't you join me?" he asked.

"I just took a shower."

"Yes, but I believe I'm filthy enough to warrant one that requires an extra set of hands," he said, putting down his book to cast her a lecherous glance. "If you think my skin's unclean, just imagine how impure my thoughts are."

"I'll give you a head start," she said with a grin, eyeing the soot on his skin. "I don't want to get ashes and sawdust in my mouth."

"Oh, you'll likely get something in your mouth regardless," Talvi snickered, then got up and disappeared into the bathroom.

Annika began to gather dirty laundry from around the room, and she spied his crumpled and filthy jeans lying by the door. She picked them up and slipped her freshly manicured fingertips into his pockets so she didn't accidentally wash anything important. In the left back pocket, she was surprised to find a smart phone, although it was locked. Talvi had never mentioned that he had his own phone. She tried a few different passwords, including their wedding date, his birthday, and even the word 'wine', but she had no luck. She put the phone back and searched the front pockets next. In the right one she found some loose change, a decent amount of folded cash, and an old flip-top lighter engraved with the words 'cheeky bastard'. She let out a snort of amusement and stuck her hand in again, finding something much more mysterious. It wasn't that she held a handkerchief in her hands, or even that it was half stained with blood. It was the initials 'MN' embroidered in dainty fuchsia lettering that intrigued her the most.

She thought about Talvi's heartfelt confession only moments earlier, and of how much she wanted to believe it. It really had sounded too good to be true. She stuffed the handkerchief back in its place beside the lighter, dropped his pants on the floor, got dressed quietly, and brought the rest of the dirty laundry down to the dungeon.

CHAPTER 22
The Upper Hand

Annika was surprised to find the kitchen floor spotless as she came downstairs for with the basket of dirty laundry. The living room had been miraculously swept up, and not one spot of sawdust remained. The once sooty rug had never looked better. Even some of the threadbare spots looked brand new. It seemed impossible, given how filthy the area was only a couple hours ago, but then, faerie magic made the impossible happen.

Patti, Charlie, and Chivanni were playing cards at the kitchen table while an enchanted spoon stirred mushroom and asparagus risotto under the supervision of faerie magic. As soon as the first load of clothes was in the wash, Annika came back up and was dealt into the game.

"I see you've found something a little more your style," she observed as she sat next to Patti, who was no longer wearing Charlie's pajamas. Instead, she wore a knee-length orange dress with a fluffy white cardigan. She grinned, setting down a card on top of the pile in the center of the table.

"Yep. Charlie and I were able to get a few things to tide me over until I can get my bed and dresser here this Sunday."

"So I guess James gave his blessing?" asked Annika, organizing the cards in her hand. Patti smiled even wider.

"I waited to ask until he had calmed down a bit, but yeah, he said he was fine with the idea."

"Did he mention anything about the pixie dust?" Annika whispered.

"Not a word," Patti whispered back.

Annika sighed in relief, glad that her friend didn't have to worry about having a place to stay, and also that the house was cleaned up from that after-noon's fiasco.

"Where is he, by the way?"

"Jack called, and then he disappeared out onto the front porch," Charlie said, motioning toward the living room. "That was maybe fifteen minutes ago." Just then, the front door opened and shut, and into the kitchen came James with some sort of list in one hand, and his cell phone in the other.

"Alright Jack, thanks for staying so late," he said, sounding genuinely thank-ful. "I'll be there in a bit to finish up, but you can go ahead and lock up." He shut his phone softly and set the list on the table before pulling up a chair, but he didn't sit down, he simply stood in place, looking bewildered.

"So what's the word?" Annika asked. "Are the paintings finally there?"

"Oh, they're there alright. All thirty-seven of them," he said quietly. It was the calmest Annika had heard him speak in a week, and she caught a glimpse of his list. It had numerous measurements on it, probably of the artwork. "I was expecting fifteen large pieces. Not thirty-seven small, medium, *and* large ones. If they were all big, I could just slap them on the walls in a couple hours, but thirty-*seven*? It will take me all night just to lay them out so they look halfway decent. Plus, Jill is still out sick, and Jack has to leave tonight for the dentist. It's his uncle that's going to fix his tooth, but he lives two hours away. He's going to try to get back as soon as possible tomorrow, but it won't be until the early afternoon. I don't know how I'm going to pull this one off." His olive skin began to turn white. His brown eyes began to water, but he blinked quickly as he walked over to the coffee grinder and began preparing a large pot of coffee. He dodged a salt shaker as it barely missed his head and headed for the stove to touch up the risotto. "I don't think I'll be coming home tonight."

"Aren't you at least going to have dinner?" Chivanni asked. "You can't work very well on an empty stomach."

"I don't think I could eat if I tried," he said. "I feel sick."

"There must be something going around, because I'm also feeling rather unwell," Talvi said, having suddenly appeared in the doorway. He gave Annika a disappointed look but said nothing as he quietly prepared himself a cup of tea.

"I can help you lay out the paintings," Patti volunteered. "I'm not trying to brag, but I *kinda* have a strong background in fine art."

"Well that would help out a lot, actually, but I know you have classes in the morning. It's going to be a really late night, I'll tell you that much right now."

"I've pulled all-nighters before," Patti smiled confidently. "Besides, I owe at least that much to my new landlord."

James looked grateful beyond words, and busied himself with brewing a pot of coffee, but something had caught his attention. His eyes rested on the spoon that had been stirring the risotto, sans hands, for the past half hour.

"Hey Chivanni?" he asked. The red-haired faerie glanced up from his cards. "Yes?" he said slowly.

"Do you think you could help me out with some faerie magic of the spoon-stirring variety? Maybe you can come to the gallery and just help us with the lights? You'd be perfect for it . . . I wouldn't have to drag out the ladder and set it up a million times. That right there would save me about two hours."

"I have done quite a few big favors for you lately," he said, raising an eyebrow before turning back to his hand of cards. "And besides, I'm in the middle of cooking risotto. You can't just leave in the middle of cooking risotto. It must be constantly stirred. The garlic needs more time to simmer."

"But it would mean so much to me. If this is how you make dinner," said James, motioning to the self-propelled kitchen utensils, "I'll bet you can make the paintings float so we won't have to lay them all out one at a time to see the best way to arrange them. Shit, if you could help me out, it wouldn't take long at all! We could even get done in time to get a good night's sleep! I'll make it up to you any way that I can."

"Hmm . . . " Chivanni trumped whatever card Charlie had just laid down, and now Charlie was forced to draw over and over from the pile, which made the faerie's wings flutter with glee.

"Please? Whatever you want, just say it," James begged.

"I don't know," Chivanni said with his impish grin. "I can't think of anything I want in return."

"Why don't you and Patti run along with James," Talvi said to him, pouring a bit of cream into his cup and standing near the stove, waiting for the kettle to whistle. "That will give you a chance to get started while Annika and I finish making dinner. We'll pack it up and bring it to the gallery as soon as it's ready." He grabbed ahold of the enchanted spoon that was stirring the risotto and took a bite. After nodding his head in approval, he turned to Chivanni.

"Who is to say that you have to name your price right this moment?" he asked, motioning to Charlie, who was still drawing cards from the dwindling

215

pile. "Don't you realize that you're in the best possible strategic situation? When someone owes you something, it's always *you* that has the upper hand, never the other way around."

CHAPTER 23
Friends of Convenience

April virtually exploded with warm breezes, frequent rain showers, and myriads of pink, purple, yellow and white rhododendrons were blooming throughout the neighborhood. Spring had come early this year, and it was a soft season, as soft as the new blades of grass that grew thick and green practically overnight. The harbingers of spring were in no rush to be done with their task of waking up Mother Nature from her winter slumber. Every flower bloom seemed to last forever, every sunset was lasting longer, and the park across the street had once again become a lush haven of rolling emerald hills divided up by mossy footpaths. A storm had drifted in from the coast and blown flower petals across the yard from the various blooming trees; it looked like the biggest wedding in the world had taken place at the park.

On the other side of the street, one house in particular was improving just as quickly, thanks to Talvi's expertise and Chivanni's help. The new cedar shingles had been put on and nearly all the cracks in the crumbling plaster had been repaired. The ceiling and walls had been painted, and the flower beds out front were immaculate.

Following the most successful show James had ever hosted at his gallery, he officially welcomed Patti into the growing home with her own set of keys to the house. He had completely gotten over the afternoon he'd come home to a sugary, sooty disaster. Charlie and Talvi had packed the last of Patti's possessions and moved her out of her dinky studio apartment in a single day, thanks to Chivanni's faerie magic. The boys would playfully bicker over who got to drive her to class, but since Charlie was working on the farm full time, Talvi seemed to always win. When she wasn't away at her classes or searching for a new car, her friends were doing their best to keep her as entertained as possible.

Annika frequently found herself getting ready for work to the sound of a saw running or a nail gun shooting or music blaring downstairs, if not all three. Each day when Talvi picked her up and brought her home, there was something new to see and admire. She wondered how badly behaved her husband could have been in his younger days, to have acquired the incredible skills he was showing off daily. James was in heaven, watching his ugly duckling of an inheritance blossom into a beautiful swan.

Things were finally falling into place for everyone under the roof. Patti was able to focus primarily on her classes, James was having record sales at the gallery, and Charlie was warming up to his new brother-in-law little by little over video games and discussions of the history of agriculture. Along with that, the band was also practicing three times a week, and sounding good enough that James had booked a couple gigs in May. Whatever time Charlie had after work and soccer was spent in the practice space above the garage, recording his drums for their new album. Considering how many new songs Annika had come up with, they had their work cut out for them.

Annika, on the other hand, had forty hours a week at the music store to deconstruct how she felt about her marriage while she re-stringed guitars or showed kids how to properly use a whammy bar. Even though she was caught up with James on her overdue bills, she still wanted money of her own without relying on her husband. She had always paid her way, and never expected to stay home and be taken care of like a pet, just because a man put a ring on her finger. If anything, she had always imagined that one day her music career would take off, and *she* would be the one keeping a gorgeous man for a pet. It kind of felt like that already, what with Talvi always arriving right on time to pick her up after work and then bringing her home to reveal something else improved around the house.

The third Sunday of the month was reserved exclusively for James, as it had always been. It was on the third Sunday in April that he and Annika stopped to have coffee and dessert at an outdoor café following a hair appointment, and then three hours of searching for one white men's blazer, size medium. Annika was convinced that it didn't exist, but she tried to be sympathetic just to humor James.

"You'll probably find one half price in three months," she said, sipping from her mug.

"If I wanted one in three months, I wouldn't have dragged your ass to every men's store downtown!" he snipped, rolling his eyes in an exaggerated way. "I wanted it three *hours* ago."

"You're a little cranky today," she teased. "What's the matter? Is Chivanni holding out on you?"

"What's that supposed to mean?" James said casually and began to dig in his bag for his cigarettes.

"Exactly what it sounded like," she said primly. She almost asked him for a smoke, but she was trying to follow Doctor Danny's orders. So far, she had done well, cutting back to just an occasional cigarette here and there. Today was the first time in weeks that she had indulged in junk food, and she was still feeling fantastic.

"He's not exactly my type," he said, looking away from her as he lit his cigarette.

"Oh please! I saw the way you jumped on him when . . . " Annika ended her sentence as soon as she saw James's confused expression. She wondered if he had any memory of the pixie dust incident, and was struggling to re-word her sentence when he cut in.

"Do you think just because he plays for my team that I'm interested? Is it because you're married, that you think you're the authority on relationships? Are you the official matchmaker of the house? You know in England they have a name for people like you . . . 'smug marrieds'," he said, and flicked the ash repeatedly, but it wasn't necessary as he'd only just lit his cigarette a moment ago. His tone of voice put her on edge. She may have felt fine physically, but she sensed she was coming down with an acute case of James. She braced herself accordingly.

"I'm not smug."

"I beg to differ," he went on, still needlessly flicking his cigarette butt every now and then. "It's insulting that you assume Chivanni and I are going to hook up just because we're both fairies."

"I don't think that at all!" she argued. "I have *eyes*, James. I can *see* the way you two look at each other."

"Oh give me a break," he sneered, ignoring her observation as he took another drag. "Besides, you're not supposed to nail your roommates. And I know you wish something would happen with Patti and Charlie, but she's just not into him like that. Even if something happened, what are you going to do when it doesn't work out and none of us can stand to be in the same room with each other? Either way you'll lose a friend, and you don't even stop to think how I feel, being innkeeper to all this potential drama. It rarely works out in the long term."

"And what exactly makes *you* an expert on relationships?" she insisted. "At least I've had boyfriends before. You just have hookups."

"I've had plenty of relationships, thank you very much!" he snapped back at her, sneering a little. "Oh my *god*, you are so closed-minded sometimes."

"What do you mean, I'm closed-minded?" Annika squealed in disbelief at what she was hearing. "I'm one of the most open-minded people I know!"

"Then you of all people would know that open relationships are just as valid as exclusive ones," he said defensively, flicking the ashes off his cigarette. "Look, I'm not trying to badmouth monogamy, but it's not for everyone, even though you think it is. And I'm definitely not going to take relationship advice from a gal who's only four months into her first marriage. Your new hubby's hot, and he's definitely not boring-ass vanilla like Danny was, but I still can't believe that you took yourself off of the market so fast. Portland has some of the best eye candy I've ever seen, next to Manhattan and Milan. You could've had a blast dating around after Danny, and instead you just got tied down to another guy. Or elf, I guess," he said, correcting himself. "But everyone knows that variety is the spice of life."

"It doesn't matter if you call it tied down or tied up . . . you can *definitely* have variety with the same person. Or elf," she said with a grin.

"Yeah, well, we all know how much elves like variety," James said with a snort, but Annika was not amused. She bit her lip and picked up her fork, digging into her slice of lemon meringue pie. James's words were not typically this harsh, and they had their fair share of fights over them, but she was determined that this would not be one of those times. She tried to distract herself with her dessert. It was tart and tangy, and the fluffy, sweet meringue dissolved slowly on her tongue. It was surprising how something so sweet could still not get rid of the sour taste his words had left in her mouth.

"Do you think people can change?" she asked after washing her pie down with a sip of coffee. "Let's say you met someone you really liked, and they didn't want an open relationship. Would you be exclusive with them? I mean, I know it depends on the person, but if you were used to sleeping with—"

"Seven people at the same time?" James interrupted, trying not to smile. "You want to know if I would ever miss something like *that*?"

"Well . . . yeah," said Annika with an embarrassed shrug. James wrinkled his nose a little, trying to come up with the perfect response. Then he rolled his eyes, because he realized that there was no perfect response for her.

"I think if I had a chapter like that in my life, it would take an awful lot for me to never want to read it again. It's friggin' *sexy*, and you shouldn't knock something until you try it. But that's just me," he said, and leaned forward to stub out his cigarette in the ash tray. "Personally, I would never get married to someone who wasn't willing to step out of their comfort zone and try new things. Isn't that the reason why you and Danny broke up? He wanted you to trade your guitar for a minivan, and spend every evening on the couch watching basketball. You don't even like sports, but you came to all of his games. How many of our shows did he come to, though? Like, *two*? And of all the art crawls at my gallery, he never came to a single one. I have to admit, when he gave you that engagement ring, I didn't think it would last, but it wasn't my place to say so."

James sat back in his chair and stretched his arms over his head, sighing contentedly before he went on.

"You know, what I like about Talvi is that he genuinely seems interested in being involved in your life. He takes the time to get to know your friends, and he helped me with my last show. Not to mention, he could have just written me a check to cover your unpaid bills, but the work he's putting into the house is worth a lot more."

"So what are you saying, exactly?" Annika asked. "That because my husband nailed some shingles on the roof that I should let him nail other chicks if that's what he wants?"

"No offense babe, but I don't think you have a clue what he wants," he said, and took a drink of his coffee.

She stuffed another large bite of pie into her mouth and was trying to decide whether or not to continue this conversation, when James hissed, "Oh my god, it's Jerry O.!" He turned his head away as two men walked out of the café and towards them.

"Cheerio?" she asked with a mouthful of meringue.

"No, *Jerry O.*! The model I met on that buying trip I took to Italy, remember? Oh my god, do you think he saw me?" he said very low on his breath.

Annika scanned her brain, trying to remember which exciting tale James was referring to. He had so many stories, after all. "Is he the one you met on the plane when you were still living in New York?"

"Yes!"

"Ah, *that* guy . . . " Annika said slowly as she recalled the story.

Jerry was model who had been doing a fashion show in Milan at the same time that James was meeting with an art dealer there a few years ago. He had the incredible luck to be seated in between what he called the 'knock-out twins' because they were named Jerry K. and Jerry O. For the entire flight they had talked about everything under the sun. They even invited James to the show, and then to the after party, but it was Jerry O. who had invited him to the after-after party. James had spent three incredible days and three passion-filled nights with Jerry O., and when he returned to America, it was everything he could do to wait three days before calling him; one of the few dating rules that he ever followed. Unfortunately, when James finally did call him, Jerry completely blew him off, crushing him like grapes at a winery.

"James Ferrari, is that you?" a full pair of lips uttered from a gorgeous, tan face. A tall man with dark layered hair was standing in front of them, and a shorter blond man stood beside him. The taller one was dressed in a sharp pinstripe suit while the blond was dressed much more comfortably in a graphic tee, distressed jeans, sandals, and trendy sunglasses. They were each holding a to-go tray of coffee.

"Well if it isn't Jerry O.," James said with a fake smile. "I haven't seen you in years."

"The last time I saw you, you were calling me 'Oh Jerry', not Jerry O.," he said, giving Annika a wink. She pretended that he was funny and forced a smile, wondering how often he used that line.

"Are you still living in New York, or do you live here now? You never struck me as a west coast kind of guy."

James tossed his tousled hair and glanced at Jerry's blond friend suspiciously, not bothering to stand up.

"I inherited an American Foursquare in Laurelhurst, and the property taxes are half the rent I was paying in the city, so it wasn't a tough decision," he said acting bored.

"That sounds really great. I'm happy for you," Jerry replied. There was an awkward silence until James decided to be courteous and ask Jerry what he was up to.

"We're doing a photo shoot down the street," Jerry replied. "And the last time we sent Lars on a coffee run, he screwed up my latte. So I snuck out to make sure he got it right this time." He gave his friend a playful jab in the ribs. The blond just rolled his eyes a little.

"Memorizing the way you like your latte is *not* part of my job description," he said. "My job is to make you look good, you pompous ass."

"That *is* a nice suit," James said, still looking at Lars curiously.

"Isn't it?" Jerry said, exuding an almost unbearable confidence. "Lars is a fabulous stylist. He's the one you should be complimenting. All I do is roll out of bed in the morning and brush my teeth. He does the rest. Just look at these cufflinks he found!"

Jerry thrust his wrist under James's nose, revealing a pale pink French cuff and a beautiful pink pearl cufflink.

"Nice work, Lars," Annika said with an approving smile. "I especially love the pink pinstripes. Very snazzy, yet subtle."

"Aren't they great?" Lars beamed. "You should see the other guys. We're doing a whole series on bringing color back into the office. We've got a two page spread in—"

"Look who's the pompous ass now? They'll see the magazine soon enough," Jerry interrupted. "Aren't we already running behind schedule?"

"Yeah, but you and your finicky almond milk skinny latte drinking—"

"Do you still have my number?" Jerry interrupted again, looking at James this time.

"I must have lost it in the move," he said coolly while he brought his frappe to his lips, but the model was unfazed by his tone of voice.

"Are you still working in the art scene? Do you have an extra card in that marvelous crocodile bag of yours? Oh wow, is that a Hermes?" he asked, taking a closer look. James seemed a little surprised, like he'd been ready to say 'no' until receiving the compliment on his beloved bag. He took his time locating a card and surprised Jerry by handing it to Lars, who grinned and slipped it into his back pocket.

"It was really great to run into you, James," Jerry said over his shoulder as they both turned to walk away. "I'll call you."

"I won't hold my breath," James sang facetiously under it. Annika noticed that his hand was trembling a little as he put another cigarette in his mouth and lit it.

"James! I can't believe that just happened!" she squeaked when the men disappeared around the corner.

"I can't believe he said he would call. He's got some nerve, that bitch," James said, taking a drag.

"He's really a piece of work, isn't he?" she agreed. She would have liked to call him something worse, but James seemed irritated enough as it was.

"A fucking Renoir," he muttered. He had lost all interest in his chocolate cheesecake. "I'm getting a box for this. I seem to have lost my appetite." He got up and left her alone with his things tucked underneath the table. She took another bite of pie when her phone started ringing.

"Hi Danny, how's it going?" she asked.

"Good, good. Hey, Ani, I was curious if you were feeling any better since the last time we talked. I've been wondering about ya," he said affectionately.

"I've been fine," she assured him. "Great, actually. I haven't gotten sick since right before I saw you. It turns out that my body can't handle meat anymore."

"Oh, I know better than that," he laughed over the phone.

"Danny!"

"I'm sorry, I couldn't help it," he said, sounding upbeat. "But I won't tell Finnish. Legally, I can't. You and I have doctor-patient confidentiality."

"Very cute," she said, trying to make her disapproval clear over the phone, but the smile on her face made it impossible.

"So I was wondering if you would be interested in coming back to the hospital for a few more tests. I figured since this is a sort of personal side project, I'd take care of the bills."

"Well, that depends on how much you need to poke and prod me," came her playful reply.

"Is this the part where I make another dick joke and you yell at me? Because I feel like you're setting me up for one."

"You know me too well," she sighed, and leaned back in her chair. "I don't mind helping you save the world, but my schedule's pretty busy with work and practice and recording."

"Yeah, Charlie mentioned that you guys have been working really hard on the new album. I can't wait to hear it when it's done. Do I still get an auto-graphed copy, since I know the band?"

"Of course you do," she said, her voice cracking as a lump caught in her throat. She had forgotten what a sweetheart he could be.

"Alright, well, whenever you have time for me, I'll be here," he said hesitantly. "Bye, Ani."

She ended the call and was about to check her calendar on her phone, when it rang again.

"Hey Patti Cake. What's up?" she answered. There was an unusually long pause.

"How far away from home are you?" asked a man whose voice she didn't recognize.

"Uh, we're downtown having dessert," she said, trying to figure out who she was talking to.

"And what are you having, besides *me* as soon as you get home?" asked the seductive voice through the receiver. Annika felt her heart flutter as she recognized it was Talvi. His voice had such a strange timbre to it, but then again, she'd never spoken to him on a phone before.

"Lemon meringue," she giggled. "It's really good too."

"Mmm, I absolutely adore lemon meringue," he sighed wistfully. "Bring me a slice, would you? I think I'll have myself a little picnic when you come home."

"You're going to have a picnic by yourself?" she asked, not seeing where the conversation was going. "I don't get it."

"Oh, you most certainly *will* get it. You're going to make a marvelous table for me to dine on. How soon will you be home?"

"Twenty minutes, give or take a few. I think James is finally sick of shopping," she said, grinning.

"Well I'm sick of waiting. You're neglecting your wifely duties. *Tsk tsk tsk*," he chided. "I've been working so *very* hard while you've been away. I think it's time for something more relaxing. When you come home, you can sit on my lap and tell me all about your day." He stopped to laugh wickedly.

"You are terrible, do you know that?" she squealed into the phone.

"I don't think 'terrible' is the word I would have chosen, but as long as the message is clear," he crooned, and paused again. "Mmm . . . you really must come home *now*. Better bring an entire pie with you. I'm not certain if one slice will satisfy my appetite. I'll likely want a second or third helping."

"You've made your point; you don't have to tell me twice. Here comes James. I'm going to tell him we need to leave right now, okay?"

"Hurry along then. Don't keep me waiting any more than I already have been."

She grinned and hung up her phone as James took his seat across from her and boxed up his cheesecake in silence, but before she could tell him they needed to leave, his phone rang. It was a number with an area code that he didn't recognize, so he refused to answer. But something inside Annika's head told her to answer it. Maybe it was that comment Talvi had made about things happening in threes, but either way, she grabbed the phone out of curiosity.

"Hello?" she answered, and James mouthed 'who is it?'

"Oh, is this Annika?" said another male voice that she didn't recognize.

"Yeah, who's this?"

"It's Jerry; we just met five minutes ago. I forgot my phone back at the photo shoot, but I told James I would call, so I'm using Lars' phone," he said cheerfully.

"Okay, well, I'll let him know that you called, Jerry. He went to wash his hands," she said, and James turned white as a ghost as he realized who she was talking to. His eyes nearly fell out of his head.

"Can you let him know that the reason I was calling is because I got to thinking how rude of me it was not to invite you both over here. We're barely a block away. Are you interested in swinging by for a few minutes for a sneak preview?"

"Wow, Jerry, how nice of you to offer. Why don't you see if James is interested? He just came back to the table," she said, and handed him the phone. James was shaking his head and mouthing a very clear 'NO!', but she just set his phone down on his to go box and mouthed a very clear 'grow a pair', and went inside to buy that lemon meringue pie. It seemed fair payback for James's rotten attitude earlier.

When Annika came back, he looked determined.

"We're going to stop by the photo shoot just long enough for me to say something witty and mean, and then we can leave," he informed her.

"So you don't think it will take too long, do you?" asked Annika as they gathered their bags and started walking down the block. "I have a hot date waiting at home for me."

James stiffened up a little.

"Your hot date can wait. I might never have this opportunity again," he said as they reached the building. They walked up the stairs and through the door, and found themselves in an empty office. It was the epitome of generic, between the cubicles and the water cooler, and even the coffee break room off to one side. There was a hubbub of activity towards the back, where the executive offices were located. A spectacular view met them in the corner office, and it wasn't the Portland skyline. A group of men were joking with each other and the photographer had stopped for a smoke break.

"Hey, Max," a man in red pants and a large pair of tinted sunglasses said disapprovingly to the photographer, "the sign said no smoking."

"For what they charged you to rent this space, Robbie, they can kiss my black ass," Max replied, taking a drag as he adjusted a lighting umbrella. All of them turned and looked at James and Annika as they peeked into the office.

"Hi guys," Jerry said, and waved them over.

"Oh, I wasn't ready for this," Annika hissed to James, clutching her shopping bag a little tighter as she surveyed the fine specimens surrounding her.

"You're telling *me*," James hissed back.

"I'm impressed that you found us inside this maze of cubicles," Lars said proudly. "Don't the boys look great? We have this concept of pastels that you can wear year round, so we have the four men representing the four seasons. Jerry is pink for spring, and Heath is the one in green. He's summer. Ricky's rockin' the yellow for autumn, and Chip makes a wonderful winter with those icy blue eyes," he said as he proudly motioned towards the pale blond man in blue.

"I don't know, Lars," said Robbie, taking off his sunglasses with a dramatic flair. "The men look smashing, but it seems a smidge on the tame side. I hate to even say the word, but contrived is coming to mind."

"How else are you going to splash up the office?" Lars said. His feelings didn't seem harmed in the slightest. "I've worked a cube job before. The only fun thing about that kind of work is the office fling you're eventually going to have."

"An office fling? Now that sounds like the perfect antidote for this setting. You know what we really need at this sausage party is a taco stand, and there's a taco standing right there," Robbie said, looking straight at Annika. His eyes immediately went down to her feet, which were adorned by her infamous red-feathered Manolo's. "What have you got in those bags, honey?"

"Huh? *Me?*" she asked in disbelief. "You can't be serious." She looked around, but she was the only woman in the room.

"Why not? You're pretty enough," argued Robbie. "What's in the bags?"

"Just some stuff I picked up to wear at my band's next gig," Annika said as she pulled a black sundress and some odds and ends from the bags. "But I'm too short! I can't do this. Don't you have to be like, six feet tall to model?" she protested, trying to escape Robbie's plan.

"Not if you're a rock star doing a cameo for me. What's the name of your band?" Annika told him and he shrugged. "Well, I've never heard of your group, so I guess you need to work on your publicity, don't you?" he said, guiding her to sit down for a crash course in hair and makeup.

"Now, some of the best shoots are improv, but I'm not making any promises, sweetie," he said with a dismissive wave of his hand as he grew more excited. "And that little black dress will be perfect. Lars! Get her a red tie! As soon as you're ready, I'll have you sit on the desk, like you're the boss lady, and your naughty office boys have been up to some no good hijinks behind your back. No one will give a shit how short you are. They'll be looking at the boys. And your gorgeous shoes."

Annika looked at James, who just smiled and shrugged.

"You better call Talvi and let him know we'll be late," she said to him before ducking into a vacant cubicle to change clothes. "He was expecting me."

"Oh, I'm sorry, did you have an appointment?" Robbie asked.

"Well, an appointment with my husband, but I'm sure I can reschedule," she grinned in excitement as she slipped into her new dress. When she came out she was rushed to a little chair and attacked by two men, one with hairspray and a comb, and one with a toolbox of makeup and brushes.

"How strange . . . your new husband seemed downright annoyed that you were blowing him off to be draped in next season's finest," James said as he walked over to where Annika was sitting. "If he wasn't such a babe, I don't think I'd tolerate his moody bullshit."

"Yeah, but that's the nice thing about being so moody; he'll get over it," she said in between applications of lip liner, gloss and eye shadow. "He always does . . . just wait and see."

"Alright, you're done," the man with the soft brushes said, and released Annika. Robbie grabbed her hand and brought her over to the desk.

"Oh my god, I can just see it now," he said, instructing them with animated hand movements. "Seriously, I need you four to be very naughty office boys! Give me some guilty looks, but not too guilty. You've been caught doing something wrong, and she's threatening to fire one of you, but she doesn't know which one to choose."

"Caught doing what?" Heath asked. "I don't know how guilty to look."

"Stealing office supplies?" Jerry suggested, making the other three handsome men snicker. Lars rolled his eyes at Jerry, but then James spoke up.

"No one wants to see guilty office boys stealing pens. Lars has put some serious work into their wardrobe; they have to look serious. And Annika is a serious musician," James pondered out loud, and his brown eyes twinkled a little.

"Max, weren't you saying that she and I need some publicity? What if we want to hire a PR company to promote the band? What if these fellas are new interns at the firm, and they're all trying to convince her why they're the best man for the job?"

"That's perfect!" exclaimed Lars and Robbie simultaneously, and Max instructed the men to do their darnedest at getting that position while he snapped photos. Her interns all gathered around some poor executive's desk and began to make their pitches to her. She took Jerry's tie in her hand and admonished him as the camera shutters clicked and snapped nonstop.

"Hey, this is kinda fun!" Annika said, and raised an eyebrow at Chip. She turned one way, and then the other, as the men pleaded around her, "Pick me, Annika! Pick me!"

When she turned her head back to Jerry, his nose was inches from hers.

"I'll get your foot in the door if you make sure James calls me," he hissed, shooting her a salacious smirk. She thumbed the soft silk necktie as she wondered about his Italian business trip with James. Surely he must have had some redeeming qualities if James had fallen so hard for the guy. She gripped his tie a little tighter.

"What's your business plan?" she demanded, making Jerry grin even wider.

"You know how good James is at pushing people's buttons?"

"Yeah?" she asked. "I'm listening."

"Well, I am even better at pulling strings."

"Then you're hired," she said, and let go of his tie.

CHAPTER 24
School Days

When Annika and James finally returned home a couple hours later, she looked out the living room window to see her husband in the backyard, soaking wet. Freshly cut grass was stuck to his wet jeans and wet skin, and he was dragging the garden hose over to one side of the garage. She saw Patti walking around the other side of the garage with a massive water gun in her hands. She tip toed over to the corner and shot him in the side of his head, and he lifted the hose, placing his thumb over the water to drench her shorts and t-shirt. She turned to run, but slipped on the wet lawn. He was at her side instantly, and he put one bare foot over the gun before she could lift it, holding the hose away from her. He appeared to ask her something, and she shook her head. He sprayed her again and as she scrambled to get up, he swiftly tackled her. He gathered a handful of grass and tried stuffing it in her mouth, but she struggled and kicked. With one arm, she grabbed the hose and sprayed him in the face until his hair was soaking and dripping.

"I surrender!" he yelled, and she stopped shooting him with water just long enough for him to snatch the hose away from her and cover her with more grass. "Sorry, Patti Cake, my fingers were crossed!"

Annika watched them frolic for a little longer, and came outside after taking off her red-feathered shoes and leaving them in a safe place.

"Hey, you're home!" Patti cried from under Talvi as she narrowly escaped another mouthful of grass. "Did you have fun with all those hot models?"

"Yeah, but it looks like you're having just as much fun," she said, trying not to look as pissed as she felt seeing her husband crouched on top of her best friend in the back yard.

"You missed out on a good time," he said, looking up at her with an aloof expression. He ran his hands through his hair to rid it of excess water and finally climbed off of Patti.

"Well I didn't forget that pie you wanted," she said with a little smile, but Talvi merely shrugged.

"You may as well just put it in the icebox. I'm not in the mood for it anymore," he said, turning his attention to the gangly girl beside him. "Patti Cake, do you mind rinsing me off? I wouldn't want to see James's face if we came inside as filthy as we are." Annika watched as Patti ran the water over his tan shoulders and down his chest while he turned around in a slow circle. It seemed that a month and a half of him being fed Annika's omelets, Patti's pancakes, and Chivanni's cheesy potato soup had finally started to fill him out to his normal weight. His cheeks were no longer hollow, his face no longer gaunt, and his muscles were lean and strong from all the climbing around on the roof and carrying around buckets of plaster and packages of shingles. Annika sat there like a third wheel as Patti gently rinsed his arms and hands, and then handed him the hose so he could do the same to her.

"Would you be a good little wife and at least fetch us some dry towels, or is that too much to ask of you?" he asked Annika. Taken aback by his coldness, she turned around and discovered Charlie and Chivanni had beaten her to the task. They came outside with their hair still wet and two towels in each of their arms.

"Man, you guys missed out!" Charlie said, smiling hugely at his sister and James. "That was one awesome water fight!"

"I think the only one who missed out on anything today was me," James lamented, watching from the doorstep. "Mrs. Marinossian was so busy playing dress up with an office full of beautiful boys, that I didn't even get a chance to tell Jerry where he can stick the business card I gave him."

"Who's Jerry?" Chivanni asked, and handed Talvi a towel.

"Who's Jerry?" Charlie repeated. "You've been living here how long and you haven't heard about—"

"Shut up Charlie," James said quickly. "He's not worth the breath it takes to say his name."

"Do you know when the magazine comes out?" Patti asked. "I wanna see what all the fuss was over!"

"Yes, I'm quite curious myself," Talvi said with a curious look. "I'd like to see just what it was that held your attention so enrapt this afternoon."

"I'm sorry I didn't come home when I said I would, sweetie," Annika said, forcing a smile. "I didn't think it would be a big deal. I mean, we do live together and all."

"No, I understand very well," he said nonchalantly. "I sincerely hope you enjoyed yourself."

One morning after Talvi had dropped Annika off at work, Patti approached him where he lay on the couch with a cigarette, blowing smoke rings.

"Any big plans today, Talvi?"

"Hmmm . . . " he hummed in response. "I believe I'm officially out of things to repair in this house. Perhaps I'll take a nap after I take you to campus. Or I might take my bow to the park across the street. I'm terribly out of practice."

"Do you, um, do you feel like keeping me awake in art history class today?" she stammered. "I'm going to fail the course if I don't stop falling asleep during the lectures." He looked up from the sofa, deeply interested in the prospect of leaving the house to do something new and different and above all, fun.

"And, um, if you wanted, I have figure drawing class afterwards, if you wanted to hang out and do some sketching."

"Your professors won't mind me sitting in on your classes?" he asked. He didn't want her to get into any trouble, but he was greatly intrigued at Patti's proposition.

"No, art history's a huge lecture class; I doubt anyone would even notice you, let alone care that you were there," Patti said with a hopeful smile. "It's barely light enough in the room to take notes. I guess that's why I keep dozing off." She now had Talvi's full attention.

"Your drawing class is likely much smaller though, isn't it? Surely your professor would notice me there."

"Well, yeah, but um, I sorta already asked her if it would be okay if you came with me, and she said it was," she said, her cheeks growing slightly warmer and rosier. "I know you're an artist too, so I thought you'd like coming to school with me."

Talvi was on his feet in an instant, and together, he and Patti hurried to pack themselves lunch and headed out the door.

They got to class early, although Patti couldn't have been more wrong about no one noticing Talvi joining her in the huge lecture hall. While the burnt-out professor seemed completely unaware of the new student as he dimmed the lights and pulled down a projector screen, there were whispers and constant glances from other students in the lecture hall, all generated by this very tall and handsome man that Patti Kaeke had brought with her. Normally she sat alone in the back, but Talvi had insisted that if she wanted to learn anything, sitting towards the front was the only way to go. Patti listened astutely and took numerous notes. He didn't have to jab her in the ribs once to keep her from falling asleep, and afterwards he carried her backpack for her while she clutched her oversized pads of drawing paper against her chest, strolling leisurely with her as they walked to a different building.

She led him down a hallway on the second floor to a large classroom filled with twenty or so drawing tables. The room was already half full with other students, but they managed to find two desks beside each other, and Patti opened a box with many different colored charcoals and conté crayons, and handed him one of the large tablets of paper. The rest of the class filed in quickly after that, and then in walked a short, round woman with wiry hair pulled into a loose bun on top of her head. She plopped a notebook on a table in the corner and waddled over to Patti, and all the other eyes in the classroom followed right along as she stepped up beside the newcomer.

"This must be that friend of yours from out of town," she said cheerfully, craning her chubby face upwards at him. "That's great that you came in today . . . "

"His name's Talvi," Patti piped up.

"Talvi, eh?" The woman repeated, sounding the name out slowly. "Is that Finnish?"

"Why yes, yes it is," he replied, flashing his most charming smile while he ran his fingers through his wild hair. "I do appreciate you allowing me to sit in on your class."

"Well, I'm glad you could make it, Talvi. I'm Professor De la Chauvignerie," she said, emphasizing her last name with an exaggerated French accent, "but we're pretty informal here . . . just call me Dee."

"Parlez-vous la langue, ou seulement votre français de nom est?" he asked.

Professor Dee's already squinty eyes became even tinier slits in her face as she clapped her hands in gleeful approval. "Oh, you are just too much, Talvi! I don't speak a lick of French."

The very rotund professor barely squeezed between their two tables before scuttling over to a large podium in the center of the room. She hoisted up one foot with great effort, even though the podium was only raised perhaps one foot from the floor. She addressed the class for a few minutes, instructing them to look at their paper as little as possible, and to draw as large as possible, and to think in circles rather than lines.

"What are we drawing?" Talvi hissed to Patti, as he realized no one had picked up their pencils and charcoals yet. Just then the door opened one more time and a dark blonde woman in a robe and flip flops stepped in, shutting the door tightly behind her.

"Alright, everyone," Professor Dee said to the blonde as they traded places on the podium. "Let's start with the usual warm up. Ten one minute drawings . . . and begin!" The woman slipped off her shoes and robe and she went right into a pose, arching her body beautifully. While Patti set straight to work trying to accurately draw their model, the girls in the room kept sneaking glances at her handsome guest, whispering under the quiet music that came from the radio on Professor Dee's desk. The corner of Talvi's mouth twitched slightly as he tried to ignore them and instead followed the curves of the model's body, transferring them into simple contours with his bit of charcoal. The time passed by leisurely, and after the warm up, they worked on an hour long pose. At the end of that hour, Professor Dee had the class pin up their drawings for critiquing.

"Have you had formal instruction, Talvi?" she asked, after examining his drawings. "These are simply lovely!"

"Not at university level, but I have years of experience capturing the female form," he replied dauntlessly. He spoke with such a confidence that the men in the room envied him, and the women in the room envied Patti. There was a universal hum of approval, however, when Professor Dee invited him to join her class for the rest of the semester.

After class, he found a sunny spot in the grass to have lunch while Patti stayed after to talk to Professor Dee about her grades. When she came back outside to meet Talvi, he had been joined by a few of her female classmates. They looked up at her, and smiled.

"We're in the same art history class, aren't we, Patti?" one girl asked.

"We started a study group a few weeks ago so that none of us have to sit through a repeat next semester," said another.

"Maybe you'd like to join?" asked the first girl.

"Um . . . " Patti said, wondering why they were asking her, especially when she had little to offer. She didn't have decent notes to study from because she was indeed asleep at the back of the class. And the only reason she knew half of their names was from paying attention during roll call. But then she looked down at Talvi's grin and understood immediately.

"When are you meeting next?" he asked.

"We're getting together Wednesday night at seven, at the coffee shop down the street."

"That sounds lovely. We'll see you then, ladies," Talvi answered for Patti. She watched as the small group of girls drifted away. After they were out of earshot, Talvi reached into his pocket, pulling out a few slips of paper, each with a string of numbers and corresponding names.

"I got you their phone numbers," he winked, unable to hide his egotistical smile. "You have no excuse not to meet with them Wednesday evening."

"I don't think that's why they gave you their phone numbers," Patti said as she took a bite of peanut butter and banana sandwich. "Did you see how soon they left when I showed up? I chased them away with my geekiness. They only asked me to join their stupid group because they wanna see more of you."

"So what if that's the only reason they asked you?" Talvi replied. "I clearly heard you say this morning that you were in danger of failing your art history examination. Aren't you more concerned with passing the course and becoming Professor Patti Cake?"

"Well of course I want to pass, but they don't even like me. They're so stuck up."

"Perhaps they just want what you have, and they're jealous," Talvi suggested. "They all wish they had your talent, and one of them envies your haircut."

"My haircut?" Patti said, squinting in disbelief. "It's only chopped up like this because I cut it myself when I'm bored at two in the morning."

"Is that how you get it to look like that? How positively charming," he said sincerely, and swatted at her blunt bob, causing her to blush. She began humming to herself while she cut geometric shapes out of her orange peel with her X-acto blade. This was the kind of girl who had a wealth of talent wrapped in a blanket of self-doubt, a girl who just needed a good boost of self-confidence from within, a girl who tripped up the stairs not because her feet were too big, but because she wasn't confident enough to walk with her head held high enough to see where she was going.

Talvi smiled softly to himself, watching her form the geometric sections into the shape of a horse. What he felt for her was tender, it was genuine, much like the adoration he held for his sisters and his female friends back home. But then his demeanor shifted, and a hesitation lingered in his tone.

"I don't know how to say this correctly . . . but it's been on my mind ever since you moved in with us." Patti shoved a piece of orange into her mouth, not knowing why he was looking at her so intently. "Even though we haven't known each other very long, I care about you a lot. I don't want to see you failing art history, or at becoming a professor. Or anything, really," he added as an afterthought. "We're keeping that date with them Wednesday evening."

"Alright," Patti said, and smiled softly.

After Talvi's first day of school, the two of them became nearly inseparable, whether at class or in between classes, sitting on the lawn and reviewing lecture notes for the final exam, which was only a few weeks away. Patti was nervous, having slept through a majority of her art history class, but she did end up joining the study group with Talvi. It turned out to be another one of his areas of expertise, as he helped make up questions that the students might be asked on their test, and gave them clues when they struggled for the answers. Apparently Patti wasn't the only one who would have benefited more by bringing a pillow to lectures rather than a highlighter and sharp pencils. There were quite a few students that were trying to study just as hard, and every once in a while, Talvi would offer up a bit of information that wasn't found anywhere in their textbooks, trying to help them understand what Van Gogh's living conditions were like at the time, and how that might have influenced him to paint so many sunflowers. When someone would make a comment like, 'How could you possibly know that?' he would just shrug, smile his mysterious smile and take a sip of his tea.

Right around the same time that her husband had started attending drawing classes, Annika started to notice him drawing away from her. Half of the afternoons that she came home from the music shop, he would kiss her on the head and go for a long walk or a drive by himself. Sometimes he didn't come home until dinnertime. Sometimes he walked in the door with his bow, and sometimes he walked in the door with his bow and a new ticket given for yet another violation. He was starting to collect them the way James collected business contacts. He'd been cited repeatedly for shooting in undesignated areas of the park, for speeding, for parking in non-parking zones, for insubordination to the police. Immediately following the first gig that the band had played in nearly a year, Talvi got arrested by an undercover cop for buying drinks for all of his fellow study group members, some of whom were minors. Although it had been a grand headache to pay the fines for all of his outstanding bench warrants before getting him out of jail, there was no better public relations strategy for the band than having the lead singer's husband escorted out of the club in handcuffs, laughing wickedly as he ordered another round of drinks on his way out the door, including ones for the officers. Even the fliers that James had so painstakingly created were no match for Talvi's inherent and effortless notoriety, which was probably the reason why he was the one to bail Talvi out that night, instead of Annika.

It wasn't enough that Talvi was going to class with her closest female friend, or that he and James had arranged that Patti's help in painting the house would be payment for her share of the rent through autumn, which freed her from having to find a job anytime soon. Annika even felt herself get annoyed when Patti had decided to set up her little painting studio in an empty corner of their practice space. It had been Annika's territory for five years, and now there was a new girl on the block. The boys all loved it, though, and in between breaks they would come over to see what she had created while listening to them play. Annika tried to be supportive, but she was clueless regarding their jargon about composition, design and the use of negative space that James, Chivanni, and Talvi tossed back and forth like a soccer ball during their critiques. Charlie didn't know the jargon either, but he knew that he liked what Patti painted.

Annika felt like she was the only one noticing that Talvi and Patti were becoming a bit more than friends. To her, it seemed he found any excuse to bat at her blunt black bob, give her hugs, or rest an arm on her shoulder as though she were his sidekick.

When Annika asked James what he thought about them spending so much time together, he didn't even bother looking up from his laptop when he informed her for the millionth time that he thought she was either being a stupid bitch or a crazy bitch, depending on the day. Oddly enough, as much as he loved to gossip, James wouldn't even entertain Annika's conspiracies for one second.

CHAPTER 25
A Matter of Time

"I'm trying to figure out how to work this sample into the song. I think I need to slow it down even more. I know I can do it if you just give me a minute." James insisted, which Charlie took as the perfect excuse for a snack break since the three of them had already been practicing for an hour. He went into the house while Annika pulled her long red hair into a ponytail and played the now familiar chords over and over through two different pedals lying on the floor. She didn't like to take breaks very often to begin with, and lately, she didn't take them at all, except to use the bathroom. She picked out the melody on her guitar, one of the songs that had been playing over and over in her mind until she finally had the guts to work on it with James and Charlie. It was so different from her previous work, she was afraid that they wouldn't like it. James played a harmony on his keyboard and ran it through the sampler, turning a few knobs on his mixer.

"That's pretty good," said Annika. "But try it a little slower. Do you think you could you draw out the notes even *more*?"

"You mean like this?" James asked, playing them again with much more deliberation. Annika nodded and played the melody again for him.

"Yeah, I like that a lot!" James gushed, genuinely excited. "It's a really different direction . . . kind of depressing, really, but it sounds more, hmm, more *authentic* than anything else you've come up with before. I know you don't have any words yet, but how do you like this for the chorus?" he asked. A few turns of his blinky knobs and switches, and a new sound met Annika's ears.

"Uh, it sounds friggin' awesome," she smiled, feeling just as inspired as James to hear the song flesh out a little. "But I can't hit all the notes I want to." She held her left hand out, flexing her fingers. Her hand and wrist had been aching on and off for the past few weeks, and at first she thought it was from being out of practice. But it should have gone away by now. She pushed the idea of carpal tunnel syndrome out of her head and came up with another solution.

"I think I'll switch to bass and get another guitarist for the sound I want," she admitted as she took off her guitar and set it on its stand.

"What?" James asked. He looked totally puzzled. "You mean, like right now?"

"Yep," Annika chirped back. "I'll be back in a little bit."

She trotted down the driveway, burst through the kitchen entrance, and called out her husband's name.

"Up here!" he chimed back. Annika bounded up the stairs to find him in Patti's room, sitting beside her in front of her computer. Patti held a box of candy in one hand and was pointing at the screen with her other while Talvi was typing, although very slowly.

"Look love, I'm writing my very first eeeee-mail!" he said proudly. "Patti Cake helped me access my electric mailbox and I had a letter from Finn waiting for me. He says that I'm to be an uncle a third time, and one of the mares is with foal and Ghassan is to blame," he let out a devilish howl of delight and pumped a fist into the air before adding, "Atta boy, Ghassan! I wonder who will be next to be put in the family way? These sort of things tend to happen in threes, you know. That's why it's such a magical number." Patti turned around and the girls shared a grin while Talvi continued to write, striking one key at a time. It was pretty adorable, that someone so handy with a hammer around the house could barely hammer out a sentence on a keyboard.

"I suppose you've never used the internet before, have you?" Annika asked. "Or computers?"

"This is all still relatively new to me," Talvi said, still focused on the screen and keyboard before him. "I tried utilizing typewriters for a time, but the damn things were so bloody heavy, and there was always all that ribbon to fuss with. Paper and ink have never gone out of style, and it travels quite well as far as I'm concerned." He turned to Patti with his mouth open wide and she tossed in a piece of black licorice.

"Do you want some?" she offered Annika, but Annika wrinkled her nose.

"Eww, no way. When it comes to black licorice, I think there are two types of people in the world; those who love it or those who hate it. I don't know anyone who is on the fence about it."

"You really dislike it that much?" Talvi asked as he turned around. Annika nodded her head.

"Yep. I won't even kiss you for the rest of the night, unless it's on the cheek. I only like the red kind."

"Well then, we are a perfect match, aren't we?" he mused, gazing at the monitor. "I don't much care for the red version. It's too sweet for my taste."

"Where's Chivanni?" she asked, looking around the room. "I haven't seen him in a while."

"He's hiding," Patti said, sharing an embarrassed glance with Talvi. "We were trying to clean up around here while you guys were practicing. It turns out he's afraid of the vacuum cleaner."

"Seriously?" Annika asked with a laugh of disbelief.

"Oh yeah," Patti said with a nod. "He's just as neurotic about vacuum cleaners as Jill's dog is, so we stopped cleaning and switched to something a little quieter." She turned to watch Talvi tap the keyboard, and shook her head at how slow he was.

"Did you have any plans after you finish your email?" Annika asked him.

"I thought I might get Patti started cutting some of the wood for another project I've thought up," he replied, still mesmerized at the letter he was magically composing on the screen.

"You think *I'm* going to use power tools without seriously maiming myself?" Patti joked with a hearty laugh, and Annika could see her tongue was black too. "I know you can fix burns and small cuts, but I don't think you can bring back the dead, can you?"

He turned away from the computer screen and smiled softly at her.

"No, I certainly cannot. I've only seen it happen once in my entire life, and I'd rather not see it happen again."

"No way, really?" she exclaimed, sounding completely gullible. "Who did it? Was it someone you know?"

"Yes, it was a friend of mine and Annika's, actually. He brought my twin sister back to life in front of our very eyes."

"Oh my gosh! Is he a doctor?"

"No, he's a vampire." He said this as if he was telling her that Talvi's sister

243

was an accountant. It was respectable, but not very fascinating. "And now Yuri is one as well."

"Are you serious?" Patti asked in disbelief, but Talvi only smiled wide.

"Not at all, you silly girl. Are you mad? Of course he's a doctor," he replied, and mussed her hair before winking at Annika.

"Was there something you wanted, love?"

"Yeah," she said, ignoring how comfortable he seemed with Patti. "I was wondering if you'd indulge us with your musical talents. We need someone to play guitar so that I can focus on my bass lines. I kinda hate to admit it, but honestly, you're better than I am. I feel really dumb for not asking you to play with us weeks ago."

Talvi was surprised yet flattered by her query. Was it some kind of peace offering for the way she'd been behaving lately? Did she really mean it? She seemed like she did.

"I don't want to be intrusive," he said politely.

Annika knew better . . . she knew how much he would love a chance to show off to her and her friends. It wasn't until Patti urged him along with Annika that he agreed to join in. Under their supervision, he finished his message and clicked 'send'.

"What happened to my letter?" he demanded when it disappeared from the screen.

"It's in your brother's mailbox now," Patti explained. "See, this little box says 'message sent'. That means it went through just fine."

"That's it?" he asked, unsure if he should believe her or not. "That's all there is to it?"

"Aw, sweetie, you're officially a twenty-first century elf," Annika said, kissing him on the cheek. "Now come on; I know you'd rather play guitar than learn how to type."

Needing no further convincing, he walked with the girls down the steps to the kitchen, where Charlie joined up with them as they made their way back to the practice space above the garage. Patti curled up on an overstuffed sectional sofa as Annika ushered Talvi to join them, motioning towards the black guitar she'd been playing only a little while ago. Talvi took a moment to regard the handsome instrument, and he imagined that the guitar regarded him as well.

"So I guess this is the guitarist you were talking about," James remarked from behind the keyboard. "Is he any good?"

"Am I any good?" he repeated with an arrogant grin. "I play quite a bit back home, though I've never played an electric guitar before."

"Well, there's a first time for everything," she told him as she plugged in her bass as she lifted the strap over her head. She thought for sure he would have had plenty of opportunities, being as old as he was. "It's already tuned."

"You've seriously never, *ever* played an electric guitar before?" Charlie asked, grinning as he and James looked on in anticipation.

"I always wanted to, ever since I saw Led Zeppelin play at Earl's Court back in '75. Badra's beard, that was an amazing experience. All five shows were sold out, and the energy in the crowd was phenomenal. When they performed Kashmir, I thought I had died of happiness and entered the afterworld."

Charlie's jaw dropped, and the drumstick he'd been twirling fell to the floor. Led Zeppelin was his favorite band ever.

Talvi lifted the black guitar from its stand, looking it over with an air of excitement before he adjusted the shoulder strap to accommodate his longer arms and torso.

"The strings are considerably thinner," he observed.

"You must be pretty good, if Annika's letting you even breathe on her Gibson, let alone play it," Charlie said, crawling on the floor to retrieve his drumstick. "I'll bet if she had her own roadies, she still wouldn't let them come near it. Or her Melody Maker. Or her P-bass, for that matter." He pointed at a cherry and black guitar, and a cream and tortoiseshell bass that Annika was now tuning.

"Why is that?"

"She inherited those from our grandpa when he died," Charlie said. "He was a studio musician way back in the day . . . played with a whole shitload of famous people. He always had the best stories to tell us when we were kids. He left me enough money to buy these killer drums, but those guitars are worth a helluva lot more. A 1960 Les Paul just like hers sold at an auction for about a third of what this house is worth, and hers is a '59."

"Then I'm extremely flattered and somewhat apprehensive about this," Talvi replied, looking at the gleaming black instrument in his possession. "Perhaps this isn't the best idea." He had no idea what a Melody Maker or a P-Bass were, besides highly desirable.

"It's okay babe, you won't hurt her," she said as she watched him. "Just be nice to Black Beauty, and she'll treat you real good."

"How adorable . . . you named your guitar after the pretty pony?" he teased. "I'd expect no less from a bird like you."

"I didn't pick that name. This series of Gibsons are called Black Beauties," Annika replied, smirking at the one who had taught her best. "It's just a nickname for the style. So, whenever you're ready . . . *giddy up!*" The anticipation was killing her. It was killing Patti and James and Charlie, too. They all looked on while Talvi zipped through a few scales, then stopped.

"My gods," he said, looking dumbfound.

"What's wrong?" James asked.

"Nothing's wrong; this sounds bloody *brilliant!*" The others laughed and settled back into place while Talvi got better acquainted with his pretty pony and played a Led Zeppelin tune.

"Ready to try something new? Do you want a chord structure?" Annika asked him.

"That won't be necessary," he said. "I can pick it up as we go along." James played the intro that he had come up with not too long ago, and then Charlie came in on the drums, playing a steady trip-hop beat. Annika waited for the right moment, and then picked out a bass line that had been hanging out in her head as long as the melody had been.

She watched her husband curiously, practically seeing the wheels in his head spinning, grasping ahold of the melodies and harmonies with uncanny ability, like he already knew the song by heart. He looked intensely at her, piercing with his eyes, and suddenly she suspected that he was inside of her head. He smiled, and nodded his head slightly, confirming that she was indeed right, that he had read her mind and she had read his.

She began to understand that he was reading all of their minds, and the fact that he had never played an electric guitar before seemed of no consequence. He was able to take in all of the directions that James, Annika and Charlie were going, and then fuse them together with the underlying chords. His long fingers reached notes that Annika never could have; his inhuman capabilities reached a range that would have given Jimmy Hendrix a run for his money.

Talvi's eyes fixated on Annika's once more, as they brought the song to the next wordless verse. The two of them gazed at each other while their left hands glided up and down the frets and their right hands picked out every note. Even with their feet securely on the ground, Annika felt like they were dancing in perfect sync with each other. It was the first time in a long time that she felt they were genuinely operating as two parts of one entity. And after months of writer's block, lyrics did indeed come out of the woodwork, exactly as her husband had promised. They couldn't have been better planned out than if they had been written down on paper in front of her, but they were only in her mind. The eerie incantation drifted to her lips just in time for her to step up to the microphone and sing:

Thought I could handle it, this kind of emotion,
Then my lust got in the way
I knew your arrival would set in motion,
Things which I did not dare to say
You know I tried to
Resist you
But when you looked at me
Like lovers do
Oh, I knew . . . it was only a matter of time.
I never thought I could feel such devotion,
Then my love got in the way
Intoxicating like a mystical potion,
And I knew not what to say
You know I tried to
Resist you
But when you kissed me
Like lovers do
Oh, I knew . . . it was only a matter of time,
Before you would be mine . . .

The haunting, hypnotic song came to a satisfying end, and Annika saw that the music had enticed Chivanni to come out of hiding and join Patty on the sofa. The two of them whooped loudly and clapped their approval, begging for more. Their mesmerized expressions told Annika that they were headed in the right direction. For years, ever since high school, Annika had dreamed of being a successful musician, touring around the world and having the freedom to do what she wanted, when she wanted. It was only a flash of a moment, only a spark of hopeful things to come, but she honestly felt like they had a shot at that future. Maybe, just maybe, her luck had changed.

Amidst the chatter among the others, Annika and Talvi remained in a private corridor, where they still lingered in each other's minds.

"*I told you the words would come when they were good and ready,*" Talvi assured her silently, looking at her with love in his eyes. "*I knew it was only a matter of time.*"

CHAPTER 26

Bye Bye, Love

Their first gig, with Talvi's post-performance show featuring the Portland police, had caused a larger turnout for their second one. This in turn caused a third and then a fourth one to be booked, and then May was suddenly over. Somewhere in between gigs and recording, Patti had taken her final exams and now her results were in. They were all A's and B's, which earned her a well-deserved night of celebration. The household was at their third bar, doing yet another round of shots, when Talvi's hand suddenly reached for his back pocket. He ducked outside without a word to anyone, and Annika wondered why he had snuck out for a cigarette without asking James to join him. After a few minutes, curiosity got the better of her, and she found herself weaving through the sea of sweaty, drunk people, and then outside in the cool, misty air. There was no sign of her husband amongst the other smokers on the front sidewalk.

The light in the rear parking lot had burned out, and Annika was careful of her steps as she made her way to the back of the building in the darkness. She didn't make a sound as she crept further along the dirt path between the brick wall and the damp rhododendron bushes. She prayed that she didn't bump into some random guy using the wall as a urinal. But then she heard Talvi's voice from around the corner, and her ears perked up. She strained to listen, but he was speaking a language she couldn't understand. It must have been on his phone because she couldn't hear anyone else talking. His hushed tones sounded serious. Then he said some kind of goodbye, and then it was quiet.

Annika started to head back toward the front door when she heard the metallic chime of a flip top lighter opening. She turned around and there stood a tall, slender figure looming over her. His face was lit by the flame briefly as he lit a cigarette. And then it was dark again.

"Spying on me, love?"

"No, just wondering where you went off to," she said, trying to calm her racing heart. "Who were you talking to at quarter after one?"

Talvi gave an amused hum and curled his arm around Annika's waist, leading her slowly along the path toward the front of the bar. "What do you think about taking a little trip? I love Paris in the springtime."

Annika was caught completely off guard. Who didn't love Paris in the springtime? "That sounds romantic," she agreed. "When were you thinking of going?"

"A few days from now. I've already made the travel arrangements, so please don't say no," he replied. Annika looked up at him, waiting for his impish grin, but he looked serious in the streetlight.

"Sweetie, what's the deal with you never giving me any notice about major decisions?" she asked while he opened the door to the bar. "You gave me less than twelve hours' notice when we got married."

"Then I'm getting better at it, aren't I?" he said as he winked, and ushered her back inside.

Three days later, they passed through the doors of Charles de Gaulle airport and found a black Mercedes waiting for them outside. Talvi handed Annika's bag to the driver, who put it in the trunk and then shut the lid, leaving her puzzled. His black messenger bag was still slung across his chest. He turned to his wife and took her small hands into his.

"I didn't want to tell you until we arrived, but there's some unfinished business I have to tend to that may take a few weeks or so. In the meantime, I've arranged for you to be pampered and looked after until I'll be able to do it myself. I know this isn't the way you had envisioned spending our getaway, but I'm certain you'll still enjoy yourself."

"What the hell is this?" she glared at him through her sunglasses and tried to yank her hands out of his, but he held on fast. "You're ditching me in one of the largest cities on the planet for a few *weeks* or more? I only asked off work for *ten days*! I guess I just lost my job then, didn't I?"

"I wouldn't have put it that way, but yes," he shrugged, not looking nearly as apologetic as she thought he ought to. In fact, he looked rather pleased about it.

"What kind of business are you doing? Something with *M.N.*, I suppose?" she demanded, emphasizing the initials. "I know you carry around her little handkerchief everywhere you go, along with that secret cell phone of yours. I'll bet that's who you were booty calling the other night behind the club, isn't it?"

She looked square into his stunned blue and green eyes, imploring him for answers, but he offered none. Instead, her thoughts became jumbled, falling and tumbling over themselves beyond her control. It was as if he had reached in with Chivanni's enchanted wooden spoon and stirred them up himself, until she didn't know reason from risotto.

The pedestrians and traffic swarmed around them while Annika's head swam in confusion. Twenty-four hours of traveling with little sleep had already taken its toll, and now this bomb had been dropped on her. She barely remembered being hugged and kissed goodbye as Talvi buckled her into the back seat of the car, told her he loved her, and shut the door. As the car began to drive away, she saw her husband head back toward the airport doors, with his phone already held against his ear. She took off her sunglasses and stared at him until the tears of anger blurred her vision too much to see anything except smears of light and dark. When the car started to accelerate, so did her sobs. She had suspected her husband of being unfaithful for so long, but having him not deny it this time had been the clincher, along with being abandoned for this mysterious handkerchief woman. She didn't care if the driver heard her crying, but she realized she wasn't the only passenger in the back seat when she felt a long, comforting arm curl around her shoulders. It hugged her close, into a warm, clean-smelling shirt, making her feel wrapped up in a cocoon of solace.

"Shhh . . . don't cry, Annika," said a deep, rich voice above her while another hand began to stroke her hair. She looked up through her wet eyelashes to see Finn peering down at her through his large brown curls, smiling gently. "Everything will be alright."

CHAPTER 27
Bye Bye, Red

"What are *you* doing here?" Annika shuddered in surprise, and wiped her hot tears away.

Finn's dark brown eyes gleamed.

"I've been appointed your guardian while Talvi is away," he answered in Macedonian, still smiling sweetly at her. He wiped the wet corner of her eye with his thumb and held her chin for a brief moment before letting his hand rest in his lap. There was something different about the way he looked since the last time she had seen him. It wasn't his clean-shaven face, his fitted light blue buttoned-down shirt with the rolled up sleeves, or the snazzy slim navy chinos he wore. There was something else that she couldn't put her finger on.

"Will you tell me what's going on with him and *M.N.?*" she replied bitterly in Macedonian as well. She assumed Finn was using it so the driver wouldn't understand their conversation.

"They work together," said Finn, giving her knee a comforting little pat. "He has some things to take care of in London before he can focus on his work here, so he asked me to watch over you and spoil you rotten until he can join us and do it himself. He wanted to make it a working vacation, because he loves to mix business with pleasure. You mustn't be so eager to believe the worst possible scenario, Annika."

"So he just managed to contact you last minute and ask you to drop everything you were doing to come babysit me in Paris, without any sort of explanation at all?"

Finn nodded, and smiled even wider. Then in English he replied, "How could I say no?"

Annika sighed and felt a wave of comfort wash over her. What was it about Finn that soothed her soul like aloe on a burn? He took his arm from her shoulders and reached into a bag beside his feet. He pulled out an item wrapped in black tissue paper, and handed it over.

"I found you a little gift while I was waiting for my tailor to finish up. I think it will help you feel more Parisian."

She opened it up and there lay a gorgeous cream colored silk scarf, decorated with purple tulips in the center.

"Oh Finn, a Gucci scarf?"

"We can exchange it if you don't care for the pattern."

"No, no, it's beautiful," she sighed, caressing the soft edges of the fabric. "Thank you so much."

"I was thinking you could put up your hair and wear it the way Grace Kelly used to."

The private car drove another few miles as Annika found a hair tie in her purse and gathered her waist length hair into a loose bun. She let Finn fiddle with tying the perfect knot around her neck, and when she put on her sunglasses, he nodded and smiled in approval.

"*Pouvez-vous s'arrêter ici?*" he said to the driver, who pulled up to the curb and Finn took Annika's bag along with his own. They walked half a block and around the corner before he hailed a cab, giving an address to the driver in French.

"Why did we switch cars?"

"Just to be on the safe side," he replied once again in Macedonian.

"Are we in some kind of danger?" she asked quietly, in the same tongue as him.

"Hopefully not, but it's always good to be cautious. How is your left hand feeling? Anything out of the ordinary going on with your ring?"

Annika had learned to not be so surprised by Finn's intuitive questions. After all, he could read open minds just as easily as he read his countless books.

"Sometimes it hurts, and other times it's fine. I usually only feel it after I've been playing guitar for too long," she admitted. "Then sometimes it's tingly. Why do you ask?"

"I frequently wonder about that silver thread," he told her. "Talvi can feel his reach all the way to his elbow. I wondered if you had noticed the same sensations."

"I do. What do you think it could be?"

"I'm still formulating different hypotheses, but you'll be the first to know once I draw a conclusion," he said, as their car slowed to a stop in front of the Four Seasons hotel.

This time, a bellhop carried their bags up to the room, and Annika tried not to gawk as they strode past marble statues and down the polished marble floor of the lobby. Chandeliers hung from the high ceilings and the walls were lined in luxe wallpaper, edged with thick crown moulding. Every chair was covered in plush velvet or silk and there were towering arrangements of fresh flowers everywhere. Even the air smelled too expensive to breathe. When Finn opened the door to their room, Annika felt light headed.

She took off her sunglasses and saw a suite sprawling before her with a luxurious sofa and a large flat screen television. Beyond that, a chandelier hung over a king sized bed, which was covered in soft blue and white brocade and half a dozen tasseled pillows. The windows in front of the bed were framed with matching curtains, which had been pulled back to reveal the most fantastic view that she had ever seen with her own eyes. In her visits before, she had never seen a view of the city like this one. The Eiffel Tower and all of Paris lay out in front of her, beckoning her to come out and play. It could have been a postcard, but no, it was just off their private terrace.

After tipping the bellhop, Finn locked the door and joined her by the window.

"I take it that you like the room, then," he grinned.

"You've got to be shitting me! Are we really going to stay here the whole time we're in Paris?" she said, untying the knot of her new silk scarf and marveling at the view.

"I can arrange something else if it's not to your liking."

"Oh I love it," she assured him. "But this must be costing you at least a grand a night."

"Damned if I know," he said, still grinning at Annika. "I'm not footing the bill."

"Now I see why you were so eager to babysit me," she said, noticing an opera house within walking distance.

"I'd be lying if I said I preferred a tent in a forest in the middle of winter," he said, and cracked his back. "But if that's what was asked of me, I would have accepted the responsibility nevertheless. I know I've said it before, but I like having you around, Annika."

"That's sweet of you to say," she said, and turned around to take in the room once again. The opulence was utterly staggering. Talvi had clearly mastered the concept that asking forgiveness was easier than asking permission. Maybe he'd even invented it.

"I hope you're alright with sharing a room," Finn said, looking apologetic. "Talvi was very specific about you remaining within my sight at all times. You know how he can be when it comes to your safety. The sofa has a pull-out bed for me, so if you'd like to take a nap, the large bed is all yours. You must be quite tired after such a trip."

"I don't know, I've been pretty amped ever since we left the airport," Annika said.

"Amped?" Finn asked, tilting his head to one side as he furrowed his brow. "Do you mean you're still upset over the sudden change of schedule?"

Annika smiled to herself. She loved it when the Marinossian boys said words like 'schedule' in their English accents.

"No, I just mean that I'm too wound up to take a nap. I'm actually not that upset anymore, even though I probably should be, considering I got ditched for another woman in the most romantic city in the world," she explained, crawling up onto the bed and flopping onto her stomach. "You really do give the best hugs. Or maybe it's just that with enough money, anyone can be bought. Maybe I found my price, and it's twelve-hundred thread count sheets with a view of Paris."

"I know a few things about gambling, and I would bet on the hug," said Finn, appearing serious. "I don't believe a woman like you could ever sell your heart, no matter what the view."

"You're right; I couldn't," said Annika thoughtfully. "But I can still enjoy the perks of it trying to be bought."

"Yes you can," Finn said, grinning wide in approval. "What's the first thing you'd like to do then, since you aren't tired? Don't you have an uncle that lives here? We could pay him a visit."

"Nah, he's in New Zealand right now," Annika said. "He's studying butterfly migratory patterns or something like that."

"Oh? Is he a lepidopterist?"

"No, he's an entomologist."

Finn laughed softly at her.

"A lepidopterist is an entomologist who specializes in butterflies," he informed her kindly, making her smile. Of course Finn would know that. It seemed there wasn't much he didn't know.

"I don't think he specializes in one type of insect," she said. "He mostly studies how climate change affects all of them."

"What a fascinating profession. I should like to meet him some day, and have a nice long chat about that."

"Uncle Vince would definitely talk your pointy ears off," she told him. "He gets pretty passionate when it comes to the environment, and how it affects his precious bugs. Personally, I think they should all go away, besides butterflies."

"Annika, Annika . . . " Finn shook his head, but spoke no more about insects or uncles. "Well, if you'd like to do something relaxing, there's a spa downstairs where you can have a massage."

She ran her hands along the silky bedding and propped her head up with her hands, resting on her elbows.

"I was thinking more about some bloody Marys and a hot tub." Finn gave a little laugh.

"That's easily done. Why don't you get ready and I'll ring the bar."

Twenty minutes later, they were walking alongside the pool in white spa robes and slippers with their drinks. Both the hot tub and the swimming pool were quiet and empty, much to Annika's relief. She set her drink on the edge of the tub and left her robe and slippers on a nearby lounge chair, then climbed down the steps into the heated water. Finn set the timer for the jets before joining her, and when he did, she clamped her lips around the straw in her glass so her jaw wouldn't fall open.

"What's wrong?" he asked when he saw the expression on her face.

She tried hard not to stare at the sleek, chiseled torso on display right in front of her face, but it was literally impossible. Who needed to buy a ticket to the Louvre when this living sculpture stood before her?

"You're . . . just . . . so . . . *ripped,*" she said, forcing the words out awkwardly as she took a few long sips from the straw.

"Bloody hell, I just got these," he said irritably, and looked down to inspect the back of the dark blue boxer style swim shorts he was wearing. "Where's the rip?"

Annika snorted so hard that a little vodka went up her nose.

"No, no, no," she said quickly, and he stopped contorting long enough to give her a quizzical look. "It's more American slang. It means you're in really great shape. You look like a piece of art."

"Oh please," he said, looking away bashfully as his cheeks reddened.

"I mean it," she said, eyeing his toned biceps. It was taking all of her willpower not to clamp her hand onto one of them and beg him to flex. "You're like a Roman god. What the hell have you been doing?"

"You name it, and it's been done," he sighed, relieved that his new swim suit was still intact, and sank into the water next to her. He held his straw aside and took a lengthy draught from his glass before continuing. "Now that Talvi's off hiatus from work, I'm back to doing most of the household chores."

"What kind of chores?" she asked, still ogling. "You don't get muscles like that from doing laundry."

"I beg to differ. I doubt you've carried many baskets full of wet laundry and hung them to dry. It's hard work. But then so is hauling trees from the forest, chopping wood, cleaning horse stalls, stacking bales of hay, and carrying pails of water every morning and evening." He rested his left elbow on the edge of the hot tub and took another drink before doing the same with his right elbow. "I'm not complaining, mind you. It has to be done and I'm happy to do it, but it's been a rather grueling regimen."

Annika's eyes moved from his left bicep to his bare wrist, which was closest to her. It was then that she knew what was different about him.

"Your bracelet from Hilda is gone," she pointed out. "Did you lose it doing all those chores?"

Finn shook his dark curls from side to side.

"No, it was removed intentionally."

"Wow . . . I'm so sorry to hear that. What happened?"

"I said something out loud that I should have kept to myself," he replied, and took another long drink of his bloody Mary, leaving it almost empty. Annika's was still three quarters full.

"What the hell did you *say*?" she asked, flabbergasted. She was astounded how that relationship could have ended so abruptly, when there had been no sign of it heading south. If anything, Annika figured they would probably be planning a wedding of their own any day now. Finn was such a thoughtful gentleman, so what horrible thing could he have possibly said to Hilda? Annika was brimming with curiosity, but Finn just looked at her and let the corner of his mouth turn upward.

"Oh, I'm not fool enough to say it again. I learnt my lesson the first time. Tell me, how are you adjusting to living with my brother? I'm certain there's a different dynamic now that he's at your home versus you being at ours."

Annika didn't hold back when she told him about Talvi wrecking Patti's car, on getting arrested and her dad having to get them out of jail in the middle of the night. She also filled him in on her husband having to pay back her parents all the fines, along with helping James max out his credit cards, all within the first few days of his arrival.

"I would say I'm shocked, but I don't wish to lie to you," Finn said, trying not to smile too wide. "Talvi likes to throw money at problems, rather than avoid them to begin with. But, you know, it's paying in spades for us." He motioned to the mural on the ceiling and the marble walls and palm trees around the pool and hot tub. Then he leaned his shoulders back against the jets and closed his eyes, sinking so low that his chin touched the surface of the water. His wet hair weighed down his loose curls so much that his softly pointed ears stood out prominently. If it weren't for his brown eyes, he could have passed for an older version of Talvi. They sat in peaceful silence while Annika sipped on her bloody Mary.

"I'm starting to get hungry," she told him after finishing the last of her drink. "Do you think we could find a Moroccan place for lunch?"

"Of course, but we'll have to order it in," he began slowly, lifting his long, dark lashes and fixing his eyes on hers. "There's something important I need to discuss with you. You're not going to like it, but it really needs to be taken care of before we can go out and enjoy the city. I have so many fun outings planned for us . . . *after* we do this one thing."

"Okay," she said slowly, cautiously.

"Remember you asked if we were in any danger? Well, I don't mean to alarm you, but it is a possibility. Do you know anything about doppelgängers?"

"Um, aren't they like body doubles?"

Finn nodded.

"That's why Talvi wants us to stay so close, because there have been some problems with doppelgängers trying to breach security by posing as someone they are not. We can't have that happening to any of us, so I came up with code names. That way if we're ever uncertain, we'll know the truth straight away."

"Where are they breaching security? Wherever Talvi is right now?" Annika asked, raising an eyebrow. "Is he like, a spy? Is that why he won't tell me anything about his job?"

"He's in mergers and acquisitions," Finn replied, but he revealed nothing else. "Now, the names I've chosen are *sludoor* and *slunchitse*. You can use them whenever you like, but especially if I start acting strange or disappear and then come back a while later."

"Can you sound them out for me again?" she asked.

"Certainly. *Sluhn . . . cheat . . . seh. Slunchitse.* And *sludoor* sounds like *sluh*, and then *doo*, and then roll the 'r' just a bit at the end." She gave it a few attempts, to which he shook his head.

"Pucker your lips more when you pronounce the second syllable."

"*Sluhdewr?*"

"Close, but not quite. You need to relax your mouth," he instructed as he gently took her chin into his hand. He tapped on her bottom lip and studied her face curiously before letting go. "Stop puckering up like you just ate a lemon and soften your lips . . . imagine you're about to be kissed passionately when you call me that name."

Annika wasn't sure if it was the vodka or his inebriating instruction that was making her feel lightheaded, but she did exactly as she was told.

"*Sludoor?*" she finally said, and he grinned softly.

"Perfect, *slunchitse.*"

"What language is that? Is it Karsikko?"

"Why yes, Annika, it is," he beamed. "Has Talvi been teaching you?"

"No," she shrugged. "I guess he's been pretty busy doing other stuff around the house. But I have plenty of time to learn, right?"

"I'll teach you some more, if you like," Finn offered. "You've already passed your first lesson with high marks. If only all my students were as determined as you."

"*Sludoor . . .*" Annika repeated with a smile. "What does it mean?"

"It means sweetness, or something sweet, but it is also used as a pet name, such as when people address one another as 'sugar' or 'honey' in English."

"What about *slunchitse?*"

"It means 'little sun,'" he said. "When you smile, your face lights up as bright as a star, and you're so petite that I thought it only fitting to call you that, *slunchitse.*"

"Aw, that's so cute, *sludoor*. I can't believe you thought I'd have a problem with learning new words. I mean, I hope doppelgängers don't kidnap us either, but I feel pretty safe with a bodyguard like you around."

Finn smiled, and then became serious once again.

"Well, here's what I am afraid you will hate; if anyone *were* looking for you, they would be searching for a redhead in Portland, not a brunette in Paris."

Annika was silent as what he was suggesting sunk in.

"Are you serious? Can't I wear my new scarf?" she whined, feeling more concerned about her hair as she did about someone sinister searching for her. "I just got my hair done last month."

"And it can be done again," Finn said in a kind but firm tone. "I have three shades for you to choose from upstairs, but we're not leaving this hotel until you pick one of them."

CHAPTER 28
I Love Paris in the Springtime

Finn read for most of the afternoon while Annika puttered around the suite, unpacking clothes, painting her toenails, and watching a movie before taking all three hair colors and an outfit into the bathroom with her. When the hair dryer had finally shut off, Finn gave a knock on the door.

"How did it turn out? Please say you're not upset with me."

The door opened just a crack and he peeked in to see Annika standing at the mirror. Her fiery red hair had been transformed to a dark chocolate brown.

"I swore I would never, ever switch to another color," she pouted, fussing with the front section of her hair. She pinned it to one side and wrinkled her nose. "I can't believe I broke my vow for veggie kebobs and couscous."

"That will teach you to swear," said Finn, chuckling to himself as he stepped behind her. She looked up at him in the mirror while trying to guess their difference in height.

"It's fifty-one centimeters," he said with a smile as he ran his long fingers up her neck and through the back of her hair, repeating the motion on each side as he watched the tresses fall through his hands. "You did a good job, *slunchitse*. It looks very natural on you. Cheers for being such a good sport. Now we can really live it up in style."

Over the next two weeks, they skipped the touristy Champs-Élysées even though it was so close to the hotel, and visited an antique book store in the Galerie Vivienne instead. Rather than battle the crowds and flashing cameras at the Louvre or Musée d'Orsay, they opted for the Musée des Arts Forains, which housed old carousels, numerous carnival games, and rides from the past hundred years. Then there was the wax museum, and the vampire museum, and a ghost tour, which were nearly tourist-free, compared to the Arc de Triumph and Eiffel Tower. Finn had taken one look at the swarms of people and suggested a picnic near the Seine instead.

Two cafés au lait and pastries were brought to the room every morning, and they would watch the sun climb higher into the sky as they sipped their coffee in their robes and pajamas and planned out their day. When they left the hotel and stepped onto the boulevards, Finn always made a point to walk on the outside. Every time Annika found herself walking close to the curb, he would gently guide her away until he was between her and the street again. Sometimes she would make a game of it, to see if she could sneak over to his other side without him noticing, but he caught her every time.

They bypassed the famous Michelin starred restaurants and instead ducked into tiny bistros that had no names on the waiting list, but an abundance of names on the wine list. Annika quickly discovered that Finn had an insatiable sweet tooth, and it seemed he had a mission of trying every dessert in the city. So far the macaroons were winning; it was a tie between sea salt with caramel, or the orange-ginger drizzled in dark chocolate.

Paris being the international hub that it was, it was a special thrill for Annika to watch Finn interact with the people. He could ask someone for the time in Farsi, get directions to a restaurant in Hindi, and then inquire if an opera was worth seeing in Italian, all without skipping a beat. This almost always led to a longer conversation, where Annika would just smile and nod every now and then, oblivious to what was being said, but fascinated none-theless. She did begin to notice a pattern, where the person would ask him a question, and he would smile politely and shake his head 'no'.

"What are they asking you when you tell them no?" she asked, after he'd had a lively chat with an elderly Greek woman. "That's like, the sixth time I've seen you do that."

"They all want to know if I play basketball since I'm so tall," he informed her with a lighthearted laugh.

He indulged her with a day of shopping for couture, and the day after that, he surprised her by taking her to a polo match to show it off. The looks they received made it clear that there were more ways to accessorize her new white Chanel sundress than with a hat, handbag, and shoes. The hot babysitter on her arm was clearly the ultimate haute couture.

Finn definitely fit in with the polo crowd in his white blazer and tie, but he seemed oblivious to the looks he was getting from other spectators. All he cared about was if Annika was enjoying herself or not, and while they sipped on white wine and watched the ponies run up and down the field, he explained the rules of the game to her. He told her how he used to play with the twins, Asbjorn, and his cousins, but that a bad fall had persuaded him to retire indefinitely.

"Lots of people get back in the saddle after a fall. How bad could it have been?" she asked innocently, adjusting her sunglasses. "You seem just fine to me."

"Well, for starters, all of these polo ponies that you're looking at are fairly lightweight. Back home, we prefer our horses to be considerably larger, so they can work the land and travel long distances. Not to mention, a fellow like me would look ridiculous on a tiny little Arabian. But heavy horses fall harder. Also, as I mentioned earlier, one of the rules in polo is that it must be played right-handed, for safety. Since Talvi favors his left, he would constantly switch hands in order to score more points. You know how competitive he can be. The others let his blatant cheating slide, but I was always quick to call him on it. It's a dangerous sport, after all, and they have that rule for a reason. It was only a matter of time before an accident happened, though I honestly thought it would have happened sooner."

Finn paused to cheer as the team he was rooting for made a goal, and then went on.

"Talvi and I were neck and neck at a full gallop. I had control of the ball, and he was trying to steal it away. I remember him leaning over with his mallet, in his left hand, of course. I was yelling at him to stop cheating, and then our mallets caught on one another, which my mare tripped on. I went over her head and was knocked unconscious when I hit the ground, and then she landed on my back, breaking it in three places," he said casually as half time was called.

"When she tripped, she had broken her neck and was dead by the time she fell on me, out in the middle of the field. It was truly a freak accident . . . usually the horses are able to get right up after falling down. I was nearly smothered to death due to her full weight upon me. I also had a punctured lung full of blood that didn't make it any easier. When the others pulled her body off of me, they all thought I was dead. I had quite a few broken ribs, and even with our heightened healing abilities, I still needed multiple surgeries to put me back together. I had to learn how to walk all over again." He paused to take a generous drink of wine, holding it in his mouth momentarily before he swallowed and continued his story. "To this day, whenever the weather shifts, or if I stay in one position for too long, I usually have a fair amount of discomfort, but it's nothing in comparison to the first few years of torture I went through."

"Oh my god, Finn! That's *terrible!*" she gasped, putting her hands over her mouth in shock. She had thought maybe he'd broken and arm or a leg, not been totally crushed by a horse falling on him at top speed. His account had her reeling in sympathy for what he had been through. "No wonder you don't play anymore! I'm sure Talvi felt absolutely horrible about it!"

"Oh, he did," Finn nodded, smiling faintly. "He felt so guilty that he was more than willing to steal me extra doses of laudanum from the medicine cabinet. He refilled the empty bottles with maple syrup so our parents wouldn't notice that it was all gone. But that ran out quickly, and I eventually sent him farther and farther beyond our village apothecary to keep up with my demands. Then one day he came back with a new medicine called morphine, and . . . well, that's not a story that needs to be told." He flagged down a waiter for another glass of wine as he finished his previous one. "Let's stomp some divots back into place, shall we?" he suggested, offering his free hand and leading her out to the field with the other spectators. "This is about as involved as I care to be with polo these days."

Perhaps the most memorable outing was their visit to the catacombs, which resulted in Finn ducking down most of the time to avoid smacking his head on the low ceilings. When he wasn't hunched over, he was rattling off information almost nonstop.

"I still don't understand why you would put so many bodies in one spot," Annika said. "This is really neat, but really gross too. Why didn't anyone think of cremation?"

"Because in the year four hundred ninety-six, Clovis, the founder of France, converted from paganism to Catholicism. In order to promote conversion throughout the rest of the country, Clovis and the Catholic church began to ban the traditions of the ancient Romans, who were pagans. One of these traditions was cremation of the dead, which made the most sense to the pagans since they didn't believe in an afterlife. Of course, this is contradictory to

Catholic belief, thus cremation was banned for centuries. I believe the ban was only lifted by the Vatican in the nineteen sixties, and even then, the circumstances necessitating it must be dire, and the ashes must still be buried. Watch out for that femur on your left."

Annika looked down just in time to avoid walking into the leg bone jutting out from the stone wall, and stepped into a cold puddle of water instead. She was quickly beginning to regret wearing open-toed sandals in this musty, dripping, endless underground maze.

"By the twelfth century, churchyard cemeteries had become terribly over-crowded," he chatted on as they walked further along the dim tunnels. "To deal with the sheer number of human remains, cemeteries began to create mass graves for those who couldn't afford the price of burial in the churchyard. There were areas where the fresher bodies were placed before they had decomposed enough to be relocated elsewhere. As you can imagine, this contaminated the city's well water, and for a long time, more people died of disease than were born. Bubonic plague ran rampant, since it was carried by the fleas that lived on the rats that were growing fat on this readily available food source."

"Wow, I'm getting hungry just thinking about an all-you-can-eat buffet like that," said Annika. They had come to yet another large room embedded with hundreds of skulls. Finn stood up straight and glanced at her.

"I didn't think to bring anything to eat whilst we were down here," he said, cracking his back and then his neck.

"I was joking."

"We can turn around if you're feeling peckish. I don't mind. I've been here before."

"Oh have you? I wasn't sure," said Annika, laughing to herself. She decided that she had met her lifetime quota of viewing human skulls *en masse*, and agreed to start heading back. "So you might as well tell me, how did Paris bounce back from having a negative population growth?"

"Well, the city was in the midst of a renaissance by the eighteenth century, and city officials needed a new plan to accommodate all the overflowing cemeteries and mass graves," he said, happy to continue the history lesson. "There were all these abandoned stone quarries on the edge of the city's epicenter, and so began the process of exhuming ten centuries' worth of bodies from over two-hundred cemeteries, and placing them in the quarries, which is where we are standing today. That's why there aren't many tall buildings in Paris, because the foundations can't be built large enough to support them. There are so many old mine shafts down here that they would likely collapse if someone were to build—"

"Eww, I just stepped in another puddle, and this one smells worse that all the other ones," Annika complained, trying not to think about their odds of a cave-in. She lifted her sandal out of the brown water and kicked a clump of pale, chalky mud from the side of it. "Where's all this water coming from, anyway? I keep getting dripped on."

"It's condensation dripping from above," Finn informed her, matter-of-factly. "And probably a little sewage. The Parisian underground is a structural nightmare. Then you have to consider there are over six million bodies decomposing all around and above us. When it rains or becomes very humid, the moisture from these sources comes trickling down, forming all these puddles. Some of them are fairly shallow, but some are quite—"

"You mean I just stepped in dead human broth and have people's shit in my hair?" interrupted Annika.

"I suppose, in a roundabout way, yes. But think about it, Annika," he said, pulling her away from a skull protruding from the wall near her head. "It's mostly filtered. When there's a large sewage leak or flood, they don't allow anyone down here."

"Finn, I have dead people sauce in my hair. I have dead people sauce in my shoes. Can we please go now?"

CHAPTER 29
Anything Goes

"I washed my hair twice and I still feel disgusting," Annika grumbled, stepping out of the bathroom in her robe with her hair wrapped up in a towel. With the hair dryer in her hand, she passed by Finn, whom she had made to stand and wait for his turn to shower. After her realization about people sauce, she had forbidden him to sit on any furniture or touch anything except the doorknob to their room. He was to put his clothes in a plastic bag with hers, to keep them from contaminating anything else.

Once Finn was allowed into the bathroom, Annika slipped into a pair of cropped yoga pants and a tank top. As she blow-dried her hair, she decided she was finally getting used to being a brunette, much to her surprise. She wondered if her husband had been the one to suggest she change her hair, or if it had been his smarty-pants older brother. Satisfied that her hair was dry enough, she turned off the blow-dryer and set it aside, reaching for the television remote instead. She was tickled pink to discover that one of her favorite zombie movies was playing, dubbed in French.

At the next commercial break, she took off the seat cushions and pulled out the mattress, then tossed on all the pillows from the big king sized bed. She climbed back up and stretched out her legs, scanning the room service menu while she waited for the commercials to end.

The bathroom door opened, and Finn snickered at her as he ventured out with a towel wrapped around his trim waist. He set the plastic bag of dirty clothes by the door and walked over to a dresser.

"You look terribly uncomfortable," he observed, digging through one of the drawers. "I assume we're staying in, since you're reading the menu in your pajamas?"

"Yep," she confirmed. "Is there anything in particular you want me to have brought up for dinner?"

"Let me see what they have," he said, and she jumped off the bed and sidled up beside him to show him the selection.

"What was that?" she asked, eyeing him strangely.

"What was what?"

"That look you just gave me. You think I still smell bad, don't you?" she accused, looking aghast.

"No, I don't think that, not in the slightest," he said, appearing flustered. "I'm sure it's the dirty laundry by the door."

"Will you just smell my hair and make sure I got all the catacomb crumbs out of it?" she pleaded, dropping the menu on the floor. "Maybe I need to wash it again?"

"Trust me, your hair is clean," he assured her in a firm tone, tightening the grip on his towel. "You're overreacting."

"Come on, Finn, pleeeease?" she begged with the most coy pout she could muster, and rose to her tip-toes in front of him. She planted one hand on his wet shoulder and motioned at her head with the other. "Just smell my hair and tell me I'm not crazy."

He gave an irritated sigh of defeat and leaned down, sniffing the top of her head. Then he exhaled softly and buried his nose in her hair, inhaling and exhaling deeply as he wandered his way down the back of her scalp. Annika's legs broke out in goose bumps as his warm breath hit her skin again and again. The birchwood undertones of his aftershave arrested her senses, leaving her woozy.

"You're not crazy, Annika," he said in a low, deep voice, "You're barking mad." In a huff, he grabbed a few items from the drawer, slammed it shut, and disappeared into the bathroom again.

"Hey, you didn't tell me what you wanted," she called through the closed door.

"As long as it's vegetarian and wine is involved, I don't care," came his aggravated reply, and then the shower turned on once more.

Annika rolled her eyes at his touchiness and opened the door to the room just far enough to kick the bag of clothes into the hall. Maybe after two weeks of sharing a suite and spending so much time together, Finn was starting to get sick of having no privacy. After all, he was used to living in a huge house with tons of personal space, and sleeping in a bedroom twice the size of the one they were in now. She tried to shrug it off and put on some lotion and lip balm while the zombie outbreak was just beginning on television, but it was still bothering her. Then she dialed room service to place the dinner order, and also to schedule a dry cleaning pickup, but she still felt frustrated. Then she dialed the country code and the number to James's gallery.

"Guess where I'm calling you from, James," she said when he answered the phone.

"God, is it still Paris?" he replied. "Or are you and Talvi in Rome? He was talking about taking you there."

"No, the Eiffel Tower is outside my window and the Champs-Élysées is right around the corner," she said, grinning. "But I'm not here with Talvi. He ditched me the minute we walked outside of the airport. He left me with a babysitter while he went to take care of some unfinished business with a secret co-worker of his that he's never told me about. And it's a *chick*!"

"Shut the fuck up!" James squealed. "It's been two weeks and you're just *now* telling me all of this? Who's the babysitter he left you with?"

"Do you still have that screensaver on your computer at work?"

"*No fucking way!*" he screamed in her ear so loud that she could barely make out the words. "You've got to be *shitting* me!"

"I gotta admit, I'm having too much fun to be pissed off that my husband left me for another woman," she said, grinning. "We've been checking out museums and having picnics and eating some of the best food I've ever put in my face. He even took me to a polo game, but first he took me to Gucci and Prada and Chanel. And the wine here is so, so amazing. You wouldn't believe it."

"Did you just call to try and give me an aneurysm, because I'm about to have one!"

"No, actually, I wanted to let you know that I found you the perfect white blazer," she said. "Finn has one just like it, except bigger. He's like, six foot eight. Should I send it to the gallery so someone's around to accept the package? I don't think you want this sitting on the doorstep all day at the house. It wasn't cheap."

"Yeah, send it to the gallery, but send Talvi's huge hot brother with it. You can't handle both of them. I'll even accept that package after regular business hours. Can you send him now?"

"I can't right now; he's in the shower," Annika said flirtatiously, glancing at the closed bathroom door. "Oh James, he's so buff. He's been doing extra chores at home, chopping wood and hauling bales of hay around the stable . . . and speaking of packages, you ought to see him in his swimsuit. He looks like he's on the Olympic swim team, but we just hang out in the hot tub drinking top shelf booze while he gives me language lessons. He says I'm a very good student."

"You are such a bitch! I think you really *are* trying to give me an aneurysm!" Then he lowered his voice to a serious tone. "Annika, please don't tell me that you're banging him, and that's why he's in the shower."

"No, no, no, I'm behaving myself. We stepped in something really nasty down in the catacombs," she assured him. "But I'm going to be gone longer than I expected. Talvi said it could be a few weeks or so, but he wouldn't tell me anything else. He just stuffed me in a car with his hot brother and bailed. He didn't even give me a number I could reach him at, even though he has a secret cell phone."

"That seems really weird. There must be something else going on that you don't know about."

"What if this mystery woman he works with is that something else?"

"I don't know, Annika. That doesn't seem like him. He's crazy about you, in case you haven't noticed. Chivanni's been telling me some pretty wild stories about those Marinossian boys from back in the day, but we all have a few of those in our vaults," said James. "Just promise me you won't do anything stupid. You've kinda got it made with Talvi. And your hot babysitter. Look but don't touch, okay? And call me if shit gets crazy. Well, if it gets crazier."

"I will," she assured him, and hung up the phone. There was a knock at the door as someone's brain was being eaten on the television, and a table covered in different sized silver dishes was wheeled into the room.

"*Ici, c'est vous plait*," Annika said, pointing to the pulled out sofa bed.

"*Ici?*" the very cute waiter asked, as if the pulled out sofa bed in front of a gory zombie movie seemed an odd place to dine.

"*Oui, merci beaucoup*," she replied graciously, and helped him lay out the different dishes on the sheets. He seemed unsure what to do with the wine, and set the two bottles and two glasses on the coffee table with a wine key before rolling the table toward the door. As Annika held it open for him, he paused for a moment in the doorway.

"You, you are American?" he asked, and she nodded, smiling. She thought he was about to compliment her on her French, but instead he asked her in halted English, "You stay here with your . . . husband?"

"No, with his brother," she answered before realizing how it sounded when said out loud. She blushed, but the waiter only gave a subtle nod, concealing his grin as best as he could. He glanced over his shoulder, and then back at Annika. He took a black business card out of his jacket and pressed it into her hand. In white lowercase letters, she read *"la Société d'Art Souterraine."*

"Oh, you're an artist? What kind of art do you make?"

"Tomorrow you visit, an' we paint, per'aps?"

Annika flipped the card over, and in the same white lettering was an address, and nothing more.

"Merci, that would be *très bien,"* she said, putting the black card in her pocket. She gave him an enthusiastic wave goodbye along with a large tip as he snatched the bag of dirty clothes from the floor, tossed it in a basket under the table, and headed for the elevator.

She shut the door just as Finn came out of the bathroom, dressed in his baby blue flannel pants and a plain white t-shirt.

"What did you end up ordering?" he asked, locking the door since she had forgotten to. Whatever had been bothering him earlier seemed unimportant now.

"Well, I decided to play it safe and not order any seafood," she said, and crawled onto her previous place on the bed.

"A wise decision," he agreed, and reached for one of the bottles of wine. Annika began to lift the silver lids and rattled off her selections.

"Provençal style ratatouille, a side of braised chicory, mezze penne with tomatoes, black olives, pine nuts and basil, and then for dessert there's a cocoa and sea salt strudel with white coffee ice cream for me, and dark chocolate and caramel *mi cuit* with pear and ginger sorbet for you. And they had like, fifty thousand wines in their cellar, so I hope you're alright having a Carmenere with dinner and the Madeira with dessert."

"That sounds fine to me," he said passively, and inserted the wine key into the bottle he was holding.

"That's actually the Madeira," she pointed out.

"I know," he said, and began to pull out the cork.

"But we're having that with dessert," she reminded him.

"Yes we are," he said, not looking at her. He sniffed the cork, set the wine key down, and poured them each a glass of Madeira. "I don't suppose you can guess when was the last time I enjoyed a pear and ginger sorbet?"

"Um, a few years?"

"Um, try never," he said, playfully mocking her American accent while he passed her one of the glasses. "It would be criminal to let something like that waste away while I bide my time with yet another ratatouille."

He handed her the dish of cocoa and sea salt strudel and settled onto the other side of the bed. He dipped a spoon into the pear and ginger sorbet and brought it to his lips, closing his eyes in bliss.

"You have to try this," he said, and passed his plate to her. They traded back and forth every few bites for ten solid, silent minutes. Finn said nothing, other than humming a little here and there in pleasure, before trading plates and repeating the happy hums.

"I'm sorry if I annoyed you earlier about smelling my hair," she finally said. "I know I can be kind of a girl sometimes."

"I'm painfully aware of your gender, but no, I'm not annoyed with you," said Finn, mesmerized by the bloody fight scene on the television. He set down his empty plate and took a slow drink of wine, swirling it in his mouth. "I'm annoyed with my brother. He chose a fine time to pick up a job. He didn't happen to call by chance, did he?"

"No, are you worried about him?"

Finn gave an uncharacteristically contemptuous harrumph and continued to stare straight at the screen.

"No. I'm worried about you and I."

Annika was just about to ask him to elaborate on what he meant by that, when he nearly shouted,

"What the bloody hell? How can she possibly have a machine gun for a leg?"

"It's a zombie movie," she laughed. "Anything goes."

"What total crap," he announced in disgust, finally turning to look at her. "Where's the channel changer?"

"It's supposed to be crappy," she said, defending her campy film. "They made it so bad that it's good. We're not changing the channel. You wanted to know about American culture, and this is a cult classic."

"No, *Casablanca* is an American classic," he argued. "This is just insulting to my intelligence."

"Cult classic and classic are two completely separate genres. I'm trying to broaden your horizons. Have you seen *The Evil Dead*?"

"No."

"*Dead or Alive*?"

"No."

"*Shaun of the Dead*?"

"No."

"*Heathers*?"

"No. What's that one about?"

"Teen suicide and blowing up a school."

"I'm seeing a rather morbid pattern here. Should I be concerned?"

"It's not like that," she insisted. "They're all hysterical movies!"

"If you say so."

Finn spotted the remote lying by Annika's feet, and he made a grab for it, beating her to it. Her hands clamped around his, and channels flipped incessantly as they fought for control of the remote.

"Something just fell from your pocket," he said, and when she looked down, he seized the chance to yank the remote away from her.

"Oh, yeah, I forgot about this," she said, picking up the black business card. Finn settled on a program about the solar system and started in on the pasta. "I thought we could go to this gallery tomorrow. It turns out that the waiter is an artist, and he gave me his card. I think he wants me to paint a picture with him, or something like that." Finn chewed his food thoughtfully and then turned to her.

"Did he figure out that you're an American tourist? He'll probably charge you an arm and a leg for something that I could do blindfolded."

"No, he has a gallery, and I'm pretty sure it's close by. Do you recognize this address?" She handed him the card and he started to laugh, and then choked on a pine nut.

"The waiter gave you this?" he coughed, and finally cleared his throat, but his eyes were still watery. "I can't believe the place is still around."

"So you know where it is?" she asked, leaning closer with interest. "Is it close enough to walk?"

Finn handed the card back and took another long sip of his Madeira.

"It doesn't matter. I am *not* taking you there," he informed her, and tried to focus on a close-up shot of Jupiter on the television.

"Why not? Is it because it's underground? I promise that I won't complain this time if something drips in my hair. And I'll wear better shoes."

Finn started to laugh quietly, and then he had to wipe his eyes. "I don't think it would matter what shoes you wore, if you wore any at all. And I would bet every last one of my books that you would complain quite a bit if something dripped in your hair at *la Société d'Art Souterraine*," he said, still laughing softly.

"Oh it's on," she challenged him. "Why don't we go and find out so I can prove you wrong? I'm all about supporting local artists."

This sent Finn into another fit of silent laughter.

"I think you might be able to find another artist to support somewhere in Paris. Let's go watch the buskers in Montmartre tomorrow instead." He wiped his eyes again and reached for the Carmenere and the wine key.

"Why won't you take me to *la Société d'Art Souterraine*?"

"Because Talvi would have my head if he ever found out," he said, gently coaxing the cork out of the second bottle. "It's not just an art gallery, Annika. To sum it up, it's an erotic art club."

"Oh shut up," she scoffed. "The waiter wasn't a pervert. He seemed like a nice, normal guy."

"I would try to seem like a nice, normal guy as well, if I was hoping to bed you on a large canvas as art patrons spread paint over our intertwined bodies."

"*That's* what he meant when he asked if I wanted to paint a picture with him?" Annika squealed, and Finn shrugged, still avoiding looking at her.

"It's one of many possibilities. It's just like you said about your zombie films . . . anything goes." He tilted his head back, finishing the Madeira in one last swallow.

"Oh my god, I gave that guy my friggin' underwear!"

Finn snorted into his glass, but said nothing.

"Why do you know so much about this sex club, anyway? I guess you're speaking from experience?"

"Well, Annika, this may come as a surprise to you, but I do have a pulse," he confessed, refilling their wine glasses with the Carmenere. "Although I mostly went for the opium. It's been years and years since those days, and I honestly don't miss them. They had their time."

"At least you had days like that to begin with," she said, sulking. "I feel like I'm missing out on something huge, and it's right under my nose."

"You know, the one problem with building up unattainable fantasies in one's head," he said, staring intently at the television, "is that they grow so large they eventually burst, leaving nothing behind but disappointment."

CHAPTER 30
You Really Ought to Know

"Finn, do we need to get you some antacids or something?" Annika asked. They were sitting in a sunny café not far from their hotel, having brunch. It was a gorgeous day outside, but Finn looked only slightly better than miserable. If he had even slept at all, he had woken up in a bad mood and been edgy ever since.

"I'm alright," he said, but his barely eaten peach crepes and half-full cup of coffee suggested otherwise.

Annika on the other hand, was feeling incredible this morning. Her senses were turned up to their maximum capacity. Everything smelled and tasted so luscious and appealing. Her nose and her taste buds seemed to be evolved only to inhale and savor this amazing French cuisine. Her ears picked up everything around her, too, and rather than being annoying and overwhelming as it had been earlier in the year, it was now a beautiful symphony of life. The bell ringing each time the café door opened, the chime of the cash register, the sound of forks and knives cutting food on plates, the restaurant staff talking in the kitchen, and the traffic outside were all part of a wondrous experience. There was a mysterious confidence and certainty flowing within her that hadn't been there a day ago, and she felt like she owned the room, the street, and the city.

When they had approached the restaurant, a man had held open the door to the café for her before Finn could reach for it. When she ordered her eggs with black truffles, their server had given her a very sultry look of approval, and his private thoughts had made Annika blush when she inadvertently eavesdropped on them. Female diners shot her occasional disparaging glances while their husbands and boyfriends stole lingering looks at her.

"I don't know what the deal is this morning," Annika said, overhearing a woman snap at her husband for ogling in her direction too long. "It's not like I'm dressed like a whore. I'm not even showing any cleavage." She glanced down at the crisp white knee-length dress that she had worn to the polo match, which she had paired with a soft teal cardigan. "Oh, well, it's just a half inch. I must have filled out a little from eating so many pastries. Do you think that's still too much to show?"

Finn nodded his head, then abruptly started to shake his head, then unfastened the second button on his shirt. He looked ready to throw up.

"Hmm. Maybe it's just too early in the day for black cat eye makeup," she mused. "I thought Parisians were all about being sexy and classy at the same time. I was just trying to go for that vintage look."

"There's nothing wrong with . . . how you *look*," he stammered as he stood up, and dropped some bills on the table with a shaking hand. "Take your time finishing your breakfast. I need some fresh air." He dashed outside, and Annika sat in her little wooden chair, bewildered by his behavior. She ate a few more bites of her eggs, watching Finn from the other side of the window where he sat at an empty table. He was inhaling the air deeply through his nose, then letting it out through his mouth, as he watched the late morning traffic hustle and bustle by.

Finally Annika couldn't sit there any longer, and she walked up to the counter to order a peppermint tea to go.

"*Combien est-ce que je vous dois?*" she asked, opening her purse, but the older man behind the bar waved her away with a grin, giving her the tea for free. She could feel his eyes on her back as she strutted out the door with her prize.

"I'm sorry you're not feeling well," she said, stepping next to Finn, and handed him the cup of tea. "I'm pretty sure mint is supposed to help an upset stomach."

"Thanks," he said, smiling half-heartedly as he took the cup from her. "But my stomach is fine. It's in my head, mostly."

"We can get you some aspirin for your headache."

"No, that's not going to help at all," he frowned.

Annika sighed in frustration. She didn't know what else to do, if he wouldn't drink tea, or take medicine, or eat any of his beloved sweets. Then it struck her why he might be acting so strange.

"Are you a doppelgänger, *sludoor?*"

Finn chuckled, smiling for the first time that morning.

"No, *slunchitse*, I'm just having a really rough time of it."

Annika threw her arms around his neck in relief and caught another whiff of his aftershave.

"Oh yay, it's still you," she sighed into his soft brown curls, taking in his scent. He smelled so good that she didn't want to lift her head, but somehow she forced herself to do so after the extra-long hug. "I mean, it sucks that you're feeling so bad. Here, I'll give you a little massage while you're sitting. That ought to help your headache."

He tried to protest, but she was already standing behind him, kneading his neck with her hands. She rubbed his temples with her fingertips in little circles, working her way through his curls from front to back, then back to front. As her hands worked their way down his neck again and onto his tense shoulders, she was surprised at how sweaty his skin was. His right hand reached up and curled around her own, gripping tight. His palm was on fire.

"Let's go for a walk," he said in a dry voice, and then took a drink of his tea.

They made their way down to the corner and then turned onto the Champs-Élysées, strolling along leisurely. Finn walked on the outside, as always. A soft breeze blew against their faces, and the longer they walked, the more relaxed he became.

"I'm glad to see you're feeling better," said Annika. "I wonder if maybe you ate something bad last night."

Finn slowed down to a crawl, tilting his head to one side. He furrowed his brow and narrowed his eyes suspiciously as he gazed down at her.

"You don't have any idea what's going on, do you?"

"Um, I just figured you were coming down with the flu," she shrugged. "I didn't think elves got sick, but you've got a fever and no appetite. Plus you've been grumpy ever since we got back from the catacombs yesterday, so I don't know what else it could be."

"Oh Annika . . ." Finn began, and trailed off, sidetracked by the number of pedestrians walking around them. "That's not it at all; not by a long shot."

"Well then, what the hell is it, and what can we do about it?" she asked, feeling agitated. The tone in his voice made it sound like she was in trouble.

He pulled her into a recessed doorway to escape the passersby, and in the little alcove, away from the breeze, the scent of his skin enveloped her like heavy fog. He leaned against the wall beside her, and she became aware of just how much larger than her he was. All six feet eight inches of him loomed over her like Michelangelo's David come to life, and she couldn't believe how small he made her feel.

"It's basic biology. We can't do anything about it. I mean, in a scientific sense we could, but the result would be disastrous for both of us, socially." For the first time since she'd known him, Annika saw something strange and new in his dark eyes . . . was it desire? He leaned even closer to her and reached his warm hand down below her navel, pressing gently against the white poplin. As if his fingers were a book of matches, her insides were set ablaze in response to his touch. "Your dress isn't snug from eating too many pastries, Annika. It's because you're ovulating. Right now, your body is flooded with so many hormones and pheromones that I can scarcely see straight. That's why so many men are paying extra attention to you lately," he said, still staring at her, still carefully palpating each side of her lower abdomen.

"They don't know why, they just know they want you. The women know that the men want you too, at a subconscious, primal level . . . so they see you as a potential threat. But elves' senses are somewhere between a human's and a wolf's, which is why I knew what was going on when I stepped out of the shower yesterday. The scalp is one of the primary places that pheromones are released from, so smelling your hair last evening was somewhat of an exquisite torture for me. It's your right ovary that is making all the fuss, by the way. Next year it will be your left."

Astounded that he knew her insides better than she did, she felt her heart begin to pound harder in her chest. "Is that why you said you were annoyed with Talvi for picking up a job?" she asked, suddenly feeling bare and vulnerable. "Is that why you said you were worried about us?"

Finn nodded his head, and his curls fell into his eyes as he looked down at her, but it didn't break the intensity of his sleep-deprived gaze.

"All I can say is that I hope this was an honest mistake, because I wouldn't wish this on anyone. He made me swear not to let you out of my sight, which he surely wouldn't have done without good reason. If he had even slightly suspected this might happen, he never would have asked me to stay with you. He wouldn't want me anywhere near you. It's absolutely *verboten*." He swallowed hard, looking distressed when he took his hands off of her abdomen to adjust himself near his belt.

"I couldn't sleep at all last night. I could only lay there, breathing you in for eight vexing hours, wondering what the bloody hell I was going to do with you. Back home, we only have two options. You either stay far away from each other for those three days, or you remain together and give Mother Nature what she's asking for. Of course, I thought about ways to keep you isolated, such as having you put in jail for a few days, but even that wouldn't protect you from the unsavory characters who will no doubt find you nearly as irresistible. You won't be apt to behave yourself much longer in this state anyhow, so I may as well take my chances to ensure you don't bear any strange fruit. You're destined to have a very important child." He put both hands on her small waist and spread his fingers out, running them up and down, evaluating her curves. He hummed in pleasure, just like when he was eating the pear and ginger sorbet from last night.

"What the hell are you talking about?" Annika asked, trembling with unease. It unnerved her to be told yet again that there were details about her life that she had no clue of, but getting knocked up by her husband's sexy older brother didn't seem like a very acceptable destiny either. Then again, what did she know about elves' values? It might be a bit arrogant to expect that social etiquette among them was the same as it was with humans. It definitely hadn't seemed the same with fairies, not when Chivanni likened lovers to shoes. Maybe elves liked to keep things in the family? She didn't know. All she knew was that the wall behind her seemed to be pushing her closer into the thick, intoxicating haze surrounding Finn. Her body began to break out in a sweat as she breathed in his scent.

"I'm speaking of the prophecy about your husband." He cleared his throat and recited, "The first male twin to be born shall be married at dawn on the same day as his conception. His bride shall be from a distant land with the blood of a samodiva and the voice of a siren. Thereafter this union, through his bride's altered body, she shall cultivate and give birth to a voice that will liberate one soul at a time, thusly anchoring these lives to the world of the living." Finn looked down at her curiously, peering into her eyes, into her mind. "I've sung with you before, Annika, and it was . . . transcendental. I watched you enchant an entire pub with your siren song that evening. Now that your body is altered due to your handfasting to Talvi, it's rather clear what your future holds. Judging by the expression on your face, I don't suppose he bothered to mention any of this to you."

"There's a lot he doesn't mention to me," she replied, realizing that her victory at avoiding motherhood may have been short-lived after all. Images of Talvi's secret cell phone and the embroidered handkerchief swirled around inside her mind and she offered them to Finn, along with the memory of Talvi's late night booty call and him straddling Patti Cake in the grass, blasting her in the face with his hose. Finn rolled his eyes, shaking his head in irritation and disapproval the way only an older, wiser brother can.

"And here I am once more, teaching you all about your destiny," he pointed out, still encircling her waist with his hands, still remaining inside her mind, and she inside his. "Where was Talvi when you were standing on a ladder, adding your name to the family tree in my library that proved you were Sariel's greatest granddaughter? Why, he was off sulking when you fell off that ladder and into my arms. Where was he when you learned that you were destined to marry him? He was warming up with wood nymphs and faerie brandy while I was bundling you up in a sweater. Why hasn't he even taught you one word of Karsikko, when you enjoy learning new languages? And *why* would he take the chance for us to be together like this, when he knows what's coming your way? I can only hope it's because he is unimaginably harebrained and reckless when it comes to you. If he orchestrated this intentionally to avoid any parental duties, I'll—"

"You don't think he would *do* that, do you?" Annika interrupted in horror. "He *really* doesn't want kids."

"Oh, I know he doesn't," Finn replied, biting his lip in frustration. "But he knows that I do. I suppose if we fall victim to Mother Nature's whims, it would be the most sublime punishment for him. As impetuous as nature can be, all she ultimately wants is to reproduce. You're built so perfectly for it . . . you really do have the ideal proportions." He inched his hands down until he was caressing her hip bones with his thumbs. "Did you know that among female humans and elves alike, there are basically only four different pelvic shapes? The wide angles of your ilium are optimal for carrying and bearing children. It's as though you were made to accommodate twins without any serious complications, which is remarkable since they run in my family. There's so much room in here . . . so much room . . . "

Annika felt her back arch against the wall in response as he rhythmically prodded the front and back of her hips, all the while murmuring facts about the physiological benefits of her waist-to-hip ratio in his hypnotic, deep voice. She shut her eyes, trying to shut his analytical words out of her head, trying to ignore how clean and masculine he smelled, trying to overlook the fact that his tender, warm hands were making her even consider the unthinkable. It did seem like that was all her body wanted, was to listen to Mother Nature and surrender herself to motherhood. All she needed was an appropriate mate. Someone strong, someone protective, someone intelligent, patient, and kind. Someone who actually wanted to have children, and please, oh please, let him be good looking. She opened her eyes and saw all those things staring right back at her. To hell with her untrustworthy husband. To hell with her music career. To hell with everything.

She felt a warm, fuzzy sensation in her womb, and could only imagine how fertile it must be at that very moment. It was probably soft and cushy, waiting desperately for just one single seed to be sown. Her right hand moved to Finn's bracelet-free wrist and clutched on tight while her left hand hooked onto his belt, bringing him closer. She looked into Finn's hungry eyes, and wondered if he ached for her as much as she did for him.

Give me what I want, she thought. A flush erupted over her face and chest, but then the ring on her left hand began to burn.

"We both know that's not what you really desire," he said in his rich, deep voice. He stopped massaging her hips but left his hands planted firmly on her. "It's just chemicals toying with our minds."

"How can this only be in our minds?" she blurted out, blinking her eyes, trying to snap herself out of the fog. She felt drunk and hypnotized by his lustful expression. "I feel it all over my body. I can see it plain as day in yours. Are you sure it's just chemicals?"

"What do you think is making our hearts beat faster? What do you think is making our breath come harder? Certainly not conscious, rational thought. This isn't rational at all. It's just instinct, it's just brain chemistry. Isn't it remarkable how something that you can't even see can bring you to your knees?"

A perfectly timed wave of heat flooded through Annika, causing her knees to buckle underneath her. She began to slide down the wall, but Finn caught her under her arms, holding her steady as he propped her against the wall.

"I'm not sure I like our options," she shuddered.

"I don't have any others to offer you. From everything I know, this only ends one way if we stay together. I'll be like a moth to a flame trying to get to you, whatever the cost of being burned by the fire. I apologize for being so uncouth, but I'm about at my wit's end with you . . . " he paused as his eyes

285

dropped to Annika's chest, "and it's going to get worse before it gets better. You haven't even peaked yet."

"But you're so smart . . . you've read so many books . . . there's got to be *something* we can do," Annika insisted. The amount of tension building up inside her was beginning to make her nauseous. She felt terrible for wanting him, but she wanted him terribly.

"I'm telling you, I've thought about it all night and all morning, and I've come up with nothing," he said, still staring at her chest. His hands had remained under her arms, and he slowly gathered the sides of the bodice tighter and tighter, forcing her breasts to swell. Another happy hum escaped him, though his eyebrows furrowed in anguish.

"What about cold showers?"

"That won't stop me from joining you."

"We could get another room."

"I'll just break down your door."

"Maybe we could have the people at the spa bury us with ice cubes in separate tubs in separate rooms?" she suggested. She was desperate.

"I might be able to last five minutes if we did that," Finn said, locking his eyes back onto hers, "but you'll only last five and a half."

A silent scream filled her head, and her blood began to course through her veins, pumping harder and faster. Why was this happening now? Was this some kind of test? Was this some form of punishment? Had she married the wrong brother? She looked at her still burning ring, feeling the pain creep up past her elbow. There was only one other way she could think of to find out if all these feelings could be blamed on a simple biochemical reaction, or not.

"If you're right, and this is all being caused by chemicals," she said, letting go of his belt, "then maybe that's how it needs to be dealt with. We could at least try fighting fire with fire, instead of just letting it burn out of control." She flexed her left hand and reached into her purse, withdrawing the black business card.

"Why are you doing this to me?" he snapped, and took the card from her, tearing it to bits and tossing it on the ground. He sunk his long fingers into his curls, grasping them out of frustration. "That's the *last* place we should go!"

"Hey . . . think about it," she said, feeling the burning sensation in her forearm and the rest of her body retreat to a simmer. "You said this place offered more than just art lessons, right?"

He let go of his hair and folded his arms across his chest, leaning against the opposite wall from Annika. His eyes began to look less hungry, and more like an astoundingly intelligent elf sweating profusely as he faced the ultimate moral dilemma. He shook his head at her in stern disapproval.

"It would seem our backs are figuratively and literally against the wall," he said through his teeth.

"Do you have anything better in mind?" she asked.

"Blast, you," he sighed, grabbing her hand. "Let's go."

CHAPTER 31
Pit Stop

The hotel was on the way to the gallery, and the two of them stopped in to gather a few things. Finn was putting the cap on the toothpaste when the phone rang, and he dashed out of the bathroom to get it, but Annika had beaten him to it.

"Hello love," she heard Talvi say in a low voice. "How are you doing? I hope you've forgiven me for switching gears on you last minute at the airport."

"Yeah, it's alright. I'm not mad at you," she said, stepping away as Finn made another grab for the phone. She clung onto it tighter. "Hang on, I'm going to sneeze."

She pressed the phone against her racing heart and turned to Finn, who was hovering over her anxiously.

"If he's really a spy, do you think it's going to help him to find out what's going on here?" she hissed, then put the phone back to her ear, turning her back to him.

"What have you been up to for the past two weeks?" she asked, trying to sound cheerful.

"Paperwork. Lots of paperwork."

Annika rolled her eyes. *Yeah right, paperwork.*

"Oh, is it for all those mergers and acquisitions you must be working on?"

"You hit the nail right on the head," Talvi chuckled under his breath.

"Will you be able to join us soon? It would be really, really great if you could."

"Unfortunately, there's so much paperwork, this will take considerably longer than I had hoped. I'm afraid it could become a summer job, but I can't get into that right now. Tell me, are you enjoying Paris? Is my brother treating you right?"

"Yep," Annika said with a stiff upper lip, looking over her shoulder at Finn, who was still standing close by. "He's doing everything he can to show me a good time. In fact, I'm pretty sure he has something *huge* planned for me tonight." Finn's jaw dropped in horror.

"That's fantastic to hear. I told him to indulge your every desire. I'm glad he's making good on that promise. Oh bollocks . . . " Talvi's phone plunked down on a hard surface, and then Annika heard what sort of sounded like high heels coming closer, and then what definitely sounded like another woman scolding her husband, wailing just how badly she needed him.

"I have to go," Talvi whispered into the phone, and then with a click, the line was disconnected.

CHAPTER 32
Paperwork

"How many times do I have to tell you that you are not to make outside calls on that telephone line?" Merriweather hollered at Talvi, still holding the phone down on the receiver.

"I'm *inside* your office, so how could that have been an *outside* phone call?" Talvi argued in his defense. He swiveled in her chair and looked up into her beautiful, angry dark eyes. A mischievous smirk flashed across his face as he gazed at her. "This is why I should have my own office, with my own private telephone line. Not a sad little table butted up against your desk. You can't even bother to suit me with a decent computer. Look how flimsy this little thing is that you've given me to use!" he picked up the thin laptop that was sitting on a stack of papers waved it around carelessly. She snatched it out of his hands, glaring at him in frustration.

"This flimsy little thing is worth twice as much as what I'm using, you stupid bastard, and even if we had free space available, why would I ever give you a private office? All you would do is lock the door and take a nap with a bottle. At least this way I can keep a close eye on you and try to teach you how to function better in a high-tech society."

"I just think you could make an exception for me, Merri," he pouted, batting his eyes at her as he leaned back in her chair. "Please?"

"That's all I've ever done for you, is make exceptions, and look where it's gotten us," she said, frowning as she walked around her desk and set the laptop down on his table. "You can't bloody type, you can't bloody drive an automobile, and you barely know how to use the smartphone I gave you."

"If it were truly smart, it wouldn't need me to tell it what to do in the first place," Talvi retorted. "And I know how to drive an automobile. Annika helped me get my license. I'm bonafide in America."

"Yes, I found your traffic record, and I have to say, I strongly disagree with that statement. You need to learn these things inside and out before you will ever work another job for me. Times are changing, Talvi. Every twelve-year old in London with a cell phone is better qualified to be on the embassy's payroll than you at this point. Now get out of my chair and get back to work!" Merriweather snapped, giving him a warning look.

"Must I really fill in all these entries by computer?" he whined as he reluctantly crawled out of her chair. She pushed him aside and sat down while he leaned against her desk, hovering over her. "It would be so much faster for me to write them in by hand than to type them."

"Spoken like a true ignoramus," Merri muttered, trying to ignore him and focus on her computer screen.

"You really ought to have an assistant for this sort of thing. I think you and I both know that I'm immensely overqualified for data entry. Whatever happened to Brigitte?"

"Transferred."

"Julie?"

"Transferred."

"Marilyne?"

"She's the one who left your cheeky lighter in her desk when she resigned."

"Really? No more lovely Marilyne?" Talvi asked with great interest, leaning down close to her. "Whatever brought that on?"

"What do you *think* brought that on?" replied Merriweather, glaring at him again. "She found out about you and Julie!"

"Oh, don't blame me. I'm not the one hiring all these chatty ladies to work in a department designated for clandestine operations," he accused with a devilish grin. "You know about me and brown-eyed girls, and you certainly know what my specialties are. I was merely doing research. Such a pity . . . Julie was a very enjoyable assistant to experiment with. Too bad she couldn't keep her mouth shut, but then, I suppose that's why we got along as well as we did."

Merriweather looked ready to slap the arrogant smile off of his face, but she resisted the temptation.

"Regardless of whoever's fault it is, we currently have no assistant to help us," she said, giving him a stern look. "I've put in multiple requests for extra help, but no one has even applied for the position. Nobody wants to work with either of us, not even the poor, naïve interns. It's well-known around here that I'm a demanding bitch and that you're a heartless womanizer."

"What a load of rubbish," Talvi scoffed, and walked over the bar. "I have a heart. Why, I have a *huge* heart." Merri rolled her eyes at him.

"Do you know what others around here say about my office door? They say it ought to read: *Director of International Relations*, not *Director of Modern Intelligence*, because of all the shenanigans that have gone on in here with you and your 'huge heart'. If I don't get you up to speed quickly and have something of value to show for it, we may both soon be out of work. So please be more grateful that you have any space to work in at all. Speaking of which, what are you bloody thinking? We have *work* to do and it's not even time for lunch!"

"Yes, but it's five o'clock somewhere," he said, pouring two glasses of Scotch. "See, I'm learning more slang every day. I'll be up to speed in no time. And now that I have my cheeky lighter back, your unlucky streak ought to lift any day now. Just you wait and see."

Merriweather turned in her chair to face him as he handed her a glass and settled into his seat across from her.

"You know, Talvi, the longer you fight me tooth and nail on this mountain of work, the longer you'll be here instead of Paris. What's it going to take to motivate you?" she wondered aloud, looking the piles of folders on her desk. She took a sip of her drink and massaged her temple, closing her eyes. "I know you can learn this. You're so good with your hands. I tell you what . . . if you finish that stack of folios by Friday evening, I'll give you a reward for all your hard work."

"And what might that be? Another stack of folios?"

"No."

"Ooh, a more comfortable work station?"

"Of sorts. You'll definitely be more comfortable this Friday evening than you are right now."

"Well, might I have it early, so I could be more comfortable now?" he said, being snarky. "Or perhaps you enjoy watching me squirm?"

"I do enjoy watching you squirm. I enjoy it quite a lot, actually, but this reward for your hard work is not something I can give you in my office. We'll have to go elsewhere," she said, and took a key chain out of her purse. She sorted through the keys and singled one of them out, dangling it seductively in her fingers. Talvi's eyes widened hungrily as he recognized where the key led to.

"Oh Merri . . . oh Merri, *really*? You're going to let me inside there after all this time?"

She nodded her head, smiling so smug, and set the keys back in her purse.

"It's good to know I can still get your attention. Now, get back to work!"

CHAPTER 33
Our Little Secret

The entire walk was filled with silence until they reached their destination. Finn opened the door to a place with a different name than what was on the business card, but the address was the same. They found themselves in a very modern art gallery, with high unfinished ceilings, and exposed brick above the white drywall where a few large abstract paintings hung.

"Are you sure this is the right place?" whispered Annika.

"Yes," Finn whispered back, avoiding her eyes.

"*Bienvenue*," welcomed a very thin older woman in a simple black dress who was sitting at a desk. She proceeded to tell them about a new exhibit that had just gone up, and led them to a larger room full of nudes in various styles. Some were abstract, some were impressionistic, some were done in broad, splashy strokes, and some in tiny, organized ones like Van Gogh. The only thing they had in common was that they were all of an elegant blonde woman lying on a chaise lounge, painted in the same tasteful pose from different angles. Some were marked as sold, and a few were marked as not for sale. The ones that were still available gave Annika a wallop of sticker shock, but then, these were not mass produced street vendor souvenirs. They were high class works of art.

"*Excusez moi*," Finn said to the woman, taking out his wallet, "but we're here for the *other* exhibit." He surprised Annika by handing the woman a black card that looked identical to the one given to her by the waiter, only Finn's was made of metal and looked very, very old.

295

"This one's on me," he said to Annika, and handed the woman a credit card as well.

"*S'il vous plait, suivre moi,*" the woman said, still holding the card. She brought them to a room at the back of the gallery. She unlocked the door to reveal countless Venetian masks on display, and instructed them to choose one. They ranged in all different colors, some were made to cover an entire face, but most were made to cover half. There were feathers and sequins and ribbon everywhere Annika looked. Some were over the top and some were plain and simple. Some featured giant ostrich plumes, some had smatterings of butterflies or dragonflies running up one side. There were human faces, cat and dog faces, ones with bird beaks, and ones with elephant trunks.

Finn chose a black satin mask with silver scrolls on the edges, and Annika selected a white one overlaid with blue stones and delicate feathers on the sides. They stepped out of the room and the woman locked the door, and pulled back a curtain beside it to reveal an old freight elevator, which she opened for the two of them.

"So why did that woman tell us that we're supposed to wear these at all times except when we're alone in our room?" Annika murmured as they headed down, tying the ribbon on her mask.

"Because they have a strict policy that what happens here stays here," Finn said, tying on his own mask. "And I couldn't agree more."

The elevator stopped and when it opened, they were greeted by a slender young woman in an elaborate black mask. Her blonde hair was held up in an elaborate knot covered in shimmering stones, and her black halter dress defined the word 'sexy'.

"My name is Nicolette. I'll be your attendant during your stay," she said in a breathy French accent, and beckoned them to follow her to a long row of private rooms. Her black stiletto heels clicked along in perfect timing, until she stopped by an open door, motioning for them to enter. The floor was covered in plush, ornate rugs and velvet cushions in different shapes, sizes, and colors. There was a low table and sofa full of blankets on one end of the room, but the piles of cushions on the floor looked much more appealing. A tin lamp hung in one corner, with tiny stars cut out of it, casting larger stars around the room. On one of the brick walls was a pair of wooden shutters, and around the other walls hung old ornate mirrors draped in various different fabrics. The thick, heavy scent of incense rose up from the fabric as Annika sank onto one of the cushions, looking around their starry surroundings. Nicolette handed Finn a menu of sorts.

"If zere is anything you desire zat is not on ze menu, don't hesitate to ask," she said, leaning forward to make sure Annika heard her. "I am very resourceful."

She gave an elegant nod to both of them before handing Finn a golden key and sliding their heavy door shut.

He stood in silence, looking over the list for a long time. He checked off a couple boxes at the top, and then sighed as he checked a third toward the bottom with a deliberate stroke of the pen. Then he set it in the hall and left the door partially open, leaning against the wall right beside it.

"It's so pretty in here," Annika said, looking up and around the room. "It's like a cozy little nest. I would never believe that it's actually the middle of the day. I feel like we're in a dream." She started to take off her mask, but Finn shook his head.

"You can take that off when our door is locked," he instructed her. "Why don't you have a look at the films playing?"

"Huh?" she asked, and followed Finn's outstretched finger, which was pointed at the coffee table. She walked over and knelt down to find a sheet of cardstock with different titles and corresponding numbers. She recognized a couple of the films, one of which was on her never-seen-but-must-see list.

"*It Came From Outer Space*," she announced to him. Finn tilted his head and folded his arms across his chest.

"What did?"

"No, that's the name of the movie I want to watch. *It Came From Outer Space*."

"Very well. Cue it up."

"It's a *cult* classic film," she sang playfully, trying to cheer him up. "Not a classic like *Casablanca*."

"I'll watch whatever you like. I don't care."

"Why are you so grouchy?" she pouted. Finn narrowed his eyes at her, not smiling.

"I still can't believe what you said back at the hotel to my brother," he said. "I know I heard you say it . . . I just can't believe that you did. It was so cruel, yet it seemed to give you such pleasure. Do you think I'm happy about being placed in this situation? I feel this is all simply a game in your eyes, and I am a hopeless pawn."

"I'm sorry; I didn't mean to hurt your feelings. I guess I have a warped sense of humor," she said, shrugging as she adjusted her mask. "I know Talvi was lying to me when he said he was busy doing paperwork. I think he's busy doing somebody else. He was acting sneaky on the phone, like he didn't want to get caught talking to me."

"Of course he didn't want to get caught speaking to you," Finn pointed out. "He's not allowed to have any outside contact when he's working."

"So then he *has* to be a spy!" Annika announced. "Seriously, who the hell gets called away out of the blue to spend all summer doing paperwork with another woman? If his job is honestly working on mergers and acquisitions, then I'm a friggin' rock star. His story reeks of bullshit, and I don't think you're buying it either."

"And what good would it do for me to share what I know?" he asked. "It's only going to upset you."

Annika stood up slowly and sauntered over to him, crossing her arms as well.

"It's really cute how you want to protect me from what I already know, but why don't you let me be the judge?"

Finn shook his head again, but his irritated expression faded away as a compassionate one entered his brown eyes.

"Annika, I don't want to hurt you. I hate seeing you cry. I'm not going to sit here and recite every wicked thing that my brother has ever done, especially not when it's taking every ounce of my willpower not to . . . "

Stiletto heels approached, and Nicolette appeared in the doorway holding a large tray with different items set upon it. There was an ornately carved wooden box, a small jade jar, and a short brass lantern with a pattern of crickets cut into the metal. Beside that rested a long wooden pipe, a box of long matches, and a long, thin rod. It was exotic and enticing all at once. Annika took the tray from Nicolette, waiting while Finn thanked her and locked the door with the golden key. He slipped off his mask and hung it on a hook in the ceiling, then slipped off his shoes and socks, setting them neatly by the door. He motioned for her to sit down on the cushions, before sitting across from her with the tray between them. He lifted the ornate wooden box with both hands and buried it in the pile of cushions behind him, casting it out of sight.

"What did you just hide?" she asked, eyeing him curiously.

"Pandora's box. I don't wish to open it."

"Then why did you get it?" she asked, grinning as she pulled off her white peep-toe heels and tossed them carelessly by his shoes. "What's in it?"

Finn pursed his lips as he lit the brass cricket lantern.

"The initials M.N. stand for Merriweather Narayanaswamy," he said abruptly, and removed the lid from the jade jar. An earthy, sweet smell rose up and Annika glimpsed inside to see a dark paste. "She and Talvi used to be partners, but now she is his director. They have an unconventional work relationship, but it works well enough for them, and so it continues. No one else can handle him except her, so you ought to be grateful that she keeps him employed. It's what has allowed us to have such a lovely time in Paris so far. It's what bought you that expensive dress you're wearing."

Using the long, thin rod, he formed a portion of the paste into a little sphere. He placed the tarry ball onto the bowl of the pipe, and rested the bowl on top of the cricket lantern, then stretched out on his side, propping up his head up with some of the pillows.

"So she's his boss then? She tells him to jump and he asks 'how high'? She has that much control over him, even though I'm his *wife*?"

Although she had been dying to know what the initials were on the handkerchief her husband kept in his pocket, she found herself instantly hating the name Merriweather. It was such a happy, sunshiny name, too. She wondered if vampires like Konstantin hated beautiful, sunny days as much as she hated Merriweather.

"Most of us have at least one person in our lives like that, if not more," said Finn. "It's typically the ones who hold the purse strings or the heart strings. They're not always the same person. You'll be more comfortable if you lie on your side as I am."

"Is this just how it's going to be, then?" Annika asked, bunching up some of the pillows as Finn had done and lying on her side across from him. "I'll always be second fiddle to Merriweather?

"I would never say second fiddle," explained Finn. "I don't wish to insinuate that I question his loyalty to you, because he is very loyal to those that he loves the most. Loyal to a fault, sometimes. I was always curious to see what kind of woman he would end up with, since the ones he bothered to bring around were very . . . "

"Skanky?"

"Forgettable," Finn said, glancing at her briefly before resuming his watch over the lantern. "When he brought you home, I saw quickly enough that you were anything but forgettable. You have a spark that can't be snuffed, and it has nothing to do with your beloved red hair that you miss so much. I mean an inner strength, a fire that burns so hot that it could forge steel. That's why your interwoven rings are so symbolic. I don't believe anyone else would have the fortitude to be my brother's wife. I do believe that he's not ready to be married to you. And you're not ready to be married to him. I understand the reasons why—it happened so fast, and you don't really know him very well. You can't trust him because you're not ready to. And he isn't ready to openly share himself with you either. But being in a relationship with someone means that you need to grant one another certain allowances. I can't tell you what those allowances are to be regarding you and my brother. The two of you will have to decide that for yourselves. All I can tell you is that jealousy tries to control love, which only tears it apart. It's trust that builds love, setting it free."

Annika took a moment to think about the thoughtful things that Finn had said. They seemed to make perfect sense, though it struck her as strange that he could harbor such wisdom about relationships when he had said something so terrible to Hilda that they had broken up over it. She glanced at his bare wrist, wondering if she ought to try asking him about it again, but she didn't want to upset him, either. It was so pleasant, lying there in the cushions with him, letting his soothing energy calm down her anger at Merriweather. Ooh, there was that happy, cheerful, evil name again.

"It's hard not to be jealous when Merriweather can call him with no notice and leave me hanging indefinitely," Annika muttered.

"She does try to accommodate him," he explained patiently, still watching the pipe and the lantern attentively. "That's why Talvi's nearly always home over the winter time. It's one of their more unusual arrangements. But yes, it's quite common for him to have little to no notice. I can't tell you how many mornings I woke up and discovered him gone. I remember when he received his summons to travel to Spain . . . he left right in the middle of dinner. He wouldn't even stay for dessert, and Anthea made lemon meringue pie, his favorite."

"Aha, that must have been where he met the Spanish princess."

"He told you about her?"

"Yep. I've been learning all sorts of juicy gossip about you Marinossian boys," she said, smiling primly as she pushed the mask to the top of her head. "I found out who sent Talvi to the samodivi of the East to return some borrowed books. I know you're not as much of a gentleman as you'd like everyone to believe, Finn Marinossian."

He stopped looking at the pipe and stared directly into her blue eyes. A mischievous light had brightened his face.

"Do you, now?"

"Oh yeah. I guess that's why you knew those samodivi of the East that Talvi found at the troll's house. You were on a first-name basis with them, and I think I know why. I'll bet you weren't much of a gentleman when you first met them, were you?"

"Now that is not a very ladylike question to ask, Annika."

"No, it's not, but I'm right, aren't I?"

"I'll let you draw your own conclusions, but let's keep my ungentlemanly conduct just between us, shall we?" he said, blushing brightly, grinning wide. He glanced at the long pipe one more time, and then passed the mouthpiece of it to Annika, leaving the base resting over the brass lantern. "Ladies first."

She inhaled the smoky vapors, letting the sweet, heavy smell fill her lungs. When she exhaled, a thick, bluish-tinted smoke rose above their heads. She passed the mouthpiece to him and he took a long pull, holding it in his mouth for a moment. Then he parted his lips, drawing the smoke out of his mouth and into his nose in a perfect French inhale.

"Oh, do that again," she said, but he passed the pipe back to her.

"It's not very gentlemanly to go out of turn," he said, snuggling into his pillow while she took another puff. They passed the pipe back and forth, and he repeated his trick for her a few more times.

It was understandable to Annika why there were so many cushions, why the room was so dim and cozy. Their dark little den was far, far away from the sunshine and merry weather up above. It made sense to her why animals burrowed into the ground, safe from the harsh elements. In the den, all was safe and secure. Even her ability to overhear others' thoughts and conversations seemed to deaden and dull into a quiet calmness. All the agitation seemed to drift up and away with the blue smoke. It caught on the star-shaped lamplight, leaving her feeling comfortably numb, protected and at peace. She couldn't even feel the nose on her face, let alone the ring on her finger, but she felt safe in this nest with Finn watching over her.

"All I smell is opium," she said, putting up her hand when her next turn came. Finn took one more long draw of smoke before retiring the pipe.

"All I smell is you," he said quietly, rolling onto his back as he exhaled and closed his eyes. "It's going to be a long, long night."

"So this isn't helping at all? I really thought it would."

"It's taken the edge off," he admitted. "But that's about all it has done."

"What does it feel like?"

He was quiet for a long time, and for a moment Annika was sure he'd fallen asleep. Then he moistened his lips and said, "It feels as though I've been crawling through a desert for weeks on my hands and knees, chasing a cup of water that is forever dancing out of my reach. The ground is hot and dry, and all I want, more than anything in the world, is a drink of that water. Just a taste of that fresh, clean, cool water. It keeps dripping and spilling in front of me, and I try to lick it off the ground, but I end up with a mouth full of sand every time. It's making me want to scream. I'm so bloody warm."

Annika moved the tray out of her way and sat up, then pushed Finn' curls up to rest her hand on his damp forehead.

"Maybe we need to open that box. Your skin's on fire."

She reached behind his pillows, searching until she felt the lid under her fingers. The box was wedged securely in place; she couldn't pull it out. She wiggled two fingers under the lid, touching some sort of wrapper, before she was yanked away and found herself sitting to his left at arm's length. His dark eyes burned in frustration.

"I told you, I didn't want to open that," he said through his teeth, gripping her arms tightly against her waist.

"Then why did you get it?" she asked again. She tried to wiggle free, but his strong arms wouldn't let her budge.

"It's a last resort, and I'm not ready to resort to it yet."

Annika grinned to herself, imagining that there weren't too many things that came in wrappers that would fit inside Pandora's box if she was as fertile as Finn claimed.

"I'll bet I know what's in there," she taunted, swinging her left leg over him and settling onto his hips while she gazed in his beautiful eyes. Images of him lifting her dress and doing despicable things to her in that private little doorway off the Champs-Élysées played in her mind like a dirty filmstrip. It was followed by a double feature of her covered in melting ice cubes, being dug frantically out of a bathtub by him, while she counted to thirty.

"Annika, please . . . don't do that," he said, looking as if he were in great pain as his breathing grew heavier. He let his grip on her arms loosen and took her by the waist, intending to push her off of him. "You're only making it worse."

"I didn't do anything," she said innocently, all the while rocking her hips gently against the hard swell in his chinos.

"Well, those weren't *my* thoughts, you *kotka diva*," he hissed while his skin broke out in another round of sweat. "Damn you . . . they are now. You must be starting to peak."

He tried feebly to push her off of him, or pull her off of him, only to realize that he was not accomplishing either. Instead, his hands stayed in place, feeling her body moving with his. A soft moan escaped his lips, and Annika felt a rush of excitement to see how much control she had over this strong, intelligent creature nearly twice her size beneath her. He was covered in sweat and his face was contorted in a strange blend of pleasure and agony. She'd never seen him tortured like this, but it didn't last long.

With a louder groan, he flung her off of him and sat up on his knees. He took off his shirt, wiping his damp face with it before taking it to his glistening skin. The high from the opium and the scent of his clean sweat mixed with his birchwood aftershave pushed Annika further into her delirium. She curled her fingers under his jaw, then reached out toward the living Roman god in front of her and gently took a handful of his curls in each fist, pulling him closer, inhaling from above his pointed ear down to his shoulder. He smelled so good, so clean and pure, just like the water he said he thirsted so desperately for.

"Why should my lying, cheating husband be the only one to have room for certain allowances?" she sighed into his neck.

"That's not how I meant that remark at all. You twisted my words, you twisted creature," Finn said, and despite himself, he tossed his shirt aside and took her by the waist once more, caressing her lovely ilium with his thumbs, humming in approval.

"Let's open the box, Finn. You said that whatever happens here stays here, right?" she whispered, running her nose along his cheekbone until it was touching his. "Or did I get that twisted too?" She tried to kiss him, but he pulled back just as her lips brushed against his.

"No, you're right. It stays here. All of this will stay right here, and we shall never speak of it again."

His hands slid up her waist, up her bodice, then slipped her cardigan off her shoulders and free of her arms. He leaned back to pull the mysterious box out from under his pillows, setting it beside him, easily within his reach. Then he took her arms in his warm hands, letting them wander from her inner elbows up to her shoulders, before sliding down again. Her skin prickled in response to his touch.

"What are you going to do?"

He unbuckled his belt, and pulled it completely free of his chinos.

"What are you going to do?" she asked a second time, wide-eyed. Her heart was thumping wildly in her chest as her pulse raced. "Talk to me."

"I'm not going to hurt you, but what I'm about to do is not gentlemanly in the slightest," he replied, opening the lid of the box. "Now close your eyes . . . and count to thirty."

She couldn't see what was inside, but she nodded because she wanted that more than anything else at that moment. She closed her eyes, and began to count. A wrapper was torn open and then she felt him take her tightly by the arm. She had only made it to nineteen.

The sensation that filled her was like the first crack of thunder rolling through her body after a season of drought. Where the earth had been scorched dry by countless days of relentless sun, there was now soft, warm rain soaking the sand, soaking into her spirit. She could feel the thrill of running naked in the rainstorm, smelling the fresh wet drops on her bare skin, on her neck, in her hair. The wind rushed in her ears until it was replaced with pulses of white noise and otherworldly notes. She gasped and shuddered as she fell back into a blue pool that had appeared beneath her, clinging to Finn for dear life as the warm waves of bliss washed over her again and again. She became an underwater thing, wet and slick like the skin and scales of a mermaid. She could imagine her long hair swirling all around her, all around him, surrounding them both in rhythm to the thunder, in rhythm to her breath, in rhythm to her heartbeat, and his heartbeat.

"Keep your mask on, *slunchitse*. You know the rules," he murmured in her ear. His hands pulled her mask back down into place every time she tried to push it off of her face. His mouth was so close to hers, his skin was so warm against hers, and his mind filled hers with images of racing through infinite oceans of space. Together they traveled, until they arrived at a source of incredible warmth and light. It was the most beautiful thing Annika had ever seen or felt. It was the origin of that source of comfort, that cocoon of solace that only existed between her and Finn. He cradled her in his arms, lying there together in the cool rainstorm. And then, the storm relented to a long, quiet, calm drizzle. And then, the rain stopped.

CHAPTER 34
So Blue Over You

Annika opened her heavy eyes and looked around the dim room. The starry lamplight was absent, contributing further to that dream state. The only light in the room was coming from a black and white film playing on the television; an evening scene of a man walking with a woman toward a telescope under a starry sky. The volume was turned completely down, and the only thing Annika heard was an occasional soft puff on the opium pipe.

She realized her head and right arm were resting on Finn's chest, and she could feel his right arm curled around her back, with his hand resting in the groove of her waist. Her entire body was stiff and sore, and her head was pounding as it rose and fell with each shallow breath he took. She wished she could shut her eyes and fall back asleep in that cozy, dark little nest, but the room was spinning and her stomach was extremely angry about something. She sat up slowly, covering her bare chest with the blanket, and turned to look at Finn. His curls were swept aside, and even though his eyes were closed, she still tried to read his expression. When he lifted his long lashes and their eyes met, there was no guilt, no remorse. There was only a sleepy and serene tranquility glowing about him.

She looked around the dark room, letting his arm slide gently down her bare body and fall onto the cushions beside her. Her white dress lay in a wrinkled heap not far from her. A few feet from that lay her white jeweled mask and her

305

teal cardigan. Her shoes seemed to be missing, along with her protective amulet.

Hesitantly, nervously, she crawled out of the blankets and pillows. Finn set the pipe down and watched her gather the bodice of the dress. She yelped as it unfurled in front of her. All over the skirt were swirls and streaks of yellow, red, and orange.

"What happened to my dress?" she asked, bewildered.

"Your waiter and his friends," Finn answered quietly.

"When did that happen?"

"Tuesday evening, I believe,"

"What day is it today, *sludoor?*" she asked, filling with anxiety.

"I don't know, *slunchitse,*" he yawned as he turned to look at the television. Annika kept waiting for him to elaborate more, as he was always keen to do, but he seemed content to watch the movie in peace. Her stomach gurgled again and she hurried to slip on her panties, dress, cardigan, and mask, taking the overnight bag with her.

"I'm going to the bathroom. Do you need to lock the door or can I just close it and come right back?" she asked, but Finn appeared to have fallen asleep.

She shut the door and wandered down the row of rooms, fighting the nausea and dizziness, realizing precisely how cold the stone floor was under her bare feet. It all seemed new to her, yet she found her way to the bathroom as if she knew it by heart. She stared at the masked woman in the full length mirror, examining her under the artificial light. She had been wearing the mask so long that it felt like it was part of her; an alter ego. It seemed to have its own personality, and she was just the body schlepping it around. She realized there was yellow, orange, and red paint on her neck, intermingled with streaks of blue. There was also blue paint on her calves. Gathering her skirt in her arms, she followed the blue trail up her legs and over her knees. She lifted the dress even higher. The paint had been applied heavier along the backs of her thighs, across her rear, around her hips, and over her waist and lower back. It was even in her hair.

What the hell did we do? she wondered, looking at her mask, as if it could confess all that it had seen.

You couldn't look and not touch, but could you touch and not taste? it seemed to ask. Another current of uneasiness ripped through her, and she let go of her dress and rushed over to the sink.

She got out the toothpaste and began to brush her teeth. Her upset stomach finally lurched and she threw up, then rinsed the basin and brushed her teeth again. She swished some water in her mouth and spit it out, trying to determine what day it was, trying to retrace her steps to her last memory, but the harder she tried to remember, the more her head pounded. There were only snippets here and there; red, yellow and orange flames crawling across her skin, blue rain drops quenching her thirst, Finn's deep voice reminding her over and over to keep on her mask, counting to nineteen, and his warm hands on her waist, her hips, her thighs. So many masks . . . so much paint.

Her hand trembled as she rested it the same place where Finn's had rested in the doorway off the Champs-Élysées, where Talvi's had rested in her bedroom so long ago. The warm, fuzzy feeling was gone, which might have been a good thing, but then again, it might be a bad thing. A very, *very* bad thing.

"Is there anybody in there?" she asked out loud, searching for any sensation that might resemble this so-called ray of light.

"Just me," a woman's voice answered, and a toilet flushed. Nicolette came out from one of the stalls and walked up to Annika, standing beside her as she washed her hands. She reached for a hand towel, and leaned against the counter, eyeing Annika through her mask with a little smile as she carefully dried her hands. "Did you change your mind about the shower?" she asked. "I did *très bien* with your lover, no? He had more paint on him than you."

"I think I'm good, but thanks," Annika stammered, blushing at the offer. That certainly explained why Finn was so clean, and why he was glowing.

She came back to the room and locked the door, dropping her mask on the ground by where Finn's shoes and socks still sat neatly where he left them. She sat next to him, watching him sleep. His breathing was so slow and quiet, she was afraid he wouldn't hear her ask her painful question.

"Please tell me I didn't get it on with the waiter and all his friends," she whispered, trying to ignore her aching body. "I kinda feel like I did." He mumbled something she couldn't understand.

"What?"

He opened his eyes and repeated, "*Kukaan ei sa koskettaa sinua paitsi itse.*"

"I don't have a friggin' clue what you're saying, Finn," she said, looking at him with concern.

"I *said*, no one but myself was allowed to lay a hand on you," he replied somewhat impatiently.

"No, you didn't. You were saying something else. It sounded like *coo-con coss ketta*."

"Ah . . . I was answering you in Karsikko," he sighed, yawning again. "Occasionally I become confused on what language to use."

"You never get confused," she frowned. "That's not like you at all."

"It is when I've been lying so deep amongst the poppies," he said, closing his eyes and resting his head in her lap. "Come lay with me in the field again, *slunchitse*."

"I think we've both had enough of those flowers," she said, brushing his curls out of his eyes. She wanted to remember what lying in the field with him had consisted of, but it was all still a blurry spot in her memory. The more she tried to remember, the more her head ached. Finn handed her the remote control in a languid motion, and she caught sight of his fingertips. They were stained with blue paint.

"Would you prefer to have volume? This is the film you wanted to see . . . *It Came From Outer Space*." Annika nodded, and took the remote.

They sat together in silence for the entire length of the film, but Annika couldn't lose herself in the story. She was lost in her head, searching for her missing memories of what they had done, and however long they had been there doing it. Had it been days, or even longer? She had no clue, but it didn't matter. What was done was done. The red paint on her dress was the ultimate scarlet letter, but she only felt bad that she didn't feel more guilty for what they had likely done. Her anxiety and restlessness were getting worse, and she was relieved when the movie was over.

"Finn?"

"Yes?"

"Do you think we can leave soon?"

"Mmm hmm," he hummed, but he didn't budge from where he still rested on her lap.

"I meant *really* soon. I don't feel good."

He nodded his head, and propped himself up as if he were physically exhausted. Then he tilted his head backward as far as it would go, and slowly arched his back, cracking it a half dozen times. When he finally sat upright, he yawned so hard that he had to wipe tears from his eyes.

Annika gathered his shirt and pants from the opposite side of the room and brought them over, since he seemed so tired and stiff. It seemed to take him forever to fasten his buttons and buckle his belt. Annika didn't remember him being so sluggish when they had first smoked the opium, but then, who knew how long he'd been awake, or how much he'd smoked. He slipped Pandora's box into their overnight bag and blundered his way to the door, sitting down to put on his shoes.

Annika started looking for her own shoes, finding one under the couch. It was spattered in the same blue paint that was on Finn's hands, and when she went to put it on, she noticed that the bottom of her foot was the same color too. She glanced over at the opium pipe, and sighed.

This is why you can't have nice things, she could just imagine James yelling at her. She started to shake her head, but then she stopped. It still throbbed mercilessly. She stumbled through the sea of cushions and tried not to throw up again as she leaned down to blow out the cricket lantern. Together, she and Finn walked to the elevator, leaving their nest of pillows, and hopefully all memory and evidence of what that room had been privy to.

They were greeted by the thin older woman, who let them out of the elevator and took their masks, and led them to her desk. She had Finn leave his email address in case Annika's amulet turned up, and then took his cards out of a locked drawer, handing them back after he signed the bill, no questions asked.

Annika's eyes were grateful that it was a cloudy day. The ominous sky was dark gunmetal grey, and it looked like it was thinking about raining, but hadn't made up its mind yet. Annika couldn't remember the last time she'd bought a pack of cigarettes, but now seemed like the right time. They stopped at a magazine stand, where Finn snagged a few scientific journals and she picked up a pack of smokes and a new lighter. While Finn paid, she noticed that the calendar was marked as the last Friday of June.

As soon as she could get outside, she ripped open a pack and was inhaling that calming nicotine, chasing away her anxiety with every desperate puff. Finn shook his head in dreamy disapproval, helping himself to one of her cigarettes, lighting it in slow motion and bringing it to his amused lips with blue stained fingers. The world raced around them, commuters, students, and tourists, as they meandered block after block to their hotel. There was no rush. There was no need. There was no schedule. Time didn't matter. Nothing mattered at that moment except a steady supply of nicotine, a light breeze, and Finn walking on the outside as he always did.

Annika caught a reflection of them in a storefront window and stopped to look at herself again, this time without her mask. Her partner in crime stood next to her, watching their reflection as well. Among the morning crowd on their way to another day of work, they remained untouched in a bubble all their own . . . him looking as content as a cat with a canary, and her, stained from head to toe by their misdeeds. She held her head high and smoked, looking at this strange colored version of herself; her unmasked alter ego. The dress, like her, may have been ruined . . . but it was still a Chanel.

"I just realized something," she said, holding her cigarette in one hand, and draping her brown hair over her shoulder with her other hand.

"And what is that, *slunchitse?*"

"Every book you own belongs to me now."

"However did you arrive at that preposterous observation?" he asked, taking a leisurely drag from his own cigarette.

"You bet me every single one of your books that I'd complain if something dripped in my hair at *la Société d'Art Souterraine*. Well, look at all this paint in my hair. I haven't said one word about it." She ran her hand down her long locks and looked up at him. It was splattered in primary colors.

"No, I distinctly heard you complain about the paint."

"I complained about it getting on my dress, but I didn't say anything about it getting in my hair," she said, looking at her reflection and grinning smugly.

"Either way, I wasn't serious."

"You made the bet and I accepted. I won fair and square. But I don't have room for all of my new books, so I'm going to let you keep them at your house. Does that sound fair to you?"

"Not at all, but I suppose that will teach me to make wagers I can ill-afford, even in jest. Perhaps I should consider myself lucky that I lost to you and not the Casino de Monte Carlo," he grinned. He draped his arm around her, still watching her in the reflection. "You know what this means, don't you?"

"That I now own ninety-nine percent of your most prized possessions?"

"Precisely," he sighed, nodding his head ever so slowly. He turned to look down at her. "And until I win them back, I'll be wrapped around your finger."

At that moment, the dark clouds parted, and a ray of light rested on the two of them, illuminating Annika's dress in its rich, radiant, fiery hues. She could feel the warmth radiate through her body, before reflecting off of it.

"Why, look at you, all aglow," Finn said softly, with a dreamy look in his eyes. "You look just like a fallen star, my little sun."

"Maybe that's because I *am* one," she replied as she met his blissful gaze, abruptly remembering something he had said to her about Talvi.

You're not ready to be married to him.

He was right.

CHAPTER 35
The Flaw in Finn

Along with their dry cleaned catacomb clothes, there was a white envelope on the floor with Annika's name on it when they walked into their room. She opened it up and discovered that it was a telephone message. She snorted when she read it, because it was literally written word for word in James-speak.

Oh my god. Shit is blowing up. Call me ASAP. —James

That could have meant anything, coming from him, but the fact that he had bothered to call her in Paris meant it must be important. James would still be asleep anyway, so Annika decided it only made sense to take a shower and put on a clean outfit. She locked herself in the bathroom, and turned the dial in the shower to the hottest setting. She pulled off her clothes, inspecting herself again in the bathroom mirror of their suite. It was uncanny, how many nooks and crannies seemed to have blue paint.

The hot water felt so good on her tired body. Her head still hurt, and her stomach was still queasy, but the steamy shower helped tremendously. She washed her hair and scrubbed her skin as hard as she could bear until every last streak of the incriminating paint had been rinsed down the drain. She put on her robe and intended to get the overnight bag from Finn, but when she opened the bathroom door, she did not intend to find him stretched out on the sofa, wrapping his belt around his arm. Pandora's box sat open, next to him.

313

"What's this?" she gasped, reeling inside from what she was seeing.

"I'm afraid that even though you're out of the woods, I'm a bit lost among the trees. I'm trying to come down to the earth as gently as I can," he explained. He then put the end of the belt in his teeth, while he reached inside the box with his right hand and curled his left hand into a fist, looking for a vein. "I just need a little more."

"Finn, wait," she said, trying as hard as she could to stay calm while she casually knelt beside him on the sofa. "Can I go first? I've never done this before."

He looked at her curiously, letting the belt drop from his mouth.

"Annika, what are you talking about? I gave you your first taste three days ago."

"Was that when you told me to close my eyes and count to thirty?" she whispered, covering her mouth with her hand in surprise. "*That's* what you did to me? Holy shit! I thought you stabbed me with something else!"

A low laugh sounded from deep within Finn's chest.

"I'm quite flattered that you think I could ever feel as good as morphine. If only." His face melted into a bemused smile as he picked up the needle and closed lid of the box. "I didn't know any other way to resist you after you crawled on my lap and put such explicit images into my mind. You were rather . . . determined. But it was absolutely brilliant of you to suggest the gallery. Opiates are known for diminishing the sex drive, although I had no idea that I would need such a large quantity to prevent *la petit mort* from happening in each others' arms. I honestly don't know how else we would have gotten through the past few days without our lovely poppies. It makes me miss them so much."

"Can I give you this dose, *sludoor?*" she asked, feeling relieved and terrified all at once. She reached her hand seductively toward his and took the needle from him. "I want to make you feel as amazing as I can."

"You already do, *slunchitse*," he murmured. He tightened the belt around his arm and held it out to her, waiting expectantly.

"Close your eyes," she hummed in his pointed ear. "And count to thirty."

As soon as his eyes were shut, Annika clamped her fingers around the syringe and snatched the box, darting into the bathroom as fast as she could. She locked the door behind her and quickly pushed the syringe's contents into the toilet. There was a knock at the door, then a pounding, then his voice trying to reason with her, growing in urgency.

"Annika, open the door," he plead from outside. "You don't know what you're doing. Annika, *please* . . . "

She opened the wooden box lined in brown velvet, and saw it was divided in half. In the front half, one longer section was filled with individually wrapped syringes. Those were the wrappers she had felt when she snuck her fingers into it three days ago, the wrapper she heard before he shot her full of this memory-erasing, mind-numbing serum. The other half of the box was divided into smaller sections, each containing a small glass bottle filled with clear liquid, though they were not all full. She lifted one out and read the label description; medical grade morphine.

"Annika, open the bloody door!" he demanded, pounding harder. "I did this for you! Do you hear me? Now let me in there! Don't make me force my way in!"

She hastily opened the bottles one by one, dumping them into the sink and then turned on the faucet full blast, rinsing them as fast as she could as he continued to threaten to break down the door. There was a hard thud, then another, then another, and she realized that he was indeed kicking the door in. The wood around the doorknob was beginning to splinter. He would be in there any second.

Her hands shook as adrenaline surged through her, and she threw the needles and the bottles into the toilet, flushing right at the moment that the door flew open.

"*What have you done?*" he screamed at her, scooping a handful of empty bottles out of the toilet. "What have you *done?*" he repeated, throwing them on the floor and grabbing the lapels of her robe. He jolted her so hard that it scared her almost as much as the crazed look in his eyes. She was being shaken like a ragdoll in his muscular arms. "Do you *know* how much money that cost?"

"Who fucking cares? You could have *died*, you dumb shit!" she yelled back. "You could have OD'd anytime over the past three days, and I was too fucking high to know up from down, let alone get you to a fucking hospital!"

"I *know* your limitations, and I sure as bloody hell know *mine*!" he insisted. "Who are *you* to question my intelligence?"

"Who are *you* to shoot me full of drugs for three days?"

"Would you rather I had put something *else* inside of you, you *kotka diva*?" he snarled, shaking her again.

"Yeah, actually, I *would*!" she choked, and started to cry. "I'd rather have your baby than have you die!"

He was so completely taken aback by her admission that the rage left his face. He sank to his knees with her still in his arms, and from behind his curls, she could see tears begin to gather in his eyes.

"That's how people overdose," she went on, afraid to move. "You're off the shit for a while, and then you think you can handle your regular dosage, then *bam*, you're dead! You think you're so smart because you've read a zillion books, but you're really just a fucking idiot!"

Finn was silent for a long time. He still held her by her robe, looking at her until his watery eyes blinked, sending tears down his face. He let go of her lapels and wrapped his arms around her, hugging her close as he buried his head into her shoulder. His hand rested on the back of her head, stroking her wet hair carefully, and she felt him take a deep breath and sigh.

"I'm sorry, Annika. I'm so sorry for all of this," he whispered.

"It's okay," she replied, and felt a surge of comfort rise up within her. She imagined that they were in their safe little cocoon, not beside the toilet clogged with syringes, sitting on the bathroom floor among empty morphine bottles and splinters of wood.

Finn let go of her and wiped his tears on his sleeve, before brushing hers away with his thumb.

"You had your hands in the toilet," she said, sniffing. "That's a little gross."

"Well, I'm certain it's still cleaner than the water from the catacombs," he sighed with a weak smile. He reached up to moisten a wash cloth under the faucet, and then shut off the water, which had been running the entire time. He gently wiped her face and then cleaned off his hands, removing the rest of the blue paint from underneath his fingernails. "Did you know, not once in three hundred and seventy-two years, has anyone ever called me a fucking idiot?"

"I guess there's a first time for everything."

He tossed the wash cloth aside and sat back, shaking his head at her.

"Oh, Annika. I've looked after my niece and nephew quite a bit, but you're more of a handful than the two of them combined. Whatever am I going to do with you?"

Annika shrugged, grinning slightly, until he grinned too. Everything was going to be alright, just as he had assured her from day one.

The sound of a key in the front door snapped them out of their private moment, and Annika yelled out,

"No housekeeping, *s'il vous plaît!*"

The door shut, and she sighed in relief. But then she gasped in horror as a tall, wild-haired figure clad in black stepped into the doorway. He did not look pleased in the slightest at what he saw.

CHAPTER 36
Busted

"What the bloody . . . " Talvi trailed off as he took in the scene of the broken door, the syringes in the toilet, and the bottles on the floor, along with his wife sitting amidst it all in nothing but a disheveled robe. He looked at her for answers, then at Finn, who looked equally as disheveled in his wrinkled clothes, but he received no explanation.

"How did you get in?" Annika asked, utterly dumbfounded at her husband's timing.

"I'm paying for this fucking room," he said, his blue-green eyes looking angry and hurt all at once. "I have a *fucking* key. Why, cheers for asking how I've been, love. It's fantastic to see you too!"

He stooped down and picked up an empty bottle from the floor, sneering as he read the label.

"So this is why you haven't been answering the telephone," he said, standing back up to resume his glare of disapproval. He dropped the bottle into the trash can under the sink. "I've been ringing your room for three days. I thought of a million awful things that could have happened to you both, but this certainly wasn't among them."

"It's my fault, Talvi. Annika didn't know what I was doing until quite recently," said Finn from where he still sat on the floor. "I tried to hide it from her, but she just found out."

"You don't say," Talvi mused, glancing at the toilet and then at the splintered door, but his tone was skeptical at best. He lifted his left leg and with his right hand he withdrew a black-handled knife from inside his boot. Annika clutched Finn's arm, afraid to even breathe. The blade gleamed brightly in her husband's hand, but he rested it on the counter while he shoved his left hand into the messenger bag slung across his chest. He pulled out his smartphone, then unlocked the screen and tapped it a few more times, bringing it to his pointed ear as he looked down his nose at the two of them.

"You'll want to start packing your things. Your Parisian holiday is officially over." He motioned with his head towards the suite, and they hurried past him, over the bottles and wood splinters, and out of the bathroom.

Without warning, Finn whisked her out onto the balcony, shutting the door behind them.

"I know you like to let your imagination run wild," he began, gripping the rail while he watched the rain pour down on the city. A cool breeze licked at Annika's neck, and she pulled her robe tightly around her chest. "But don't you *dare* spend one single second thinking about our misadventure. Fill your mind with sunrises and cafés au lait out here with me. Fill it with the scent of the catacombs and the sound of polo ponies running across the field. Let your mind wander to the dressing rooms at Chanel, but don't you ever, *ever* let it wander to the depths of *la Société d'Art Souterraine*, do you hear me?" He turned to face her, and when Annika saw his grave expression, she felt a chill run down her spine. "I wasn't joking when I said Talvi would have my head if he ever found out that I took you there. We're skating on very thin ice, *slunchitse*."

She nodded quickly and darted back inside as soon as Finn opened the door. The silence in the hotel room was only broken by her husband's one-sided conversation. Annika strained to listen in as she and Finn gathered their clothes, shoes, and souvenirs, and began stuffing them into their luggage. Talvi's voice was low and biting as he knelt down and began picking the paraphernalia out of the toilet with his knife, adding it to the bottle in the trash can.

"So how soon can you get me three first-class plane tickets to Sofia?" Annika heard him say as she stuffed her painted dress into its garment bag. There was a short pause.

"Bit of a family emergency, Merri. I'm sorry, but I won't be back in time for what you and I had planned this evening."

Long, long pause.

"Yes, but if we've waited all this time, what's another week or so? If I can return sooner, I will." Talvi's voice shifted from sounding irritated, to sounding downright lecherous. "You know how badly I want to see what you've been hiding from me down there. It's been so long I've almost forgotten what it looks like. Such a shame, really. You know how much I love it when you let me loose in there, and give me whatever I want."

Annika's heart crawled up into her throat just far enough to make her nauseous, before sinking down into the bottom of her stomach. She had never felt more repulsed by a man in her life, but then, this was no man. As much as she didn't want to hear the rest of the conversation, she couldn't turn back now. She hoped desperately that she was misunderstanding something, and she strained her ears again, only to hear him say, "Trust me Merri, I'll wrap this nonsense up and come back as soon as I can. I can't wait much longer, either."

Two hours later, the three of them were on a plane forty-thousand feet above France, with Annika sandwiched in the middle of the Marinossian brothers. Talvi had claimed the window seat and Finn had the aisle. She shared looks of sympathy from him and looks of condemnation from his brother, but words were scarce between those three; both telepathic, and spoken aloud. After his phone call to Merriweather, Talvi had rifled through their luggage, searching for any hidden paraphernalia. Annika thanked her lucky stars that Finn had torn up the incriminating little black business card from her wanton waiter, letting it drift away in the breeze down the Champs-Élysées.

Talvi dragged his messenger bag out from under the seat and pulled out a small stack of folios and a laptop computer. He pushed the bag back in place and put the laptop on his fold-down tray, setting the folios in his lap. When he opened the screen, he angled it so Annika couldn't look at it without being obvious. He opened the top file on the stack and began to type at a steady, fluid clip, which left her almost speechless. Had he really been telling her the truth when he claimed he'd been doing paperwork for the past two weeks? On top of that, the last time she had seen him type, it was strictly of the hunting and pecking variety.

"What are you working on, *sludoor?*" she asked, trying to break the silence between the three of them.

"Paperwork, *slunchitse*, as I told you on the telephone," he quietly answered, not looking away from his task.

"Can I see what kind of paperwork you're doing?"

"You can . . . however, you *may* not," he said, and continued to type away.

This grammar lesson wasn't the answer Annika wanted to hear. She frowned, feeling irritated, and anxious. Finn unbuckled his seat belt, grabbed an airsickness bag, and disappeared into the lavatory.

"I just remembered, I'm supposed to call James as soon as possible. *May* I use your cell phone when we land?"

"No," Talvi replied without missing a beat.

"Why are you giving me the cold shoulder?"

"Because I have a mountain of work to complete before I can move on to my next project, and dealing with your bullshit has now made things exponentially worse," he explained, still typing. "I've been watching my accounts, keeping track of how much you've been spending, and where you've been spending it. I thought it odd to see no charges since Tuesday morning; however, not answering your telephone since then is what aroused my suspicion. I never expected it was because the two of you were getting as high as kites. And here I thought you'd been kidnapped by doppelgängers or Finn had acquired a debt with the wrong crowd. He does love his cards, but I guess he likes gambling with opiates more. Either way, I am fairly disgusted with you both, hence the cold shoulder."

"Oh, and you expect me to believe that you've been a total prince for the past two weeks?" she asked. "Or maybe you *have* been, Prince Talvi. What did you have planned tonight with Merriweather that you can't wait to get back to do with her, hmm? I heard the way you were talking to her in the bathroom, you ass."

Talvi said nothing, although his typing slowed down considerably. His lips were pressed together in a tight, thin, angry line. His eyes grew dark, like the black clouds of an approaching storm.

"I know you can't wait to get back and get it on with her," Annika taunted. "I know no one else but her can handle you at work. I'm sure I know exactly how she handles you. You said she gives you whatever you want, and that it's been so long you've almost forgotten what she looks like down there. I'll bet she's pretty, isn't she?"

"No, Annika. She's not pretty at all," he replied softly, catching her off guard a second time. A cruel smile played on his lips as he stopped typing and closed his eyes, resting his head against the back of his seat. "She's absolutely *stunning*. Her skin is rich and dark like maple sugar, and when she lets her long black hair down, it just barely covers her perfectly shaped tits. She smells like jasmine and tastes like spiced vanilla, although sometimes she tastes like scotch. I used to pour it down her neck and drink it out of her lap, but now when I come inside her office, she has me use a glass like everyone else. Regardless, I'll do whatever it takes to please her, because she makes me want to work so bloody *hard*."

He moaned quietly to himself, then opened his eyes and blinked a few times before resuming his typing as if nothing had happened. Annika raised her hand to slap him, but he caught her arm in mid-swing. She tried to jerk it away from him a half dozen times but it was pointless in his iron grip. All she wanted was to pull off her ring and run away, but she was unable to do either.

"Why would you *say* something like that?" she hissed, feeling horrified and repulsed.

"I thought it would be more effective than simply telling you to shut up," he said with a brazen smirk as he finally released her arm. "I hope it worked. I have a lot more reports to read through before we land, and the sound of your voice is quite unbearable."

Annika, however, was aghast at the image he had planted in her mind of him and his boss.

"You are the biggest douchebag I've ever known!" she cried, trying to reign in her anger so the entire plane couldn't hear her, except for maybe the row behind her. And maybe the row behind them. "Oh my god, I hate you *so* much! How am I even married to you? You're like, the king of the douche lords! What's wrong with you, that you would say something like that to me?"

"I've tried saying everything else I can to stifle your insecurities, and it doesn't seem to make any difference. I suspect deep down, that's the sort of thing that you wanted to hear all along. If you must insist upon thinking the worst of me, I may as well try and meet your expectations. Isn't it a husband's duty, to make his wife happy? All I've tried to do is make you happy, my little dove." He paused long enough to bat his lashes at her, feigning innocence as no one but he could do. "Shall I elaborate further on the many ways that I used to ask my director for a raise? Because I can, if it pleases you. She certainly gave me a lot of them."

"I think I've heard enough!" she snapped, turning her back to him right as Finn returned and settled into his seat. He reclined his chair as far as it would go and covered up with a blanket. His curls were damp with sweat and his skin looked clammy.

"Finn, what's wrong?" she asked, brushing his curls aside, but he seemed afraid to open his mouth. It was probably for the best. He looked like he might throw up again. Annika draped her own blanket over him and smoothed his hair, trying to be as comforting as their airplane seats would allow.

"He's going through withdrawal," Talvi informed her casually as he resumed his typing. "He'll live. He'll just feel like he's dying over the next few days."

To Annika, the next few days seemed to take forever to pass by. She couldn't even imagine how long they must have lasted for Finn, who was fighting an upset stomach, hot sweats, cold chills, an aching back, a runny nose, and insomnia, all while traveling the long hike to his family's home. He had little to say other than moans, groans and the occasional sigh. Annika didn't have much to say either, after her little chat on the plane with her charming husband. Instead, she focused on taking care of Finn however she could, wiping away his neck and forehead with a cool wet cloth when the sweats came on, and keeping him bundled up when the chills arrived. She rubbed his shoulders whenever he needed to stop and take a break, and was always quick with a sympathetic smile and bottled water.

Strangely, even without his morning tea, and even though he was for the most part being ignored, Talvi seemed happy as a lark throughout their journey, humming every now and then as if a great weight had been lifted from his shoulders. After the plane had landed in Sofia, they had taken a taxi north until they reached a gravel road in the middle of nowhere. From that point, they got out and walked, and walked, and walked through the foothills of the Balkan mountains until they reached a familiar waterfall just as the sun was setting. They stepped over the stones and behind the falls, into a cave dwelling that Annika hadn't seen in the better part of a year.

"Runa . . . Runa lagoona," Talvi called playfully, but there was no answer. The huge hearth hadn't had a fire in it recently, either, though there were soft furs lying on top of the little wool mattresses. Talvi pushed them together to accommodate his height, but when it was finally time to go to bed, Annika found herself turning her back to her husband and inching closer to Finn.

They spent the night there and left right away in the morning. Other than beautiful scenery and miserable silence broken by Talvi's cheerful humming, nothing exciting happened until midday, when a black raven came out of nowhere and landed on Finn's shoulder.

"Cazadora," he sighed in relief, nuzzling into her soft feathers. "Please, please fetch Asbjorn. Tell him to bring us three horses as fast as he can."

It was the most he had said in days.

CHAPTER 37
Checkmate

"Go on ahead. I'll be right in as soon as I turn the horses out," Finn offered as they arrived at the sprawling Marinossian hacienda.

Annika followed Asbjorn and Talvi through the yard, past the gardens, into the kitchen, down the hall, and into the round shaped conservatory, where Talvi's older sister sat on a brown velvet chaise lounge, staring at a chess board on the coffee table. Next to the chess board sat a plate of cookies. Sloan was sleeping in the crook of one arm while she tapped her fingers silently on the velvet cushion with her free hand. Talvi's mother was relaxing in the chaise lounge across from Anthea, tossing a ball of yarn back and forth with Stella. A pitcher of milk sat on a tray with some glasses on top of an empty wood burning stove.

"Who's winning?" Asbjorn asked as he stepped between the arched windows and the chaise lounge, greeting his wife with a kiss on top of her head before starting to rub her shoulders.

"Who do you think?" Anthea grumbled as she frowned in concentration and moved a chess piece forward. Then she looked up and her irritated expression melted into a happy one.

"Annika, it's *so* good to see you!" she exclaimed as loud as she dare, while Sloan slept on. "And Talvi, it's good to see you too, but oh, Annika, I'm so glad you're well." She patted the empty space beside her on the chaise and Annika took a seat.

"We were so worried when the boys and Runa and Dardis returned without you," said Althea, giving her a warm smile. "But you seem to be alright."

"It's been a little crazy, but I'm okay," Annika said, grinning at Anthea and then at Althea. It was so nice to have someone kind talking to her for a change.

"What happened to your hair like the fairies?" Stella asked, frowning Annika with suspicious eyes as she clutched on to her ball of yarn.

"Oh, I changed it. What do you think, Stella? Do you like it, or should I go back to the way it was?" Annika asked, running her fingers halfway through her brown hair before they got stuck in a snarl. All that horseback riding had been unkind to her hair.

Stella pinched her little mouth from one side to the other, thinking hard.

"I like the red better."

"I do too. I'm going to change it back as soon as I can," Annika agreed, smiling as Stella put the yarn ball in her mouth and crawled towards the tall arched windows on her hands and knees. She looked like a little panther, prowling under the potted plants that sat along the windowsills. Annika had to admit, her niece was pretty adorable. And smart.

"Mother, do we have any of that jalapeño cheese left from last night?" Anthea asked. "It was so good, that I can't get it out of my mind."

"Is this what you were just asking for?" Ambrose replied, having just come into the room with a plate of sliced cheese.

"Yes!" she hissed. He handed his daughter the plate, and then looked briefly at the chess board before making his move.

"Checkmate," he said, his eyes twinkling merrily.

"Really, Father?" she whined, frowning at him as he sat down beside his wife. Anthea took a slice of cheese, placed a cookie on top of it, and shoved it into her mouth, careful not to get crumbs on Sloan. The happy sigh that came out of her made it clear that this was a winning combination.

"I'll warn you now," said Asbjorn with a wry grin, still rubbing Anthea's shoulders. "If anyone else wants a cookie, you better act fast."

"Oh, there's more in the kitchen," said Althea, rising up from the lounge with a motherly smile. "I'll go get them."

"Is it really that good?" Annika asked, seeing how delighted Anthea's expression was as she put another cookie on a second slice of cheese and ate it. Anthea nodded enthusiastically, and Annika reached for a piece of jalapeño cheese to see what all the fuss was about.

"Thanks, *sludoor*," she said to Talvi as he offered her the plate of cookies.

Seeing they were snicker doodles, she took two, and put the piece of cheese under one of them before eating it. It wasn't anything like what she was expecting, but spitting it out wasn't an option. She smiled at Anthea as if jalapeño and cheese flavored snicker doodles were the best thing since sliced bread.

"Oh, Annika, you're learning Karsikko," Anthea said happily. "How lovely to hear you speak it. Have you learned any other words?"

"Well, I know *slunchitse* means 'little sun', and I got called a *kotka diva* a couple times, but I don't know what it means," she said, with her mouth full of cheese and cinnamon goo. "Is that Karsikko?"

Ambrose snorted and stroked his beard in amusement, while Asbjorn stopped rubbing Anthea's shoulders and said he needed a glass of milk. Anthea's eyes were wide, and her mouth was pinched in a screwy, tortured smile.

"Yes, and I suppose you heard that from my darling brother," she said, glaring up at Talvi, before looking down at Sloan, who was resting peacefully.

"Mmm hmm," Annika nodded; her mouth still full. With trembling hands, Talvi shoved the plate of cookies into her lap and left the room in a hurry. Anthea shook her head and looked at her father for help.

"You may as well tell her what it means, since you two seem to be enjoying those disgusting cookies so much," Ambrose said, grinning mischievously.

"It's a very crude term for a lady when she's ovulating," Anthea explained quietly, leaning closer to Annika so Stella couldn't hear. "It translates to 'wild female cat', but it refers to when they come into season. They yowl and carry on, and rub up against your legs constantly, because they are so desperate for . . . for kittens. They are unbearably annoying until they get what they want from the male cats. Why ever would Talvi call you such a name, unless you had your three days with him? Are you not telling us some rather exciting news? Am I finally to be an aunt?" Anthea's brown eyes lit up while she cradled Sloan close, waiting for an explanation.

It wasn't Talvi who called me a kotka diva. Annika thought, panicking as she struggled to swallow the disgusting jalapeño cinnamon mush in her mouth. *It was Finn. He called me that when we were in Paris together, before Talvi came to get us!*

"No!" Anthea cried out, startling Sloan awake. "Oh my gods, *no!*"

Meanwhile, Talvi had stormed out towards the stables in a fury, and met his brother halfway across the back yard.

"Is it true, the reason why you didn't answer your telephone for three days?" he demanded, his voice shaking. A wild, fierce look had overtaken him, and he looked like a black panther ready to pounce. "What did you *do* to Annika in Paris?"

"I slipped up, Talvi. I made a mistake," Finn admitted in a calm voice, trying to avoid looking into his brother's furious eyes. "I know I never should have done what I did to her, but there was no other way around it. I had no choice. I swear I didn't hurt her. I was as gentle and careful with her as I could possibly be. She wanted more . . . she begged me for more, but I only gave her as much as I thought her body could safely tolerate . . . "

"Anthea, what's wrong?" asked Asbjorn, rushing to her side immediately. "Is it the baby?"

"No," she said, still looking at Annika as if she were about to cry. "Not *our* baby!"

"Oh, no, no, no, I'm not pregnant," Annika said quickly, wishing she had a glass of that milk. She was positive it wasn't the cookie she'd just swallowed that made her feel like throwing up. Anthea still appeared astonished as she tried to coax Sloan back to sleep.

"But you and Finn were together for your entire three days . . . " she pointed out weakly, unable to comprehend what she had learned. Ambrose and Asbjorn shared an astounded glance before resting their eyes on Annika.

"Yeah, I know," Annika replied, studying the plate of cookies in her lap to escape their stares. What a lovely, normal conversation to be having with her new in-laws. She looked at Stella, who was peeking out the window with the ball of yarn still in her teeth. How best could she answer everyone without saying it out loud in front of the children? How best could she answer without unintentionally revealing a play-by-play of that week? They didn't need to know about her waking up naked in Finn's arms. They also didn't need to know about the blue paint, and everywhere it had been.

"We found a way around it," she said, still staring at the plate in her lap.

"There is no way around it, Annika," said Asbjorn, sounding doubtful. "Not if you were together. You wouldn't have been able to keep your hands off each other. You can't even sleep through it. The pull is too strong."

"It turns out that morphine is stronger," she whispered, afraid to look up at him. She stretched out her left arm and pointed her right finger toward her inner elbow, making a motion like she was shooting herself. Anthea's worried eyes softened, and the tension in the room eased up.

"So *that's* why you came to visit so unexpectedly . . . to make certain that Finn wasn't left alone after such an ordeal," Ambrose sighed, stroking his beard again. "I'm amazed that it worked. He had a long, long battle with that after his polo accident, you know."

"He mentioned it, but he didn't go into much detail," said Annika, feeling relaxed enough to look at him.

"He would have healed faster if he wasn't out of his mind for so long, but we had no idea how bad it really was until I relocated the herb garden."

Annika wrinkled her forehead in confusion as she looked at her father-in-law.

"I don't understand how that helped you find out about Finn. Did you dig up a bunch of poppies?" she asked. Some of the seriousness left Ambrose's face as he helped himself to a snicker doodle from the plate in her lap.

"Well, at one point they were poppies. I had the horses all hitched up, thinking it was going to be a simple project, and then the plow turned up a crop of something I'd never seen in the soil before," he explained. "I discovered that Talvi had been burying all of Finn's empty morphine bottles under a clover patch on the edge of the gardens. He spent the rest of the spring digging glass out of the dirt, and I'm certain that's why the herb garden thrives where it is, along with getting better sunlight. I made him sift through the soil until there wasn't so much as a pebble left in it. I couldn't have the horses stepping on that, let alone anyone digging in it. But I'm just grateful that he was too lazy to dig much deeper, or we might never have realized the extent of Finn's addiction until it was too late. He nearly died in the polo accident . . . we certainly didn't want to lose him to something that we could have prevented."

"When he finally got the morphine out of his system, he swore he would never do it again," Anthea added, "but of all the reasons to risk walking among the poppies, I don't believe I can think of one so understandable, dire as it is."

"Mummy, look at Uncle Talvi and Uncle Finn!" Stella giggled as she pressed her hands and nose against the window in between two huge ferns. "They're hugging!"

"That's nice, dear," said Anthea, playing with Sloan's curls as she shifted him on her lap. She turned back at Annika, looking quite stern.

"Are you still taking it?"

Annika shook her head.

"When was the last time he did?"

"Friday morning, I think. He was drifting in and out of consciousness when I woke up. He didn't know what day it was, and he kept confusing English and Karsikko. But I flushed the rest of his stash, so you don't have to worry about us bringing any here. I don't put up with that kind of shi—I mean, stuff," she corrected herself, glancing at Stella and then at Sloan.

"I'm glad to hear that," Anthea said. "But I'll warn you now; don't take anything that he says or does personally in the near future. He's quite mercurial when his pretty flowers have been taken away."

"Mummy, look! Now they're hugging on the ground!" Stella squealed.

"What?"

Anthea turned to look out the window, along with Asbjorn, and cried out again, waking Sloan for good this time. The brothers were wrestling on the lawn with their arms interlocked, until Talvi broke free. He threw a flurry of punches to Finn's head and body, but Finn kicked the back of Talvi's knees with one of his long legs, grabbed him by the neck when he hit the ground, and managed to climb on top of him. He delivered a few solid right hooks to Talvi's head and ribs, and a couple of mighty kidney punches before he got jabbed in the throat.

"I think I need to go break that up," Asbjorn said, frowning with concern as he came to the window and picked up his daughter.

"They'll sort themselves out," came Ambrose's unconcerned response. It didn't stop him from getting up to see what all the fuss was over, since the ferns in the windows were obstructing his view. "They haven't had a good scrap in a while."

"I don't think that's a scrap," Asbjorn said, plunking Stella beside Annika before darting out of the room. Ambrose and Annika looked out the window just in time to see Talvi nail Finn in the jaw with his left elbow, slashing him open. Bright red blood spilled down Finn's throat, and down the front of his shirt. Talvi raised his elbow again and this time he brought it down on the side of his brother's head. A trail of red began to run into Finn's ear and down his neck. Talvi shoved his right forearm against Finn's throat, and with his left hand, he started to pull the knife from his boot.

"Dear gods—he's going to *kill* him!" Ambrose exclaimed, and rushed outside after Asbjorn.

"Come along, Annika," Anthea said in a commanding voice, standing up with Sloan and heading toward the hallway. "Can you keep the children entertained in the music room across the hall while I go help?"

"Of course," she said, trying not to cry. Holding Stella close in her arms, she followed Althea out of the room. She took one last look out the window, watching both Ambrose and Asbjorn pull Talvi off of his brother, and even then, he still tried to kick Finn as he was being dragged away.

CHAPTER 38
Father Knows Best

Ambrose wasn't an elf known to be easily angered, but he was positively livid as he and Asbjorn hauled Talvi to the shed behind the stables and threw him to the ground, tying his hands securely behind him. While Asbjorn kept one boot firmly on Talvi's back, Ambrose disappeared into the shed and returned with a rusty shovel.

"I can manage now, if you'll see to Finn," he growled, and pressed the shovel between Talvi's shoulders while Asbjorn raced over to Finn. Ambrose forced his youngest son to walk in front of him, past the horses in the fields, and into the forest of towering silver poplars and white birch trees that lie beyond the gardens around their home.

"How *dare* you lay a hand on anyone like that in my home, in front of my grandchildren? How *dare* you do that to your own brother?" The twinkling in his blue-green eyes was long gone and his knuckles were white around the shovel's handle.

"How *dare* he do that to *me*!" Talvi shouted, his heart still pounding loudly in his chest. "He acted like what he did was some kind of accident, and then went on about how sweet and gentle he was when he was having his way my wife! He told me she begged him for more! Gods, I'm going to be sick . . . "

Ambrose dropped the shovel and grabbed the collar of Talvi's shirt, which was spattered with Finn's blood, jerking him close.

"He didn't have *any* way with her!" Ambrose roared in his face. "He gave her

335

morphine to keep her subdued, and then he filled himself with so much of it that he might have *died*, all to spare you and Annika the heartache of her carrying his child!" The wild ferociousness evaporated from Talvi's face as this fact registered in his mind. "She told us everything while you ran off like a half-cocked dilettante to deliver your misguided revenge. I'm losing count of how many times you've almost killed him, due to your recklessness!" Ambrose pushed him away and took the shovel once again, forcing his son to continue walking in front of him.

Talvi was silent for a few minutes before he took a deep breath and shuddered when this grave error in judgment finally registered in his brain. Unfortunately, the anger and adrenaline were still coursing powerfully through his bloodstream, and had nowhere to go.

"I wasn't holding the needle, so how can it be *my* fault?" he asked, tossing his head arrogantly.

"Because you're old enough to know better!" Ambrose spat, pushing Talvi with the end of the shovel to keep walking onward at a fast clip. "Because your new bride is not. Because you left her alone with your brother without knowing when her three days are. She was born a *human*, Talvi—she doesn't *know* these things about us! She's only twenty five, and you're three *hundred*! You ought to be the one guiding her along this new path, not abandoning her when the timing is inconvenient for you."

"I didn't exactly have a choice," Talvi argued, ducking under a low hanging tree limb. "I made a deal with Merriweather in exchange for finding Annika."

"Always excuses with you, Prince Talvi," his father said, frowning as they stepped over a fallen log. "You are but an observer of chaos, never the cause. Nothing is ever directly your fault, is it?"

"I made a promise!" he insisted. "I couldn't break it!"

"And what are marriage vows? Are they not a promise?"

"I don't recall the exact terms we agreed upon in our contract," Talvi snapped. "It was nearly half a year ago at sunrise. I was tired. Why don't you ask Dardis and Chivanni? They were there."

"Why don't you ask them yourself?" Ambrose snapped right back. "Speaking of the fairies, where's Chivanni? Did you leave him at the London embassy?" Talvi said nothing, and his father's eyes widened. "You're supposed to be responsible for him." Still, Talvi said nothing, and his father's eyes were nearly falling out of his head. "You didn't leave him in *America*, did you?"

"So what if I did?" Talvi spat. "They have fairies there, too, you know. He'll be fine."

Ambrose glared daggers of rage at his son as they walked along. He had never wanted to hit him so hard in his life, but he somehow found the strength to keep the shovel in his hand instead of swinging it upside Talvi's head.

"You think you know everything, but you know nothing of marriage. Do you know your wife's birthday? Do you know how she prefers her tea in the morning? Why, I would bet she doesn't even take tea, since most Americans prefer coffee. Do you even know her middle name?"

Talvi sulked in silence. He didn't know any of these things.

"Every successful marriage is different for everyone who is in one," his father went on, "but they all require the same thing."

"Love?"

"Surprisingly, no. There are plenty of successful, yet loveless marriages out there in the world."

"Well then, what is the elusive missing ingredient they all require?" Talvi sneered.

"They all require the merging of two lives, not just two bodies. I know you're adept at merging bodies, but you know absolutely nothing about merging two lives. Think about it, son. Do you realize that you've never had one authentic relationship with a lady?"

Talvi started to name a name, and stopped. Then he tried another, and stopped again. There were so many named and nameless faces floating around in his mind, but none of them were anything he had ever thought of as a relationship. Then one dark-haired elf came into mind.

"What about Zenzi? She was a sort of girlfriend."

"More like a sort of nightmare," Ambrose said with an incredulous face. "I'd rather have a case of poison oak than see her face again. At least the rash goes away when you stop scratching it."

Talvi snorted to himself.

"She is quite like a bad rash, isn't she? Perhaps she'll finally get the hint if I have the displeasure of running into her and she sees my wedding ring."

"Do you honestly believe that a bit of metal will be your shield from relentless females like her? Talvi, you have no idea what it means to be married. You must yield to one another, trust one another, respect one another, and *worship* one another. Simply slipping a platinum band on one another's fingers does not a marriage make." Ambrose guided him to the right, and began to look around more closely at the pale trees in the forest as they continued to walk.

"But I love Annika so much. I am so utterly under her spell, and she is so utterly unaware. I can scarcely believe that I just tried to kill my own brother over her!" he lamented with tears in his eyes. "That woman will be the death of me."

"More than likely, if you keep behaving like this," Ambrose said and slowed down, though he kept walking. "I mean that, Talvi. If you cannot get your act together, it will be me digging your grave instead of you digging mine. Your chosen profession does not lend itself well to married life."

"What does it even matter?" Talvi said bitterly after a while. "I think she's afraid that she married the wrong brother. I don't know how she learned to keep things from me, but what I do know is that she trusts Finn more than she trusts me."

"I think that's the most rational observation that's come out of your mouth in ages," Ambrose said, and stopped walking. He turned to his son, who looked at him in confusion. "Annika has no reason not to trust Finn. She has hundreds of reasons not to trust you. She is a wise woman to be wary of handing over her heart to someone who doesn't even know her middle name. Your current marital status does not erase what you were and what you still are. You have ruled successfully for decades in your current position, Prince Talvi. You'll not be dethroned overnight."

"So what am I supposed to do? I can't change my circumstances, but I love her madly. I've told her those things again and again, yet it doesn't sink into her head! How am I supposed to mend things with her when she doesn't trust me completely? I think she hates me! She said I was the king of the douche lords. I'm fairly certain that's American slang for the worst name you can call someone."

Ambrose didn't laugh, though his eyes started to twinkle once more.

"Perhaps you should think about why she gave you the new title," he said, resting his hands on the handle of the shovel, "You have a lot of complicated questions. I believe you're going to have to dig fairly deep to find all the answers you're looking for."

He tapped the ground between them with the shovel, and leaned the handle against Talvi's chest. Then he walked behind him, took the confiscated knife from his back pocket, and cut the rope around Talvi's hands.

"Are you really going to make me do this, after all these years?" Talvi asked, taking hold of the shovel before looking back at his father.

"You know that I am very fair in my judgments. If you're going to act like a child, then you shall be treated like one," Ambrose said, putting Talvi's knife back in his pocket as he started to walk in the direction of their house. "And if you are going to act like a sociopath, then you shall be treated like one, which means my house will no longer be your home if anything like this ever happens again. I'll come visit you tomorrow, and see what you've turned up."

CHAPTER 39
That Chatty Brother-In-Law of Yours

Back in the music room, Annika was trying to keep Stella and Sloan entertained, but their attention spans were about as short as hers. It was just as well; they were exactly the distraction her fraught nerves needed. The door opened and Asbjorn walked in, scooping up Sloan in his large arms and swinging him gently around in a circle.

"Thank you for watching them while we got the situation under control," he said in a calm, collected voice, assuring her that there was no need to worry any longer. "The rest of us are in the kitchen, if you'd like to eat something tastier than snicker doodles with jalapeño cheese. Unless you truly enjoy that sort of thing."

"Eh, I think I'm just going to hang out in here for the rest of the night," Annika said, even though her stomach was growling. "Maybe I'll sleep in here, too."

"Why ever would you do that?" he asked, furrowing his blond brows at her. "It wouldn't be very comfortable."

"I'm feeling a little out of place right now," she replied. "I don't know what I'm going to say when I see Talvi. I'm not even sure I want to stay in his room with him tonight, after what he did to Finn. Is he alright, by the way?"

"Yes, he'll be fine," Asbjorn assured her, swaying from side to side with Sloan in his arms. "It's just a scrape, compared to the polo accident. He'll need to keep his stitches in for a couple of days, but it could have been much worse.

341

As far as Talvi goes, he won't be home tonight, so you don't have to worry about what to say to him right now. You'll have his room all to yourself."

"What do you mean? Where did he go?"

"His father sent him off to think about what he did," Asbjorn said, and set Sloan down. The little boy started to toddle after Stella around the edge of the room while he watched affectionately. He sighed and shook his head before turning back to Annika. "I think this is the first time the brothers have ever fought over a lady before."

"They weren't fighting over me. Finn was just defending himself," Annika said, brushing off the comment, but Asbjorn shook his blond curls.

"No, those were offensive moves he made, not defensive," he pointed out. "He's incredibly strong. He might have even won that fight if he was in better health and Talvi hadn't started in with the elbowing. Pulling his knife wasn't very honorable either, but then, he tends to be a dirty fighter. I imagine his training took over and it couldn't be avoided."

"His training?" Annika asked. "For what?"

"He's highly skilled in hand-to-hand combat," Asbjorn said with a mysterious smile. "I thought you would have picked up on that by now. Have you ever tried to get away from him? Or, what I really ought to ask is, have you ever *successfully* gotten away from him? Talvi is akin to death itself . . . if he rests his gaze upon you, it's unlikely that you'll escape him."

Annika thought of when she'd attempted to slap Talvi on the plane. His reflexes had been lightning fast. She also thought back to their first morning together in her bedroom, playing cat and mouse with him in the shower, and then failing to escape him when she got out of the shower. Plus there was that tango in her living room that she couldn't escape. She shook her head at her brother-in-law.

"You know that I was gone for a year before I was able to come home, don't you?" asked Asbjorn, resting his hands on his hips. "When I returned, so much had changed. I had expected my children to be a year older, but I was astounded to find that Talvi was married, and even more shocked that Hilda and Finn had parted ways. So naturally, I had to wonder what, or *who* did they have in common that wasn't there before I left? Why, it was a strange young human lass whom I only saw for a brief second before she disappeared into a closing portal. And now here you are, and those Marinossian brothers are literally at each other's throats."

"What are you getting at?" she asked, giving a prim smile. "Finn and I are just friends. Sure, things got a little crazy in Paris, but I didn't have anything to do with him and Hilda breaking up. What happened, anyway?" Annika didn't know Asbjorn at all, but she was leaning towards liking him.

"She waited almost thirty years for him to be sure about his feelings for her, and then suddenly, she ended it. I don't think any of us saw that coming."

"Thirty *years?*" she squeaked. "Finn told me that the reason they split up was because he said something he shouldn't have."

Asbjorn nodded, causing his loose blond curls to sway.

"Well? What did he say?"

"I think he told her something to the effect that he felt he knew you in another life, if not in numerous lives."

"But that's a really sweet thing to say," Annika remarked, feeling confused. "I don't understand why they would split up because of that. I know I've felt like I've known people in other lives before. He's probably one of them. What's the big deal?"

"He's an atheist, Annika," he said, with yet another mysterious smile. "He believes in science and facts and logic and reason, not gods and myths and previous lives and such. You may have mistaken his knowledge of the esoteric to mean that he believed in it, but that was incorrect, until recently. Then he met someone who made him question those beliefs. And then he considered them. And then he began to believe in them. It was a bit much for Hilda to accept, after waiting all that time for him to have that same level of faith in their relationship."

"Why didn't he say something when I first met him?" asked Annika, but she felt she already knew the answer.

"Why would he want to? Who do you think always got the ladies, between those two?" Asbjorn said with a knowing look. "Finn's very selective to begin with, and he's such a gentleman, that by the time he felt comfortable telling a lady that he fancied her, his brother had already paid her a visit. Perhaps that's why he got involved with Hilda to begin with, because Talvi has only thought of her and Runa as sisters.

"Also, if he had said anything to you, it would likely have caused the three of you pain. We all knew you were destined to marry Talvi. It was written in the stars, and Finn didn't want to interfere with these unseen forces that he had just started to believe in. One way or another, he wanted to have you be part of his family. That's why he worked so tirelessly to help Talvi and the fairies create your rings and plan your wedding ceremony. He knew that was the only way to have you in his life."

"I, I don't know what to say," Annika said quietly, realizing how much went on in the world around her without her knowledge. "Does Talvi know about this?"

Asbjorn waved a hand in dismissal, chuckling as he did so.

"No, Annika, your husband hasn't a clue, and unless you tell him, I doubt he would ever figure it out. Clever and cunning as he is, I don't think Talvi is able to comprehend that level of pure affection free of any expectation. That's not a derogatory statement about him. It's simply an observation of how his mind operates. He has many expectations of your relationship. It's incredibly rare to truly love someone without having any expectations of them. I know I don't feel that way about Anthea. I love her very much, but I have a lot that I expect from her, such as being a loving and supportive wife, a patient mother, and so on. And you wouldn't believe the expectations that she puts upon *me*!" He raised a brow at her while he smiled warmly. "I told her I wanted to wait another few years before we added on to our family, and look how that turned out."

He walked over to the end of the room where Stella and Sloan were playing and gathered both of them in each of his strong arms. "What am I going to do when there are three of you to hold next April?" he asked them with a happy smile.

CHAPTER 40
Fallen Stars

Annika mustered up the courage to follow Asbjorn into the kitchen. She saw Finn sitting at the large wooden kitchen table beside a ceramic bowl of red-tinged water, holding a damp cloth against the entire right side of his face. Anthea was packing up her surgical kit while her mother was making sandwiches.

Finn motioned for Annika to sit next to him while Asbjorn sat down with the children. She tried her best to push the conversation from the music room out of her head and took a seat right as Ambrose entered the kitchen through the heavy side door.

"I am fairly certain, of all the silver hair on my head *and* in my beard, only three strands are not from Talvi," he announced, and strode up to Finn. "Let's have a look at Anthea's sewing job, shall we?"

Finn took the bloody cloth away from his face to reveal a ghastly, long cut along the edge his jaw, and another one running up his hairline. The stitches were neatly done, but the jagged wounds still looked painful and swollen.

"Your brother did a number on you, but your sister did a fine repair job," Ambrose said, looking close at his oldest son's face. "You likely won't have much scarring, if you have any at all." Finn dipped the cloth in the bowl of cool red water, wrung out the excess, and held it against the side of his head once again.

"Lucky me," he muttered.

345

"You *are* lucky, Finn," said Anthea with a disapproving frown, and went to help finish making the sandwiches. "Father, what did you do with Talvi?"

"I took him to dig a hole."

This made Anthea and Finn laugh, but then he winced, pulling his stitches accidentally.

"Why is it so funny, to dig a hole?" Annika asked.

"It's a punishment that Father used when we were adolescents, and he hasn't done it in years," Anthea explained. "He takes you out to the woods and leaves you there to dig for answers to your problems. You're not allowed anything but a canteen of water and a shovel. You're not even allowed to come back to the house. When he visits to check on your progress, if he's not happy with what he finds, you have to keep digging. At least, that's what I know of it. I never had to dig a hole, and Finn did not see much of it, either. It was mostly reserved for the twins' bad behavior."

"And that works?" asked Annika skeptically.

"It's a simple, yet effective way for a hot-tempered lad or lass to burn off some steam," Ambrose answered. "And you know what else helps?"

"Uh . . . no."

"A dull shovel."

"Really?"

"Absolutely," Ambrose said to her. "A dull shovel makes it that much harder to dig with, so I gave Talvi the dullest, rustiest one I could find. And I was in such a hurry that I forgot to bring any water for him."

Finn laughed again, and grimaced as he inadvertently pulled his stitches again.

"Can I come out with you when you check on Talvi tomorrow?" he asked with a mean look in his eyes. "I'd like to fill the hole back in with him still in it." Anthea gave Annika a *see what I mean?* glance as she brought over two plates piled with cheese, tomato and cucumber sandwich halves.

"Then you are no better than him," his mother said in a tone that kept him from commenting any further.

Annika was glad to have the children around for a much needed distraction while she ate her sandwich. As she was finishing the last bit of her light dinner, she noticed that Finn had only taken one bite of his sandwich.

"Aren't you hungry?" she asked, looking concerned. "You haven't had a whole lot to eat over the past week. I've only seen you drink ginger ale and water."

346

"It hurts my jaw to chew anything," he said tersely, still holding the cloth against the side of his face. He took the bowl of water into his free hand as he got up from the table. "I'm just going to go lie down for a while."

Annika sighed as she watched him leave the room, and reached for another half of a sandwich. Even when he was in a bad mood, he was still too nice for his own good.

"I feel so bad for him," she said. "When my brother Charlie had his wisdom teeth pulled, he had to eat soft foods for a week. I made him chocolate pudding every day." She looked over at Finn's mother. "Do you have cornstarch and some cocoa?" Althea nodded with a warm smile, and Ambrose went to light a fire in the cast iron stove sitting beside the large hearth while she retrieved the different ingredients from the pantry and cabinets. "How about eggs and milk?" Annika asked as she took a clean bowl off a shelf and was handed a few measuring spoons.

"That's such a kind and sweet thing of you to do for him," Althea said as she placed a sauce pan on one of the stove burners. "You're going to have to learn your way around our kitchen for when you come home for winter. The fires in the stove and the hearth never go out, and the cooking never seems to end, either."

"Oh, well, Talvi and I haven't really figured out a schedule yet," she said, feeling a tiny bit nervous with her new mother-in-law. "Until last year, I've always spent Christmas with my family."

"Then you ought to keep spending it with them," Althea suggested in a gentle, but firm tone. "I can't imagine how your mother's heart ached when you were gone. You and Talvi can celebrate Christmas with your family, and then come here afterwards and celebrate Yule with us."

"Aren't those holidays at the same time?"

"Yule is actually a few days before Christmas, but I don't think anybody here would complain about celebrating it twice."

Asbjorn and Stella both smiled wide and shook their heads.

"I definitely wouldn't mind doing that every year, if you want to keep your tradition with your family," Ambrose said.

"I would mind," Anthea joked. "I'll never be able to leave the kitchen."

"Yes you will," her mother assured her. "You'll have Annika and Talvi here to help. He's not too bad in the kitchen, you know," she said, looking at Annika.

"I find that hard to believe," she said. "I don't think I've ever seen him cook.

He stirred some risotto once, but Chivanni's the one who made it. Usually he's just hanging out, letting other people do all the work."

"Yes, he does tend to believe his mere presence is inspiration enough, but he'll help if you know how to ask," said Althea with all the authority a mother would have regarding her child's habits. "The thing about Talvi is that he wants to be the best at everything he sets his mind to. The trick is getting him to set his mind to what you want him to do." She collected a drop of water from the pump in the sink and flicked it into the pan on the stove. It sizzled and she motioned to Annika that it was ready, then sat back down with the others.

Thirty minutes later, Annika carried a warm, covered dish down the hall and up the first flight of stairs to a landing, and saw that Finn's door was closed. She knocked softly.

"Come in," his deep voice answered.

She walked into the room lit by the colors of a gorgeous sunset, and shut the door behind her. He was lying in his bed, pulling out the stitches closest to his chin. She set the dish on his nightstand and sat down beside him.

"What are you doing?" she asked with concern. "That's going to leave a scar if you do that."

"I know it will," he said. "That's what I want."

"That has got to hurt like hell," said Annika, as he pulled out another stitch and let it fall to the floor.

"You know what really hurts?" he asked her, looking angry. "Lying crippled in bed all day, unable to sit up without help, just because it's going to rain or snow, because your stupid little brother wanted to beat you at a game decades ago. At least now whenever he looks upon my face, he will remember what he tried to do to me today. He might finally learn something from his older, wiser brother."

"I hope so, too, but I wish you would leave your stitches alone."

"I wish you could have seen his face when I told him how gentle I was with you throughout your three days," he said, surprising Annika by smirking exactly like Talvi always did. "It was absolutely priceless. You would have thought it was I who was holding the blade against *his* throat."

"Yeah, it was a huge misunderstanding," she pointed out. "But you're both going to be fine."

"I'm not so certain about that. It seems a pity that I have paid for a crime which I did not commit," he said, smiling as cruelly as Talvi had on the airplane. He placed one warm hand on her knee, guiding it slowly up her thigh. "Perhaps I should send Cazadora to inform him that his wife is in my bed after all. Isn't that why you've come to me now, so that I might justify my wounds?"

"Knock it off, Finn!" she gasped. She slapped his hand away and leapt to her feet. "I used to think you two were so different, but unless that's the morphine talking, you're a lot more alike than you know!"

"We *were* a lot alike, at one point in our lives," he admitted, caressing the warm spot where she had been sitting. "Did you know that The Picture of Dorian Gray was inspired by the two of us?"

"You mean the book by Oscar Wilde?" she asked, and he had her full attention. She'd read the book a few years ago and remembered it was about a beautiful man who did terrible things, and those things were reflected in his portrait rather than on his handsome face. Either of the brothers could easily have starred in such a novel.

"Yes, we first met Oscar at a social club in London. I can't recall how the introduction was made; it was such a blur of pixie dust and absinthe, of cards and men, of women and wine and song. We ran into him a few years later in an opium den, and he was so impressed with our level of carousing and the lack of wear and tear on our faces, that he wrote a story about it. I'll bet you didn't know this, but the first version was rejected by his publisher for being too indecent and immoral for the general public. He had to water it down considerably for it to be accepted, and even then, it still caused a great deal of scandal. Sometimes the truth is less believable than fiction."

"Yeah, no shit," Annika said, eyeing Finn cautiously from where she stood at his bedside. "I'm sure learning a lot more than I ever expected to about you Marinossian boys. Asbjorn told me what you said to Hilda, by the way."

The cruel look left Finn's face as he withdrew his hand from the blanket, and stared into his lap.

"That wasn't something that you needed to know."

"I guess Asbjorn thought differently. He had no problem going into detail about why you wanted me in this crazy family to begin with," said Annika. "After all you and I went through, I'm surprised that you would try to hide this from me, like it's something to be ashamed of."

"Well, it needn't be shouted from a mountaintop, either. I didn't want you to misunderstand what I meant . . . or the manner in which I meant it," Finn explained. "I certainly didn't want to tell you after you made a comment about my body looking like a piece of art. You need to try a little harder to keep your private thoughts private, instead of overindulging in them. If you find yourself laden with inappropriate ruminations, you best push them into the corners of your mind, and don't ever venture there again. Otherwise you'll get us both into more trouble, if that's even possible." He raised a stern brow at her and she covered her embarrassed and blushing face with her hands. "Asbjorn is not only my sister's husband; he's also a very dear friend of mine, and I trust that he explained my standpoint accurately. I hold no expectations of you, Annika. I only want you to be happy being part of my family. All I desire from you is to see your face light up whenever you are here. I want to see it light up as often as I can. Perhaps we can one day share wine and desserts again, and I might try and watch one of your cult films and understand whatever it is that you see in them."

"Well, I brought you a dessert, and we did watch *It Came From Outer Space*, remember?" she said, smiling faintly at his sweet sincerity.

"I hardly remember anything about those three days after we opened Pandora's box, other than Nicolette giving me one hell of a scrub in the shower," he said, and dipped his finger into the dish, humming in satisfaction as he tasted the warm pudding. He crawled out of his covers and walked over to the large desk in front of his even larger window that revealed a bright orange and purple twilight outside. He reached into a drawer and withdrew something small enough to conceal in his hand. "But that does remind me; speaking of things coming from outer space . . . " He stepped back over to the bed and sat on the edge near where she was standing.

"One of my astronomy students gave this to me as payment for tutoring, but it's too small for my fingers. Perhaps it would fit one of yours? I noticed on your passport that your birthday is coming up soon, and I've little left to give you that you don't already own."

He opened his hand, and there on his palm lay a dark silver ring. It was simple and smooth, and when she picked it up to look closer, she saw uneven striations all over the band.

"What is it made out of?" she asked as she sat down beside him and tried to put it on her right middle finger. It was too small. Next she tried her pinky. It was too big. She slipped it onto her right ring finger and it fit perfectly, as if it had been created to rest exactly there.

"Meteorite," he said, looking intently at her hand. "It's a fallen star, *slunchitse*. I may not remember much of your film, but I do remember you being lit up as brightly as a falling star when we were walking along the Champs-Élysées back to the hotel. I told you that until I won my books back from you, that I would be wrapped around your finger. Now you won't forget . . . although you don't have to wear it if you don't care to. Unlike your wedding ring, there are no strings attached to the one that I'm giving you."

Annika held both her shaking hands in front of her, looking at the two rings. On her left hand, there was a flashy, twinkling platinum band inscribed with a promise of enduring love that would go the distance. On her right hand, there was a modest and unassuming fallen star that already had. It had journeyed from the edge of the universe, through space and time, just to be with her. Tears came out of nowhere and her throat choked up as she recalled telling Asbjorn so easily that she felt she may indeed have known Finn in another life. Maybe this was the proof. It surely couldn't be coincidence.

"Should these be switched?" she whispered, looking through her tears from one ring to the other. "Did I make a mistake?"

"Your name is on our wall down in the library, and that's not a mistake," said Finn gently. "Your wedding ring is irremovable, and that's not a mistake."

"But I'm scared that it is. I trust you so much more than . . . " she couldn't speak, she was crying too hard. He folded her into his chest, holding her tight as she sobbed. The protective warmth of their little bubble returned and surrounded her with an overwhelming sense of peace as he began to speak, soothing her with his deep voice.

"I care for you so much, *slunchitse*, but if you had married me instead of my brother, you would have remained a human. You would have grown old and died in front of all of us within a fraction of our lives. How could I ever be so selfish, to allow your flame to burn out so quickly, all for a fleeting handful of years to call you my own? I feel as though we've already spent a past life together, if not more. I have no scientific evidence to prove my theory. I only have faith in it, but it feels like the correct explanation. I don't know what else could rationalize this force between us. It's my belief that the universe meant for you and I to be together in a different capacity this lifetime."

He tilted her face up toward him and brushed away her tears with his thumb, gazing at her lovingly through his loose brown curls. His soft brown eyes watered as he looked at her soul and said, "I know I've told you this before, Annika, but I really do like having you around."

CHAPTER 41

Mr. Fix It

After breakfast the next morning, Ambrose filled a canteen with water from the pump at the kitchen sink and handed it to Annika.

"Let's go check on that husband of yours, shall we?"

The two of them started off in silence, though it was more of the peaceful type than the awkward type.

"I hope you didn't stay up too late crying," he remarked casually as they ambled past the horses in the pastures.

"How did you know I was crying at all?" she asked, suddenly feeling less peaceful and more awkward.

"I have a wife and two daughters, and I'm the father of one notorious heartbreaker," said Ambrose, smiling ever so slightly at her. "Trust me, I know the look."

"I slept alright," she said quickly, almost tripping on a root sticking out of the ground. "I slept just fine."

"What's one lass to do with so much love given so easily and freely to her?" he said, lifting a dark eyebrow at her.

"I don't know," she shrugged. "I don't think I'm that big of a deal." She felt unsure of offering up anything that had been said the previous evening in Finn's room, and she definitely didn't want to share any of the things that had not been said.

"I know you don't think you are a big deal. That's the problem. You are, in fact, a rather *big* deal." Ambrose hummed to himself in thought before he continued. "I can't imagine how difficult it was for you to go home after everything that happened to you here, and try to go about your normal life. Your family and friends thought you were quite unwell, didn't they?"

"Yeah," Annika said quietly as they passed under a low branch of one of the endless giant white poplar trees surrounding them.

"When we were speaking about holiday arrangements, it made me curious. Do you ponder much that you'll outlive them all by a dozen lifetimes?"

"I don't really think about it," she mumbled. Ambrose slowed his pace and turned to her, looking at her sympathetically.

"Annika, you don't have much more time with them, compared to what you have with us. I understand why you're driven to cling to your former life. It's secure; it's comfortable; it's familiar to you. However, you only have perhaps another ten to fifteen years before your family and friends begin asking why you haven't aged along with them. I can assure you, it will upset them, even scare them, the more time that goes by and leaves you unchanged. If you were to have a child within the next dozen years or so, it will only magnify the situation. You ought to know, they don't grow nearly as quickly as human infants."

"Yeah, about that," Annika began, "How old are Stella and Sloan? They only look like they're two and four, but that can't be right. Talvi once told me that he's twelve times older than me."

"He is correct," Ambrose explained patiently. "They appear that age in human terms, but Stella is forty-eight and Sloan is nineteen."

"That's so crazy," Annika said, shaking her head in disbelief. "And Anthea's totally fine with changing diapers for another twenty years?" Ambrose gave a soft laugh.

"I don't think anyone particularly enjoys that task," he remarked. "It does make one think twice before making a baby. However, with you coming from a human family, you will have to think more than twice before making that decision. I know there is a lot in front of you that you would rather not deal with anytime soon. I would suggest, speaking from experience, to try and open yourself up to the realm of the uncomfortable and unfamiliar sooner rather than later. The humans in your life don't know you the way we do. They certainly don't know you the way Talvi does."

"But that's been the problem all along," she pointed out. "We got together so fast that we hardly know each other! How can he know anything about me?

Plus I know he keeps a lot of secrets. Sometimes I feel like I don't know anything about him beneath the surface."

"You knew enough about him to marry him in the first place," Ambrose said, smiling to himself. "Surely you saw something in his soul that you couldn't live without. When is the last time you looked at it, anyway?"

Annika shrugged. She couldn't remember the last time she lovingly gazed into her husband's eyes and lost herself in them, but now that she thought of it, it was probably right before, during, and immediately after their wedding.

"Do you know why he hasn't a clue what your middle name is, or when your birthday is?"

"Well, I was gonna say it's because he doesn't give a shit, but I get the feeling you're going to tell me it's something a lot sweeter."

"You are every bit as saucy as he claimed," Ambrose said with a snicker. "But the reason he doesn't know isn't because he doesn't care. It's because when his eye is on the target, everything else falls to the wayside. He has seen the essence of your soul, Annika, and possessing your heart is all that matters to him. He knows only too well that you haven't given yourself to him completely, and I told him that no one could honestly blame you for it. Don't let his legions of fawning flatterers fool you; Prince Talvi is not the easiest to love, but there's a diamond hiding deep within that mess of coal. He has a reputation about him as strong as any suit of armor. I'm afraid he'll be trapped in it for long time, even though he'd like to be done with it. It is his own creation. You both have a lot of hurdles to overcome, to be able to trust one another, but please understand; now that you're within his inner circle, he will fight for you to the death. You almost saw that yesterday, but thank the gods for Asbjorn stopping him just in time. I'm certain that the only thing which will enable Finn to forgive his brother is his incredible fondness of you."

He looked at Annika, glanced down at the meteorite ring on her right hand, and then looked back up at her, letting his blue-green eyes shine. Annika tried not to blush, but it was too late.

"I know Talvi is incorrigible, impudent, impatient, and infuriating at times. I didn't raise him to be that way; it's simply who he is. But just as he is wild like the blizzard he was conceived in, he is also as loyal as the cold is to snow. I know your biggest fear is that you can't trust him, but I think if you can learn to accept him for who he is, you'll be able to let that fear go. Then you will know what to do with all of the love that's being offered to you . . . from *everyone* around you. And then, you will understand what a big deal you really are."

They walked for the next fifteen minutes in silence, until Annika smirked and finally asked,

"So, are you saying that it's okay that he doesn't know my middle name or my birthday?"

Ambrose let out a soft laugh and shook his head.

"No, that is really unacceptable," he said quietly. "Please forgive me; I am not trying to make excuses for my son's bad behavior, but you need to understand that he has never been in a serious relationship before. You might consider adjusting the learning curve for him. He has a lot of catching up to do. Now I know I left him right around here somewhere . . . " He peered around the tall silver poplar trees, looking for a sign of his son's whereabouts. Then his eyes caught sight of a few tall mounds of dirt behind some bushes. He motioned for Annika to follow him a few paces behind, raised his forefinger to his lips, and together they walked closer to the mounds of soil, rocks and roots. Then he abruptly stopped and looked down.

"Badra's beard, that's quite a deep hole you've dug there, Talvi," he said, dodging a shovel's worth of dirt. "Surely you have found a few solutions to your problems."

"A few," came the reply from below.

"Care to share, so I can decide if you need to keep digging or not?"

"Why yes, I would, actually." Another load of dirt came flying up and Ambrose walked to the other side of the hole and sat down, motioning for Annika to do the same a few feet behind him.

"Alright then, I'm listening."

"Well, I admit I may not know much about merging two lives together, but I don't think Annika knows much about it, either. She ought to be out here with me, although I doubt she could dig very deep, little thing that she is," he said, sending another pile of dirt up. Ambrose winked at Annika and looked back down at Talvi.

"Why do you think that?"

"Oh, for starters, she was going to go to work the very next day after Chivanni and I arrived at her house. I spent almost three months getting to her door, missing her terribly as I tracked her down, and then she simply said to me, 'Sorry, I have to go to work.' Can you believe the nerve?"

"That was incredibly insensitive of her. What did you do?"

"I wouldn't have any of that nonsense, so I set her straight and made her stay home." A wicked laugh rose up from underground and a large pile of dirt came flying up after it. "I told her that she was being a rude hostess and her wingless faerie friend agreed."

"You're right, she was being a very rude hostess," Ambrose said, and shook his finger in silent reprimand at Annika. Her cheeks flushed in embarrassment as she recalled being punished for her bad manners.

"She also lied to me from the get go. She thought she was pregnant, so instead of telling me right away, she tried to hide it until her mother accused her of having morning sickness. It turned out she was merely getting sick from eating animals, but still; my own wife lied to me, Father."

"That can be a difficult thing for a lady to be forthcoming about, Talvi, especially when she knows her partner wants nothing to do with children. Your mother and I weren't ready for Anthea when she came along, but such is life. It's different when it's your own child, but you won't understand that unless the time comes."

"Fair enough, but after all the trouble I've had in the past with Zenzi, surely you can understand—"

"That is in the past, and we are discussing your future," he replied quickly, looking down at his son, which intrigued Annika greatly. "Do you have any other complaints about your wife that need sorting out?"

Talvi hooted a laugh and was all too happy to indulge his audience with his opinion.

"Her wingless faerie friend owns the house she lives in, and she owed him quite a bit of money, so I paid him in trade and she got angry at me for it."

"Why did she get angry?" Ambrose asked. "I would feel relieved if someone did that for me."

"That's what I thought as well! I think she was brassed off because she wanted to pay the debt herself and I did it for her. I had the funds, and I didn't want her to worry about it. Perhaps she's jealous of my income. Those modern girls are really touchy about their finances."

"Are they, now?"

"Oh, Father, you wouldn't believe it! She was downright insulted that I should want to take care of her financially."

"Well son, perhaps she is overcompensating a bit," said Ambrose, stroking his graying beard thoughtfully. "Though you take for granted that on Earth, women have been subjugated by men for ages, and still are to this very day.

Why do you think Anthea hates to travel there? It's because she doesn't want her children to be influenced by the blatant misogyny that still runs rampant in human society. It's not the way it is here, where we value the attributes and celebrate the differences of *both* genders. Times are changing, thankfully, but you must be patient with those modern girls. They are trying to rectify centuries of oppression and backward thinking. It's quite a task they have." He winked at Annika and she winked back, nodding her head in complete agreement.

"Yes, I believe you're spot on about that," Talvi replied, and was silent for a few thoughtful moments before sending more dirt flying out of the hole. "But speaking of modern girls, Annika's friend needed a place to stay, so I asked if she could move in, and that caused an entirely new set of problems. You'll never guess her name. It's the bee's knees."

"Her name is Bees Knees?" Ambrose asked with a grin.

"No, dammit, but I don't believe you'll guess it, so I'll save you the trouble. It's Patti Cake. Her last name is Kaeke, which is a sort of drum. Now how charming is that?"

"I'd say that redefines the word charming. So what's the trouble with a charming girl named Patti Cake?" Some rocks and roots came flying out of the hole as Talvi went on.

"She's such a delightful girl to be around, though she's terribly clumsy and accident prone. She can scarcely go a day without injuring herself in some fashion, so it's a good thing for her to have me around, but Annika acts as though I'm looking for any bloody excuse to grope her friend. I told her she was being irrational, but she didn't believe me."

"Were you inappropriate with her friend?"

"I didn't think so, and Patti Cake didn't think so, and the wingless faerie and Chivanni and Annika's brother Charlie didn't think so, but I'm not married to them, so what does it matter?"

"It matters to you, Talvi."

"I don't think how I feel matters very much to Annika. I'm just her toy, her pet. Perhaps that's why I like Patti Cake so much, because she treats me like a friend instead of a lap dog. Annika leaves me home all day to go to a job she doesn't particularly like, let alone need, and then I'm expected to be waiting faithfully when it's time for her to come home. I want to take her to Rome, and she wants to sell guitar strings to snot-nosed children. I understand it's because she wants to earn her own money, but I know that's not the way she wants to do it. Since she was always away at work, I found myself spending more time with Patti Cake than with her, and then she became jealous of that too!" The irritation in his voice began to escalate, which corresponded with the amount of dirt flying out of the hole in the ground.

"And let me tell you something about Patti . . . she went so far as to ask her professor in advance if I could attend her drawing classes, because she knew how much I would enjoy it. I can't think of anything similarly thoughtful that Annika has done for me, but Patti Cake is as sweet as her name would suggest. You would adore her. She's tall and artistic like Yuri, and sweet and silly like Runa. She made me forget about being homesick for them."

"I didn't think you got homesick, Talvi," Ambrose called down to him, offering a sympathetic glance to Annika before peering back down into the hole.

"Why shouldn't I, from time to time?" Talvi asked. "Yuri and I were nearly inseparable until about a year or so ago. It's like having half my heart ripped out of me."

"Yes, I can't even imagine how it must feel for you, being separated from your twin so suddenly after sharing a womb and a life together."

"I'm getting on."

"She sends her regards, by the way," he said delicately, but it was met with an unimpressed harrumph.

Ambrose sat back, wearing a frustrated and disappointed expression. Annika was heartbroken to hear the hurt in Talvi's voice as he uttered these secret confessions so freely to his father, and tears stung at her eyes. She thought she had him all figured out from day one, that all he really cared about was booze and sex, and not necessarily in that order, but she realized that she had no clue about his feelings, about his desires, about a lot of things. She tried to recall doing something sweet and thoughtful for her husband, but all she could remember was forbidding him from going with her to her mother's salon, worrying sick that he was going to drop her like a bad habit when he had tried to tango with her, choosing a room full of hot models over him when he had asked her to please bring home a lemon meringue pie, making jabs about his past on their very first morning together, and a whole list of other slights against him, not to mention threatening to have his abortion.

She thought back to when Finn had told her that she wasn't ready to be married to Talvi, that she wasn't ready to trust him. It finally clicked, what he meant. Annika wiped away a few tears as she came to the realization that Finn had said it for her benefit, definitely not for his own.

"Father, when we get back home, I might ask Mother if I'm really your son."

"*What?*" Ambrose asked, whipping his head back towards the hole again. "Of course you're my son! You have my eyes! Why would you even say such a thing?"

"Because here, I'm Prince Talvi. And Annika proclaimed that I am king of the douche lords. I'm confounded as to where all this royal blood in my veins came from."

Annika stifled a laugh with her hands as Talvi's father leaned over and scooped a large armful of dirt back into the hole.

"I'm not sure either, but I do know that wherever you are, it's better to be a king than it is to be a prince," he replied, grinning wide. "Did you think about why your fair lady gave you the new title, your majesty?"

"Oh, I know exactly why she gave it to me," he chirped from below. "I said something absolutely horrid to her about my history with Merriweather. Annika insists that I must still be shagging her senseless because she's one hell of a lass with one hell of an ass, and I can't convince her otherwise, no matter what I say, so I gave up trying. I can't tell you how bloody fantastic it felt to stop defending myself to her. I have to get back to London right away, so I'll have the two of them meet face to face. That ought to settle things."

"Do you feel that's a wise thing to do?" Ambrose asked with a doubtful expression as he glanced at Annika, who didn't appear to like the idea one bit. "That might not go the way you hope it will."

"I'm aware of that, but Annika already thinks so little of me, so what else have I got to lose? Ha, I could sell quite a few tickets to that cat fight," Talvi called up with a loud *meow*, and flung a large pile of dirt high into the air. "Seriously though, I'm running out of options. I intended to keep my work private from her, but it only seems to encourage her to trust me less. She claims husbands and wives ought to have no secrets between them, but I of course couldn't disagree more. There is so much that I simply can't tell her. If she understood the nature of my trade, she might trust me better. Perhaps that's why she trusts Finn more than me, because he doesn't have anything to hide and I have everything to hide. Why shouldn't she wonder if she married the wrong brother? She truly cares for him, and he would make an ideal husband, doting on her every day and being home every evening. Plus, he loves Anthea's little larvae. He would probably want as many of them as Annika could tolerate.

He would never leave her in the middle of the night to wake up alone, and come back months later, unable to say exactly why he left or where he has been."

"Stop digging and have some water," Ambrose said, taking the canteen from Annika and dropping it down to his son. "You're blinding me with your brilliance."

There was a pause as Talvi took a long awaited drink, and then sighed.

"I feel so awful about what I did to him," he said so quietly that Annika could barely hear. "I'm grateful that he's stronger than he's ever been, though I'm pissing blood because of it. He got me good in the kidney." He uttered a rueful laugh before continuing.

"I've thought a lot about he and I, and I have to admit, there has never been a single time when we came to blows over a female. If we both fancied the same one, he let me have her every time. Whenever we fought, it was always over chores or something petty like that. I have no reason not to trust him, either. Perhaps you'll think me mad, but I want to ask him if he'll be my *korvaaminen*."

"Yes, I'd have to say I think you are a raving lunatic to entertain such a notion right after what you did to him," Ambrose said slowly. "Even if you were on the best of terms, that's not an agreement to be entered lightly into. You'll be lucky if he were to even speak to you before you leave." He paused for a moment to look at how far down Talvi had dug, shaking his head in disbelief. "Although it seems you've spent some time seriously considering it. Given your profession, and given the extreme lengths that Finn has already gone to for you both, I am tempted to give my approval. But now is not the right time to make this decision. He is not in a state to give it any proper thought. Neither are you, really. Let's discuss this another time."

Ambrose stood up and glanced down into the hole, running his fingers through his hair just like Talvi did from time to time.

"I'd say you have another couple feet to go, and then you may fill the dirt back in. See you at dinner."

He motioned for Annika to get up and follow him back to the house. This time they walked at a faster pace, and she found herself trotting to keep up with his long legs.

"He's got a lot on his mind," Ambrose said as quietly as possible, looking serious. "That was the deepest hole he's ever dug, and he's dug quite a few."

"I had no idea . . ." Annika began, feeling herself tear up again. "He never mentioned anything to me about being homesick or missing his sister."

"Perhaps he didn't feel comfortable enough to share those private things with you. No one likes to feel so vulnerable to someone else, but if you are ever going to grow as a couple, you both need to start baring your souls instead of baring your teeth," Ambrose said a little louder, now that they were safely out of sight and earshot.

"He may have been born winking at the midwife, but he doesn't need to be picked apart constantly by someone who's only doing it to avoid facing her own troubles. You're in denial of what your future entails, but I also don't believe Talvi has helped you very much on your way. Did you read the books that Finn sent for you?"

Annika recalled the pile of books that Talvi had unpacked on his first day at her house. The titles she could recall were the book about the samodivi, and the guide for new vampires and their loved ones. She had thought that they looked interesting, but somehow she put off reading them due to work, or band practice, or recording, or going shopping with James, or getting her hair done, or . . . or . . . or. She shook her guilty head at her father-in-law.

"Do yourselves a favor when you get back and read them aloud . . . *together*," he said, shaking his finger at her again, but this time his eyes twinkled merrily.

CHAPTER 42
Those Marinossian Boys

Squeaky clean and wearing a soft white t-shirt and dark green cargo shorts, Talvi walked barefoot down the hallway to the landing where his brother's room was. He knocked on the closed door twice; both times there was no answer. Silently, he let himself into the room, and saw Finn sleeping beside a pile of French science journals, with one lying open in his hand. Talvi walked over and sat on the edge of the bed, gently taking the magazine from Finn's long fingers. He stirred, opening his eyes with a start when he realized who was sitting in front of him.

"What's this?" he asked suspiciously as his heart began to pound faster, "You've come to finish the job, then? Now I know how some of your victims feel right before you strike. What did you bring? Your blade or your poisons?"

Talvi held his bruised, empty hands up.

"I brought nothing but my deepest apologies. Father confiscated my knife indefinitely. He says that it's cursed now."

"He's right. It *is* cursed."

"You don't believe in curses."

"You don't know what I believe," Finn retorted.

"I believe that's quite the beauty mark you have there," Talvi said, looking at his brother's jawline apologetically. Finn reached up and held the curls aside from the right side of his temple, revealing another dark pink scar.

"Annika informed me that chicks dig scars, so I suppose now I'll have to test that theory," he said dryly.

"See there, I actually did you a courtesy," Talvi said, trying to joke. "But you did manage to kick the piss out of me . . . I daresay I'd rather have been punched in the stones than in the kidney."

"Now there's a theory I don't wish to test."

Talvi sighed and took a long look at his brother, bundled up under his covers on this warm early summer day. He was still suffering from his withdrawal symptoms, although they were much less severe than they had been a few days ago.

"I'm so sorry . . . " he began, but Finn held up his hand.

"I know you're sorry," he said, not smiling. "I have heard apologies from you before, and I know that you're genuinely sincere when you speak them, but I don't want to hear it this time." He sat up gingerly and motioned toward his chin with his hand.

"What I want to know, is if you've learnt anything. Tell me what you see."

"I see you need a shave," Talvi said.

"Is that all?"

Talvi pursed his lips.

"You're so much like Father," he said, shifting uncomfortably on the quilt. "You're both always so apt to teach me a lesson. I know full well what you're trying to tell me. You're going to do as he did and point out that I am dangerously mad about my wife, and blinded by what I feel for her. But I don't know how else to be. It's as though I'm under a sorcerer's spell. I've never felt this way about anyone . . . not even Yuri."

"Trust me, I know you haven't felt this way before," said Finn. "You're in love for the first time in your life, and rather than growing gradually, this love smacked you all at once, harder than a troll's club. It's a bit terrifying, how much it controls you."

"You're telling me," said Talvi, looking at his bruised knuckles with regret.

"I *am* telling you," he said, crossing his arms as he leaned back into his pillows. "I'm concerned for your safety. All of the family is, but especially Father, because he knows the risks you take better than any of us do. Yuri walks among the undead, and look how upset he was to learn about her fate. If your judgment were impaired by your intense feelings for Annika, and you . . . if you . . . " he paused as he swallowed a lump that had unexpectedly formed in his throat. "You're a right bastard sometimes, and I find myself disliking you immensely more often than not, but you're still my little brother. It would break our parents' hearts to lose you, damnable troublemaker that you are."

"I know," he said soberly. Then he looked back at Finn, and ignoring his father's advice, he cleared his throat and asked, "That reminds me; I wanted to ask you a question."

"And what is that?"

"Given the risks I take, should anything ever happen to me . . . I wanted to know if you would be my *korvaaminen*."

Finn's eyes looked at his brother's with perplexed curiosity.

"Are you honestly asking me this, after all that happened in Paris? After what happened yesterday?"

Talvi nodded.

"Perhaps I struck you in the head one too many times, to cause you to ask me such a thing?"

Talvi shook his head.

"Did you discuss this with Annika?"

Talvi gave a little shrug. "Not yet, but I think we both know she'll be quite keen to the idea. She's clearly very fond of you."

Finn unfolded his arms and pushed back his covers, and fanned himself with one of the science journals.

"Blast these never ending chills and sweats," he muttered, but he didn't seem terribly inconvenienced by them. "You really are asking me this, aren't you? Are you certain you're not doing this merely to win me over, so you don't have to feel remorse for what you did to me? You can't bargain with Annika like this, using her as if she were a stack of poker chips."

"I'm not trying to up the ante here, Finn. I know what you went through, and it showed me how much you care about what's best for her. You risked your life to protect her, even if it was from yourself. There's no way that I could have ever resisted her, but you found a way. I couldn't trust anyone else for this role, which is why I'm asking you. It would mean the world to me if you said yes," Talvi said, giving a hopeful smile.

"I'm not certain this is a good idea. I want to accept, but I wonder if this is an act of bad judgment on both our parts."

"If that's your concern, Father already gave his approval," Talvi assured him. "I don't expect an answer straight away. I know you'll need some time to consider such a request, since you can't change your answer once it's been agreed upon."

"If Father gave his approval, then I don't need to consider it for a second," said Finn as he continuing to fan himself.

"So you'll be my *korvaaminen* then?" Talvi asked, expectant in his unwavering gaze.

"Yes, Talvi, I'll be your *korvaaminen*, but I'm only doing it for her, not for you," said Finn, stretching out his hand to shake Talvi's in agreement. "Though, perhaps I'm getting in over my head with her. Your little wife is quite a handful. Did she tell you that I lost every single one of my books to her in a wager?"

"Come off it," Talvi snickered. "You would never be so daft as to bet all your books to anyone."

"But I *was* daft enough," Finn admitted, shaking his head in disbelief. "I made the bet, she took me up on it, and she won fair and square. She's much more intelligent than she'd have either of us believe. You better watch yourself." This time it was Talvi's turn to be shocked.

"Finn! I've seen you escorted from over a dozen casinos for bleeding them dry at blackjack and baccarat! How could you lose a bet to Annika? What*ever* was the blasted wager over?"

Choosing his words ever so carefully, Finn tossed the magazine aside, put on his best poker face, looked his brother straight in the eye and said, "It was about her hair."

"Ha, no wonder you lost!" his brother howled. "Her mother's a hairdresser and she can change it right back to red. You clearly don't know the first thing about modern girls and their hair!"

"No, clearly I don't," said Finn, looking on with a wry smile as his brother had a healthy laugh at his expense. When it died down, Talvi's smile faded into the most humble expression. It was a look he rarely wore.

"I still can't believe you discovered how to resist *kotka divas*. I wish I would have known about that a couple years ago. It would have saved me a lot of trouble."

"Avoiding Zenzi altogether would have saved you a lot of trouble," Finn replied, sneering as he rolled his eyes in disgust. "She is the epitome of the phrase, 'never moisten your quill with unpredictable ink.' I half expected her to arrive at your and Yuri's birthday party with a black-haired babe in her arms. You have no idea how lucky you are that your predicament turned out the way it did."

"No, Finn, you're wrong there," Talvi pointed out with a cavalier grin. He reached into his pocket, giving his 'cheeky bastard' lighter a squeeze through his front pocket, and headed for the door. "I know exactly how lucky I am."

The moment Talvi left the room, Finn peeled back the covers and stepped in silence to the door, locking it as his heart began to race again. He turned around, leaning with his back against the wall, and shuddered in relief.

"And *I* know exactly how lucky *I* am," he whispered to himself.

CHAPTER 43
Field Trip

"I really don't want to do this," Annika said to her husband as they walked up the steps of the London embassy. "Can I just wait outside?"

Talvi smirked and pointed to a sign on the side of the building that said 'no loitering' before he rang the buzzer on the side of the massive doors.

"Ugh, seriously?" she groaned. Even though she and Talvi were on speaking terms, things were still not remotely back to normal. Annika wasn't even sure if there would be such a thing as normal for the two of them. The two of them hadn't spoken much after he had returned, bathed, and sat down to dinner with his family as if nothing unusual had happened. It was a performance that only a serious actor could have pulled off . . . or a very good spy. Annika thought about the little clues here and there about her husband's livelihood; the 'training' that Asbjorn said he had, him refusing to explain where his income came from, the fact that he always had some sort of weapon on him, his stealthy way of sneaking in or out of a room unnoticed, and Finn not arguing with her when she had suggested it in the first place.

And then there was Finn. For getting into such a serious bare knuckle fight while going through morphine withdrawal, he seemed to be in a fair enough mood when he had given his goodbye hugs to Annika. When Ambrose had told her to embrace the unfamiliar, she wondered if raging non-human hormones, opiate junkies making leaps of faith, and secret agents completely losing their shit were what he had been referring to. If that wasn't the unfamiliar, she didn't know what was.

Gerald opened the door, wearing less tweed this time, and looked at Talvi patiently.

"Good afternoon, Gerald. Do you happen to know any place nearby that makes a decent lemon meringue pie?"

"As a matter of fact, I do, Talvi. Won't you come in?" he said, and motioned with his hand for the two of them to step inside.

"Annika, this is Gerald, one of our doormen," Talvi said, introducing them. "He keeps the riff raff out of the embassy. Gerald, this is my sweet little wife, Annika."

Gerald's stoic face transformed into a surprised one. He fussed with one ear and leaned closer.

"I'm sorry; did you say your *wife?*"

"I did indeed," Talvi said, and took Annika's left hand, kissing her ring. He let go and nudged her gently. "Go on love, where's your manners?"

"Sorry, this is my first time here," she blurted, and stuck out her right hand to shake Gerald's. "Nice to meet you."

"A pleasure to meet you as well, Annika," he replied as he gave her a gentle shake and let go, unsure if he was being taken for a ride or not. He shot a perplexed glance at Talvi.

"I believe Merriweather is conducting an interview, but if you wish to wait outside her office, I could give Annika the tour."

"That won't be necessary," he chirped, grabbing ahold of her hand. "I'll take her myself."

Caught off guard again, Gerald took a key from his pocket to unlock the door on the right side of the small foyer, and gave a gentle wave as Talvi led Annika down the narrow hallway to an elevator. Talvi inserted a key of his own into a little brass box, before selecting the second floor. When the polished brass elevator doors opened and Annika stepped out, she looked with wide eyes at the scores of computer equipped work stations in the center of the main room in front of her. Sitting at the desks were a couple trolls, many elves, and a few wood nymphs, along with other magical beings that she couldn't even begin to name. She saw a small pink orb of light zip by that could only have been a faerie, and she followed it as it rose up toward the ceiling of the thirteen story atrium, full of chandeliers and skylights. Upon the chandeliers was an array of multi-colored orbs, all radiating as brightly as the pink faerie, and she realized that there were probably hundreds of fairies resting on the light fixtures. It cast an ethereal glow upon the rest of the room, even in the late afternoon light.

"What *is* this place?" she asked under her breath, so as not to draw any attention to herself.

"A safe haven for political asylum, but mainly a research facility, focusing on intelligence, criminal activity and justice, although for a while, it acted as a hostel for misplaced travelers," he answered. He leisurely led her past sofas, chairs, lamps and tables that were only broken up by the scores of bookshelves between them. There must have been hundreds of thousands of books on that floor alone. And then Annika realized that half of the floors above them were exactly the same. "It's much less chaotic now than it was a few months ago."

"Why was it so chaotic?"

"Because there used to be another embassy in Paris, exactly where you fell when you disappeared from my world and landed in your own," he explained. "That one dealt more with accommodating travelers, issuing passports and exchanging currency, so it's been a bit overwhelming, to have an entire embassy disappear."

"What happened to it?"

"I can't say."

"Oh, right, it's probably classified information," she said, grinning primly, and he raised a curious brow at her.

"I can't say, because I don't *know* yet," he said, squeezing her hand gently.

"Is that why you brought me there in the first place? Finn said you wanted a working vacation out of this whole ordeal."

"That was the original plan, but that didn't pan out too well, now, did it?" he asked, touching the tip of her nose affectionately.

They walked to another wing of the building, with a few long wooden benches outside of the hallway, and came to a tall set of doors. With another key, he opened them up and they walked into a large, empty, round room filled with wooden tables and heavy chairs, all facing forward in a half circle. It looked like a cross between a senate floor and a courtroom.

"My father spent many a day here, debating and creating laws, and overseeing countless proceedings," Talvi informed her. "That's why my family spent so much time in London when I was younger. Now he's mostly retired from the embassy, and only gets involved in very difficult cases."

"Is he like a judge, or a politician, or what?"

"He is and has been many things. A judge, a diplomat, a mayor, a consigliore . . . "

"Oh my god, like Tom Hagen in *The Godfather?*" she squealed, making her voice reverberate off the walls and ceiling of the huge room.

"Shhh, love," he said with a disapproving look, touching his forefinger to his lips. "There's no need to scream so bloody loud when I'm right here beside you."

Annika was just starting to wonder what sort of family she had married into when she caught a whiff of jasmine. Her stomach turned a little, her heart started to beat faster, and her palms began to sweat.

"Hello Talvi, and hello at long last, Annika," a crisp female voice said from behind her. Annika turned around to see a tall elven woman with long black hair standing there. She looked sharp as a tack and sexy as hell in her well-pressed white blouse, black vest, black pencil skirt, and black high heels. She was more stunning than Talvi had described. Her shiny hair did indeed come down to her breasts, and her flawless skin held the golden brown hue of a perfectly toasted marshmallow. She wasn't wearing much makeup, other than a bit of lip stain and mascara. Her lashes were so long and dark that her eyes naturally appeared to be lined with soft kohl.

"You must be Merriweather," she said, trying not to frown as she gave the sophisticated woman a once-over. She found herself wishing she'd worn something more stylish than jeans and sneakers.

"I am indeed," she replied confidently, looking at Annika with her large, dark, unreadable eyes. "I've heard so much about you."

"Yeah? Well, I've heard too much about you," said Annika, trembling with anxiety. It was painfully easy to imagine her husband's hands on Merriweather's bare hips, and his face buried between her thighs, lapping up her very best scotch. Merriweather's eyes widened subtly, and she glanced at Talvi before looking back at Annika.

"I've gone through all of your reports, Merri," he said, avoiding his wife's gaze as he patted his messenger bag. "Did you want to have a look at them in your office?"

"No, I'll not waste the time going back up there if you've truly earned that reward I promised you," she said, walking over to one of the desks. She patted the spot beside her, prompting him to join her. "Besides, my new assistant is filling out a few forms and would appreciate the privacy."

"Your new assistant? I thought you were only having an interview," said

Talvi, taking his laptop and the stack of files from his bag and setting them next to her.

"It was a second interview," she said, looking very pleased with herself as she flipped her hair behind her shoulders and crossed her arms over her chest. "I believe we've finally found the perfect candidate. *He* just graduated from a military academy, so following orders comes naturally to him."

"Ah, see Merri, I told you that your luck would change. You shouldn't have kept my lighter for so long. Perhaps you should give your new assistant one of his own so mine doesn't get nicked again?" Talvi said playfully; perhaps a little too playfully for Annika, but she just stood in the background and kept quiet, trying to ignore the long-legged, exotic and elegant creature that was perched beside her husband as he booted up his computer.

"He doesn't smoke, you cheeky bastard," she said with a lofty roll of her eyes, and motioned for him to show her his work.

"These two reports contain multiple discrepancies, which I thought you should have a look at," he said quietly to her as he handed her the top two folios. "You'll want to re-examine these statements."

Merriweather was silent as she opened the cover and let Talvi point out a few pages to her. She looked up at him, and then Annika.

"Annika, would you mind giving us a few moments?" she said, motioning to the doors that had been left open.

"No problem; I'll just wait in the hall for you," she replied, relieved to have an excuse to not be in that room. The relaxed banter between them wasn't proving much to her except that they definitely had a long, unconventional history together. She hurried out and shut the doors behind her, and sank into a bench in the hall.

As soon as the doors were shut, Merriweather turned to Talvi, steely-eyed.

"Why did you tell her about the last time you asked me for a raise?"

"I don't know what you're talking about," he said, running his fingers seductively through his hair.

"Well I know that you only do that thing with your hair when you don't mind getting caught lying. You think you have everyone believing that's your tell-all giveaway, but I know you better than that. You're the best liar I ever met." Talvi's eyes flashed darkly as she pointed this out, but he said nothing.

"I'm not certain why you felt the need to share that information with anyone, especially not your new wife," she said, shooting him a severe glare. "You know full well that everything that occurs within my office is supposed to be confidential. You are risking an awful lot, and I'm not certain where this carelessness is coming from."

"It comes from the fact that Annika doesn't trust me as far as she can throw me," he said quietly. "She thinks the worst of me half the time that we're together. It's been up and down like a damned yo-yo with her, trying to soothe her suspicions. I just can't seem win her completely over."

Merriweather looked like she couldn't decide whether to laugh in his face or slap it.

"My very best raven flies away on hiatus because he has some personal problems and a long-awaited prophecy coming to a head; he returns two years later wearing an irremovable wedding ring, and then he's baffled that his new, human-born bride is suspicious of how he earns his keep. Is that what you're telling me? Because that's what I'm hearing."

Talvi thumbed the ring on his finger and tossed his mane, looking sullen as she went on.

"I'm amazed that we're even having this conversation, given that you earn your keep by getting others to trust you, women in particular. Did it ever occur to you to try and treat her like one of your assignments? Speaking of which, I thought of a fantastic cover for the reason you'll never take off your ring. You can claim that you are a poor, young widower, and that you promised your wife on her death bed that you would always wear it. It's really a good story, don't you think? I know if I were being seduced for information, I would gladly tell you anything you wanted to know after hearing such a maudlin tale. It's a shame that neither one of us had thought of it earlier, but you'll be able to test it out soon enough. I have an assignment lined up for you, and I need you on top of it as soon as possible."

A faint burning sensation began to form around his ring, traveling up his arm and into his shoulder. Talvi closed his eyes and saw himself and Annika in a snowy clearing in a dark forest, just before dawn. They were surrounded by a circle of white candles, kneeling on soft pillows. He watched as he slipped her wedding ring onto her finger, and then she placed his on his finger. He remembered how clear and intense the sunrise had been on that winter solstice, how it illuminated their matching wedding bands and made them twinkle and shine. The rings hadn't moved since. He saw her cut his palm with his now cursed knife, and then him cutting hers, before their bleeding hands were tied together, as he promised that his love for her would cross any distance. He remembered her crying, telling him that she didn't want him so far away, telling him that she needed him near her. He remembered crying also, and most of all, he remembered promising that he would in fact, be right there for her.

He bit his lip and looked at the woman who he had spent a significant portion of his lifetime working with. Then he glanced at the closed doors, where his wife sat on the other side waiting; waiting for their life together to truly begin.

Out in the hall, Annika heard footsteps approaching. A well-dressed young man with very short dirty blond hair that was longer on top stopped in front of her. He held a folder in one hand, and carried an air of indifference about him, along with incredible posture.

"You haven't by chance seen Merriweather Narayanaswamy come this way, have you?" he asked.

"She's in there," Annika answered, pointing unenthusiastically to the closed doors. "She's having a private little chit-chat with my husband." The man's indifference fell aside. Suddenly he was very interested in who sat on the bench.

"You're not Talvi Marinossian's wife, are you?"

"Yeah, actually, I am," she said, wondering why he was looking at her so strangely with his dark grey eyes. "I'm Annika."

"How nice to meet you, Annika. I'm Merriweather's new assistant, Stephan," he said, outstretching his hand to shake hers. He seemed to hold onto it a few seconds longer than she thought necessary, but she swept the thought out of her mind as he took a seat next to her on the bench, sitting rigidly on the edge rather than sinking his back into it.

"So it's your first day here and you already know who my husband is?" she asked, trying to make conversation.

"A lot of us know who your husband is," was Stephan's prickly reply, and without any further attempt at explanation or conversation, he opened his folder and reviewed its contents in silence.

"Talvi, are you even listening to me?" Merriweather asked, forcing him out of his mind and back into the room where they were sitting. "I said I have a job for you."

"I'm not interested," he said, shaking his head.

"I wasn't asking if you were interested," she replied with a stern voice.

"I'm serious, Merri," he said, and when he looked up, she was shocked to see his eyes had become glassy with tears. "I thought perhaps I could compartmentalize things to the point where I might still be able to carry out my assignments, but things honestly are different since I saw you last. Even if it's my cover, I find the idea of telling another woman that Annika is dead unthinkable. Just saying it out loud is . . . " He turned away from her, trying to discreetly wipe the corners of his eyes. "I never wish to say it again."

Merriweather looked at him carefully, thinking back to his first days of employment. He was the only natural born raven that the embassy had ever come across. When they realized that he had written the book on the art of seduction, and he was told that he could get paid for his prowess, provided that he gather intelligence and do away with a few bad apples on the side, it had been a perfect match. The embassy didn't have to teach him a single thing, other than how to collect his paycheck. For decades, he had been their most efficient operative, audacious, arrogant and worth every penny, until this little matter of Annika Brisby had come up. Now, to Merriweather, the most magnificent and legendary raven she'd ever known just looked like a caged blackbird with clipped wings.

"If that's how you feel, then there's no need for us to go downstairs to the weapons locker after all. I'll let you keep the phone since you did read through all these reports as I asked you to. However, I will need your laptop and your keys," said Merriweather quietly while her dark eyes burned. She closed his laptop, stacking the pile of folios on it and gathered everything into her arms. She made no attempt to beg him to take the assignment, to shower him with compliments about how irreplaceable he was, or to try and find a pithy desk job to offer someone of his esteemed value. That simply wasn't Merriweather Narayanaswamy's style.

Stunned and feeling separated from his body, he watched as his left hand pulled his keys out of his pocket, and handed them to her. The motion seemed unreal, but it was really happening.

"It's not every day that I get to train an assistant how to deactivate an operative," she said coolly as she stood to leave. "Now come along. I have to lock the doors behind you."

They stepped into the hall and Merriweather was surprised to see her new assistant loyally waiting for her.

"You're already done with the forms I gave you?" she asked, and he nodded, standing up to take the pile of folios and Talvi's laptop out of her arms.

"Looks like you hired me just in time," Stephan said, motioning to the items he held. "Do you need me to stay a while longer and get started on this?"

"I would love it if you could stay, but we have something else more important to take care of first," she said, glancing at Talvi, who looked completely bewildered by her and her new assistant. Shifting the workload into one arm, Stephan outstretched his hand and introduced himself. As Talvi shook his hand half-heartedly, Annika thought that once again, Stephan held on a little too long. Merriweather locked the doors with Talvi's keys and then started to walk away with her new assistant. She turned back and said,

"It was a pleasure to meet you, Annika. And Talvi . . . you know how to reach me if you change your mind."

Annika peered up at her husband, who stood frozen in the same place as when he'd come out of the room, except that he was staring at Merriweather's back with a dazed expression. His eyes moved down to meet hers as she approached him slowly.

"Are you alright?" she asked, concerned by the look on his face, noticing his damp eyelashes. With his left hand, he reached out and took hers, knocking their rings together gently with a soft *clink* when they intertwined their fingers.

"Do you remember when we were married, and you were telling me how you didn't want me across the meadow?" he asked, looking at her with bittersweet inquisitiveness. "You said you needed me right next to you, and I promised I would be. Do you recall that promise I made to you?"

She nodded her head, surprised that he remembered.

"I've told you in the past that I keep my word. I try not to make promises I have no intention of keeping."

"What are you trying to say?"

"Well . . . " he paused to look at his messenger bag slung over his shoulder. It appeared much lighter without the computer and folios inside of it. "I hope you still need me around as much as you let on during our wedding. I'm not certain if I just quit, or if I just got sacked. Either way, I don't work here anymore."

Annika's jaw dropped.

"What happened?"

"You," he replied, and leaned down to touch his forehead against hers, squeezing her hand tight, then letting go and pulling her as close against him as he could. He stroked her long brown hair and nuzzled against her ear, telling her ever so softly, "*You're* what happened. What do you say, my little dove . . . shall we skip the rest of the tour and go home?"

CHAPTER 44
Reconciliation

After booking their flights home via Talvi's phone, they stopped at a wine shop before checking into a hotel near Heathrow airport. He nabbed a wine key from the bar and had a bottle of Tempranillo uncorked before they even reached their room. Annika didn't even wait for the door to shut before dragging her bag into the bathroom. After a week of hiking and only one bath, she felt she deserved a very nice, long, hot shower. She was dismayed when she realized that she had left her special conditioner at the hotel in Paris, leaving her hair rough and full of snarls when she stepped out of the bathroom.

Talvi had been lying on the bed, flipping through menus and nursing that bottle of wine until it was half empty. When he rose, his eyes ran from her head to her toes, then back up again, before he gave her a dismissive kiss on the forehead. He took a hearty swig and carried the wine with him into the bathroom.

"Why don't you be a sweet little wife and find a place you'd like to order dinner from while I take my shower?" he called out to her, and shut the door.

"Babe, you didn't tell me what you wanted," she called through the closed door.

"As long as it's vegetarian, I don't care," came his disinterested reply, and then the shower turned on once more.

A current of déjà vu rippled through Annika's mind, but she shrugged it off. After she struggled to put on her t-shirt and yoga pants over her damp skin, she found herself cursing once more that she had forgotten her conditioner when she began to comb it out. She flipped on the television and her annoyance was replaced with sheer bewilderment. The same zombie film that she'd watched with Finn was playing. She stared at the screen, then at the bathroom door, then at the restaurant menus, and then back at the screen.

What the hell is going on here? Am I dreaming? she wondered, and searched through the menus until she found the number to a Chinese restaurant. After placing her order, she settled into the bed and continued watching the movie, holding her comb absentmindedly, half expecting Finn to come out of the bathroom when the door opened.

But out stepped Talvi, in his worn out cargo shorts and soft white tee. And even though it was wet, his unruly black hair still managed to rebel in every direction. He reached into the bag from the wine shop and opened a second bottle, this time a Bordeaux, before settling beside his wife.

"I think a white would have been a more appropriate pairing with Chinese," she pointed out. She winced as the comb caught on yet another snarl, ripping a few more strands of hair from her head.

"Bollocks to that rubbish," he said, taking a sip from the bottle. "I'll drink whatever I like with whatever I please, and I'm partial to red." He passed the Bordeaux to her and took the comb away with authority. "Come along now, scoot up so I can sit behind you," he said, rapping her on the thigh with the comb. "I'll get this mess sorted out in no time."

"I can do it myself," she insisted.

"It's about as painful for me to watch you do this as it is to watch a bird fly into a window," Talvi said. "Now move your bum so I can have a go." Annika did as she was told without further argument, and focused on the wine and the zombie outbreak on the television. She had to admit, Talvi was as gentle as a lamb while picking carefully through her snarls and tangles. He worked with such determination that he wouldn't even pause to take a drink of wine when it was offered to him.

"How did you get so good at this?" she asked, running her fingers through a finished section of hair.

"I used to brush Yuri's hair every night before bed," he replied quietly. "She couldn't fall asleep otherwise. When I began working away from home, she would remain awake for days at a time, much to my family's frustration."

He snickered at a funny scene in the zombie movie, and then gathered another handful of her hair.

"How long did you work at that job?"

"Just over seventy years."

"Seventy years?" Annika repeated, mystified at the number. "That's an insanely long time to do one thing."

"My unique skill set rarely allows for me to do just one thing," he replied casually as he took the comb and worked it through her hair. "It was the perfect fit for me, but now that you're in my life, I seem to have outgrown elements of it, the way one outgrows a pair of shoes. Speaking of which, you may have to reign in your spending a bit until I sort out how I'm to take care of you. I told Merri about those red-feathered Manolo's of yours, and she showed me how much they cost. I didn't realize you had such expensive taste until Finn took you shopping. For a girl who complains so much about spending money when I'm around, you seem to have no trouble spending it when I'm away."

"Yeah, that's called retail therapy, babe, so I hope you'll think twice about taking me on vacation and then ditching me without an explanation," Annika said, gloating confidently. "And I can get another job to support my shoe addiction. I've been taking care of myself for a while. I don't need you to worry about it."

"I'm not implying that I'm skint," he said, appearing nettled as he reached around her for the wine. He took a drink before he went on. "I've plenty of savings, and I'm not concerned about living comfortably, but I'll be damned if I'll let you spend all of your time working away from home for a pittance when I've given up my entire career so that we can be together."

"And I appreciate that, but we can't live off of savings forever," she said, trying to reason with him as a zombie on the television met a gory demise.

"Tell me something, my little dove," he asked, passing her the bottle, and then resumed combing out her hair again. "Why are you so dead set against letting me take care of you? Is it because you're female and I'm male? Would this even be an issue if you were male and I were female?"

"I just don't think in this day and age that a woman should expect to be taken care of by a man," Annika shrugged, and took a sip of the wine.

"In what fashion?" he implored, leaning in closer to her as he spoke. "Financially? Physically? Emotionally? Spiritually? Husbands and wives are expected to take care of one another, wouldn't you agree? Or should they all be so bloody independent that they don't need one another after all? Then what is the meaning of a marriage in the first place? Isn't that what's wrong with the modern world, that loss of compassion and connection, that loss of strong and trusting relationships? Isn't that what's wrong with us? I know we have something solid and real which we can build upon, but you must give me *something* to work with."

She turned away from the movie and saw his hypnotic blue and green eyes hovering in front of her. The corner of her mouth twitched as she glanced at the bottle in her hand.

"You said you wanted something to work with?" she asked him.

"Yes, Annika. Please . . . anything," he begged.

"You can work on this," she said, grinning to herself as she passed him the bottle of wine.

"How dare you steal my own joke and use it on me, you saucy girl?" he crooned, letting his incredulous expression melt into a softer one. "Theft is a crime in most places. You must want me to punish you again."

"I shouldn't be punished at all. I can't help it if I didn't learn my lesson the first time. You're just a bad teacher."

Talvi eyed her lovingly and exasperatedly all at once while he dropped the comb and raised the bottle to his lips.

"Annika, if money were no object, what would you do with your time? Would you focus on your music or would you rather spend five days a week in someone else's shop just to prove that you can buy yourself a pair of pretty slippers every now and again?"

"Well . . . if money were no object, I wouldn't work. My music would be my work," she admitted.

"Then let your music be your work, you stubborn, silly girl, for money is no object."

"What kind of money are you talking about?" she asked, now turning her body to face him. "Are we talking private yacht money, or private island money?"

"Oh, I don't know, Annika. I was never interested in purchasing either of those things," he said breezily, setting the Bordeaux on the nightstand. "I wish you would stop thinking of it as my money. It's *ours*. And if you think I use it to control you, you are sorely mistaken. You actually have more control over me than I ever imagined, until the other day. I only pray that Finn has truly forgiven me."

"He seemed really happy when we left," said Annika, glancing at her meteorite ring from him. A warm, comforting feeling drifted over her as she thumbed it.

"He was happy to see me leave," Talvi replied.

"No, that wasn't it at all," Annika said. "Did it have anything to do with that *kormanin* thing you were going to ask him?"

Talvi's eyes narrowed suspiciously.

"How would you know anything about that?"

"I was with your dad when he came out to the hole you dug," she confessed, causing her husband to scowl. "He said you had a lot on your mind because it was the deepest one you'd ever dug."

"I said some very private things to him . . . I didn't intend for you to be listening in."

"I guess he wanted me to hear what's going on in your head," Annika said, and put her hand on his knee. "He said we need to talk more. I'm trying to be a better listener, but you need to open up outside of your comfort zone."

Talvi pursed his lips and tossed his mane, looking like an irritated black cat that was undecided whether to stay and be petted, or slip out a window.

"So what's this *kormanin* thing you were talking about?"

"I asked Finn to be my *korvaaminen*," Talvi replied in a serious voice. "You know how children are born and they have faerie godparents?" Annika nodded. "It's similar to that, but for couples. It's a promise to care for someone if their partner were unable to. It's a bit old fashioned and not very common, but I thought my circumstances necessitated it. If anything happened to me, I wouldn't trust anyone else to care for you as you rightfully deserve."

"Aww, I think that's really a sweet gesture," she said, running her fingers through her hair again. "Do girls get to pick a *korvaaminen* for their husbands?"

"Absolutely they do, if they feel there is a need."

"Then I would pick Patti Cake for you," she told him.

"Pish Posh. You're only saying that to be nice," he said, trying not to smile.

"No, I mean it," she said. "When you told your dad that Patti, James, Charlie, and Chivanni all agreed that you weren't being inappropriate with her, it made me feel really stupid for thinking that in the first place. I can see how she reminds you of Runa and Yuri. Plus I know you're a huge flirt. I knew that when I met you, but I just figured you would stop being one after we got married."

"You may as well have expected me to start wearing curly-toed shoes and begin making toys for good girls and boys," he said with a contemptuous snort. "I am what I am. I was dead serious when I told you that you were stuck with me and *all* of my habits for the rest of eternity."

"Were you really born winking at the midwife?"

"So the story goes," he said, and shot her a seductive wink. "She warned my mother that I was going to be quite the charmer. You take it so bloody serious, but I'm only having fun. And you certainly don't seem to mind when it works to your advantage, such as when we went to the bank and I made friends with Sandy." He paused and sighed irritably before he went on. "It's been exhausting to constantly prove my loyalty to you. That's why I became so angry on the airplane, in addition to arriving at the hotel to find what I found, and then you didn't even give me a kiss, or tell me that you missed me. I'm very sorry for what I said about Merriweather, but I've really had enough of your insecure feminine nonsense. You're not an insecure woman."

Annika was silent as she thought back to what Finn had told her back in Paris, when they were in their safe little den deep underground.

I don't believe anyone else would have the fortitude to be my brother's wife . . . being in a relationship with someone means that you need to grant one another certain allowances.

Maybe allowing him to be his flirtatious, outrageous self was the kind of allowance Finn was referring to all along. Her moment of clarity was shattered when Talvi let out a delighted howl.

"Oh, that is just bloody brilliant!" he hooted in glee.

"What is?" Annika asked, glancing at the television screen, to which his eyes were fixed upon.

"Our heroine has a M4A1 carbine assault rifle for a leg," he pointed out. "How perfect is that for killing zombies?"

A warm, sweet sensation seeped into Annika's skin as she recognized her husband's appreciation of her favorite genre of films.

"It's okay for being caught off guard, but I think the noise would just end up attracting more zombies," she pointed out. "Wouldn't it make more sense to use a knife or a sword?"

"True, a blade is ideal for stealth," he agreed, running the comb effortlessly through her untangled hair. "Even guns with silencers are not really silent when the firing pin strikes the primer. A knife in a skillful hand can remove a throat or a heart without making a sound. However, they require far more intimacy than a gun, and the last thing one would want is to come into contact with zombie blood. It might lead to infection, so the rifle is clearly the optimal choice in this situation."

Thoroughly impressed with her husband's rationale, Annika turned to smile at him.

"If the zombie apocalypse ever comes, you're definitely the one I want to have by my side."

"Aww, love, you know I would kill every last one of them if they dared touch a hair on your head," he said, and kissed her on the head before continuing to run the comb along her scalp. She understood how such a soothing motion could have lulled his twin sister to sleep. It was just as relaxing as the wine, if not more so. He set down the comb and began to run his fingers through her damp hair, not catching on a single tangle.

There was a knock at the door, and Talvi stopped playing with her hair.

"Get down on the floor," he ordered, pointing to the side of the bed farthest away from the door.

"What for?" she asked, wrinkling her nose in confusion. "It's just our dinner, babe. I got us Chinese."

He looked at her skeptically, and in a few short strides, he darted in and out of the bathroom, before peering through the peephole at their visitor. When he cracked open the door, Annika noticed that he was holding his straight razor in his hand. She sat silently on the bed, observing as he folded the blade out of sight of the person, put it back in his pocket, and took out his wallet instead. After he paid, he locked the door and brought their dinner over to the bed, acting as if nothing out of the ordinary had happened.

"What was that all about?" she asked, eyeing him suspiciously.

"All that discussion about zombies put me on edge," he said, flashing a smile before sniffing the take-out boxes. "Did you order ma po tofu for me?"

"Yeah," she said slowly, still perplexed about the business with the blade. "You said you'd been craving it for a long time."

"I didn't think you would have remembered that," he replied, kissing her on the cheek before unwrapping a pair of chopsticks. "The last time I had this was when Yuri made it for me nearly two years ago. No one else in the family likes it."

"Then I hope this is half as good as hers," Annika said, digging a fork into her rice and vegetables. "I'm sorry I never thought about how much you must miss her."

"Let's not speak about her right now," he replied in a quiet voice in between bites.

"Alright, well, I'm sorry about bugging you so much about your past. Your dad said that I was only focusing on you to avoid focusing on all the changes happening with myself. I think he's right."

"You mean to tell me that my father came to my defense?" Talvi asked in disbelief.

"Oh yeah," said Annika with her mouth full. "He told me that I need to adjust my learning curve for you, because you've never had a girlfriend before. Is that true?"

"Well . . . yes, it is," he admitted, still surprised to learn what his father had told his wife.

"I thought Zenzi was your old girlfriend," said Annika, remembering a distinctly annoying elven girl who hung all over Talvi the first time he took her to the Tortoise and the Hare. "Hey, did something crazy happen between the two of you?"

"Let's not speak about her right now, either," Talvi said, focusing on the television. "I don't wish to ruin this peaceful moment with you." Annika laughed to herself, because only he would call this a peaceful moment, when there was the rattle of machine gun fire mixed with brain-obsessed, bloody zombies screaming in the background.

"Alright, well, is there anything you want to ask me, since we need to learn how to communicate more?"

"Yes, actually there is," he said after swallowing another bite. He waited until Annika turned to face him. "What's your middle name?"

"It's Jane," she confided with an embarrassed smile. "My mom got to pick my first name, so my dad gave me my middle name from a song he liked." Talvi's expression became more intrigued.

"Sweet Jane?" he asked, to which she nodded. "Why, you weren't yet a twinkle in your father's eye when that song came out. I have that record album at home. I just love Sweet Jane."

"Why am I not surprised?" she murmured, smiling softly.

"When were you given that name, sweet Annika Jane?" he asked. "I don't even know your birthday."

"It's July third."

"That's only two days from now," he hummed. "I've already got a gift in mind for you, but it won't be ready until next April. Is there anything else you would like in the meantime? Something expensive? Something rare?"

"I'll opt for something rare since neither of us have an income right now," she said, grinning even wider at him. "You can make me dinner . . . without using any faerie magic."

"Ah, that is rare indeed," he said. He set his dinner on the nightstand, then took hers away and put it beside his. He pulled her into his lap, wrapping her legs around his waist. "Do you have anything in mind that you might enjoy tasting that evening? How many courses do you think you can manage to fit into your little body?" His fingertips walked lazily up her spine and then slid back down and curled around her waist. "Three? Four? More? I have a feeling you're going to be thoroughly stuffed by the end of the night."

"I have a feeling you're not talking about my birthday dinner," she said with a coy smile, ready to make up with him, ready to move in perfect harmony and sync with him, and feel that connection that had been absent for too long. She pushed his hands down onto her hip bones, guiding them to rest on her ilium. She curled her fingers under his jaw, then reached out toward the wicked creature in front of her and gently took a handful of his wild black hair in each fist, pulling him closer, inhaling from above his pointed ear down to his shoulder. Her nose ran along his cheekbone until it was touching his, but when she went to kiss him, he didn't return it passionately like she was expecting. Instead, his response was benign and disengaged. His hands let go of her hips and he leaned back, resting on his hands. He tilted his head to one side, then the other, looking at her with a quizzical frown.

"What's wrong?" she asked.

"Something is throwing me off . . . it feels so different with you now," he said in a serious tone. "I'm trying my damnedest not to let it affect me, but I'm not certain I can cope with how badly behaved you really were in Paris."

Annika's stomach turned as she snuck a glimpse into his blue-green eyes, trying to scan his thoughts for any trace of what his suspicions were. She had tried to follow Finn's advice to the letter, pushing all inappropriate memories into a corner of her mind and keeping them there. Then she saw him indulging in his pear and ginger sorbet, and the blissful expression on his face. She heard Finn's deep voice give a happy hum and her heart thumped a few times. Maybe she hadn't done as well as she'd hoped.

"What do you mean?" she asked nervously. Talvi reached out and ran his fingers through her hair once more, letting his gaze rest on the strands that fell slowly from of his hand. He looked absolutely heartbroken.

"I think you know very well what I mean . . . " he answered, shaking his head in disapproval while he reached for his smartphone on the nightstand beside the wine. "It's messing with my mind every time I look at you, not to mention the rest of my body. I don't believe we'll be able to reconcile properly until you're a redhead again. I say it's high time to allow a rooster other than James into the henhouse. Now tell me the telephone number to your mother's salon, so I can get this matter resolved as quickly as possible. I really, really would like to reconcile with you."

CHAPTER 45
Homecoming Queen

"I hope James doesn't rip my head off when we get inside," said Annika as their taxi pulled into the driveway of their house. "I was supposed to call him back over a week ago. He said it was important."

"What was important?" Talvi asked, unbuckling his seatbelt.

"I don't know," said Annika, grabbing her purse and a couple smaller bags as she opened the door. "All he told me was that shit was blowing up."

"Why didn't you tell me it was an emergency?" Talvi cried, looking worried. He paid the driver quickly and peered at the house while he walked to the trunk and took out their luggage. In that last half-hour before sunset, he could see the beautiful flowers were still blooming and the trees were full and happy. The lawn was freshly mowed, and it appeared that a fresh coat of paint had been applied to the wood trim. The once-dilapidated house was now one of the prettiest on the block, if not in the neighborhood.

"Sweetie, nothing's literally blowing up," she assured him as he followed her up the steps to the side door. "It's more slang. It means something's happening."

"Such as . . . ?"

"I don't know, let's find out."

She opened the door and as soon as she shouted her hello into the kitchen, James went off on her.

"Oh my god, where the hell have you been?" he demanded as he stormed in

389

from the living room, with Chivanni zipping in front of him. The faerie barely gave Annika and Talvi time to drop their bags before enveloping them in tight hugs, sending his wings aflutter while James ranted on.

"I've been leaving a shit-ton of messages at your hotel and then they told me that you checked out days ago and I'm totally trying not to freak the fuck out, but you really need to be better about getting back to me! And why the hell didn't you just get a fucking international calling plan and take your phone with—"

"James, do I need to put you in a time out?" Chivanni interrupted in a calm voice. James tossed his tousled brown hair and rolled his eyes before admitting that no, in fact, he did not need a time out at all. The shift in his attitude was drastic, and didn't go unnoticed.

"Where's Charlie?" Annika asked. "And Patti?"

"At the farm," James answered. "One of the cheese makers is leaving, so Charlie's teaching her how to make mozzarella by hand. I had no idea how much that girl likes cheese, but it's pretty much the perfect job for her."

"And they can ride to work together, since Patti still hasn't found a car she likes," Chivanni added.

James spied a garment bag marked Chanel and snatched it the way a child snatches candy at a parade.

"Um, let's take that upstairs," Annika said. She had no desire to look at her formerly white dress. James and Chivanni followed her and Talvi up to their room, where they set their bags on the bed and began to unpack.

"You said things were blowing up, but everything looks just fine to me," said Talvi, looking around their room. "What exactly were you referring to, James?"

"Do you remember your wife's photo shoot with Jerry O. and the rest of the boys?" he asked, getting excited.

"Ah yes, I'll not forget that day very easily," he said, smirking at Annika. "We were supposed to have a romantic picnic, but I got the brush off for some other blokes instead. Are you bored with my repertoire already, love?"

"No," she said, blushing as she gave him a playful shove.

"Well Jerry O. called me and we went out to dinner, and he pulled some strings last minute, and the band got a blurb in the magazine!" James informed her.

"I can't believe it," Annika said, staring at him. "You went out to dinner with Jerry?"

"Annika, did you even hear what I said about the band?"

"Yeah, and that's super cool, but I'm really surprised that you went out with him again, after what he did to you."

"Oh, who gives a shit?" came James's irritated reply. "Let me go get the damn magazine so you can see for yourself what I did for the greater good."

He traipsed out of the room and went downstairs while Annika tossed dirty laundry into the hamper.

"I don't think I care for 'Oh Jerry'," Chivanni said with a sigh. "James said he only met with him for professional reasons, but I worry that he's playing with fire."

"He probably is," Annika said, giving Chivanni a sympathetic look. "He got burned pretty bad last time, but there's nothing anyone can do to . . . " she trailed off as James climbed up the steps and joined them in the room again. He plopped the magazine down on top of the luggage on the bed, and opened it to a two page spread marked with a green sticky note. There was Annika, surrounded by four handsome fellows in colorful suits, perched on a desk in a little black dress with her red-feathered shoes. She aggressively held Jerry's silk tie in her fist while he flashed a dazzling smile at her. She was astounded at how glamorous the photo looked, how perfect the lighting was, and how sexy and rock-and-roll she came across. In the bottom right corner of the page was a summary of what their band sounded like, along with her name and a link to their official website, and instructions on where to download the songs that they had available online.

"People have been downloading our stuff like crazy ever since this came out last week," James said, gloating at her with pride. "Especially the song that Talvi helped us with. People are going nuts over it! We might actually get a decent paycheck for once!"

"Wow . . . " Annika said, picking the magazine up and looking closer while Talvi looked over her shoulder. "This is just, this is really amazing. Jerry said he could pull strings better than you can push buttons, but I guess I didn't have a clue how connected he is."

"Yeah, well, you're *welcome*," James snapped, and grabbed the Chanel garment bag from the bed. As he unzipped it, he gasped in delight, then gasped in horror.

"Annika, what the hell did you *do*?" he demanded, holding the dress in front of him as he looked at the red, yellow and blue paint smeared all over it in disbelief. "You've got to be shitting me! You ruined a Chanel? Oh my god, you ruined a fucking Chanel!"

"Um, I was, um, supporting a local artist," she stammered as her face grew warm. "It's an abstract painting now."

"I think it's pretty," said Chivanni, gathering a section of blue hemline in his narrow hands. "All white might be a bit boring."

"No, it's supposed to be pure white," James insisted, shaking his head in grief at the once perfect dress. "What's wrong with you? You do not finger paint a Chanel! Thank god you weren't wearing this the day we ran into Jerry and his stylist, or you would've gotten both of us banned from the photo shoot!"

"If the dress is truly ruined, then why bother keep it?" Talvi asked, taking the last of his things from his bag.

"Because it's still a Chanel," James said crisply. He gave the dress one last look and zipped the garment bag to hang it in the closet. "You're not supposed to defile such a sacred thing, but you also don't just kick it to the curb, either."

CHAPTER 46

The Rooster in the Hen House

Talvi followed Annika into the very cozy, very crowded salon the next morning, which happened to be a Sunday. An emergency bulletin must have gone out among the hens, because every seat in the coop was taken. Even the hooded hair dryers were occupied, although they weren't running. Talvi ran his hand through his hair and grinned like a Cheshire cat as he was paraded past the flock.

"Is this the mysterious Mr. Lewd and Lascivious?" Beatrice asked, putting her hands on her ample hips.

"Yes, Beatrice, this is my new son-in-law," Faline replied while she gave Annika a hug.

"How delightful to meet you, Beatrice. I do like the alias Mr. Lewd and Lascivious, but you can call me Talvi for short," he said, letting his eyes twinkle brightly as he reached for her hand.

"There's nothing short about you, is there?" Beatrice replied, looking him up and down as she extended her right hand toward him.

"No, there really isn't," he said, kissing the back of her hand. "My loving wife can attest to that."

Rather than attest to anything, Annika swatted his rear for being so cheeky. Beatrice just laughed and motioned for the two of them to take a seat in the swivel chairs.

"I like him already," she said, and mussed Talvi's hair. She took a second look at his ears before walking behind the counter to the mini-fridge, but didn't say anything about them. Other than the strange shape of his ears, he looked like any other six and a half foot tall Portland native, in his slim-fit jeans, t-shirt, and Chuck Taylors.

Faline introduced a white-haired woman named Agnes and the other older ladies seated around the small salon and then Beatrice returned holding two champagne flutes with a raspberry resting in the bottom of the glass, and handed them to the new arrivals.

"These don't look like mimosas," Annika observed, sniffing her drink.

"No, we're having champagne screws made with Finnish vodka in honor of Talvi finally getting to meet the ladies," her mother explained, and then turned to Talvi. "Your first name is Finnish, isn't it?"

"I honestly prefer Talvi, but yes, the origin is Finnish," he said, and took a sip of his drink, nodding in approval to Faline, and then he turned to Beatrice, flashing a debonair smile. "I believe you've discovered the path to my heart, Beatrice. I certainly wasn't expecting to receive a screw in my honor when we arrived, but there's really no better way to begin a day, now is there?"

Beatrice shot Annika and Faline a surprised look as she blushed, but Annika just shrugged and laughed.

"Hey, you're the ones who came up with the new drink idea. I've never had a problem with mimosas," she said to Beatrice and her mother after taking a sip. "Is there really vodka in here? Are you trying to get hammered before you fix my hair?"

"When Talvi called two days ago and told me that you colored your hair dark brown from a box, I wasn't sure how else I would cope," Faline joked. "But I put extra orange juice in mine just to be on the safe side. I sure don't want to make it any worse."

"It's not that bad, Mom."

"It's not the shade that's bad, hon, but this isn't going to be as simple as your regular touch ups, either," she explained. "Boxed color is a pain to deal with, and I'll have to lift all of the brown out before I can add your red back in. That's why I told you two to dress comfy." She paused to glance skeptically at Annika's colorful and poufy silk and organza skirt, accented with strings of shimmering sequins. "I hope you realize that you're going to be sitting in that skirt for at least a few hours. This is no quick fix, unless you don't mind cutting your hair as short as Patti's." Avoiding Annika's glass, Faline secured a black cape around her and tied it behind her neck.

"I definitely don't want that," Annika sighed, looking at her skirt like she wished she had worn something else with her sleeveless top. "Short hair is cute on her, but I don't think I could pull it off."

"Please don't ever cut it that short," said Talvi. "I love how long it is now."

"You've been red ever since I've known you, Annika. It's so strange to see you as a brunette," said Beatrice, leaning against her work area beside Talvi's swivel chair.

"So you see the dilemma I've been dealing with here," he replied, making his case to the group of women as he motioned to his wife. "I took Annika to Paris, went away for business, and when I returned, there was a brunette bird in the hotel room, insisting that she was my wife. I can barely even kiss this woman sitting here, because every time I look at her, I keep thinking, 'this is *not* my wife'. I simply want her to appear as untouched as she was when I left her. Is that not too much to ask?" A few of the women sighed in admiration, agreeing with him wholeheartedly.

"Whenever I get my hair done, Harold doesn't even notice," piped up a crabby faced lady.

"I have a feeling Harold is a bit daft, not to notice something as significant as his own wife's hair," Talvi replied sympathetically and took another drink from his champagne flute. His comment was met with an enthusiastic nod of agreement from the crabby woman, and more clucking from the hens.

"Well, I'll get her back to normal soon enough," Faline assured him, and began combing through her daughter's long hair and sectioning it off.

"So Talvi, tell us a little more about yourself," asked Agnes. "What do you do for a living?"

"I'm actually taking a break from mergers and acquisitions. My office in London was making some demands that would have prevented me from being a very good husband, so we parted ways." A series of clucks and coos sounded from more than half of the women.

"What a good man, putting his family first," said one of them.

"Speaking of families, when are you two starting one?" another asked. "I'll bet you'll have beautiful babies."

"You hens are quite skilled at the open ended questions, aren't you?" he remarked.

"You have no idea," said Faline, glancing at him and then at her daughter. "So, how long until I get some grandchildren?"

Annika was at a loss for what to say, and looked to Talvi for help. She remembered what Ambrose had told her about human babies growing faster than elven ones, and how it would upset her family to bring home a baby that seemed not to age at all.

"We're planning on traveling extensively, now that neither of us is tethered to a job," Talvi replied, reaching over to take Annika's hand in his. "We have all the time in the world to raise a family, but every year, Venice sinks further into the Adriatic Sea. Have you ever been there, love?"

"Nope," she said, smiling gratefully at him.

"Then we'll have to be certain to spend some time there on our way to Rome. There are so many places I want to take you, and so many more where I want to take you again and again." His wistful expression assured her that all he wanted was to take her again, and again . . . just not in the traveling sense.

"Pardon me for asking, but if you quit your job and plan to travel, what are you kids going to do to make ends meet?" asked another.

"I've actually been saving nearly all my income ever since I began the position," Talvi explained. "I never had a steady sweetheart to spend it on until I met Annika, so there's quite a bit set aside. We're going to be fine."

"I can't believe you've never had a girlfriend," Beatrice accused in a light-hearted tone. "Not someone as good looking and smart as you. Annika said you speak nineteen languages. Did I hear that right?"

"Oh yes," he chirped, happy to brag about himself. "I traveled a lot growing up and also for work. After about six months of total immersion, it's not that difficult to pick up a language. Although I must admit, it took me close to a year to fully grasp Japanese, and English slang has just gotten ridiculously out of hand these days."

"You can say that again!"

"English slang has just gotten ridiculously out of hand these days," he repeated, winking at one of the hens. "Did you know, that if something is happening, it is now referred to as blowing up? Annika said that yesterday when we arrived home, and I thought the bloody house had caught fire!"

"Kids these days," muttered one of the group.

"Do you know German?" Beatrice asked him. "Agnes speaks it." She motioned to the white-haired lady.

"*Wie geht's,* Agnes? *Freut mich, sie kennenzulernen. Ihr Haar ist so schön wie der erste Schnee des Winters,*" he replied, and Agnes beamed as though a lantern had been lit inside her eyes.

"*Danke,* Talvi. *Du bist ein sehr charmanter junger Mann,*" she replied, and her cheeks grew rosy. "*Ich wünschte, mehr Männer hatten Ihre Manieren.*" They chatted for another moment and then Agnes gave a contented sigh.

"You did alright with this one, Annika," she said with a delighted smile of approval. Annika gave her husband an equally delighted smile as her mother began applying a creamy concoction to her brown tresses.

"What do you like to do for fun, besides making the newspaper more entertaining to read?" Beatrice asked Talvi.

"He's quite a handyman," Faline told her. "He fixed the roof and built a new staircase to the basement of their house."

"I wouldn't say I did that for fun, but because it needed to be done," he clarified. "I couldn't risk my poor little wife and her flat mates falling down those old rotted stairs. I'm rather fond of them, even James, what with that foul language of his. I've met sailors who swear less than he does."

"That young man needs his mouth washed out with soap," said the crabby woman.

"I keep wondering when our faerie friend is going to do something about that mouth of his," Talvi chuckled, then paused to take another generous sip of his drink. "It's only a matter of time before it gets washed out with something."

Annika clamped her jaw shut to keep from spitting out her drink and laughing. Her husband was better entertainment than cable.

"So Talvi, I have to ask . . . are you an archer, since you obviously must be an elf?" Beatrice inquired in a sarcastic tone. "I noticed your pointy ears."

Annika looked at him, curious what his response would be.

"Why yes, I am an archer," he confessed, smiling confidently at her before glancing sideways at his wife with a wild and wicked spark in his eye. "Annika can tell you, I'm quite skilled with my bow. I never miss my target. I love to practice as often as I can, and if uninterrupted, I'll typically shoot until I've no more arrows left in my quiver. Trust me, it holds a lot of them."

"You should take him to Washington Park," she said to Annika before looking back at Talvi. "There's an archery range there that you can use for free, and it's open from dawn till dusk."

"Really?" Talvi replied, his interest piqued. "And where is this? Is it very far away?"

"Oh, no, not at all," said Beatrice with a dismissive wave of her hand. "It's probably a fifteen minute drive from here."

"Annika Jane, how could you neglect to tell me such a thing when you know how much I love to shoot my bow?" he scolded, wagging his finger at her just like his father did not too long ago. "There you go again, being a rude hostess with such bad manners. *Tsk, tsk, tsk* . . . for shame, Annika!"

"I didn't know there was an archery range there," she said defensively. "But I promise we can go anytime you want to. We could even go after we're done here, if you want."

"No, I have other plans after we're finished here," he said, and tipped the bottom of his glass up so that he could eat the raspberry that had been resting at the bottom. "But perhaps we'll go to the range tomorrow."

"What kind of plans do you have?"

"The kind I am apt to make, my little dove," he said with a smile, and then revealed no more.

Three and a half hours later, they returned to what appeared to be an empty house.

"Where is everyone?" Annika asked, dropping her purse into an empty chair at the kitchen table.

"I've arranged for us to have the house to ourselves while I give you your birthday present," he said, letting a mischievous spark enter his eyes as he walked to the counter near the fridge. He turned around, leaned back on his elbows, and beckoned with one hand in a come-hither motion.

"Oh, I'll bet I know exactly what you wanna give me," she taunted, draping her long red hair over her shoulder as she sauntered over to him.

"I'll bet you don't," he taunted right back, taking her waist in his hands. Instead of pulling her close and kissing her, he turned her to face the living room. "Why, whatever is that on the coffee table?"

Annika went out to investigate, returning with an exquisite pot of dainty white flowers.

"Sweetie, these are beautiful!" she sighed, breathing in their spicy fragrance. "What are they?"

"They're dove orchids, my little dove," he said with a smile. "They only bloom after it rains, and they're endangered in their native habitat, so you'll need to take good care of them. These little doves flew in all the way from Panama."

"I thought I said I didn't want anything expensive," she reminded him, smelling the orchids again before setting them on the kitchen table. "Not that I'm complaining. These are gorgeous!"

"Yes, but you opted for something rare, and sometimes those two things cannot be mutually exclusive," he said with a wink. He reached into the fridge, withdrawing a bottle of champagne and two chilled glasses, taking care not to knock them together. She stood nearby, gazing at him sweetly while he popped the cork and topped off their drinks.

"No champagne screws?" she asked flirtatiously.

"No, love, just champagne," he replied. "Why don't you sit down and relax, while I prepare our dinner?"

"No way. I just sat at my mom's salon for three hours," she pointed out, taking a sip from her glass. "I'd rather stand right here and watch you work."

"If it pleases you," he said, and walked back to the fridge. He gathered an armful of different vegetables, laying them all out on the counter, before taking out a cutting board, a honing steel, and a large kitchen knife.

"What are you making for me, anyway?" she asked as he began to expertly sharpen the knife with the honing steel.

"For the first course, we'll have artichoke and tomato bisque," he informed her, testing the sharpness of the blade before giving it a few more passes with the steel. "For the second course, I've planned a fennel and mint salad. The main course will be butternut squash and pear ravioli, with rosemary sauce." He paused to put away the honing steel and wipe the knife with a kitchen towel, then began to chop some carrots. "I wanted to keep the meal light enough so that you'll have plenty of room for dessert. I'm afraid I have a ridiculous amount of it, but I couldn't bear to see it wasted."

"Oh really? What's for dessert?"

A smirk played on Talvi's lips, and without stopping his slicing, he replied, "Me."

Annika felt surge of ravenous hunger bolt through her body, and as hungry as she was for that gourmet dinner, all she could think about was the dessert that awaited afterwards.

"It's been a long time," she said, watching him slice up an artichoke with as much effortless ease as when he had first used his straight razor in front of her. No wonder he never cut himself shaving; his blade seemed to be a natural extension of his arm.

"Trust me, I know it's been a long time," he agreed, now slicing tomatoes at a furious pace. "It's been exactly four weeks and two days. That's seven hundred and twenty hours. Or forty-three thousand and two hundred minutes. Or two million, five hun—"

"Hey, if you're complaining that it's been too long since you got laid, you did have an opportunity in London, but *somebody* didn't seem up for the task," Annika interrupted, glancing at her orchids.

"Yes, well *I* married a *redhead*, not a brunette," he said, setting the knife on the cutting board to scoop the vegetables into different dishes. "I had no idea that you changing your hair would have such an effect on me. Please, Annika, don't ever do that again. And don't ever cut it too short, either. I meant it when I told the hens at the salon that I felt as though a strange woman had taken your place. I never want to experience that again."

A tender, melting sensation now wafted over Annika's heart. Her smile gave way as her bottom lip trembled and her throat swelled. Without warning, there were tears in her eyes.

"What is it, my little dove?" he asked, taking her gently into his arms as he looked down at her inquisitively.

"It's what you said about my hair," she said, wiping her eyes as more tears arrived. "You couldn't even cheat on me with *me*. You really *are* as loyal as the cold is to snow."

"I've been trying to tell you that for months. Do you mean to tell me that we could have avoided all this trouble if I had merely purchased a cheap box of hair dye from the drugstore?"

Annika shrugged, sniffing as she smiled halfheartedly.

"Well?" he implored, leaning down close enough for his forehead to touch hers. "Is that truly all that needed to be done, for you to trust your little bumble bee to only take nectar from his favorite flower?" Annika's weak smile faded, and her face became serious.

"Not exactly, but it sure helped," she said quietly as she looked him straight in the eye. "I want to trust you completely, Talvi, but there's no way in hell that you were working as an investment banker. I wish you would stop treating me like I can't handle the truth about you, or thinking I'm too stupid to figure out that you were working as a spy."

"I don't think you're stupid at all, Annika," he said, blinking his long black lashes slowly. "I think you're a very clever girl. I never once claimed to be an investment banker. I was telling you the absolute truth when I said that I specialize in mergers and acquisitions for the London Embassy."

"Then what exactly did you acquire for them, that you sometimes had to leave in the middle of the night and be gone for months at a time?" she asked, raising an eyebrow.

"This and that," he said, not even bothering to hide his bold grin.

"Did you ever have to merge with an enemy agent to acquire *this* and *that*?"

"From time to time," he said, with a twinkle in his blue-green eyes.

"Did you ever kill anybody?"

"Trust me, love, you're much better off not knowing the depths of my dark side," he replied in his velvety smooth voice. "One mustn't go around poking tigers, especially not lovely lady guitar players. You'll lose those skillful fingers of yours, and I'm ever so fond of the things they can do." He took her left hand in his and gently kissed each fingertip, dialing up the charm with each touch of his lips.

"Don't think you can woo your way out of this, Mr. Lewd and Lascivious," she said, reclaiming her hand so she could press her index finger into his chest. "If you have to wait another forty-three thousand minutes, so be it, but I'm not letting you inside of me until you let me inside of you." She reached up to tap the side of his head with her finger, unafraid of poking this tiger.

"I recall telling you that some things are best left unsaid, no questions asked." Talvi's eyes grew dark with intensity as he spoke. "I don't want to see any details from your Parisian holiday with my brother. I've already considered every possible outcome, and I will tell you, I don't have many regrets in my life, but that's one of them. I absolutely abhor that I put you both in that situation. I'm just grateful that you're both alive. Next year I'll see to it that Runa stays with you instead, so that I don't wind up an uncle to my own child. Although who knows? Perhaps I am already? I'd certainly love to see the look on your mum's face when you try to explain how *that* happened!" He let out a diabolical roar of laughter when Annika's jaw inevitably dropped.

"How can you laugh about that?" she gasped in revulsion.

"I told you, love, I considered *every* possible outcome," he reminded her with a maniacal grin, batting his lashes at her. "Either way, we'll know for certain if you don't bleed within a fortnight."

"But we didn't do it!" Annika screeched. "I'm not remotely pregnant!" She felt her stomach give a feeble flip and she turned her back to him, reaching for her champagne that had been sitting on the counter. "I can't believe you thought that was funny!"

"Yes, well, I can't believe I was so bloody stupid to arrange such a situation to begin with," he said, blushing in shame, but the devilish smile remained on his face as he returned to his slicing and dicing. "If you're going to have any larvae crawl out of you, I should hope that they would be my own."

"But I know you don't want kids, so when you said you'd adore ours, you really had me convinced that we could pull it off. Were you teasing me then, too? I don't want any right now, but I might want one someday, if they'll be anything like Stella and Sloan."

"I meant what I said, love," he said softly. "In all truth, I was actually scared shitless, but that's why I told you we would get through it together. I certainly couldn't do it alone, especially not if we had twins. I suppose a vainglorious part of me wouldn't mind seeing what sort of progeny we might create, but I don't wish to explore parenthood when we have so much yet to discover about one other."

"I know," she said, taking another sip of champagne before turning to face him again. She reached up and twirled his hair into two little peaks that resembled devil horns. "That's why you need to let me inside of your mind, so we can start discovering those things. You can't keep so many secrets from me."

"Annika, if I let you inside my mind, I can waltz right into yours. Remember what I told you about putting too much sugar in the lemonade? You can't undo it once you've put it in the pitcher. Are you certain you want to risk letting me see what's in there?"

Annika focused her eyes on his deft hands as the sharp blade made short work of the rosemary, feeling a chill of shame at her behavior in Paris. Even if biology and body chemistry were to blame, she couldn't separate it from her memories of Finn's warm hands running up and down her waist in that doorway of the Champs-Élysées. It would definitely be easier to pretend like nothing had happened. But then the unstable foundation of their marriage would keep decaying from below, until it caved in on them like a sinkhole after a flood.

"I guess that's a risk I'm willing to take, though it sounds like you're the one who's more afraid to take that same risk," she said, putting on a brave face. "If we're going to have an honest, trusting relationship, we've got to start building it somewhere. It ought to be right here." She tapped the side of his head again.

Talvi set down the knife, and wiped his hands on the kitchen towel. He took a generous drink from his champagne flute and took her face in his hands, touching his forehead to hers with a reluctant, yet knowing sigh. He closed his eyes as though he was regretting what he was about to do. When he lifted his lids, the harrowing stare he assaulted her with pierced her soul. Overwhelmed by his intensity, she felt like she was falling into a black abyss, the dwelling of the devil himself. Her stomach turned, her skin felt clammy, and her pulse quickened with adrenaline. But as frightened as she was about opening herself to him in this moment, she was more afraid to look away. Instead, she let her mind wander into his, taking in the scope of his dark side.

A vision came into view that appeared to be in the not so distant past. He was tip-toeing barefoot down one of the dark hallways of his home, where he slipped into a room near the end of it and closed the door without a sound. Annika recognized the neat and tidy room, with countless displays of butterfly collections on the walls. A tall Japanese screen stood in the corner with silk undergarments thrown over it, and not far from that, Yuri lay in her bed. She was reading a book by candlelight, with her hairbrush resting beside her. Her brown eyes looked up from her book and she smiled as her brother climbed under the covers with her. The gentle smile morphed into a sneer of disdain when he touched his cold feet against her bare leg. Her expression softened, however, the moment he picked up the brush and began to run it gently through her hair again and again, until she had fallen asleep in his arms. This scenario repeated a few times, until one night when Talvi slipped into Yuri's room and found her already asleep. This time a letter was held in her limp hand instead of a book, and when he leaned down to read it, he saw that it was from Konstantin. His eyes burned like blue flames, encircled in green wheels of fire; green with envy, and wet with tears.

Another scene came into view of him donning an old fashioned suit, playing the part of a piano instructor. He was sitting on the bench of a grand piano beside a well-dressed and bejeweled young woman that may very well have been the Spanish princess. Annika could see him take one of her pale hands off the ivory keys and turn it up so that he could kiss her palm, then her wrist, then her inner elbow. He looked up at her seductively and said, "I could probably just ask you who's on the guest list at your father's private meetings, but I would much rather have you sing them to me." He reached around her waist, sliding closer to her as he continued to whisper sweet nothings into her ear, while the other hand reached under her beautiful gown, prodding her for information, no doubt.

In the last vision, he was dressed in his black suede traveling outfit and had pulled a robust, older man in a three piece suit into a bathtub.

"I'm not telling you anything!" the man insisted, as Talvi pulled him close, with his back against his chest, exactly as he had held Annika in her bedroom before tying her up. Using the same knife that he had taken to Finn, he softly ran the tip of the blade over the man's mouth, leaving not so much as a scratch.

"I'm fairly certain I can persuade you to spill your guts," he crooned into the man's ear, standing outside of the tub. "It would be better for us both if you just tell me where the plans are."

"I'm not saying a word, you fiend!" the man growled at him.

"Very well," Talvi sighed, and unfastened the man's necktie, rolling it up and stuffing it into his mouth. "Have it your way."

In a heartbeat, he sank his knife into the bottom of the man's belly, and yanked upward through his vest so violently that his entrails spilled out of his abdomen and into the bathtub. Talvi stood there patiently throughout the muffled screams, watching the gush of bloody intestines splash all over the walls and white porcelain. He let the body slide out of his arms and carefully wiped the blade on the man's lapel before walking to the sink. Then he rinsed his knife under the faucet, washed his hands, and returned his knife to the sheath inside his boot. He casually dabbed at the red spatter on his face, and fussed with his hair in front of the mirror at some length until he was satisfied with his appearance. Then he walked back to the tub and rifled through the man's pockets, until he pulled out a piece of paper from inside the man's jacket. He unfolded it, looked it over carefully, then took out his lighter and set it on fire in the sink, letting it burn to a crisp before slipping out of the window and disappearing into the night.

"Now do you understand why I keep so many things private from you?" Talvi asked when Annika pulled away from him, letting the corridor between their minds dissolve. "Do you see why I don't wish to share everything about myself? Some things are indeed best left unsaid."

Annika knew she had two options as she stood there, speechless from what she had seen. On one hand, she could be terrified to know what kind of horrors that her husband was capable of. She had never imagined he could be so manipulative and cunning, so dangerous and deadly. And if these were the memories that he'd cherry-picked out of seventy years' worth, what sort of things was he keeping private?

Or, on the other hand, she could trust what his father had told her; that Talvi would do anything for her, and that there was a diamond hidden deep inside that dark, tainted exterior. She also recalled Chivanni claiming that he wouldn't want anyone else for a friend, and that Talvi would shower her with steadfast love and protection. There had to be some weight behind a statement like that, if they had been friends for nearly sixty years.

Talvi stroked her hair gently, then guided her chin to face him. He looked at her as though he understood her anguish all too well.

"I'm sorry you had to see all that, but I hope it alleviates some of your concerns. I don't know if you've noticed, but I can be a right bastard sometimes."

"Oh, I noticed," she assured him, wide-eyed and reeling from the visions. She covered her face with her hands, taking deep breaths to calm herself down. He was right about one thing for sure; she couldn't undo what she had seen.

He took a final drink and set his empty glass on the counter beside hers, pulling her into his arms.

"Now, is there anything else that needs addressing?"

"Yeah, but I can't deal with it right now," she admitted, inhaling the familiar scent of his shaving soap. Honeysuckle, fruit trees, and cinnamon greeted her nose as she rested her head against his chest. "It's too much to process. My brain feels like it's going to explode."

"Oh, now, we can't very well have that, especially since you banned the use of faerie magic for the evening," he replied, kissing the top of her head as he began to sway from side to side with her. "If you thought the mess from the sugar and soot was bad, you don't even want to know how difficult it is to get bits of brain out of a rug."

"You're right; I don't want to know," she said, shuddering at the thought. "I don't want to think about any of this right now."

"Would you like a distraction?" he asked playfully.

"What kind of distraction?"

"I'll give you a little clue. It's in my front pocket," he replied. She turned around and started to reach into the right pocket of his jeans, but he shook his head.

"No, no, the other one."

She slid her hand into his left pocket, and reached around until she came across what clue he was referring to. He grinned and laughed wickedly, but said nothing.

"That is *not* a little clue," she said, blushing as she took her hand out of his pocket.

"I didn't think it would be," he smirked. "I told you that I had an overabundance of dessert waiting for you. Perhaps you'd like a taste to be certain you'll enjoy it, since we have so much?"

"I'm pretty sure I'll enjoy it, but you can still give me a taste," she said, licking her lips in anticipation.

He tilted her chin upwards, stooping down to deliver the sweetest, softest kiss he had ever given her. He smelled like cinnamon and tasted like champagne; it was a dessert unlike any other. Happy memories of his drifted into her mind this time; the freedom of driving a car, the thrill of dancing a tango in the living room, and the joy of playing an electric guitar for the first time in his long life. There was no urgency in his caress when his hands gathered her long red hair in his hands. There was no impatient grasping of clothing when his hands let go of her hair and encircled her waist. They had all the time in the world to be in that moment. Her blood felt as effervescent as the bubbles in their champagne glasses, but then the moment ended.

"What do you think, birthday girl?" he asked. "Would you like more dessert, or would you prefer we move on to the bisque?"

"I'm liking the dessert, actually," she said with a grin, readying herself for another kiss, but he slipped out from between her and the counter, and started walking towards the kitchen table instead. He picked up the orchids and disappeared into the living room with them. When he returned, he pulled off the tablecloth where the flowers had just been sitting, gave it a quick shake, and replaced it back on the kitchen table. Then he marched over to her, swooping her up so that her legs were wrapped around his waist, and began to carry her away.

"Where are we going?"

"You didn't think we were going to eat on the floor, did you?" he asked, setting her down on the kitchen table. He lifted her arms and pulled her shirt up and over them, casting it aside. Cupping her breasts through her bra, he gave her a skeptical look. "Well? Did you?" She shrugged, smiling as she lifted his t-shirt over his flat stomach and smooth chest, before he pulled it over his head and dropped it beside her shirt. He reached around her back and unfastened her bra in a heartbeat, and she giggled when his sideburns grazed her chest. She tried not to shudder as he kissed and fondled each breast again, running his hands over the smooth skin. He gave her an impatient squeeze before lifting his head.

"Annika, love, where's your amulet?"

"I don't know . . . maybe it's still in my luggage."

"No, it wasn't there. I went through everything when we unpacked," he said. "I assumed it was in your purse."

"Probably," she said with a shrug, drawing his face against her chest. The truth was, the last time she had seen it was in Paris, underground, and not in the catacombs. But she didn't let herself think about her amulet's whereabouts for a second longer.

"You had better hope you find it, otherwise nothing's going to save you now," Talvi said, laughing wickedly in between taking tastes and deep breaths of her skin. "I think your dessert is almost ready. Shall I check the oven?" he mused, and reached underneath her skirt, sliding his hands up her thighs. A thrilled gleam of delight entered his expression.

"I take it that means it's ready," she said, smiling primly at him while unbuckling his belt. He nodded, coaxing her panties down her legs until they landed on the collection of clothes on the floor. When she unzipped his jeans, he sighed in relief and curled his hands around the backs of her knees, pulling her to the edge of the table.

"Do you want me to take this off?" she asked when he reached under her rainbow skirt again.

"No," he instructed, with smoldering, starving eyes. "It makes you look like an exotic bloom, so leave it on. That way, your little bumble bee can take all the nectar he likes from his favorite flower." He kicked off his shoes and maneuvered out of his jeans before taking her into his arms and kissing her deeply again. The scent of fruit trees toyed with her nose, and the taste of champagne danced from his mouth to hers. She felt herself being gently guided to lie back, and she fully expected him to melt into her, but he surprised her by restraining himself, resting his hips against hers while sheer pleasure radiated from every pore of his skin.

"I never thought I could feel such devotion, and then my love got in the way," he began to say, his mouth hinting ever so subtly at a smile. "Intoxicating like a mystical potion, and I knew not what to say." He leaned his head down above hers as his hands coaxed her lower back to arch upwards against his hips. "You know I tried to resist you, but when you kissed me like lovers do, oh . . . I knew . . . it was only a matter of time . . . before you would be mine."

"I'm so glad you like my song," she smiled, looking up into his eyes. "Of any song I've ever loved, I think that one's my favorite. I hope that's not too vain, to love your own creation more than anyone else's."

"How could you not love what our passion produced?" he asked, nuzzling into her cheek. "We created it together."

"I never could have finished it without you," she confessed. "You were right about the words. They came to me at the perfect time."

"It's true, the timing was perfect, but did it not strike you as odd, that they came to you as though they were whispered in your ear?" he asked.

"No, actually; it didn't seem odd at all," she admitted, as he rocked his hips ever so slightly from side to side between her legs. "It was the first time I stopped overthinking the words, and just let them come to me. I gave in and lost myself in the moment, like you said I should do. I don't know exactly where the words came from." She looked up into his eyes, and saw that familiar twinkle in them. "But I'll bet *you* know."

"They were my mantra while we were apart, Annika," he said, teasing the corner of her mouth with a flick of his warm tongue before focusing his gaze upon her. "Those words played over and over in my mind nearly every moment of every day that I spent trying to get to your door. I walked countless steps to their cadence, in forests and fields, through the snow and over ice, never knowing they would be put to your music one day, allowing for all the world to hear how much I love you. Now, let me help you sing."

The smell of cinnamon and the taste of champagne returned as their lips met once more, and after laying everything out on the kitchen table, and after months of dissonance and discord between them, Annika and Talvi finally fell into perfect harmony.

CHAPTER 47

It's All in the Eyes

"It's about time you guys showed up!" Patti shouted through the din of the noisy and crowded bar to Talvi and Annika. Charlie, James, and Chivanni were all about to join her for a round of shots, but they waited as two more were poured for the birthday girl and her husband.

"We would have been here earlier, but Annika forbade me from having any assistance in the kitchen," Talvi explained, taking a shot glass that Charlie passed to him, and handing it to his wife. "I've never made a meal like that before, and I had no idea of the amount of preparation, let alone actual cooking to be done."

"Did you have any leftovers?" James asked, passing him another shot. "Your menu sounded incredible!"

"Yes, the meal was absolutely delectable, but the food is in the icebox, wrapped up in aluminum," Talvi snickered, reaching out to touch Annika affectionately on the nose as she was given a shot glass.

"Wrapped up in *what*?" James shouted through the noise.

"Aluminum!" Talvi repeated, louder this time.

"What?" James shouted again.

"Aloo-MIN-yum, you deaf bastard!" he howled. "Piss! You did that on purpose, didn't you?" James probably would have responded, but he was laughing too hard at Talvi's accent. Chivanni just shook his head and smiled.

"Alright, alright, let's drink these before we spill them," Charlie said, raising his shot glass. "Here's to my little sister getting a little older. Happy birthday, Ani." The others followed suit, and passed their empty glasses to the bar as another round of drinks was ordered.

The contented grin on Talvi's face faded when his hand reached for his pocket. He pulled out his phone, glanced at the screen, and then stuffed it back into his pocket.

"Who's calling you?" Annika asked.

"Who do you think?" he replied, and put his arm around her. "I'm not going to answer it, though. She can leave me a message if it's that important."

"I have to say, Talvi, I'm really surprised that you made Annika dinner," Patti said, sipping her drink. "I thought all you knew how to make was lemonade."

"Oh, you just hush your mouth, Patti Cake," Talvi scolded with a smile. He rolled his eyes and took his phone out of his pocket, and Annika frowned when she saw that Merriweather was calling him a second time. He pushed the button that sent the call straight to voicemail and put it away.

"Why is she calling you right now? Isn't it like, three in the morning in London?" Annika asked amidst the chatter.

"It's five," he replied, hoping not to elaborate further.

"Did she not get the memo that you don't work for her anymore?"

"Apparently not, but she'll figure it out soon enough," Talvi said, kissing her on the head and then nuzzling into her neck. "I for one cannot wait to write some new songs with you. We make such beautiful music together, if I do say so myself." He tried to pay attention to what James and Chivanni were now discussing with Patti and Charlie, but he could tell that Annika was not enjoying herself much at all.

"This may be daft of me to ask, but is there something upsetting you?" he said into her ear so that only she heard. Annika rolled her eyes at his question.

"Uh, *yeah*," she said, turning to face him so that her brother and their friends wouldn't see the irritated look on her face. "When we were at the hotel in Paris, I clearly heard you tell your boss how much you loved it when she let you loose, and let you take her however you wanted. You were dying to hook up with her, and you didn't even try to hide it, just like you're not even trying to hide the fact that she's booty calling you on my friggin' birthday!"

"Oh, Annika," he began, with a sorrowful and sympathetic expression in his blue-green eyes, but he was trying his damnedest not to smile. His cheeks turned a deep shade of scarlet, which then spread to the tips of his ears as he

410

took her by the shoulders. "When I was speaking with Merri at the hotel, I was referring to something entirely different. I can see how you would misunderstand that conversation, now that I think about it, but . . . " he drifted off, distracted by an outburst of Chivanni's laughter. "Merri's had a dreadful time keeping an assistant, and it's more or less my fault, so I completed a backlog of tedious paperwork for her. My reward was to be a trip down to the weapons locker, not down on *her*. The locker is in the basement of the embassy, and she has one of only three keys to that room. That's why she and I would have to go down there together. I haven't been there in ages, but she's always let me take whatever I wanted in the past. You can understand why I would be so eager for the chance to see what she has down there. It would be the same as someone taking you into the finest guitar shop and letting you have your pick of instruments, free of charge."

He bade Annika to lose herself in his eyes once more, and she caught the sight of him being let loose in a well-lit room, bypassing the assault rifles and handguns, and instead running his hands over the pommels of swords, gauging the weight of different daggers in his hands, and hurling razor sharp throwing knives at a target, all under Merriweather's watchful eyes as she recited the specs of each item he showed interest in.

Now it was Annika's turn to blush. She felt the heat creep across her face and ears, and even down her neck and chest. How ridiculously humiliating, that she had taken his conversation so far out of context, and for so long. Maybe this was her punishment for eavesdropping.

"I'm sorry that there was such a misunderstanding between us, but you don't exactly help things by assuming the worst about me, either," he said. He reached up to tuck a strand of her long hair behind her bright red ear, then began rubbing her shoulders as he tried his best to comfort her. "Though, to be fair, there's a lot that's quite unsavory. But sharing details of my former profession is not wise for either of us. In fact, I've probably told you too much as it is."

"Yeah, you sometimes overshare," she said, reaching her arms around Talvi to cuddle against his chest. "But I forgive you."

"Bloody hell, I ought to turn this damn thing off," he muttered when his phone started to ring a third time.

"Maybe you should just see what she wants," Annika suggested when she noticed that Talvi now had two voicemails along with his two missed calls. "If she's calling you this early in London, it might be really important."

"Perhaps, but I'll still try to make it snappy. Don't you go anywhere," he said as he tapped her affectionately on the nose and hurried outside to take his phone call.

"So Patti, I have a question for you. Actually, I think we all do," Annika said, folding her arms over her chest. "It only makes sense to have you do the artwork for our new album. Are you interested?"

"Oh, and we could have the album release party at the gallery, featuring all of your paintings from school!" James added enthusiastically. "I'm all for it, so you damn well better say yes."

Patti grinned wide, turning to Charlie, but he was only wearing the same hopeful smile as Annika.

"Of *course* I'll do it!" she laughed. "I'd be insane not to! There's starting to be a serious buzz about the band now that you've got some demos out. Speaking of which, when are you guys having another show?"

"I guess whenever works for the guys works for me," Annika replied, looking at James, and then at her brother. "My schedule's kinda wide open now. Talvi wants me to take some time to focus on writing more songs, so I guess I could start booking us gigs now that the album's getting mastered."

"Wow, that's really exciting!" Patti squealed with glee. She waved at Talvi as he made his way towards them through the crowd. "You're lucky that he's so supportive of your art."

"Yeah, I *am* pretty lucky to have someone like him in my life," she agreed.

Talvi came up behind her, slipping one of his arms around her waist while he handed her a shot.

"Drink up, dear," he said.

"What is it?" she asked, sniffing the little glass.

"A surprise," he said, watching her expectantly. As soon as she'd taken the shot, he took the glass from her, looked at her friends and brother, and gave them a wink and a smile. "I'll be right back."

He took Annika by the arm, guiding her to the rear of the bar, and led her through the kitchen.

"Dude, you guys can't be in here," one of the cooks said.

"We were just leaving," Talvi replied, not bothering to look at who was speaking to him. Instead, they headed straight for the door, and stepped cautiously into the night.

"Where's your car?" he asked, once he saw that they were the only ones out back behind the building. He reached between two of the trash barrels positioned against the wall, and pulled out a dark brown backpack. "I can't remember where we parked, but I have something special for you in it," he said, and slipped the backpack over one shoulder.

"Um, it's down a block and a half over there," she said, pointing into the trees before digging the keys out of her purse and handing them over. He took them in his free hand, but his other didn't move from her arm as he ushered her along the sidewalk at a fast clip, staying in the shadows of the side streets.

"Why are we going so far out of the way?" she asked.

"Because it's easier for me to get away with this, my dear," he said, and stopped walking just long enough to pull her against him, aggressively copping a feel while kissing her hard on the mouth. "If that's what you feel like through your clothes, I can't wait to discover what you'll feel like when I take them off."

"Seriously? You want more dessert?" she hooted. "Well then, we might have to call it an early night."

"That sounds like a fine idea," he said, and tossed the shot glass under some rhododendron bushes before resuming walking.

They arrived at her car and he helped her into the passenger side before climbing into the driver's seat. He adjusted the chair back so he was sitting with good posture instead of reclining like he usually did, then pulled quietly out of the parking spot and got onto the highway.

"Sweetie, you told everyone that we'd be right back," she pointed out as they merged onto 84 east. "They're going to worry if we're gone too long. I'll text James and let him know about our change of plans." While she dug her phone out of her purse, Talvi rolled his window down. Then he extended his right hand out to her.

"Let me see that for a second."

"No way. You're not supposed to text and drive," she said with a grin, but it didn't stop him from snatching the phone out of her hand.

"One, one-thousand," he counted, then chucked it out onto the highway.

"What the *hell* did you do *that* for?" she yelled at him.

"I don't want us to be disturbed during our alone time," he replied, rolling the window back up.

"Yeah, well you could have just turned it off, you jackass!" she hollered. "I've got a zillion pictures saved on there and all my contacts and stuff! That was a real dick move you just made! And speaking of dicks, I hope you don't think you're getting laid again, you ass!"

"Oh, I'm pretty sure I still am," he said, without a care in the world.

"Oh my god, Talvi, what's gotten into you? You're being such a douchebag! Give me a cigarette already!"

"Sorry dear, I don't have any."

"What the hell? You always have . . . " Annika trailed off, noticing that the tail lights and headlights of the traffic were starting to blur. She rubbed her eyes and strained to see them again, but they were even blurrier than before. It looked like they were exiting onto 205 north, toward the airport, but the letters on the signs overhead morphed into an incongruous smear. She clutched her hands together, twisting her meteorite ring around her finger, and an image of Finn giving her a very important language lesson bounced into her mind.

"Why don't you have any cigarettes, *sludoor?*" she asked, suddenly feeling suspicious, sick, and drowsy all at once.

"Because they're bad for your health."

"What was in that shot you gave me, *sludoor?*" she asked, feeling more nervous, nauseous, and tired. She could barely keep her eyelids up. She thought about holding them open with her fingers, but her arms were like lead weights attached to her shoulders, rendering her hands useless.

"I told you, Annika, it was a surprise," came his prickly response. He glanced over at her, watching her head loll from one side to the other, before eventually coming to rest against her window. "Are you starting to figure it out?"

"Where are we going, *sludoor?*" she managed to mumble through her numb lips.

"We're going to visit a friend of mine," he said. A nasty smile spread across his mouth, and an even nastier expression filled his soulless dark grey eyes. "Although at some point we should get to know each other a little better. I *am* your husband, after all."

"Hold on a moment, Merri. I'm almost outside," Talvi called into the receiver of his phone as he slipped through the crowded bar and beyond the front door to where it was quieter. Once he was out in the cool, fresh air, he reached for his back pocket and pulled a cigarette out his case, then casually lit it with his cheeky lighter. "What the devil is it now? Have you suddenly forgotten that I don't work for you anymore?" The response that followed was so loud and unintelligible, he had to hold the phone away from his head. He took a long drag, rolled his eyes, and smirked as he brought the phone back to his ear again.

"I'm sorry, Merri, I couldn't understand a damned word you said. It's five in the morning there in London. Shouldn't you be asleep, instead of interrupting my wife's birthday party with your feminine hysterics?"

"You're *vile!*" was all he could make out of the screaming.

"Oh, I know I'm vile, along with all the other things you've called me over the years," he chirped. "Although, if you really telephoned just to whisper sweet nothings in my ear, I know you can do better than this. Remember our assignment in Budapest? My gods, I'll never forget the wicked things that came out of your mouth, not to mention what came in it." He snickered shamelessly and took another drag, holding the phone at a safe distance as he braced himself for the impending onslaught of insults.

"I did NOT say *you're vile*, you bloody bastard! I said *your file! File*, with an F, as in, you are a *feckless, fucking FOOL!*" Merriweather yelled from the other end.

"What file are you talking about, Merri? I gave you all the papers I was working on when I left. Have you misplaced them already?" he asked, making a concerted effort not to start laughing again.

"Your personal file!" Merriweather replied in a frantic tone. "I think Stephan stole it!"

"Stephan?"

"My new assistant, whom you met right before you left the embassy!" she reminded him. "Talvi, he's a doppelgänger! He disguised himself as *me*, and walked right up to our security guards last night and asked them to let him into my office! Don't you remember, when you were leaving the embassy, he insisted on shaking your hand! And the very first thing I taught him after that was how to deactivate your file. I just discovered that there was a charge made in my name for a plane ticket to Portland, and I think you and Annika are in danger! You both need to get out of town *immediately!*"

Whatever smirk had been on Talvi's lips was now long gone.

"Cheers for the warning," he said and hung up. He threw his cigarette on the sidewalk, not bothering to stamp it out before going back into the bar. He pushed his way through the sea of people around him until he saw his friends. He did a quick head count, but the only redhead present was Chivanni. There was no sign of his wife.

"Chivanni, come here a moment, would you?" Talvi asked him. The faerie smoothed his long bangs aside and hopped over, as Talvi leaned down to ask discreetly, "Where's Annika? In the loo, I hope?"

"Are you that intoxicated already?" he replied with a grin. "Have you forgotten what you did only a moment ago?"

"What do you mean?" Talvi asked. "All I did was step out to take a phone call. Where did Annika go?"

"You took her into the kitchen," the boy replied with a shrug. "You said you'd be right back, but I assumed you would have returned with our guest of honor."

Talvi could feel his stomach begin to turn, and his throat begin to close up, but he forced out a few more words.

"Did I do anything else? Tell me exactly what I did, even if I so much as sneezed."

The boy wrinkled his little freckled nose, and shrugged again.

"You gave her another one of those little faerie-sized drinks, and then you took her that way," he said, pointing to the door to the kitchen. Talvi took him by his thin arm and guided him through the door.

"Dude, I already told you once—you can't be back here!" the cook said, but Talvi shot him a dark glare and picked up a fillet knife lying on a nearby counter, shutting him up. His desperate eyes darted past the sinks and stoves; then his nose picked up a familiar scent amidst the perfume of burnt cheese and fryer grease. He followed it straight through the main kitchen aisle, pulling Chivanni along with his free hand, until they had walked outside. It wasn't until the door closed behind them that Talvi's heart started to pound in his chest, sending such rivers of rage and adrenaline into his veins that his entire body shook.

"Talvi, what's wrong?" Chivanni asked as he caught a glimpse of the furious aura surrounding his friend. "You look like you're ready to kill someone!"

"That's because I am," he snarled through his clenched jaw, tightening his grip on the knife in his left hand. "Someone disguised as me has taken Annika, and when I find him, he will be begging the gods to have mercy on his soul, for I will have none. Apparently he is unfamiliar with the phrase; You never mess with a Marinossian."

Before you go . . .

I was wondering if you could do me a quick favor. It won't take long.

Leaving reviews is one of the most kickass ways to support authors. You're also helping other readers decide if our books are right for them. If you have a minute, I'd LOVE a review from you!

Review The Silver Thread on Amazon

Review The Silver Thread on Goodreads

Thanks so much!

Emigh Cannaday

Fans Only
VIP SECTION

Dying to know when the next book will be released? Love going behind the scenes?

Join Emigh's reader group!!

As a VIP you'll have access to exclusive content, deleted chapters, a private Facebook group, author updates, the hottest new Fantasy and Paranormal Romance reads, and be notified of new releases before anyone else.

Sign up at emighcannaday.com/mailinglist

Also by Emigh Cannaday

The Annika Brisby Series
Dark Fantasy/Paranormal Romance

The Flame and the Arrow

The Silver Thread

The Scarlet Tanager

The Darkest of Dreams

Song of the Samodiva

The Faerie Files
Urban Fantasy Romance

Wiretaps & Whiskers

Catnip & Curses

Hexes & Hairballs

The Novi Navarro Chronicles
Dark Fantasy/Paranormal Romance

Prince of Persuasion

Crown of Contempt

The Sloane Spadowski Series

Dirty Rom-Com/Contemporary Romance

Jerk Bait

Slip Sinker

Catch & Release

About the Author

Fun Fact: Emigh sounds just like "Amy"

Emigh Cannaday lives in Wisconsin with her rock star/winemaker husband and a rambunctious pack of Welsh Corgis. She grew up drawing and painting but now uses words to illustrate her offbeat & elaborate daydreams.

When she's not hoarding houseplants or cuddling corgis, she spends her free time testing out new recipes on her friends & family.

Made in the USA
Middletown, DE
25 September 2022

11195757R00257